LEGAL TENDER

(THE RELUCTANT HUSTLER BOOK 5)

BY

J. GREGORY SMITH

OTHER TITLES BY J. GREGORY SMITH

Thrillers

A Noble Cause (Thomas & Mercer, Kindle Bestseller US, UK, and Germany)

The Flamekeepers (Thomas & Mercer)

Darwin's Pause (RedAcre Press)

The Reluctant Hustler Series

Quick Fix (Book 1, RedAcre Press)

Short Cut (Book 2, RedAcre Press)

Easy Street (Book 3, RedAcre Press)

Fast Cash (Book 4, RedAcre Press)

The Paul Chang Mystery Series

Final Price (Book 1, Thomas & Mercer)

Legacy of the Dragon (Book 2, Thomas & Mercer)

Send in the Clowns (Book 3, Thomas & Mercer)

Young Adult

The Crystal Mountain (RedAcre Press)

Short Stories

"Heroic Measures" (Amazon StoryFront)

"Blenders" (*Insidious Assassins*, Smart Rhino Publishing)

"The Pepper Tyrant" (*Uncommon Assassins*, Smart Rhino Publishing)

"Something Borrowed" (*Zippered Flesh: Tales of Body Enhancements Gone Bad*, Smart Rhino Publishing)

"Street Smarts" (*Stories from the Ink Slingers*, A Written Remains Anthology, Gryphonwood Press)

"Powder Burns" (*A Plague of Shadows*, Smart Rhino Publishing)

"Short Order Crook" (*Asinine Assassins*, Smart Rhino Publishing)

Published by RedAcre Press

Printed in the United States of America

First Printing, 2024

ISBN 978-1-7353889-3-9

For Julie

CHAPTER 1

Philadelphia, Pennsylvania: Fishtown

I took my usual morning walk to clear my head and stretch out my rehabbed knee. If I wasn't lazy, the joint would feel almost normal, thanks to a good doctor and a lot of physical therapy.

I was grateful to the field surgeon over in the Sand Box who specialized in IED injuries, but that was years ago, and now I only saw him in my dreams. As for my physical therapist, I woke up most mornings next to her. Sandy joined me on my walk sometimes but had to go in early today, leaving me to my thoughts.

Just as well, I wasn't going to be good company since I'd just been fired. Well, not fired exactly, as I had been the boss and owner, but shoved aside nonetheless. Long story short, until recently, I'd owned an import company that specialized in high-end furniture from the Middle East. I ran the port facility and the trucking to get the product to a guy in Ohio who sold the merch through his growing chain of stores.

The same guy also held the note on the whole operation, and I'd been paying him over the last couple years, with interest, while he built up his business here in the States and left behind his old reputation as a shady businessman who escaped Iraq.

Apparently, I was considered part of that shady past, and he no longer wanted to be associated with the likes of me and my crew, so he had called in the note and bought me out. Just like that. I'd be okay, but I felt for all the workers the guy was going to replace.

I heard the approaching car just before the hairs on the back of my neck stood up. Too late, I turned toward the old-school station wagon with tinted windows. The window slid down to reveal Fishtown's answer to the Angel of Death.

Kevin "Killer" Cullen. "You're slipping, Kyle," he said. "I could have been anybody."

I tried to play it off, but I was shaken. "Maybe you still got it. Ever think of that?"

The guy leaned on the window frame, and the morning sun illuminated his pale skin and large, oft-broken nose. His cold, blue-eyed stare burned into me, and I remembered how, when I first met him, it was indoors. I'd thought his eyes were black, the pupils were so dilated. I'd wondered if he could see in the dark.

"I need to talk to you."

I gestured with a phone. "I'm not hard to reach."

"Or find." He pointed to the passenger door. "Get in."

Cullen pulled away from the curb before I could even shut the door, much less fasten my seatbelt.

"So, how's retirement treating you?" I hadn't quite mastered chitchat with the Philly Irish Mob's deadliest hit man.

"Trying to stay busy, I guess." He must have seen my expression as I attached awful meaning to the word "busy." "Don't be an ass."

"What's going on?"

"I have a problem, and I thought you might be able to help."

We weren't exactly friends and definitely not colleagues, but over the years we had developed an understanding. Since he'd stepped away from working for the Irish, I hadn't seen him around much.

"What can I do for you that your old bosses couldn't?"

He glared at me. "It's not something I could ask them."

I realized the anger was just a mask. He was embarrassed. "What is it?"

"You asked about retirement. Well, that's just it. I'm trying to stay retired."

"You lost me."

Cullen pulled the car over and stared at me. I was more comfortable when we were on the move. "All right. When I left the old life, I took the money I had saved and bought a rental property."

Relief flooded though my body. "Why didn't you say so? We rehab old properties all the time. You need some work done? Help with city inspections? You *did* come to the right place."

"That's not it."

I was still in the dark, but my stomach sank. "What, then?"

"What about squatters?"

I blinked. "You mean tenants who won't leave?"

He nodded. "Or pay."

I tamped down the urge to laugh. "You're telling me some idiots picked the most dangerous man in the city to stiff on the rent?"

He didn't smile. "They don't know anything about that. Did you miss the part about I'm out? I'm trying to live lowkey, and handling business the old way ain't gonna help. The place is in my real name and everything."

I began to see his point. "Dumb question, but by any chance have you tried to get them evicted—you know, through the legal process?"

"You own enough places to know how long that takes—if it even works." Cullen ran his fingers through his salt-and-pepper hair. "All my money is tied into this place. I can't carry deadbeats."

The interminable delays were a big reason we never went the official route with our own properties. "That part I get, but I still don't see why you couldn't 'encourage' them to pay or leave for their own safety."

His eyes got that hard, predatory look. "Kyle, I'd like nothing better. And yeah, they could go away without a trace." He paused. "But I'm seriously trying to stay out, and I don't need any investigations into my life at this point. Besides, now you know about them."

My heart pounded. "I'd never . . ."

His lips pulled back in what for him was a rare smile. "That was a joke."

"Don't give up real estate for stand-up," I said, trying to salvage my dignity.

"So, will you help me?"

"Can you be more specific? What do you want me to do?"

"Make them leave. Without them taking me to court and stuff. Name your price."

I thought for a moment. "Okay. You can owe me a favor. Fair enough?"

Cullen knew favors were like hard currency in our world. We shook on it.

I'm a pretty big guy, but my hand vanished in his. "I'll be in touch."

CHAPTER 2

Philadelphia, Old City

I'd picked up Sandy at her place. It was a cool location in the heart of Old City, surrounded by history and a ton of eateries. Across the street, we could visit Ben Franklin's grave, and Market Street was only a block away. The early fall sun made for a pleasant walk. Her physical therapy clinic was still growing, and if she needed to expand, I'd have to help her find another location. Unless the vape shop next door could be tempted by a buyout offer.

"You know," I said, "if you left your apartment, the rent you save could go to more retail space." I tilted my head toward the vape shop.

"Leave those guys alone. They're okay. We have enough room for now." She broke into a smile that still hit me right in the chest. "I thought you wanted to cling to bachelorhood."

By now, my first marriage was well in the past. Sandy and I had gotten pretty serious, and I was reaching the point where her moving in to my place officially wasn't so scary. I squeezed her close. "How's this for clinging?"

"Any more and you'll squish me," she said.

I relaxed my grip. "Sorry."

She hadn't addressed my point. She stepped back and a pair of skateboarders rolled between us and scraped to a halt in front of the vape shop, where they hopped off their boards.

Sandy had tracked their progress with a smile. "Some of those daredevils are my youngest clients," she said.

We crossed the street and hit one of the hoagie shops.

After we got our food, we sat at a table.

"What's left for the wind-down of the port?" she asked.

"Boring stuff." I tried to wave it away.

"Hard stuff."

I could only nod at that. "Yeah. I worked with some of those guys from the time I was with Delivergistics. It wasn't easy to shift the operation into an import company. Cliff may be done with management and ready to retire, but not the drivers."

"You said you'd be able to find them jobs. Plenty of demand for good ones."

"Sometimes," I admitted. "Sometimes not. This was good, steady work."

"And didn't you say the crane guys and some of the others would stay on?"

"Turns out Ali didn't have a plan in place for them." I felt a twinge of satisfaction. "Did I tell you they said they were willing to step down for me?"

Sandy looked up from her sandwich. "No. You're not going to take them up on it, are you?"

I relished imagining the look on Ali's face if that happened. Ungrateful prick. "I appreciate their loyalty, but without a port, my crane operator needs are light."

We finished our hoagies, and the silences that were usually comfortable felt labored. Outside the shop I tried again. "What do you think about what I said? You giving up the apartment and moving into the house?"

We got all the way across the street before she answered. By then, the food had balled up in my belly. Sandy played with her hair wrapping a strand around her finger. "Can we talk about it later? I'm going to be late getting back."

It wasn't that late, and I'd been expecting her to jump at the chance. "I thought this was what you wanted."

"Why the rush?" She shrugged. "Sometimes it's nice to get away and hear my own thoughts."

"What's that mean? I don't let you"—I searched for the right word—"express yourself?"

"Your place, your life. *That* life," she said, lowering her voice. "It still feels like Ryan's place. And world."

My friend Ryan's ghost loomed over the house. It was true. It had been his home and the whole hustler lifestyle that went with it had lived on after he died. I'd thought Sandy had accepted all that.

"What changed? That's nothing new."

Sandy took a deep breath like she was measuring her response before speaking. "Maybe the thought of committing to that scene, full-time. It feels like a big step."

"You sound like Ali. You're saying you want to keep your distance from a lowlife crook like me?" Sometimes when words jumped out of my mouth, I wished they had strings to pull them back.

Her face went stony. "That was uncalled for."

I was about to agree and apologize when a flurry of movement caught my eye. The entrance to a nearby drugstore erupted with a group of young men all dressed in dark hoodies and masks, and they were racing right towards us.

I couldn't see faces, but the whoops of glee made them sound like teens. They carried bags stuffed with merchandise, some spilling out onto the sidewalk.

"GO, GO, GO!" Laughter mixed with cursing. They were almost on us. Focused on me, Sandy had been a beat slow to turn toward the commotion. As she did, the big guy in the lead plowed right into her. She yelped in surprise, and her hair whipped into the air when she slammed to the sidewalk.

I saw it in slow motion even as the thieves swarmed by me. The guy who'd knocked Sandy down paused to look back and swear at her. He'd just turned to run again when I flipped into gear and charged him, lowering my shoulder and catching him right in the midsection. The punk went flying and landed with a heavy thump halfway into the street. His bag opened like a torn piñata and pills and makeup containers scattered.

In my rage, I wanted to kick the guy into next week, but some of his pals were heading toward Sandy, who was still off her feet. I saw she was probably just stunned. I moved over her to protect her and shoved a couple more guys when they got too close. They kept their feet and ran away, in no mood to fight. I kept my head on a swivel, watching hands that might be reaching for a weapon.

The guy I'd flattened was up and running away, and I was happy to see him doing so with a limp.

As fast as it started, it was over. Finally, a bewildered security guard emerged from the store. I heard cars screeching away, one after another, and stared while all three raced up Market Street and took the entrance to I-95. They were too far away to get a look at the license plates.

I turned back to Sandy. "Are you okay?"

She was working her feet back under herself. "I think so." She held up one arm that had some scrapes that looked like ripe strawberries. Painful, but not serious. I stared at her face and head, relieved to not see any bruising or bleeding. I helped her up, and she hugged me.

I felt her breath hitch as she pulled herself together.

"Thanks for playing matador," she said. "What was that?"

"Flash mob robbery. New twist on the video craze some years back. Now instead of dancing, a bunch of kids coordinate over their phones and hit a store all at once." I checked Sandy for her balance. "You're good?"

She nodded and glanced at the security guard, who'd taken a knee. He was an older guy, with short gray hair and a cut above his swollen eye.

"You all right?" Sandy said. She'd worked as a paramedic before switching to physical therapy. I followed her to the man's side. "You want an ambulance?"

I saw a nameplate on his chest that read "Shaw." "Damn knuckleheads." Shaw took out a handkerchief and dabbed the cut. He swore when he saw the red. "Second time this month."

"The same group?" I asked.

"They didn't sign the guest register, but yeah, I'm not blind yet. It was the same ones."

"What did the police do?" Sandy said.

Shaw barked out a bitter laugh. "Same thing they'll do when they get here. Take a report and sit on they ass."

"Did you see who sucker-punched you?" I pointed to Shaw's eye.

"Yeah, the big one. He was slow enough to grab. Probably should have just let him go. That's what the managers are going to tell me."

On cue, and no doubt because the coast was clear, I saw a short, bald guy peek out the door and only then notice that his employee was still on the ground. Sandy knelt in front of Mr. Shaw and checked his pupils for signs of concussion. I knew the store would have called medics by now, but a look couldn't hurt.

The manager came over. "Are you okay, John?"

"Been better, but I guess I'll live."

"His eyes look clear." Sandy touched Shaw on the arm. "Keep the pressure on that cut." To the manager: "Did you call an ambulance?"

"Huh? Who are you?" The manager looked more stunned than any of us.

I wasn't keen on making it into any official reporting, but unless we ran off, we'd probably have to give some sort of statement. "Innocent bystanders. They ran right over us." I caught Shaw's eye. "That big guy you mentioned knocked her down and uh, bounced off me. He landed hard over there." I pointed to the scattered merchandise and for the first time noticed something else.

A cell phone.

I looked at the manager. "Keep an eye on him. I'll scoop up what I can from what they dropped." I moved fast to corral pill bottles and makeup containers—and palm the phone with my back to him.

By now, we had drawn a bit of a crowd. "You two need anything, Kyle?" a bike shop owner a few doors down asked me. I knew most of the small business owners around here. Sometimes I could help solve problems for some of them. Big chains like the drugstore had little use for someone with my connections.

Another couple workers from the drugstore emerged with bags and began collecting the piles of stuff I'd made. I handed over what I'd gathered—all but the phone.

"Thanks for your help." The manager kept looking up and down the street. The crowd soon got bored—not enough blood, or maybe they'd seen this movie before—and moved on. "Where are the police?" He glanced at Shaw. "And the ambulance?"

On cue, a siren sounded in the distance.

"This same thing happened earlier this month?" I said to the manager.

"Are you a reporter or something?"

I let the sharp tone go. He was pale and sweaty. "Not at all. I was just wondering what the cops said."

I watched him, fascinated by the internal struggle between the company line and the real person. "They took a report. Bet they have a whole pile of them at the station. They wanted to know if anyone was hurt or killed and gave me a copy of the paperwork for the insurance company." His expression and Shaw's told me everything else about their frustration.

The ambulance arrived before the police, and I left my number with the manager in case the cops needed a statement. He told me he doubted they would. Security footage from inside would tell the story. Sandy already said she wasn't going to bother with charges, as we didn't know who crashed into her. She also refused the free Band-Aids and ointment from the store.

We walked back to her office. She was quiet, and I was about to say something when I heard the phone in my pocket ding.

"Was that the guy's phone?" Sandy said when I pulled it out.

"Yeah." Even though the phone was locked, a line of the text message appeared.

Everyone get out alrite?

The screen went black again, but not before I got a glimpse of the owner's face on it. He wasn't wearing a mask. I touched the home button and the face returned on the lock screen.

"There's your man," I said.

Sandy looked. "Looks young. But that wasn't just a prank."

"It sure wasn't." I looked back at the phone and stopped walking.

"What?"

"Are you okay to get back to the office on your own?"

"Yeah, I'm fine, but—"

"What would you do if you realized you lost your phone?" I began to move back toward Market Street.

"Retrace my steps," she said, "and if that didn't work just use 'Find my phone' . . . Oh."

"I'll catch up later." Now I jogged away. The last thing in the world I wanted was to lead this clown and his merry crew to Sandy's workplace.

Would this guy return to the scene of the crime so fast? Why not? I figured all he had to do was get dropped off nearby without his hoodie and mask and he'd be a civilian again. I also didn't think he'd be dumb enough to come with a pack of friends, but then again, this was a bold crime.

I took out my own cell and called the tech expert on my team. I had some ideas, but she'd know the best play. I called the number for VP, short for Vox Pox, her cyber nickname in the hacker world. Maybe someday she'd get around to spilling her real name but the only important thing right now was that I could reach her.

"Yo." She skipped the pleasantries.

"Got an iPhone from a goon in a flash mob who crashed into Sandy and dropped it when I checked him into the boards."

"Is she hurt?"

"Scrapes and bruises, nothing serious. I'm fine, by the way."

There was a pause. "Oh yeah, I see the scanners are saying it was a looting at the drugstore there. What do you need?" She was tapped in to more sources of information than I could understand, but this one would link to the police radios.

"I think the guy will be back for his phone, maybe soon."

"So, you got a hot potato?" she said. "It's locked?"

"Yeah, think you can crack it?"

"Forget it. Those things are a pain. They lock out after a few bad tries. It takes a lot of juice to pull that off. Just ask the feds."

"I thought so. I was going to plant it and have a talk with the dude when he shows up."

"You're alone? Sure that's a good idea?"

"He's just a kid."

"Big enough to flatten your girl. And 'kids' are blowing each other away every day in this city, or hadn't you noticed?"

"All right, how about I hide it nearby and take his picture?"

"Didn't he see you?"

She had a point. "Close enough to smell the hoagie I ate on my breath."

"Gross. Tell me how you're sure it was his phone."

I explained about the flash of text and the locked screen picture.

"Dude. Take a picture of that and send it to me."

I should have thought of that. "That'll be enough?"

"Ye of little faith. Quick, send it, and I'll tell you right away."

She ended the call, and I switched my phone to camera and touched the guy's phone. I declined the passcode screen, and it settled on his lock screen. I took a few shots, not sure how close to get but figuring VP could choose among them.

I looked around for a sign of anyone looking. Not yet. I decided to chance going back to get my truck. I sent the pictures to VP, then drove a short way to the sixth police precinct. I debated about turning in the phone to the cops then remembered the manager's frustration with their response.

Screw it. Let the kid sweat the location if he followed it here. But I didn't have all day, so I got out and pretended to tie my shoe while I tossed the phone into the sewer.

CHAPTER 3

Fishtown, Kyle's place

When I checked back with Sandy at her work, I quickly felt like I'd overstayed my welcome. She was fine physically, and we'd been through a lot worse in terms of dangerous situations. Still, I could tell she needed some space, so I headed back to my place.

While the house no longer looked like my childhood friend's home preserved from when we were still in high school, it remained in legal limbo, though probably not for much longer. My friend Ryan was gone, but to the world he was still just missing. I had it on good authority that when he finally got declared legally dead, I would be named in his will as the owner of the place. But that was merely paperwork. The house was already mine, and as for what else he left me—a list of contacts and schemes that I'd not only taken on but expanded—I also had to own the life I led now.

VP had texted me that she was on the way over. That was usually a good sign and always meant she had more to say than she wanted to discuss over the phone.

I knew when she'd arrived well before her distinctive *tap, tap, tap* on the back door. After years, she still refused to come to the front door. The security system she'd designed let me know when she entered the backyard. Cameras captured her stroll across the grass to the back steps. She wore her usual gray hoodie and a backpack. The ordinary-looking door hid a steel frame and thick locks that rivalled a prison cage.

I let her knock anyway, as if it might be bad luck to just open up.

"You made good time," I said when I finally pulled it open.

She gave me a fist bump and a hug. "Yo. Glad I caught you before you got called in for a tryout with the Flyers." She flipped her hoodie back to reveal a young lady with short mouse-brown hair, mischievous eyes, and a crooked grin.

I always took it as a compliment that she was comfortable enough around me to smile openly. She was normally self-conscious about the slight droop on one side of her face, courtesy of a stroke she'd suffered as a teen.

I let her raid the fridge and parked myself at the kitchen table.

"You want to stick around for dinner later," I said, pointing at her snack, "if this doesn't ruin your appetite?"

"Can't, thanks. Steve wants to try out a new air fryer. I should take advantage before he decides to find a way to weaponize it." She laughed.

Steve, aka Starvin' Steve, was the MacGyver of our team. Like the old TV show's namesake, he was a gadget-head of the first order. Unlike the actor on the show, Steve was a tall, gangly guy whose red hair and freckles brought to mind an even older character for geezers like myself: Howdy Doody.

I was glad to see he and VP were doing so well.

"I guess you were able to use the pictures I sent," I said then told her what I'd done with the phone.

I thought she'd laugh, but she looked up from the laptop she had been firing up. "Wait. Where exactly?"

I told her the police precinct. "The sewer just across the street, actually."

VP's fingers flew across her keyboard, punctuated by scrolling with her mouse. I peered over her shoulder and saw folders open and close. "That's it," she said to herself as much as me. "Open sesame." I saw her login to what looked like a Philadelphia City Police website.

"Is that a good idea? Won't they know you're peeking?" I wasn't sure what she was looking for.

"Any idea how many servers this is bouncing off of?"

"No."

"More than they can shake a nightstick at." She must have been having fun, since questioning her methods usually earned me a lash of caustic sarcasm. "If you must know, it looks like I'm coming from a local radio station's traffic desk."

It started to make more sense. She opened a camera feed from one of the poles on the street downtown. I recognized the street in front of the police precinct. It offered a perfect view of where I'd dropped the phone.

"Grate view, eh? *Graaate.* Get it? Get it?"

She *was* in a good mood.

"Whatever," she said. "Let's take advantage of our premium access, shall we?"

I wasn't sure what she meant by that, but a few clicks later, I saw she'd opened up the time-lapse recording. As she rewound the footage, figures and cars rushed by backward at cartoonish high speeds.

"And heeere's Kyle!" She paused, and sure enough there I was, stepping out of my truck. "Nice technique, boss. You really have to look for the drop."

"Thanks for the review, but—" Then, it hit me. "You think?"

"Let's go forward a little slower." VP advanced the recording, and the cartoons moved in the right direction. I watched the timestamp. About an hour after I'd left, we saw a van pull up. A group of guys got out. They wore hoodies or caps, but otherwise didn't stand out other than that there were several people together.

One of them held a tablet and turned in circles.

"He doesn't look familiar," I said. "That dude looks half the size of the one who dropped his phone. Can you go back there and pause?"

She did, and the camera got a glimpse of the side of the guy's face. "Yeah, who the hell is he? The guy I crashed into didn't look anything like these people. Neither did the rest of the crew coming out of the drugstore. This guy—hell, all of them look more like a protest group. See that arm?"

"Let's see what they do," VP said.

She let the clip run forward, and the guy with the pad zeroed in on the sewer. "So much for coincidence," I noted. "And they know about the street cameras. Notice how we barely get a glimpse of their faces?"

"Yeah," VP said, "especially after they figured out where the phone is."

We watched the tablet guy say something to the driver, who pulled the van up right in front of the sewer.

"What's this?"

"Oh, snap," VP said. "Check it. They're blocking the view from the police station."

The door slid open, and the tablet guy tossed the device inside, then reached deeper and emerged with a crowbar. He gestured to the smallest person, who had to be only a kid, and the two of them pried open the manhole cover near the sewer. The leader guy pointed meaningfully into the slot, and when the kid hesitated, the leader shifted his grip on the crowbar like it was now a club. The kid got the point and clambered down what I imagined to be slimy, filthy, ladder rungs into the sewer.

"Yo," said VP, "these are some devoted anarchists."

The leader called down through the jet-black slot and pointed. A minute later, the kid emerged with a phone clenched in one grimy fist. His gray hoodie was smeared with streaks of algae and probably stuff I didn't want to know about.

The leader pointed to the van, and the kid disappeared inside. Another guy with legs like pipe cleaners helped the leader replace the manhole cover, and then they hopped into the van and were on their way.

"Not a peep from the police station," I said.

"They moved like they had training." VP couldn't disguise her admiration.

"Yeah. But who the hell were they? Did you see anything to link them to the guy on the phone?"

VP logged out of the video clip. She brought up a larger version of the pictures I sent and then rolled out her research for me. "This guy—the one you and Sandy met earlier—has a big footprint, and I don't just mean his shoe size." VP opened a series of mugshots. He had a shaved head and dark, cold eyes. In a later shot, I noticed a scar above one eyebrow.

"Not his first rodeo, I see."

"Not hardly. His name is Andre 'The Giant' Rogers, big dude as you already found and not quite a kid at twenty-two, but a long résumé nonetheless."

"Robbery, assault, car-jacking, hit-and-run. Drug and weapon possession. A well-rounded fellow. He couldn't have done much time and stayed so busy."

"Nope," VP said. "Probation, parole, time served. Charges dropped. Lesser charges plea bargained. The system at its finest."

"Considering the cops' interest today, I don't expect they will be adding to the charges."

"What if you'd given the cops the phone?" VP asked. I couldn't be sure if she was giving me crap or just playing devil's advocate.

"He was masked during the rip-off, and only I know he dropped the phone when I planted him in the street. I can't prove it. I'd probably get charged with stealing it."

"We'd pull the bail together for you," she said.

"I know I can count on you as a character witness." As even I didn't know her real name, I'm sure she would have been thrilled to chat up the police.

"Maybe in a way it's good they aren't interested. At least not in you." VP saw my point. "But the important thing is that Sandy"—she paused—"and you are okay."

"She seems fine. But what was with this crew of run-of-the-mill punks tag-teaming with anarchists? The two groups didn't seem like they'd normally hang out."

VP nodded. "Yep, it's weird all right. But unless I'm missing something, is it *our* weird to figure out?"

"What do you mean?"

"Dude, what do *you* mean?" She wasn't just yanking my chain. "I got your big guy's address and no way to trace that we know it. But what do you want to do about him? Set up on him? Work him over with muscle?"

VP was tweaking me a little, like such measures were so out of the question, but if Sandy had been really injured, the answer might well have been different. I wasn't proud of it, but it would have been nothing for me to call in a favor or two. "Yeah, and tell me you wouldn't feel different if it was Steve he'd ploughed over."

She smiled at that.

"But you're right. What's our move? Not exactly a profit center to steal deodorant and vitamins back for the drugstore." I shook my head. "It was a hell of a weird, random encounter."

"Interesting times in an interesting city," she allowed.

"Thanks for the fast work, and for coming by."

"Always good to practice."

CHAPTER 4

Kyle's place, the next day

Rollie was at the door ten minutes early, right on time for him. Old enough to be my father, the lean, fit former marine sniper had taken me under his wing when my marriage fell apart and stuck by me when I'd followed Ryan into this Robin Hood lifestyle. Rollie ran a side business with me where we bought run-down houses and fixed them up, sometimes to sell, other times for rent to carefully screened tenants. We liked to help those who needed it and could pay us back with their own work, learning repairs and cultivating a trade and, if all went well, on to staffing our budding contracting business.

It all sounded great on paper, and we had enough wins to stay in business, but renters at this rung of the economic ladder sometimes had more baggage than we could carry. We dealt with it as needed, which was why Rollie was here today.

"You scoping the want ads these days?" Rollie said as he stepped inside. He'd never had anything to do with my work at the import business, unless saving me several times when goons tried to take the place by force counted.

"Just wondering how I had to time to deal with the port and get anything else done."

"You let Cliff run the place. How's he doing?"

"He's happy to retire. I don't think he'd work for Ali even if he'd asked."

"Good for him. I'm still pissed for you that that prick thinks he's too good for you now. We should have kept those diamonds." Rollie grinned.

"Screw him. Let him learn the hard way how much crap I kept off his plate so he could build his sanitized new life."

Rollie nodded, then glanced around. "Sandy at work already?"

"I guess." I paused before I spoke, and he noticed right away. "Ah," I went on, "she was at her place last night. I'm sure it's nothing."

Rollie waited.

I told him about asking her to move in full time.

"And she came to her senses and said no?"

"Bite me. She didn't say no."

"But not yes."

I could only shrug. "Thing is, I don't think it was me, exactly. She said it would mean she was saying yes to the whole life." I told him what I'd popped off with to her after that, and he winced.

"What did you say after you pulled your size eleven out of your mouth?"

"The subject got changed." I gave him the quick version of the bizarre encounter with the flash mob.

"Talk about saved by the bell. Or was it alarm?"

"I don't know if it helped or hurt, but . . . we've talked and all, but it has that awkward surface feel. You know what I mean?"

"I was married for fifty years. I know it well." Rollie smiled. "She hit a nerve and you hit one back. Give her some space. She'll come around."

I chewed on my lower lip. "You think? Maybe she's right. It's a weird life, to be sure. We are sort of crooks, when you get down to it."

Rollie waved this away. "Crooks are bad guys. We're outlaws. Rogues."

"I guess."

Rollie laughed. "If you can pull a squared-away old jarhead like me into this life, anything is possible."

"I don't want to *pull* Sandy into anything. But she knows the ones who make the rules never seem to play by them. We just try to even the odds." I'm not sure who I was trying to convince.

Rollie cocked his head at me. "You okay, kid?"

"I'm fine. The port thing with Ali just came out of nowhere. It was the most legit business we had going."

"The houses are okay, if you don't look closely at our seed money. Put more time into those. You aren't exactly a master carpenter yet."

"I hope you're right about Sandy."

Rollie started to say something, then pulled the plug.

"What?"

He frowned in thought. "Well, if it doesn't work out with her, would you mind if I tried my luck?"

He blocked my punch to his shoulder and grinned at me through a boxer stance. "Ready to get down to business?"

"If you're done breaking my balls."

Rollie shrugged. "For now." He turned serious. "You said something about a squatter issue? That's news to me. Which place?" Rollie ran a tight ship.

"Not one of ours. And you or Franklin would know before me if it was, anyway."

"Who, then?"

"You're going to love this," I said. "Cullen."

Rollie stared at me. "'Killer' Cullen?"

"Yup."

"What's the punchline? We're supposed to dispose of the squatters' bodies for him?"

I explained about Cullen's predicament and need for a lower-key approach. "He's on the paperwork for the house, so he wants discretion, which does make sense."

"And these goobers don't know who they're dealing with?"

"Not a clue."

We just stared at each other for a few seconds, but it didn't get any less weird.

"And you're serious?" he asked. "Cullen wants us to handle it?"

"He'd consider it a favor." Which was the same as saying he'd paid us up front in cash.

"I'll be damned. So, what are we up against?"

"The short version is that he rents a bedroom to a kid, some longhair named Lin. Next thing he knows, Lin has two other buddies who'll chip in."

Rollie shook his head. "Sublets? Rookie mistake."

"Cullen is new to straight gigs. Anyway, a few months go by and the rent starts coming late, then stops. Cullen checks on them, and they stop him at the door and, get this, read *him* the riot act about all their rights and how he can't come in to the place without permission."

"Talk about poking the bear."

"Right? He said they were usually high, but I have to think they're also pre-wired for stupid."

"Why not just change the locks when they aren't home?"

"An easy fix," I agreed, "but can you believe, not legal?"

"But it's his house. I still don't get it. It's not like we haven't rousted people before."

It was true. We were careful, but things happened. "That's the catch. This Lin punk has connections with protester groups who will sue and cause high-profile disruptions. Cullen wants to avoid all that."

"So, you're saying we need to get creative?"

I held up two sets of paperwork and a set of keys. "Feel like a little staycation?"

CHAPTER 5

Philadelphia, Old Richmond

Like a lot of the neighborhoods near Fishtown, the streets could be a mixed bag of run-down row houses and rehabbed gentrified places. I could see why Cullen wanted to look after his investment. It was obvious he'd put a ton of money into the place. The outside sported a fresh coat of paint, the windows had all been replaced, but I could already see that some of the blinds were bent and askew.

Starvin' Steve drove Rollie and me down in one of our vans. "You guys need a hand?" he asked.

"Nah, the ride is enough for now. Thanks." Rollie hoisted a large green duffel bag onto his shoulder and carried a big tool case in one hand.

I had another couple of bags. "Depending on how it goes," I told Steve, "maybe VP will give you a pass to stop by." He turned his reddened face away from us. The guy was just too easy to rib.

As for me, I had all the "pass" I could want after another tense exchange with Sandy. She knew Cullen, even helped him out of a serious jam once, but knew what he was and was not happy we were involved with him.

What could I say? Sure, we had people to bring in on projects, but some things required the personal touch and anything involving Cullen had to go well.

"Let me know." Steve closed the door from the driver's seat and drove off before the car behind him on the narrow city street had a chance to start honking.

"Got a feeling the inside won't be as neat and tidy as the exterior." Rollie had noticed the tatty blinds too. "You ready, in case they're feeling froggy in there?"

"Yup. I'll go first." I didn't think, based on the descriptions, that we were dealing with heavies, but idiots sometimes surprised. Which was why I was glad to have Rollie with me. Idiots were also likely to underestimate an old guy like him.

"Going to knock?"

"And spoil the surprise?" I dug a set of keys out of my pocket. The lock was in good shape, as was the door, despite the dirt and scuff marks that made me think some people kicked the bottom with filthy boots instead of pressing the doorbell.

I opened the door wide and fast to give Rollie space to come in right behind me. "Luuuucy, I'm home!"

The first thing that hit me was the stench of weed and sight of food bags and empty cans and bottles all over the place. A flat-screen television rested on the floor below the broken wall mount where it belonged.

We tossed our luggage on the floor to free our hands. I listened, but it was so quiet I began to think nobody was home.

"Well, that was easy," Rollie said.

As soon as he said it, one of the bedroom doors upstairs opened and a figure clad in only in boxers came pounding down the stairs screaming every swear word he knew. He was thin enough that if he fell on the stairs, he looked like he might slip between the balusters. He had so much ink on his torso I almost mistook it for a tight T-shirt. Just the way Cullen had described.

Oh, and he had a baseball bat in his hands.

Amid the torrent of cursing, I grasped that he was curious about who we were and how we got inside. We waited for him to reach us. Rollie looked amused, but like me, he watched to see if the guy was going to wind up for a swing.

"Lin, buddy," Rollie said. "I guess we should have called first."

He recoiled like I'd just doused him with cold water. "How . . ."

"You look like a 'Lin,'" Rollie said.

"Who are you people?"

I jingled the keys at him. "Great news. We're your new roommates."

Confusion swam across his face. "Bull. You can't come in here."

"Au contraire," Rollie chimed in. "A little French lingo I picked up in the service. Which branch were you in?"

The bat wavered in Lin's arms, then he raised it again. "Get out. Now."

"Why?" Rollie asked.

"I'll crack your skull, old man. I'm not playing."

The guy was several inches taller than Rollie and probably fifty years younger. Still, it wasn't even remotely fair. Rollie closed the distance, and by the time Lin tried to use the bat, Rollie was barely an inch away and Lin only bumped him with an elbow as Rollie jammed the swing.

Before he could try again, I stepped up and snatched the bat out of his hands. "No ball in the house."

Rollie seized Lin by the throat and squeezed his windpipe while he backed him against the wall at the landing for the stairs.

"Son, you're getting on my bad side. That's a mistake. Housemates should get along."

Whatever Lin tried to say came out as a gurgle. I noted the crimson color his face was turning and checked the time. We didn't want to make the lad stupid. Or stupider.

"Maybe we should start over," I suggested.

Confusion, anger, and that underlying arrogant façade gave way to fear. After fear could come understanding, but after that came sleep.

"What do you think, Lin? Sound like a plan?" I asked. "We're good guys once you get to know us."

It was hard to tell what Lin thought about that, but judging by his feeble pawing at Rollie's iron grip, he was open to negotiations.

"We'll take that as a yes." Rollie released his hold, and Lin sagged to his side on the floor. His chest heaved and the dragons on his back looked like they were ready to fly away.

"What do you want?" Lin finally managed to croak out.

"Peace, love, and understanding," Rollie said. "But for now, we'll just settle for understanding."

"The peace part will be up to you and your buddies," I said.

Lin coughed, and I could see the rage build in his eyes. This guy didn't get challenged like this often. Or ever. "What the fff—" Lin cut himself off, reconsidered. "What are you talking about?"

"I'll break it down for you," I said. "I'm Mutt, and this is my friend Jeff. We live here now with you and your friends. Got that so far?"

"Is this a joke? You can't live here. You have no right, and I'll call the cops."

Rollie already had a phone in his hand. "Way ahead of you, partner. Call 'em up, but you also might want to put some clothes on. People might talk."

I took out a copy of our paperwork and made sure our names were covered up. "And make sure you show them this."

Lin looked from the phone to the papers and decided to see what I was talking about.

"Recognize Mr. Cullen's name? You can pull all the squatters' rights crap you want and now that Rollie and I are here are on the lease, so can we. See how this works?"

"No way." What passed for wheels turned in Lin's head. "This ain't over. You don't know who you're messing with. I got resources."

"Oh no! Not resources." I covered my mouth in horror.

Rollie didn't smile. He stepped to Lin, who moved up a couple stairs. "Do what you think you need to, but if you ever pull any kind of weapon on us again, we're going to play for keeps. Do we understand each other?"

Rollie wasn't even talking to me, and I still got the chills.

"Whatever. I hope you like parties." Lin's voice cracked, and I saw his hands shake. We'd be careful, but I suspected Rollie's warning had landed.

* * *

Cullen's rental, a few hours later

We'd unpacked in one of the bedrooms upstairs after we'd tossed some other guy's junk into the hallway. Worn clothes, a bong, and assorted junk all went out the door. A cheap hunting knife went out the window and onto an adjacent roof.

As soon as we cleared out the nest, the next thing Rollie did was break out his tool bag and hardware. While he installed a heavy deadbolt and exterior lock on the room, I followed Steve's instructions and put up a wireless camera for the inside of the room.

Rollie tested the locks. The doors were nice wood ones, not junk, hollow-core cheapos that would give way from a hard glance. "This'll do for now. How's our bunkie doing?"

"I'd think he's decided to burn the place down, judging by all the smoke coming from under his door. At least, if it didn't all smell like skunk."

"I'm going to torch these clothes when this op is done," Rollie said. "He sounded rather excited for a while there, didn't he?"

Despite being hard of hearing in my left ear thanks to a bomb blast over in the Sand Box years ago, I could hear the guy loud and clear with the other one. Mostly he was screaming for his friends to get back home. "If his idea of cavalry is the two people Cullen mentioned, we should be fine."

"You going to be okay here for a bit, kid?" Rollie asked me. "I need to get some more supplies."

"I'm good. Tell Steve the camera was a piece of cake. If he has some more, we could use them."

Once Rollie was clear, I left the room and locked it up. I decided to give myself a tour, as Lin appeared to be feeling antisocial.

Overall, the place was a mess inside. The guest bathroom looked worthy of a hazmat suit. They hadn't broken anything, at least that I could see, but I could have written my name in the soap scum layered on the shower floor. I could only imagine what the master bath looked like.

I went downstairs looked at the poor couch. The cushions were stained and dusted with crumbs. A pizza crust stuck out from one seat like a bony finger. On one wall what used to be a Van Gogh print of *Starry Night* could now be titled "Holy Night," as several darts pinned the canvas to the wall and other misses remained embedded in the sheetrock.

On to the kitchen. "Whoa . . ."

Dishes perched in the sink to the point I wondered why they bothered with a pretense that they'd ever be cleaned. I opened some of the cupboards. As I suspected, there weren't many unused plates left. I opened the dishwasher and heard broken glass shift inside. I closed it up.

Roaches and ants raced away when I moved an overflowing trash can. I checked the microwave and smears of tomato sauce decorated the bottom tray, while something cheesy had exploded and vulcanized onto the top.

In the fridge, I found condiments, leftovers in Styrofoam containers, and a couple six-packs of beer. I pulled out a couple cans and shook them up. With a couple others, I gave the tabs just enough of a pull to get that gentle hiss.

I was about to close it up when I spotted a bottle of ScorchAss hot sauce. I took it out along with the leftovers and gave the pizza and pad Thai a zesty refresher.

By the time I left the kitchen, the soles of my shoes were so sticky they sounded like Velcro tearing with each step.

Down in the basement, things were a little better. There was a washing machine and a dryer. They both looked like they'd had a tough time but were still functional. I checked the lint trap and pulled out enough to make a sweater. Detergent powder caked the rim of the clothes washer.

The furnace and water heater looked fine, but that didn't mean Rollie and couldn't come up with some improvements.

I heard footsteps above and muffled voices. The cavalry, I presumed. I went upstairs and saw two figures in the living room. One guy had blond hair shaved on one side and went almost down to his shoulder on the other side. The second had crazed red hair and milk-white skin.

They both sported ratty jeans and old T-shirts. Lin perched on a step about halfway up the staircase.

"Where's the other one?" the blond guy said.

"He left," Lin said. "It's time this one did too."

The blond guy wasn't scrawny like Lin, but his bulk was soft. The pale redhead was short and had a nervous energy that made me wonder what he was on.

"Gentlemen. Lin seems to have forgotten his manners. I'm Mutt, and you are?"

"Showing you the door," said Blondie. "We live here, not you." He had a pry bar in his hand.

"How un-communal. Plenty of room for everyone." I looked to the stairs. "Lin, didn't you explain we have every right to be here?"

"I didn't explain shit. You don't have that senior-center psycho with you. Do the math, and get lost."

I was sorry Rollie wasn't here. He'd have loved his new moniker. "I thought we settled that. Rollie and I are going to take care of the place.

Not to worry, you guys can help. Who wants to start in the kitchen? I'll take the other to scrub the bathroom."

They all looked at each other as if I'd just started speaking in tongues.

"Lin said you locked your stuff in my room." Blondie hefted the pry bar. "First your crap goes out the window, then you, if you don't get a clue."

I tried to picture any of these jerks being able to lift me to toss me from a window. "This isn't the welcoming, nurturing space Mr. Cullen told me to expect. He said we'd get along."

"The only thing getting along is you." Blondie tried to shove me out of the way, so he could climb the stairs. I was braced and didn't budge.

"One of us needs to hit the gym," I told him. "Either me to lose weight, or you to beef up a little." I shoved back, and Blondie fell over the coffee table. He dropped the pry bar and sputtered curses.

"Get him!" Lin shouted from the safety of his perch.

The redhead squatted to pick up the pry bar, but I got there first and stepped on it. Blondie got to his feet, and the redhead tried to punch me in the groin. I pivoted at the last second, so he hit me in the thigh.

I kicked him, more to push than hurt him, and he was so light he kind of sailed right onto the couch. I glanced to see if Lin was going to join the party, but he looked indecisive.

Blondie wasn't, and took the opportunity to land a haymaker on my nose. The pain exploded like he'd punched me right in the temple.

"Bastard." I charged into him and drove him back into the wall by the front door. I buried my fist into the guy's solar plexus. He folded around my arm and lost his lunch.

My reflexes kicked in, and I dodged the not-so-happy meal. I let him sag to the floor coughing and struggling for breath.

I glared at the remaining two and picked up the pry bar. "We done?"

Red's brief flight on Air Kyle seemed to have cleared his head. He looked at his friend. "Jason, you all right, dude?"

Blondie, aka Jason, wasn't, but he would be. He tried to answer and only managed tiny gasps.

"What did you do to him? He's suffocating."

"I knocked the wind out of him. Along with whatever he ate today." I stood over Jason, careful to avoid the mess. "Don't try speaking. It feeds the sense you're drowning in the air."

Right on cue, he sucked in a deep lungful of air and rolled onto his back. The guy on the couch looked a bit relieved that his friend wasn't dying.

"You got a name?" I asked him.

"Caspar." The guy stared at Jason.

"Caspar and gasper, what a pair. Lin, are you going to come down and help your friend? How about you help clean this mess?"

"Screw you," Lin said. "You don't like it, leave. There's the door."

Caspar gained courage from Lin, who I decided was the Moe of these Three Stooges.

"Suit yourself."

Lin waved his friends up the stairs. "C'mon. Forget him for now."

I waited until I heard the door close to Lin's bedroom and then returned to the space Rollie and I had claimed.

CHAPTER 6

Old Richmond, Cullen's rental

I tried to clean up my face and change my shirt from inside the room. The boys were quiet inside the master bedroom.

This was a dangerous time, as they still thought they had the upper hand, and might elect to try something stupid. The point of this exercise was to ensure nobody got killed, but I didn't have complete control over that.

I heard the door across the way open and some whispering. Now someone was on the steps. I put my head against the door on my good ear side and picked up a chuckle, and then I think Lin said, "Go ahead. We got you."

Adrenaline spiked in my guts. I wished I'd thought to drill a peephole, but too late now. I reached into my bag and tucked a small revolver into my waistband that I prayed would stay put. I also picked up a handheld stun gun. Footsteps came closer. My mind raced.

At the last second, I put on a pair of sunglasses in case they tried to blast me with pepper spray. It wasn't ideal, but I'd at least avoid being blinded.

Someone rapped on the door.

"Yes?" I slathered on false cheer.

"Open the door." A shrill feminine voice. More whispering. "Mutt?"

"Just a sec." I unlocked the door and cracked it open with my foot positioned to keep it from opening all the way.

The stooges were all behind a short young lady with close-cropped magenta hair and a black sleeveless Che Guevera T-shirt. Her pale arms

30

were folded, and I could see a yin-yang symbol on one forearm and an anarchy logo on the other. Large-framed glasses completed the look.

"Lin," I complained, "you didn't tell me we were getting company. I would have straightened up."

"Can it," she said. She reached into her pocket and pulled out a business card.

I took it and glanced at it, keeping watch for any sudden moves from the stooges. "Rose Thorn, attorney with the World Citizen Project. Is that a stage name or something?"

"Hilarious. Want to tell me what you think you're doing?"

"I'm just trying to get along with my new roommates." I took off my shades and flashed a big grin.

"You assaulted two of them, and your friend tried to strangle Lin."

"That's revisionist history." I wasn't getting pulled into this game. I took out my phone and snapped her picture, then one of her card.

"You don't have permission to take my picture." She held out her hand. "Give me that."

I dropped the card into her palm and sent her picture to VP.

"You need to delete that. And where did you send it? I'll get an injunction."

I put my phone away. "Get an injunction, an outjunction, and maybe even a *Petticoat Junction*."

I thought she was mad before. "You can't throw my clients out of here. They have rights, and the landlord hasn't even filed any paperwork for eviction. But you are trespassing."

I got the rental agreement and held it up, again concealing our names. "We're just as legally, and we meet our rental obligations. Unlike these deadbeats."

"Give me a copy of that."

"How about no?" I pulled it away and saw she'd been reaching for her phone to get a shot. Too slow. "You waltz in here and flash a card with a goofy name and start issuing demands. How do I know you're a real attorney and rep these clowns?" I looked over at the guys. "Just an expression."

Her face turned brick red. "You'll wish you never met me."

"Way ahead of you on that."

31

She muttered something.

"Sorry, was that Latin, counselor?"

* * *

The next morning

I regretted asking Rollie to wait until morning. I hadn't gotten much sleep, as the stooges had played rap music at top volume right outside the room all night. They'd retreat when I opened the door but then another speaker downstairs would start.

But the kicker was when it finally got quiet and I'd just drifted off only to awaken to loud pounding on the door. I jumped up and grabbed the stun gun and pistol. I figured they were hopped up enough to make a charge.

I wasn't even close. It wasn't pounding; it was hammering. The fools were nailing me into the room.

"Faster!" I heard Lin say.

"What do think this is going to accomplish?" I called through the door.

More hammering, even faster, which gave it a desperate edge. They were still scared of me, which was something.

"You rented a room, and you got one," Lin said. "There's a window. That's your private entrance now." High-pitched pot giggles baited me from the hall.

When they were done, they remembered to put the music back on.

Now that the sun was up, Rollie called me when Steve dropped him off.

"Kept you busy, eh, kid?" Rollie wasn't as full of sympathy as I'd hoped. "Okay, I brought coffee, but you're going to have to lower down my cordless out the window, okay?"

I went to the window, and Rollie was a sight for sore (and tired) eyes. I found some twine in Rollie's kit and used it to lower the plastic case with his tools.

Minutes later, I heard some commotion from downstairs. "Hey, you can't do that." It sounded like Lin.

"Move that couch, you brats," Rollie barked in his marine drill instructor voice. "It won't work any better than that stupid chain."

Rollie had the keys just like I did, so I figured they tried a barricade when he unlocked the door. As for a door chain, Rollie was lethal with bolt cutters.

"Jeez, it stinks in here. Who puked? Disgusting. Make yourself useful, and get a mop from that closet."

Face-to-face made the punks a little more polite, but not more helpful.

"No? Fine. This place is gonna be squared away, believe that." I knew Rollie was keeping an eye on everyone just in case, but I also knew he was having a blast. "You, Lin. Was that your idea to lock my man in his room?"

If Lin answered, I couldn't hear it.

"That's funny?" Rollie asked. "Outstanding. We've got plenty of jokes to share."

I could hear his footfalls on the floor below.

"You must be Jason, and that leaves you as Caspar. You get one warning, and I don't give a crap about your hippie lawyer either."

Now I heard him on the steps.

Rollie knocked on the door. "Top of the morning, kid."

"Just in time. Thanks. How we looking out there?"

"Strictly amateur hour. Hang tight. Your coffee won't even get cold."

Good as his word, after a few nail-screeching, wood-splintering minutes, Rollie had me free.

"Thanks." I clapped him on the shoulder.

"Which one was it that got you in the nose?"

"That bad?" I was trying not to touch it.

"Swollen is all. Go on, I have some calls to make."

When I got back, I heard a shout from the kitchen. "What the . . . shit!" It sounded like Jason. Now he yelled up the stairs. "What did you do to my food, asshole?"

I peered down over the stair railing and waved. "I was locked in my room all night."

The guy was sweating and wiping his mouth on his sleeve. Clearly, he wasn't the resident chili head.

"Crew is on the way," Rollie told me when I got back to the room.

'Great idea." I wasn't looking forward to splitting all the work just between the two of us. We used young people from the low-income rentals as a sort of apprenticeship program, and then ones who liked it and did well went on to work with Rollie rehabbing properties. It could be grueling work, but enough had prospered in it to make it seem worthwhile.

"We'll have to watch over them in case these goobers want to hassle them," I said.

"Oh, I think those characters will respect our privacy." Rollie smiled.

* * *

An hour later

Lin and company showed no signs of heading off to work or whatever it was they did with themselves during the day. Their plan seemed to be to bombard us with constant racket. Cullen had warned me that nuisance calls to the cops went ignored these days.

If Cullen ever saw the extent of the damage inside the house, these guys would die hard and wind up as fish food off the Jersey Coast.

Rollie's phone rang. "Be right out." He hung up. "Crew's here."

I followed Rollie down the stairs. The stooges were draped on the couch watching some stupid game show with the volume going full blast.

"We're going to tidy up," Rollie announced to the crew. "Don't let us bother you."

Jason and Caspar looked to Lin for guidance. He saluted Rollie with his waterpipe.

Rollie opened the door and waved in five of our people. They were some of our regulars, and I was glad to see a brother-sister team who kept things running smooth. The sister, Zoe, high-fived me then her face scrunched up in disgust when she looked around the room. "*Dios.*"

"Yeah. Do what you can."

Her brother, Angel, a recovering addict who hated drugs, smirked. "Bet, Mr. . . . uh . . . Mutt." He pulled out a full-face respirator and called out in Spanish to the other three guys. They all donned the respirators like a SWAT team about to deploy tear gas.

One handed a mask to Rollie and tossed me one. I slipped it on and made sure it was working. Rollie called out to Angel, "Son, you got any more of those?"

Angel smirked behind the plastic and gave a big shrug. "*Lo siento*, Senor Jeff."

Two of the crew went outside and one returned with a rolling mop and bucket kit. Another carried a plastic gallon jug slathered with warning labels.

Lin blinked at the cleaning service dressed for a biohazard zone. "What the hell is this?"

"We asked for help. You all said no," I said, raising my voice to force it through the mask. "You made a big mess, and these folks need to break out the good stuff to do the job right."

Rollie stood next to me while the crew got ready. The guy with the bucket went to the kitchen to get water from the sink.

"We don't have enough masks for everyone," I explained, "so you might want to clear out for a while."

"Bullshit," Lin said. "We're not going anywhere." The other two nodded along with him.

I walked over to the front window to raise the blinds, and one fell off the wall. I opened the windows and felt cool, fall air flow in.

The bucket rolled in, and as Luis, the guy with the jug, approached, he gave a meaningful look to the rest of our team that set us all to double-checking the seals on our breathers.

I held up a finger and looked at Lin. "You sure you want to stay?"

He held up a different finger back at me.

I nodded to the guy with the jug. "Okay, Luis."

Luis cracked the seal and poured a clear liquid into the bucket until I could see the white fumes jump off the water.

"Christ!" Caspar covered his nose and jumped over the back of his chair.

"Really clears out the old sinuses, eh?" I said. The three stooges coughed and scrambled away from the source. "Just the ticket for getting rid of that puke stink."

Luis put down the jug of full-strength ammonia. He made sure it mixed with the water, then he dunked in the mop and began to clean the floor.

The stooges retreated to the kitchen. I followed. "They'll be in here soon and, of course, the rest of the house."

"No way, dude." Lin had more on his mind but the fumes were too strong. As he coughed and teared up, his friends were already working the locks on the back door.

"Good idea," I told them. "Fresh air. They will be a couple hours. You won't even recognize the place. You'll see. Leave it all to us. We'll take care of everything."

Lin was about to continue the debate, but another worker came in and started on the kitchen floor. It must have seemed like they were cleaning the place with smelling salts.

I followed Lin outside to the small backyard. Jason and Caspar were hunched over with hands on their knees like they were trying to keep from coughing up a lung. Lin joined them, and I pulled up my mask. Even a whiff from the open back door told me it had been a good idea to make sure they all got out.

I grinned at them. "No pain, no gain, yeah?"

Lin recovered enough to point a bony finger at me. "You try to lock us out, and we'll get the cops here. You don't have that right."

"Wouldn't dream of it, champ."

CHAPTER 7

Old Richmond, Cullen's rental

Not long after the stooges had left, I heard a vehicle pull up outside the backyard fence. I recognized the van. I went to the gate and opened it to let Starvin' Steve in. He was wearing white painter's coveralls and a breather mask with a tinted face shield so he looked like some sort of invader from outer space. Steve's tall, thin body swam in the large suit. He carried a pair of metal suitcases.

"Shall I take you to our leader?" I said.

"Nanu, nanu," he replied in a passable Robin-Williams-as-Mork voice.

"Wasn't that show before your time?" We walked to the back door, and I almost forgot to mask up until a whiff reminded me.

"They invented a thing called reruns, boss." I assumed he was smiling.

Steve leaned in close and spoke into my good ear. "Are these kids suicidal?" He didn't know Cullen like I did, but everyone in our circles knew who he was.

"They're all assholes, but yes, in a way this is a rescue operation." I failed to suppress a yawn. I pointed to the TV. "They're making it damn tough for me to maintain my tender feelings for them, though. With them blasting their hip-hop, I don't think I got an hour sleep."

Steve smiled, and I realized that his mask was custom, and the entire face shield had cleared once out of the sunlight, like a pair of auto-darkening lenses. "Show-off."

"I can take care of the TV for you. The music too." Steve nodded toward the basement. "Shall we start down there?"

* * *

Cullen's rental, the basement

Rollie clomped down the wooden steps to the basement. His breather was in his hand. "Gas masks are now optional, boys and girls."

Steve and I peeled ours off.

Steve had looked over the equipment and was already digging into one of the aluminum suitcases he'd brought. "These ought to do the trick." He held up a pair of wireless controllers. He looked at Rollie. "You're sure those clowns won't be able to get down here to mess with anything?"

"That's next," Rollie said. "It'll be like a vault when I'm done." He looked around us, shaking his head. "Also, the lads are sure hard on those nice wooden bedroom doors upstairs. I think Mr. Cullen would appreciate it if we took them to our shop for repair and repainting."

I caught the plural and burst out laughing. "*All* the doors?"

Rollie smirked. "Why not?"

"What will those things do?" I asked Steve, nodding at the controllers in his hand. I usually like the technical details explained to me like I was a kid.

"Once I get them on, I'll add an app to both of your phones." Steve started in on the water heater.

"Anything I can do that'd be helpful?"

Rollie pointed to his toolbox. "You can take these bedroom doors off. Just leave them to the side. I'll get them later."

"Oh, I almost forgot," Steve said. "VP said for you to call her when you got a chance, Ky—Mutt. Low key, she said."

"Do you call her VP at home?" Rollie asked him. "You know, when . . ." He trailed off and Steve flushed crimson. Man, he could be touchy about their relationship.

"Maybe." We assumed Steve knew her real name, but he never slipped up. She was big on protecting it, and by now any real name would sound strange to me anyway.

I went to the backyard and called VP. "Low key" meant using a burner phone. Usually if she didn't leave a message or anything, it meant she'd found good information.

She picked up right away. "Yo, how's camping?"

"Damn kids kept me up all night." I gave her the short version.

She laughed. "Something tells me you'll get the last word."

"Gonna try. Steve said you had something."

She turned serious. "Got a minute?"

"Yeah. I'm alone." I liked to let her know I'd be able to talk more openly, though we were always careful on a phone line, even with a burner.

"Something is weird. Your little lawyer friend."

"You found her?"

"Yeah." She settled into an uncharacteristic pause.

"What?"

"She was hard to find, and I'm not talking about because she has a dopey nom-de-plume-sounding name."

"What was the problem?"

"On the surface, she has a small social media footprint. I mean, she appears as an attorney for that group the World Citizen Project, but that site is just window dressing."

"There's no such group?"

"Oh, no. They exist all right, and they *are* big, but they're like a hydra, offshoots that have offshoots that sit on boards, that send funds to this and that, nonprofits here, foundations there, all funded from . . . somewhere."

"I'm not sure I follow."

"That's the idea." VP sounded frustrated. "I feel like I barely scratched the surface, and that's with me digging and hitting some serious firewalls."

"I hope you were careful."

"Please. I could spot their trackers a mile away."

"All of them?" She'd taught me a few tricks.

"That's what's the strangest: A place has to be pretty geeked up in the first place to try backtracking someone poking around, but leaving clumsy trackers for me to spot and get past while more sophisticated countermeasures are waiting, takes serious juice."

"Slow down. They tried to track you, but you evaded and were able to keep searching. But then they had more traps than that?"

"Something like that. Imagine having a password on an account and making it super easy to guess. When someone figures it out and it looks like they're in, but in reality, they just get to poke around a fake site while countermeasures trace the intruder to their source."

I felt tension cinch up my shoulders. "They did that to you?"

"They tried. They chased me all the way back to the IRS, and I disappeared. If they were as smart as I think, they bailed before the IRS IT gang detected them."

I laughed. "You built a fake IRS?"

"'Course not."

My laughed dried up. "You don't mean you went through the *actual* IRS?"

"Don't ask a magician how she does her tricks, mmmkay?" She sounded like she was beaming.

I made myself take a breath. VP knew what she was doing. "I wouldn't understand anyway," I said. "I just picture you tiptoeing through a lion's den on the way to twist the tail of the wolves next door."

"You *do* get it. But the wolves would be crazy to chase me back, wouldn't they?" She laughed. "Besides, I figured that if there *was* anyone poking around, it might just be an agency like the IRS. That, or they'd think it was something worse that would keep them up at night."

"So, is Rose Thorn just a ghost?"

"Well, in her guise as an activist lawyer, definitely not. I found her on documents as attorney of record for a number of cases."

"Sounds real enough."

"Right. But there's a pattern. It seems our girl's specialty is defending anarchist types during violent protests. She was around in both Portland and Seattle a while back, and she put together an amazing track record. And she's kept it up."

"How so?" I was trying to picture this lady in court, but I assume she had more than T-shirts in her wardrobe.

"She never loses. I mean like, ever. All her clients are repeat offenders, busted for assaulting cops, throwing incendiary devices, torching police cars—um . . . 'allegedly' and stuff like that. All the cases got tossed."

"All? How does she manage that?"

"Don't know. In all the cases, the prosecutors reduced the charges to something like a ticket for trespassing or loitering. The accused were out and back on the streets in no time."

"Robo-lawyer."

"Yup. And now she's here, and wouldn't you know, she's off to a great start here in Philly? Not in bulk yet, but my guess is she's just getting warmed up."

"Any idea why?"

"Why here? Why her?"

"Why any of those things?" I said. "It doesn't make sense. Why does this place she works for pour so much effort into her running interference for troublemakers?"

"I can dig looking out for people who get jammed up by heavy-handed cops, but this is firebombs and riot stuff." VP let out a sigh. "I dunno. Lots of missing pieces. Guess we'll have to shake the box until some more fall out."

"Let me know if you find out anything else. Meanwhile, we'll keep trying to shake up a few deadbeats around here." I ended the call and headed back inside to help. The cleaning crew was still here, and I assumed the stooges were smart enough to stay away at least until they were gone.

I went inside and felt proud of the group we'd put together. The kitchen looked functional again, and the dishwasher was working on the first of a couple loads to catch up.

The living room looked even better, with the exception of the still dismounted TV and the dart holes in the wall. Rollie and I could sort the TV, and the wall just needed some paint and spackle. The couch looked reborn, and all the stains were nearly gone.

I went upstairs with the hammer and screwdrivers I'd taken from Rollie's toolkit earlier.

The cleaning crew was working up there. I had them shove all the guys' clothes and junk into closets and strip the beds, so the sheets could be "sent out for laundry service." Soon after, I had all the bedroom doors off their hinges.

Luis came up the stairs with some shower curtains. "Mr. Kyle, Mr. Rollie said to put these in to replace the doors—you know, to respect their privacy." It was good to see the kid having fun.

Steve joined me upstairs. "Rollie is finishing up in the basement. Can I see your phone for a minute?"

I handed it over after unlocking it. Steve held his own phone, and his thumbs danced on the controls. I heard a ping from mine.

"What are you putting on there?"

"It's a custom app we came up with," he said. "Looks like you just have access to a smart house, but there are some extra features."

"Yeah?"

He showed me. "See? This here controls the hot and cold water."

"How much control?"

Steve smiled. "Ever been taking a shower when someone flushes the toilet?"

"Of course." I thought about the sudden blast of hot water. "Good test of reflexes."

"This one will close the hot, or cold, in a flash."

"Nice. Any ideas for those damn speakers?"

"Are they up here?" Steve asked.

"Yeah. I'm still tempted to kick them in, only they are their property and I don't want to give any ammo to that crazy lawyer. We're on solid ground as tenants putting in work as part of our agreement, even if they find it inconvenient. We're fixing stuff they broke."

"VP said the lawyer was a real piece of work."

"Sure seems that way. I still don't know what to make of these clowns, or her, but we have a job to do."

"Yup," Steve agreed. "I might be able to tamper with the speakers if you like. They won't know, unless they're electronics experts."

"Will it take long?"

"Nah. Show me where they are. I have to plant the bugs anyway, assuming you still want them."

"Hell, yeah."

"You got it. I'll slap some limiters inside the speakers so they'll barely make a sound no matter how high they try to crank the volume. When they want eleven, they'll get a two."

"You are beautiful, man."

Steve joined Rollie and me downstairs a few minutes later. "Almost forgot," he said. "Let me help you with that TV. We're all set upstairs. We can record or monitor them live."

"We can get it," Rollie said. "It's just a bracket."

"Oh, I know," Steve said. "I was just going to lock it onto the shopping channel."

"Oh my God." Rollie looked at him. "You stay up at night thinking of stuff like this?"

"I guess it's a gift."

My phone rang, and I saw it was Sandy. Rollie waved me off, and he and Steve set to work on the TV.

CHAPTER 8

I stood outside to take the call. I hated the anxious zing in my gut when I saw it was her. "Hey."

Sandy sounded like she'd started to talk midsentence and was speaking *much* faster than usual.

"Honey, slow down. What's going on?"

I heard her take a breath and collect herself. It took a lot to get her rattled. "Can you get down here?"

"Yeah. Are you okay?" I realized I didn't have my truck here because we were trying to stay low key at this place. These fools didn't need to see what I drove.

"Yes, I'm fine, but Jessica got mugged on her way back from lunch. Broad daylight."

"Is she all right?" I liked Jessica a lot. She'd been one of the first physical therapists that Sandy had hired when her business had begun to grow.

"Yeah. A guy stole her purse and ran off with it. She held onto the strap and got pulled down, but that was it. Still, she's pretty shaken up. And that's not all. Bitsy's car got broken into."

"I'll be right there."

* * *

Old City, Philadelphia

Rollie let me use the junker he had for our mission at Cullen's rental. No way he'd have let those goofballs see his real car, the souped-up Blue Bomber. This old Chevy ran fine, looked like hell, and stood a decent chance of getting overlooked by would-be thieves.

I pulled up to Sandy's office and parked in a reserved spot at a small parking lot next door.

Sandy was watching out the glass door at the front of her office. She came out to meet me. I gave her a hug. "I got here as fast as I could."

"Quicker than the damn cops, that's for sure."

She led me inside, and I kept my mouth shut while we walked past an open area that looked like a cross between a fitness center and a medieval torture chamber. The usual soundtrack: several older folks were working with physical therapists and complaining, but the staff wasn't buying.

Inside Sandy's office, I saw her staff member Jessica. "I'm so sorry. How are you?" She had some gauze bandages on one arm and a light scuff on her cheek that looked like she'd decided to go crazy with rouge but had come to her senses before she did the other side.

"Hey, Kyle. Been better, but it could have been worse." She forced a small smile.

"So did the cops finally show to take a report?"

Both ladies tensed.

"Assholes," Jessica whispered. "They might as well have been using a crayon and scribbling for all the attention they gave my answers."

"What did they say?"

"After getting my information, they told me they'd let me know if they had any leads."

"So don't hold your breath, in other words."

"Yeah. You know, if the creeps had asked, I'd have given up my money. All my IDs and credit cards were in there."

I thought about what else might be in there. "Your keys? For your place, I mean."

Jessica paled. "Oh, shit. And they have my license. They know where I live."

I held up my palms. "All your cards can be replaced. A pain, but nothing more. Let's go over to your place now. I know some lock people;

I'll guard the place until they get there. You'll have a new lock by dinnertime. You need to get on the phone and report all the cards stolen and all that."

"Seriously? You'd do all that?"

Sandy gave me a little smile that warmed my heart.

"No problem," I assured Jessica. "I'm not a cop, but can you tell me anything about the thief?"

"Thieves. One guy, scruffy white kid with a big paper face mask, distracted me with some stupid question." Her jaw was set. "He mumbled, and before I had a chance to respond, I heard footsteps behind me and then came a hard yank on my purse."

"Tag team," I said.

She nodded. "I resisted by pure instinct, but they caught me by surprise and off balance."

"You didn't see the second one, did you?"

"Only from behind. He was darker but also masked. Saw the straps on his ears. Both of them wore jeans and gray sweatshirts. They took off and jumped into a silver sedan that was waiting for them. Don't know what kind, sorry."

"No, you did great." I asked her exactly where it happened.

She told me. "Why do you ask?"

"Street or traffic cameras might have caught something." I blurted it out before remembering that, while I'd known Jessica for a while, she was part of Sandy's work world, not my outlaw life. She seemed to take it in stride though.

"Like the cops will lift a finger to check," she said.

Sandy shot me a look as if to remind me not to reveal too much.

"I'm sure you're right," I said, "but I might know someone who could try. The cops don't run the cameras themselves."

"You don't have to go to all that trouble," Jessica said. "But, thank you."

"Let me call my lock guy, and we can get moving." I still had my small revolver, better than nothing if those clowns decided to press their luck.

Just then another staffer, Bitsy, tapped on the glass window on the office door. I called her Ditsy Bitsy, and not without reason, but never to her face. I might have been a hypocrite, but I was at least a polite one.

Bitsy spoke to Sandy like I wasn't there. "Did you tell him about *our* car?"

Bitsy, great at physical therapy, was the opposite in her financial decisions and choice in boyfriends. Combining the two, the last boyfriend left her holding the bag and her old car got repossessed. I'd loaned Sandy the money for a decent used car for her, so that way Bitsy could repay her instead of me. I'd joked that that way I wouldn't have to send out the leg-breakers if she defaulted.

"I'm pressed for time, Bitsy." I glanced at Sandy for help. "You called the police?"

"They put me on hold. Press one for property crime under a thousand. I hit the other button, and by the time I was done, I thought they were going to arrest me for complaining about a smashed window." Bitsy looked like she'd been crying.

I asked where she'd parked. She told me.

"That's pretty far." I didn't know of any cameras near that side street. "What's wrong with the parking lot next door?" I had a camera of my own watching that one.

"They're soooo expensive there," she said.

For the area, their rates were fair. It was Philly. But no point arguing. I scribbled an address on a Post-it Note and handed it to her. "Take your car there. Tell Ray I sent you. He'll give you a good deal, better than your insurance even, so you don't have to tell them and get your rates jacked up."

"Can they come get my car?" she said.

I glanced at Sandy again and forced myself to count to three. "No. And you aren't allowed to complain to them about that or anything else either. Let him do his job, and pay when he asks. Understand?"

"What? I never complain."

I left with Jessica.

* * *

Darby Township, Pennsylvania

Zach the locksmith almost beat us to Jessica's place. I'd called him on the way, and I guess he must have dropped whatever he was doing to head over.

"How do you get such good service?" Jessica asked me.

"Oh, we used a lot of contractors and such at the old port. I guess he appreciated the business." That, and I helped one of his employees avoid a traffic offense that could have cost him his commercial driver's license.

Basic residential locks were a simple task for a pro like Zach, and he would be done in no time. I asked him to add a Ring camera so Jessica would know if anyone came to her door even when she was away.

While Zach was working and Jessica was inside cancelling cards, I got a couple alerts on the phone app that Steve had modified. Shower number one was in use. Must be the main bedroom, where Lin felt safe. Not for long.

I toggled the switch from hot to cold and back again to give the automated valve a real workout. After a minute, it showed the shower as off, and I received a call from Rollie.

"Kid, was that you?"

"What happened?" I stepped away from Jessica's doorway out of Zach's earshot.

"I could hear that turd screaming all the way through our reinforced door, that's what."

I burst out laughing. "What did they say about the missing bedroom doors?"

"What could they say? Owner's orders, and I can't put back what isn't here, can I?"

"Time for the lights to come on in the middle of the night?" I asked.

"You know the wonky wiring on these old places. Oh, and next time you come, bring a cooler and some sandwiches. I have a feeling the fridge might be unreliable," he said. "And the other clowns just went to the store too. That's a shame."

"I know they're going to get hungry with all the smoking they're doing."

"Forgot to tell you about the smoke detectors Steve left me. They are super sensitive to cigarette and other types of smoke."

"I hope you brought earplugs," I said.

"Not these. When they detect smoke, they trip some industrial-strength air fresheners. Made to dump a whole spray can once triggered."

"What if they like the smell of pine?"

"They'll have to go somewhere else. Steve called it 'gingko and dead muskrat potpourri'."

"Rollie, that's taking one for the team." I hung up the phone.

I saw Zach was finishing up. He knocked on the door, and Jessica came out to get her keys. He explained how the Ring camera worked.

"This is too much," she said. "What do I owe you?" It was good to see she looked calmer.

Zach glanced at me.

"It's on me," I said. "You have enough to worry about. And I get a great discount, right, Zach?"

"I'll charge him double. Don't worry." Zach laughed, and I said goodbye to Jessica after she thanked me again. I walked him to his truck.

I pulled out a couple hundred bucks. "I really appreciate how fast you took care of this. She was shook up."

Zach hesitated. "You know you don't need to pay." He glanced around. "Or is this for show?"

"Consider it a tip. And you can't eat favors, right?"

"In that case." Zach pocketed the cash. "But you should know, business is booming these days. Break-ins and rip-offs everywhere. She's lucky I had this model in stock. It's nuts out there."

"I believe it." I shook his hand. "Stay safe, okay?"

"You too, brother."

CHAPTER 9

Old Richmond, Cullen's rental

It was well past dark by the time I got back to the house. Rollie was in the living room by himself, sipping on a beer and reading a paperback spy novel.

"Just you?"

"Yeah," he said. "They went out about an hour ago."

I got a whiff of something awful. "Ugh. Is that what I think it is?"

"It's worse upstairs. Tell Steve he outdid himself." Rollie tossed me a small jar of Vicks. "You'll need this. I reloaded the sprayers and hid them in a different spot, but I'd be surprised if they tried that again here. I think they went out to light up."

"Thanks for holding the fort."

Rollie smiled. "Those punks are itching for payback, but they can't figure out how. I'm sure they'll get some bright ideas when they get high enough. Just be careful."

"I think I can handle them tonight. They're going to be pissed if they try to blast me with the speakers again."

"Sure you don't want me to stay?"

"Nope. If I need help, I'll call. Get some rest, and maybe a beer that's actually cold."

Rollie shrugged. "I told you the fridge might not work. Plus, somebody keeps leaving the door open. See you tomorrow, kid."

Once Rollie left, aside from the lingering stench from the air "freshener" it was nice to have a moment of peace and quiet.

After a moment, I felt boredom creep in and flipped on the television. I hit the remote for a sports channel and thought about grabbing a room temperature brew. Pass. The channel changed, and I saw a glimpse of a football field before the set flipped to the shopping channel.

I tried again and cracked up when it jumped right back to some offer for a horrible bracelet made with "over sixteen carats of pure aquadidium!" I'd forgotten about Steve's little mod on the set.

* * *

I must have dozed off in the living room. Adrenaline jolted me alert when I heard the storm door on the front open and a key hit the lock. This was no place to be caught napping.

I heard voices whispering and looked up to see Lin leading the group. He took one look at me and glanced over his shoulder. "It's the other one."

"Welcome back, boys. It's not even after curfew. Slow night?"

Jason and Caspar filed in behind Lin. Their droopy, red eyes confirmed Rollie's earlier speculation that they'd taken in more than just fresh air.

"You guys gotta leave," Jason declared. "You're violating our rights and stuff."

"How do you figure?" I noticed Lin whispering into his phone. Something was on their minds.

It was Caspar who popped off. "You told us you were brought in to fix things, but since you and that old psycho got here, you broke everything."

"Rome wasn't built in a day."

"Huh?" Caspar tried wrapping his head around that one.

"We're dealing with some significant damage. The owner is very particular."

Jason stepped up. "No bedroom doors, the shower is jacked, the TV doesn't work anymore, and the old guy owes me money for groceries."

"He ate your food?" I played innocent.

"No, he wrecked it by leaving the refrigerator door open."

"He does get forgetful," I allowed.

Lin hung up his phone and looked at me, then opened the front door.

Rose Thorn stepped inside. "I've heard enough," she said. "This is obvious harassment. Either you get out of here, or we'll sue you and the owner. By the time I get done, these three will own the place themselves." Her ego towered over her compact body. She wore the same black T-shirt with the anarchy symbol.

"Is that a uniform or something? Do you wear that get-up into court, counselor?"

"Have your fun now. You'll see." She glared at me. "What is that stink? Is that what you were talking about?" she asked Lin.

"Yeah. Wait till you see the doors."

Rose nodded. "Privacy violations."

"Now hold on," I said. "The owner has a strict no smoking policy, and I can tell you these three are a bunch of chimneys with bad haircuts." I gestured to Rose's hair. "No offense. And just because they don't like the owner's choice of air freshener to combat the effects of their violations, not my fault."

"Bull."

"As for the doors. There are perfectly good shower curtains in their place, and we promise to knock on the doorframes. Meanwhile, your clients—do they even pay you?"

"That's none of your business. Put the doors back. And there better not be anything missing from their property."

"As I was trying to say before being so rudely interrupted, your clients damaged the doors, assaulted myself and my colleague, and barricaded me in my room. I'm sure some sort of fire code violation or imprisonment crime."

"Yet here you are."

"Remember your case law? Incompetence does not negate intent."

She frowned at me. "You made that up."

"It's in there somewhere. Gotta be."

"And my clients will swear that you attacked them." She took out her phone.

I took out mine, so we could record each other.

"You don't have my permission . . ." she began.

I leaned toward her phone. "And you don't have my permission either."

We put our phones away.

"I need your name and your friend's name."

"We'll get right on that for you."

"You think this is a game?"

I did. But it seemed impolite to say it out loud. "I can't help but wonder, isn't this small potatoes for an attorney of your caliber?"

"What is that supposed to mean?"

"What's your interest in these goobers?" I looked to the three. "Again, no offense, but shouldn't you be busy with bigger cases, like arson, assault on police officers, inciting riots? You know, same as in Portland and Seattle."

The color drained from her face and her arrogant demeanor collapsed. "How—"

"What brings you to our fair city, anyway?"

She ignored me and turned to the group. "Upstairs, now."

"First shower curtain on the right," I called up after them.

I listened to their footsteps on the second floor, and when I was satisfied that they weren't coming back, I opened my phone and tapped the access to the bug Steve planted in the master bedroom. I put in my earbuds.

Rose spoke in a hiss. "Who *is* that guy? What did you tell him?"

"Nothing. The owner sent them to do all this shit."

"I swear, if you said anything . . ."

"We know who we work for," Lin said.

"Do you? I told you to keep a low profile."

"Maybe you should have given him rent money, just saying." It sounded like Caspar. I could only imagine the icy glare. "Bad joke. Sorry."

Now Lin: "Do you think you can get them out of here?"

"I'm about to write you all off. Were you paying attention? They are asking the wrong questions."

I had to disagree. Seemed like we'd hit a real nerve.

"Okay, well if that's what you want, we will need some more muscle," Lin said. "They're tougher than they seem."

"The old guy is crazy, like he's stuck at war or something." I think that was Jason.

"Listen up, and do exactly as I say." I could hear Rose still speaking, but it was drowned out by rushing water in the sink and flushing toilet. The white noise made it too hard to pick out the conversation.

Rose may have looked "out there," but she wasn't stupid.

After about twenty minutes and I don't know how many gallons of water, they shut off the sink. I could hear stomping around, but if they were talking, it was all too far away for the bug to pick up anything.

Then, I heard them on the stairs. Jason led the way, followed in single file by Caspar, Lin, and Rose last. The three guys wore their oversize camping backpacks, and each carried a black plastic trash bag full of clothes. Only Rose was emptyhanded.

"I'm not sure the backyard is big enough for a campout, but you're welcome to try." What was going on here?

None of the guys said a word. Only Lin bothered to look in my direction. His gaze said he wanted to fight, but his body never broke ranks as he followed the others straight for the front door. He stopped before stepping out into the night and pulled the keys from his pocket. He looked at me again and let the keys drop to the floor.

"What's this?"

Rose stepped to me. For a moment, I didn't think she was going to say anything, but then she ended our brief staring contest. "You win." She turned on her heel and joined the guys out on the street.

"Just like that?" I called after them.

Nobody answered, and I was left alone to stare at the group until they rounded the corner.

I closed the door and stared at the keys on the floor. As far as I knew, only Lin had a set of keys to the place. The other guys always showed up after he did, but they could have made copies.

Gone, just like that? Couldn't be. Way too easy.

What the hell were they planning?

It was late, and I was exhausted but far too hyped up to relax. My imagination tended to go into overdrive when I got punchy. I locked the door and picked up the keys. I used the security chain and felt around my waistband to confirm I still had my pistol.

I took out my phone I fired up the bug app and listened on the earphones. What was I expecting to hear? A ticking time bomb?

I wanted to laugh at myself but failed.

Four went up, four came down. You have been here all night. The back door is closed and locked, and you would have heard anyone else come in.

All true. Yet I was feeling jumpier by the second. I started up the stairs. My room had been locked. The bug signal was all quiet. So was the top of the stairs. Steve's stink bomb was still going strong.

I was happier than ever about the shower curtain doors. I had friends who were soldiers over in the Sand Box who described the tension of house-clearing when an ambush could be behind the next closed door.

Here someone would have to snatch the curtain aside like Tony Perkins in *Psycho*.

Okay, that didn't help at all. I put my hand on the butt of the pistol and checked the first room, where Jason and Caspar slept. I made sure to look for trip wires or boxes that made my mind jump to booby traps like the one that hit my truck years ago.

Stupid. These idiots weren't Jihadists; they were stoners.

I moved into the room, checking the corners. Empty.

The place looked like I expected from slobs who'd left in a hurry. Random bits of trash littered the floor. Empty cans and some candy wrappers.

Other than the bed, the only furniture in the room was a white painted dresser and a bedside table with a ceramic lamp. I checked the dresser first. I opened the drawers one at a time using a slow, steady pull while looking inside for trip wires or anything else dangerous.

I gave the drawer a gentle, steady pull, and my heart jumped when I heard a scraping sound. It sounded like a dry leaf dragged across a piece of slate. My imagination turned that into a rigged wooden match being drawn along a striker surface, a second away from igniting a nasty surprise. I stopped and saw that the drawer was now open almost the width of my hand.

I took out my phone and hit the flashlight and camera. I panned it around on video and when I looked into the drawer, I saw the rest of it was empty all except for a small pale blue square of paper caught in the back. When I moved the drawer again, I realized that was what had made the scratching sound.

I opened the drawer the rest of the way and pulled the paper free. It was blank on one side, but the other was covered in childish scribble.

I took a picture of it and then snapped on the lamp, so I could read it for myself. It listed a phone number and then the following:

Homework Assignments: To add new phones, put "Looking to make a DIFFERENCE" for Action, or "Looking to make 1% GO TO 99%" for Work. Imp. Never both on same phone.

It was late, but I couldn't resist sending the image to VP. I didn't add much detail other than to say it was an interesting find and for her to get in touch when she had a chance.

The capital letters struck me as a specific coded message. But why leave something like that behind?

I pictured the two roomies, Jason and Caspar. Particularly the rush they'd left in, and the state of their droopy red eyes that had told me I wasn't dealing with James Bond here.

But the three of them were sure here for some reason, and in the short time we spent together, I never got a glimmer of any purpose other than full-time slacking.

They went to all the trouble of renting the place, and then there was the weird connection with Rose Thorn. They answered to her, and while Jason and Caspar seemed to be idiots, Lin appeared to have more on the ball.

I shook off growing fatigue and searched Lin's room. There was less trash strewn about—no notes or other scribblings. It occurred to me that he could remember the instructions without a cheat sheet.

I began to wonder what Lin—or, more importantly, Rose Thorn—might say if they knew the clowns had left that tidbit behind.

I grabbed some speed loaders for my revolver out of my room and a blanket and pillow for some couch duty until morning.

CHAPTER 10

Old Richmond, Cullen's rental

My phone rang, and I jumped out of a deep sleep hard enough to slip off the couch and hit the floor.

I looked to see who was calling before I checked to see if I'd broken my ass or just bruised it.

It was VP.

I hit the button. "What time is it?"

"Too early? I waited until after six."

"It's fine. Rough couple days. Must have crashed after all." I groaned as I climbed back onto the couch.

"Complete with sound effects," VP said. "Anyway, I thought you might want my thoughts on what you sent."

"Yeah. Better in person?"

"Maybe later. I'm mostly spit-balling here."

I rubbed my eyes. "What do you got?"

"Well, I didn't do much with the phone number itself, like calling it, but I can confirm that the number is a burner."

No surprise there. "And the other stuff I figured was a code," I said. "Or maybe just lingo I'm not up on."

"A little of both, I think," she said. "It looks like it's a system to sign up to get group text messages."

I felt the cobwebs start to clear. "Okay that makes sense." I fished the paper from my pocket. "But what about the part about separate phones?"

"The different messages, one for 'action' the other for 'work,' must be for distinct tasks."

"Meaning what, exactly?"

"My spit balls don't reach that far," VP admitted. "'Work' implies for money. The part about one percent to ninety-nine percent I'm not sure about."

My brain was doing better than expected without coffee. "Well, who or what is one percent?" I asked.

"The rich?"

"I think so. And the ninety-nine?"

"The rest of us?"

"Probably something like that. I think they're talking about taking from the one percent and redistributing to the rest, except I suspect in their case they mean rich companies."

VP was with me. "Snap! Like rich drugstore chains, other businesses?"

I pictured the stampede onto Market Street. "Exactly."

"Not bad, dude. And the other?"

"The word 'action' is pretty broad. Could be anything."

"How about we sign up on a burner account and find out?" VP suggested.

"You think it will work?"

"Can't hurt to try," VP said.

I filled her in on the rest of last night, wrapping up with the oddly docile exits of Rose Thorn and the stooges. "If these guys are professional troublemakers, why not stay and fight?"

"Good question."

"It was clear the lady was in charge," I said, "and she said something about not wanting to draw attention."

"Laying low until the right time."

"Yeah. And time for what, I don't know."

* * *

Two hours later

"Kid, why do you get all the fun?" Rollie had arrived with food and a huge plastic spray bottle with a new concoction Steve had made up to neutralize his stink bombs. "I would have given anything to see their Waterloo march."

"It was too easy," I said.

"Easy? You checked a mirror lately? You look like you haven't slept in a week."

"I feel the same." I smiled. "We gave them both barrels, but it was the way that lawyer reacted that gave me the creeps."

"Lose the battle to win the war, kind of thing?" Rollie asked.

"Yeah. Just like that."

"We'll figure it out. In the meantime, I still say they all owe us their lives, and we need to get to work making sure our friend gets his place back better than new."

Rollie went upstairs and soon returned. "This stuff works great."

I sniffed the air. "Seems much better. You have people coming over to help?"

"Angel and Luis are helping Steve load up the doors. I finished them yesterday. He should have new hardware for the locks. The rest of the work should be routine."

"Great. I could use a trip home and a long shower."

"All good, amigo. We have it from here."

* * *

As I drove back to my place, I felt bad leaving Rollie with all the aftermath grunt work, but I knew he loved that sort of project. The hard part was keeping him from adding his own improvements, but he understood that anything like that that Cullen might want, he could request. As it was, we'd put in a bit of investment turning his place into a non-lethal house of horrors.

It was all right. Some favors are more equal than others, and having one from Cullen in the bank was like an insurance policy I hoped I'd never need.

When I pulled up to the house, I saw a young kid riding a bike back and forth in front of the place. He looked bored and managed the bike while holding and staring at his smartphone.

I didn't know him, and I recognized most of the kids in the neighborhood. Not that there were many. We had more seniors on the block. Maybe this was someone's grandkid.

I might not have known him, but he seemed to know me, or at least who I was. He looked up from the phone and stared right at me as I parked and got out of the car. I met his gaze and watched his hands in my peripheral vision. Kid or not, he was old enough to pull a trigger. I closed the distance.

"Something I can do for you?"

The kid's dark eyes looked hard and older than the rest of him. He wore a dark wool cap and light windbreaker. He put away his phone, and I made sure his hand came back empty.

"Yeah," he said. "They want to see you."

"Which 'they' is that?"

I enjoyed the moment of confusion that took years off the guy's face. He thought for a moment then said, "I work at the bakery." He was trying hard to be discreet.

"The doughnut shop? I swear I was going to pay this week." Now, I was just messing with him.

"No." He lowered his voice to a whisper. "Heather."

Heather Bakery, home of the worst selection of baked goods in Fishtown, but the highest concentration of Irish mobsters, run by the co-bosses William and Charlie O'Brien.

"Ah. I get you." I pointed at the bike. "Am I supposed to ride on the handlebars?"

The kid looked shocked. "What? No. I'm just the messenger." He looked around. "I can't be seen with you." He rode off.

Okay, I guess that made us even. When even wannabe mobsters are too good for you . . .

* * *

Fishtown, Heather Bakery

I took advantage of the VIP parking in front of the bakery. One goon moved the orange traffic cones out of the way for me. "Thanks. I'll get you on the way out," I said like I was going to tip him.

The door opened to the usual gritty, dusty entrance to the bakery. One table sat unused in view of the grime-coated window. Glass display cases showcased the day(s?)-old assortment of baked goods. Stale tobacco overpowered the faint odor of lace and Irish oatmeal cookies.

A guy named Jimmy greeted me. He was what passed for a doorman to the place and in a pinch, could pretend to serve customers if anyone was dumb enough to blunder past the guys in front.

I'd long since graduated the typical frisking most visitors would get. Instead, he just pointed to the back hall. "You know the way."

I did. I wasn't considered "family" in any sense of the word but couldn't deny that I worked *with* the Irish. I'd stumbled into becoming the guy who ran their small loansharking business. It was kind of a franchise arrangement, where I got the leads from them and they got a cut of the action from any loans I generated. It was a pain in the ass, and despite the ugly name, a money loser for me. I'd agreed in order to help a friend in trouble and had been stuck with it ever since.

On the plus side, the Irish kept the drug and gambling addicts for themselves, as they liked the chance to sink in their claws. For my part, I got to help down-on-their-luck people in the neighborhood. Because I'd never send out leg-breakers, those who couldn't pay ended up owing me a favor, which was what made my oddball outlaw operation tick.

But I hadn't been summoned to an audience with the bosses to talk small-business lending practices. Something was up.

When I got to the heavy door at the end of a dark hallway monitored by cameras, I just nodded to the guy sitting on a stool. I knew what to do when I heard the door lock buzz.

Inside the plush but outdated apartment suite, not much had changed over the years. I heard heavy footsteps that preceded Charlie, the bigger and crankier of the two O'Brien brothers. Since I'd first met him, he'd lost some hair and a couple of fingers but otherwise maintained his intimidating presence.

"About time." Charlie shook my hand, and I tried to avoid the stumps of his pinky and ring fingers.

He waved me inside the living room and headed straight to the bar to pour the mandatory glass of whiskey.

"Ever think of using a faster way of communicating than Wannabee Western Union?" I accepted the drink and raised the glass for a polite sip.

"If they can't handle little stuff, how can you trust them with bigger jobs?" Charlie took a generous gulp.

"They grow up so fast," I quipped.

"When they get a chance." Charlie had seen the alternative too many times, I knew. "So, how's life in the unemployment line?"

"I cashed out of a business I developed. Just looking for the next opportunity." I felt a flash of anger, no doubt just what Charlie wanted.

"I heard they shoved you aside like yesterday's news," Charlie said with a laugh then sobered up all at once and added, "We could have made a mint with that port if you'd only seen the opportunity right under your nose."

"That was never going to happen." The last thing I'd needed was for the place to have been shut down for smuggling.

"I guess we will never know," said the second brother, William, as he stepped into the room. He was a wiry man with an intellectual appearance, especially alongside his hulking brother. Both cultivated their images, but William was much tougher than he appeared and Charlie was no fool, despite playing the part of the knuckle-dragging heavy when it suited him.

"Why are you so interested in the port now?" I asked them. "Good luck negotiating with Ali. He thinks I might tarnish his reputation. Imagine what he'd make of you two."

"Dear brother," said William, "I believe we've been insulted."

"Just trying to keep up," I said. "So I'm assuming you two didn't get me here just to roast me."

"That's just a bonus," Charlie said. "How's it feel to have the so-called decent folk look down their noses at you?"

"Sucks. There, you happy?"

"I'll take it," Charlie said.

"We heard a few things about this Ali character," William said. "Perhaps you're better off without him. People putting on airs can be most unreliable."

"It's done," I said. "Now what's on your mind? Seeing as we're all being honest."

"Fair enough," William said. "We—and by that, I mean your interests and ours—have a problem."

"And I was worried it'd be good news," I said.

William ignored my remark. "Friends of ours in the business community are concerned about the increasingly hostile climate in the city."

"I'm aware, believe me."

"Screw the euphemisms." Charlie glanced at his brother. "Businesses that kick up to us are getting run out of town. They pay for protection and expect it."

"I hear things." I wanted to be careful here. "I didn't think it was my place to get involved, so I try to stay out of it."

"Smart, but in this case we're all involved," Charlie said. "We keep trouble, like the city, off their backs, and make sure nobody else is pressing them for the same services."

"I understand the principle." What were they really getting at?

"The specific problem, as everyone can see," William said, "is the spike in street crimes."

I mentioned getting run down by a flash mob the other day.

Charlie nodded. "Exactly. That crap's everywhere, all the sudden. We look bad to our customers, see? In the past, we were able to handle local problems, and they wouldn't go near the place again."

"I've never operated like that," I began.

Charlie waved me off. "We know. We know. Saint Kyle can't get his hands dirty."

"Oh yeah?" My faced flushed hot, and my mouth was running on its own. "Your memory must be shot, Charlie. Care to count to ten for me?" Here, I had in mind me risking my life rescuing him from a filthy room where he was being tortured by having two of his fingers chopped off.

William stepped between us as his brother drew himself up. He glared at Charlie, then looked back to me. "Enough."

I shrugged like I was stepping down reluctantly, but the truth was that my blood had already cooled sufficiently to remind me of my just about nonexistent chances against Charlie O'Brien in anything approaching a fistfight.

"However you choose to handle matters, Kyle," William went on, "I'm betting you have seen the same challenges."

"Some," I admitted. "And I agree, whatever is going on is getting worse."

"And why wouldn't it?" Charlie groused. "What's to stop them?"

"Okay, since you brought it up, why *can't* you lean back on the thugs?" I was curious.

"Contrary to popular belief," William said, "we can't just mow people down in the streets."

"Not and get away with it," Charlie added.

"Which gets to the point. In the past, we had a certain understanding with the prosecutor. He couldn't stand for any Wild West antics, of course, but would accommodate a more tempered approach."

I nodded. "I dealt with him a few times. Very fair, as long as he ended up looking good at the end." I saw William nod. "Of course, that's out the window since he wound up face-down in a plate of fettucine." By all accounts, it wasn't foul play. The guy had died from a widow-maker heart attack.

"His replacement has been less accommodating," William said.

"Oh, you think?" Charlie looked at his brother. "Can I talk straight?"

"Feel free."

It looked like a mask fell off Charlie's face. "That piece of shit! I didn't like the last guy, but at least he got it that if we backed off, we could expect the cops to step up and do their part." Charlie jabbed a finger in my chest. "You never heard me say this, but we could use a good police crackdown around here."

William shook his head. "For all the good it would do. We have a prosecutor who refuses to prosecute. The punks that pull the robberies are out the same day. No bail, no anything."

"Not only that, our guys inside the force tell us that they are being straight out told to stand down."

"Do they say why?" I asked.

"Nothing that makes sense," William said, "beyond the fact that anyone who pushes back winds up riding a desk or gets early retired."

"And we know for sure if we started taking out the trash, the guy would have no problem prosecuting us."

"How do you know that?"

Another glance between the brothers, then Charlie spoke. "This asshole is on another level. He's squeezing us. Believe that? Just so he will stay off our backs."

I couldn't suppress the start of a grin. Charlie caught it and leveled one of his finger-stumps at it. The smile withered on the vine, but he kept pointing at where it'd been. "What's *that* about?"

"You don't think it's ironic that he's running a protection scheme on you?"

"Is that supposed to be funny?" Charlie spoke through gritted teeth.

"I guess not. Look, I'm seeing the same thing out on the streets. It's getting bad out there. But what do you expect me to do? My people aren't heavies."

"That's not what we need," William said. "At least, not exactly. You have . . . unconventional approaches."

"True. What were you thinking? Getting some dirt on the prosecutor?" I tried to imagine what to say to convince VP to spy on the guy.

William smiled. "Even if you could, are you asking us to support something that goes to the feds?"

Right. "Not the résumé enhancer you were after, eh? What, then?"

"You help your friends' businesses out, no?"

"Sure."

"Do they pay you?"

"Including favors," added Charlie.

"Yes, but—"

"But nothing," William said. "You'd be helping their businesses from the same kind of scum that is hitting *our* protectees. Hell, probably the exact same scum, with this revolving door crap."

He had a point there.

"You wouldn't hover over me telling me how to do my thing?" They saw me weakening.

"If you get the job done," William said, "we don't care."

I thought about it. "If we both fail, not only do we lose face, some of these guys are going to form their own vigilante squads. Then, it will really hit the fan."

"Maybe it should," Charlie said.

"Careful what you ask for," I said. "All right, I'm in." The math was easy. Better to work with these guys than against them. "Which are the businesses you are protecting?"

William took out a list he'd prepared for our meeting, a real tell that showed just how desperate the O'Briens had become.

CHAPTER 11

Fishtown, Kyle's Place, the next day

I'd called a meeting of the brain trust of our group. Rollie, VP, and Steve all sat in the living room. Only Sandy was missing, since she was busy at her work and I knew she wanted a little space from our ventures. I didn't know if that was going to be permanent and what it might mean for us, but I had plenty of problems on the front burner at the moment to distract me from the issue.

"You're asking us to work for the Irish?" VP's face scrunched in disgust. Steve held his peace, and Rollie waited to hear more, but his expression wasn't encouraging.

"Not exactly," I said.

"Not *not* exactly either," VP shot back.

"Can we try to focus on who we'd really be helping? The businesses we look out for are no different from theirs. Right next door, sometimes, and we all see what is happening out there."

"Why can't they fight their own battles?" Rollie said. "They've managed in the past."

"We've gone to war alongside them before. This isn't new," I pointed out.

"That was different," Rollie said. "We were under direct threat ourselves."

"And we're not now?" I said. "The streets are becoming a war zone, and people we all know are right on ground zero, whether they like it or not."

"What do they expect us to do?" Steve asked.

"That's the good part, I guess. They said whatever it takes." The whole group reacted to that, but I cut them off: "Hang on. I say that means we get to decide what *not* to do."

"Damn straight," VP said.

"Right," I said. "Think about it. If we sit it out, what do you expect the Irish to do? They won't just roll over to the threats."

"Blood in the streets," Rollie said. "But that's never been a problem for them."

I explained their issue, especially with the pressure from the new prosecutor. "We've never faced this scale of lawlessness. Neither have they. Think of this as an opportunity to solve their problem in a different way and protect the business owners at the same time. Not to mention regular people bound to get caught in the crossfire."

VP side-eyed me. "Dude, you're getting good at this. Ever think of going into politics?"

"That's a hell of a thing to say to me. What'd I do to deserve that?"

Rollie and Steve smiled.

"So," Steve said, "if we're in it for our mom-and-pop stores, where do we even start?"

"Hence the meeting," I said. "Places are getting hit by these flash mobs. We've gotten some intel that they are organized. VP, anything new on those text numbers left behind at Cullen's place?"

She pulled out a couple burner phones. "I followed the directions like that note you found said to do. I didn't get any hostile response or third degree, but no invitations to rip off a store or cause other trouble either. Guess we wait and see."

"It was a long shot, I suppose. Maybe something will turn up." I faced Steve. "We made those squatters' lives hell. Any ideas on what we could do to discourage looters?"

He smiled. "Sure, plenty. The real question is what can we do in sight of the people we are supposed to protect? That's more high-profile than we usually roll."

"Good point. No sense guessing. Maybe while you come up with some approaches, how about I drop in and chat with some of the businesses from the list the O'Briens gave me?"

"We'll work up some options," Steve said.

"I'll be at Cullen's place putting it back in order until you need me," Rollie said.

* * *

Philadelphia, Jewelers' Row, Sanger's Diamonds

After the smashed front window, the first thing I noticed at Saul Sanger's store was a uniformed cop just inside the door. That was new. He wasn't taking a report; he was just sitting there. I nodded to the guy and realized I knew him.

"Derek?" He'd only just joined the force a year ago and had worked at my port last summer while he was still in college. He'd joined me on a couple long-haul truck runs when we were short-staffed during a large shipment. A hard worker who'd never complained. Smart too. If he hadn't been such a straight arrow, I could have seen him finding a place on our team. As it was, I was glad things were turning out so well for him in the real world.

I felt bad that I'd lost touch since he'd joined the force. Had I been avoiding temptation to develop a new source with the police?

"Kyle, good to see you." He shook my hand. "Sorry to hear about the port. I really enjoyed working there. Are you going to be okay?"

Every time I started to feel better about being shut of the place, little things like this were a painful reminder. "Yeah, thanks. *I'll* be fine. Some good people will leave, not all of them will land on their feet." I tried to play it off.

"Not your fault. I heard you were bought out." Derek was as sharp as I remembered.

"He who has the gold makes the rules, as they say." I gestured around us at the store. "What about you? Moonlighting? Or is Saul in tight with the Commissioner?"

He shrugged. "Gotta make ends meet." He pointed to the plywood and jagged shards of glass that still clung to the window frame. "Plenty of work around. You sure you aren't looking?" He smiled.

"Nah, thanks," I said. "I'm keeping busy."

I heard a door behind the counter open with a chime.

"Kyle? Come on back."

A young guy farther down the counter returned to his jeweler's loupe and picked up a ring as an older guy stepped out from the doorway.

A big banner on the wall of the store read "Don't Look Back in Anger. Go to Sanger!" I could hear the old guy's voice from the radio spot in my head.

"Saul, thanks for making time."

He waved me through.

When we were out of earshot in his back office, Saul began to speak. He stood about five feet even and his white hair contrasted with the bright red skin under a constellation of liver spots.

"Kyle, I agreed to see you as a courtesy." Sanger gestured for me to take a seat.

"I appreciate that. The brothers asked me to come—"

"Screw them." I'm sure my eyes popped wide at that. "At least *you* showed up," Saul steamed on. "Those two can't be bothered. You know how long I've been kicking up to them?"

"Actually, no. I usually stick to my own work."

"Twenty-five years. I know the score, and I never made trouble for them. Ask anyone."

"I'm sure," I began, but the guy was hot.

"But it's gotta be a two-way street. I get that it's like insurance, you hope you don't need it, but you saw my front window." He was waving his hands around while he talked.

I nodded because he wasn't going to hear me if I spoke anyway. He needed to vent, but I was beginning to get worried he might stroke out on me.

"That's twice in the last month. Twice!" Spittle flew from his mouth. "I don't even put the good stuff out there now." I noted a row of floor-mounted safes.

"That's why I'm here."

"To what? Collect? For what? Tell them to walk in and take what they like. Everyone else does. Hope they are happy. I'll be out of business in a year like this."

I held up my hands in surrender. "I'm not their errand boy, Saul. I came to help, if you'll let me."

That slowed him down. "I'd help myself if I could. Never been a gun guy, but I'm ready to learn, even at my age. My grandson's still finishing law school, and I won't have my Sarah getting hurt over this."

"I noticed you seem to have security covered." I gestured toward the front of the store.

"What else can I do? The regular police fill out paperwork, and that's it. File a claim, they say. I did, but my agent said they'll cancel my policy after this one goes through."

"I'm sorry about that, Saul."

"Now, I have to hire the police out of my own pocket. Maybe those cockroaches will think twice next time." Saul pointed a finger at me. That was okay. I knew it was really at the O'Briens he was seeing when he did it. "And you can tell those cowards at the bakery that the cost of his pay comes out of their end."

My heart jumped. I wasn't about to toss that kind of a gauntlet at the O'Briens' feet. They knew that sort of dissention could be contagious, and they'd be pressed to make an example out of him.

Still, he had every reason to be furious. What could I offer that a real officer at the door couldn't? Rather, what could I do in full view of a real cop? I wouldn't want to put Derek in the position of looking the other way, if he even would.

"Hang on, Saul. Tell you what." I reached into my pocket and pulled out a wad of cash. "I'll cover Derek's pay if you kick up as usual to the Irish. They know about the problems and that they're different than what any of us are used to seeing. But I'm here, okay?"

"But what can you do?" Saul looked at the cash. "I don't need a loan, least of all at your vig."

I shook my head. "No interest. This is me putting my money where my mouth is. I need a minute to figure out how to help, and if I can't do better than your arrangement with Derek, then I'll cover it myself."

Did I really just say that? I'd run my little empire into the ground if this kept up. But if nothing else, Saul's head didn't look like it was going to explode anymore. He took the bills. "You can have this back if this works out. You have to understand, I speak for a lot of places that are too scared to pipe up. We're getting wiped out here."

"I hear you," I said. "Can you tell me more about what did happen?"

"Bastards. This last time, we were just about to close." Saul tapped on a laptop and spun it around so I could see what was a recording of a security camera feed.

I recognized the same man with the jeweler's loupe behind the counter. He was talking to a young man and showing diamond rings. I'd been that lad once, long ago, versed in all the Cs: color, cut, and clarity. All forgotten now. Motion by the big window (now plywood) caught my eye just before the glass shattered, making the two in the store jump. In the next instant, the door burst open and masked thieves filed in.

I was struck by the almost military precision the crew moved with. They split off to apply hammers to select cases and left others alone. Three of the group ran straight to the counter.

Right away, I saw the leader was a big guy. He pointed a pistol at the clerk, who showed his hands. Another robber threw the young customer to the floor. The big guy, who sure could have been the one I knocked down, dragged the clerk half over the counter and kept the gun in his face while another guy swept the rings into a black sack. The others scooped up what they wanted and sprinted out the front.

"Fast," I said. "Did he hit the alarm?"

"Didn't have to," Saul said. "They did it themselves when they broke the glass. Not that it mattered."

I counted about half a dozen in this group. "Do you have any feeds for outside the store?"

"Only out the back," Saul said. "Sansom is a narrow street. I'm sure several places must have cameras that could have caught something. The cops never even asked that much. Does it matter?"

"Can't hurt. The more we know how they work, the better chances are we can help."

"I'll kick in for a rocket launcher if that's what it would take."

Saul and Rollie would get along. "I was thinking along less messy lines, but good to know."

Saul smiled for the first time since I stepped in the door.

* * *

After I left the jewelry store, I glanced around for obvious cameras and saw one at a traffic light and more perched to cover store entrances.

Might turn up something, but now that I thought about it, I wasn't sure how useful it would be after all. I'd seen firsthand how these guys moved, and the key elements were surprise and speed. I was curious if they would use the same vehicles, but if they did, I doubted they would have the same tags.

And they were evolving, their operations swelling. Part of it was that they were getting bolder and really, why not? What did they have to fear? The only increased caution seemed to be that they realized a place like a jewelry store might be a harder target. So they'd escalated the chaos by waving guns around. They'd shown some restraint (somewhat) this time, but how long would that last?

My cell rang, and I saw that it was Sandy.

CHAPTER 12

Philadelphia, Jewelers' Row

"Hey, babe. What's up?"

"Hey." I could hear already she was upset.

"Are you okay?"

"Yeah. I'm all right." Sometimes my protective streak annoyed her. Not this time. "Mr. Penney got jumped on the way to our appointment. Not a block from the front door."

My heart sank at the image of the kindly old guy getting injured. He'd already been through the wringer after a car wreck which saw him and his wife badly hurt and then screwed over by a crooked lawyer. We couldn't help before he lost his wife, but our group did a number on the lawyer and got him the money he deserved. Sandy had performed miracles with his physical therapy, and he acted as an informal buffer to some of the folks in the community who saw me as an all-purpose complaint department.

"Is he hurt?"

"He's okay. Shook up, but also really pissed."

"That's good to hear."

We fell into an awkward pause that I let Sandy break.

"Yes," she said, "it's good that he's not hurt, but, well, can you come by?"

"Sure. I'm not far. See you in ten."

Even though Sandy didn't want to say more on the phone, I knew I didn't have to run any red lights to get there in a panic. Along the short drive, I noticed more plywood sprinkled along the storefronts. Not most stores, but more than I could ever remember seeing.

* * *

Old City, Philadelphia

As I got out of my truck, the streets looked normal, but there was an undercurrent of tension. Everyone moved with a sort of furtiveness I'd not seen before. Little cues—looking around, walking faster, no eye contact.

I crossed the parking lot and went inside the entrance to Sandy's therapy center.

A couple of her staffers were working with clients on some of the strength machines. Usually, the machines were all taken, and a therapist sometimes juggled several clients at the same time. Not today. It was strictly one-on-one.

I saw Sandy in her office, and Mr. Penney was seated with her. I waved to the staffers and headed back.

Sandy came out from behind her desk and gave me a hug and quick kiss. "That was fast."

"Kyle, my boy," Clarence Penney stood, which made me feel better. Maybe he really was okay. He shook my hand instead of a hug and kiss. Also okay.

He wore his signature suit, which looked like something out of the Godfather movies, complete with his Homburg hat, only now I could see it was scuffed and crushed. He treated the outfit like his uniform, including insisting on bringing a change of clothes for his therapy sessions.

"I hope you're doing better than your hat."

"Little monsters pushed me down, but other than a tear in my pants"—I just noticed a small bloodstain by the knee—"and a bit of a scrape, I am unharmed. I landed on my gym bag, which they promptly stole."

"I'm so sorry."

"They also took my cane."

That's what was missing. Even more than the trademark hat, Penney always strutted everywhere with a polished wood walking stick topped with a solid gold cap.

"I'm sure Sandy can lend you a cane until we can get it replaced."

Sandy nodded. "That's what I was just telling him. It won't be as stylish, but it'll give plenty of support."

Penney stared at the floor. "And I was just telling Sandy, as much as I appreciate that, another cane won't restore my confidence. And I must say, and this is no reflection on you, my dear"—he touched Sandy on the arm—"but I feel I have to warn the people in our community here at the center that this area isn't safe."

Sandy pressed her lips together but said nothing.

"What do you mean?" I said.

"After the indifference of the police just now, I'm sorry, but I can't let our friends come down here if nothing changes."

I realized that the bulk of Sandy's clients were older folks coming back from hip and knee surgeries. Aside from her skills at rehab, the location was ideal as a convenient spot for locals.

"Things have been rough all over," I began, "but I'm sure—"

"I feel like a coward saying so, but it isn't just for me. My friends trust my opinion, and I can't send them into harm's way."

I could see he was upset. Sandy, who could be ruthless in pressing effort during her therapy sessions, had never experienced this sort of resistance. "Mr. Penney," I said. "You know I understand how important the work that gets done here is to folks' recovery. You could set yourself and others back months, even years."

"Even if we could all dance like Fred Astaire as a result, better to muddle through a recovery at home than a fresh batch of injuries from roving bands of hooligans."

I could see his hands trembling.

"I get it," I said. "How about I give you a lift home, and we sleep on it?"

Penney looked at me and smiled. "Thank you. I appreciate that. But as for the other, what will change overnight?"

"I'll let you know," I said. Just as soon as I thought of something.

"I have some men's sweats in the back," Sandy said. "How about you try your session anyway, as long as you're here?"

I met his gaze. "If you are up to it, of course." Sandy would never have suggested it if he'd been seriously injured.

I saw a spark of pride in his eye that warmed my heart.

"I can take it."

"Kyle, help me find them, huh?"

I took the hint and followed Sandy back.

"That was sweet," she said. "Thank you."

It was nice to hear, but she was chewing her lower lip. "You're welcome. But . . ."

She sighed. "But . . . this is a real problem. Even if he's exaggerating the danger, if he scares off the neighborhood clients, I'm screwed."

I took a deep breath. "Hon, I don't think he is. And I worry about you all myself. It *is* getting bad out there. Just like what we saw, and it seems to be spreading."

"What do you expect me to do, then?"

"First things first, Penney and the other seniors will stay away if they can't get to your place safely."

"Sums up current events," she said with a brittle edge. Sandy was stressed, I reminded myself. I didn't need to take the bait.

"Yeah, so if they had a reliable way to get here, say door-to-door with someone tougher than the average Uber driver, think that'd change some minds?"

She looked at me. "What are you saying?"

"Well, I know some truck drivers who are in the middle of getting phased out and they might welcome the chance to make some short-term cash."

"That's some expensive Ubers," Sandy said. "And no, I don't think you meant that I'd have a procession of eighteen-wheelers pulling up to the front door."

I smiled at the mental picture.

"Don't worry about the expense," I said. "This is a stop-gap, but I can't think of any group better suited, this side of actual mercenaries. Remember, several of these guys drove with me over in the Sand Box. They don't scare easy."

"You think they'd be willing to do that?" I heard some hope in her voice.

"I can be very persuasive when I try." I grinned at her. It was nice to see her smile back.

We found a set of sweats for Mr. Penny.

"Do your thing," I told her, "and I'll call around. He'll be done in an hour?"

"Yeah." Sandy squeezed my hand and gave me a kiss. "Thank you."

* * *

I went out to my truck, in part for some privacy to make some calls and to keep an eye on it. I heard standard city noises, but every siren had an added sense of urgency to my ear. Maybe it was just me.

I knew who to call first: "Diesel" Dan, the senior member of our truck crew at the port. He was nearly sixty and could fix a truck in the middle of a war zone.

"Kyle?" Dan said when he answered. "Who told you?"

Huh? "Told me what?" Confusion washed through my body.

"I know you're plugged in, but it *just* happened." His voice sounded strange.

"What did?"

"I got jacked. On my last day, believe that shit? I thought it was some weird goodbye ritual from Ali."

"You got what? I haven't heard anything."

"Right in front of the port. I had just left with a load of furniture to take to Ohio. My replacement was going to deadhead the truck, and I was supposed to take a damn bus home. New rules: no riders."

"But what happened to you?"

"Some pricks blocked the intersection with a truck and acted like it was stalled. I swear the hair on my neck rose. Just like the old days."

"Set-up?"

"Sure as shit," Dan said. "Never expected it like that here." He continued, "Next thing I know, this little dude in a mask hops up on my door and points a gun at the window and screams at me to get out."

"Jeez."

"Well, like he asked, I did, only I was kind of fast about it and hit him with the door, and he fell. One shot went right through the tire, but not me, at least."

"Are you all right?"

"Compared to what?" Dan chuckled. "I went down after him and got a good kick to the little bastard with the piece, and he dropped it to worry about his ribs."

"Good for you."

"Yeah, great for me. But he had friends." Dan wasn't laughing anymore. "Someone clocked me from behind. Glad I have a hard head. Another knocked out one of my front teeth, and it gets hazy from there. I heard a bunch of yelling, but it sounded muffled, like I was under water."

"Dan, I'm sorry."

"Why? You didn't hijack me, did you?"

I laughed, but my stomach felt sour.

"Anyway, I guess it was a good thing they were in a hurry, because they might have done a real number on me."

"Where are you now? Did you get to the hospital?"

"Just left. Oh, and the new manager is a piece of shit: He wanted to blame *me* when I called it in. I'm on the phone and getting my scalp stitched under a local painkiller, and he all but calls me a crook."

"Want me to straighten him out?" I meant go explain things to him . . . but maybe I meant more than that.

"I told him what I thought about him and hung up." Dan laughed again. "Not my best exit interview."

"What did the police say?"

I had to wait for Dan to stop swearing.

"Would you believe the idiot they sent out actually asked me if the merchandise stolen was valued at more than nine hundred bucks?"

"You're shitting me." But I did believe it.

"I told him the tire that got shot cost more than that, and the trailer was full of furniture. The guy just looked at me and said, 'Is that a *yes*, sir?'"

"Unreal."

"I told him 'Yes, your father should have pulled out.'"

I cracked up. "I'm sure that helped."

"Made *me* feel better. Screw them. I don't even care if they find the truck or not."

"Are you going to be okay?"

"I passed the concussion protocol. I have stiches and a shaved patch on my skull, but it wasn't my week for the calendar shoot anyway." Dan paused. "Wait, if you hadn't heard what happened, why did you call?"

I almost forgot. "Oh yeah."

I told him about Sandy's situation. "I can get my hands on some vans, just need some drivers. Since you're on injured reserve, any thoughts on who might be up for a side hustle?"

"Don't count me out so fast. I just lost my job, remember?" Dan chuckled. "Okay I might need a couple days to get fixed up so I don't scare the passengers."

"You got it, and please don't rush on my account."

"I'm okay. And yeah, a couple guys jump to mind. Try 'Cab' Calloway and 'Shred' Davis."

"Think they'd be interested?" They were solid guys on my list to call.

"Good bet," he said. "From the way Cab reacted when I let him know they were about to be canned, they might already be gone by now."

Cab would be a hell of a get for us. He got his nickname because he bore a slight resemblance to the famed musician, enhanced because he grew a vintage mustache. He may have been a skinny guy, but he had balls of steel.

I knew Davis from the Sand Box too, and more than once, I'd seen his come in after getting shot up and rolling on just the rims.

"I'll try them next," I told Dan. "Sorry about what happened."

"It won't happen again." No laughing there.

* * *

The other two were happy to sign on with us. Like Dan had implied, both of them were in the middle of dropping their trucks off at the port and resigning on the spot. I told them I'd pay cash and they could start tomorrow.

I also made sure they understood that this was a temporary measure. Or at least, I sure holped so. They deserved to be on to more lucrative driving jobs, and I couldn't match those kinds of salaries. Even with the paltry sum I could part with, this little gesture was going to be a money pit for me.

More important, though, was the glaring fact that this situation in the city could not keep going like this.

On that score, I was right. It got worse.

CHAPTER 13

Philadelphia, Old City

I saw it was time to get back to check on Mr. Penney. Inside the office, he sat and retied his shoes, which looked odd, as they were leather dress shoes sticking out from rolled-up-at-the-cuff sweatpants. Of course, his running shoes would have been in his stolen gym bag. His face was sweaty, and wisps of shock white hair clung to his forehead.

"How'd you make out, Mr. Penney?"

He smiled at Sandy. "I believe the young lady is trying to kill me."

"You did great," Sandy said. "Especially under the circumstances."

Penney fished out a money clip from the pants pocket of his suit. Sandy had given him a spare canvas tote bag bearing the logo of the local PBS station. "Please, let me give you something for the bandage and the first aid."

Sandy held up her hand. "We talked about this. You just gave me a chance to practice my paramedic training, is all."

Penney bowed his head. "I'll miss this place."

"You were going to hear me out," I said. "Don't you trust me, Mr. Penney?"

His head snapped up. "Kyle, if it weren't for you and your friends, I would be in the poor house and crippled as sure as I'm standing here."

"I don't know about all that." Actually, that was true. "But you know I help if I can. Well, I think I can."

I explained about the van arrangement. "Sandy, your team can help coordinate with the drivers, can't they?"

She gave me a glance that made me feel warm. "Absolutely."

"That would be more than satisfactory," Penney said. "But what would that cost? Remember, not all of us have ample settlements at our disposal."

I waved him off. "Not a thing. This is all temporary. It's the least we can do until things get back to normal."

"In that case, I can't wait to tell everyone." He checked his watch, another thing I'm glad hadn't been stolen from him. "We should be getting going."

"I'll meet you at the door," I told him. When he left, Sandy gave me a hug. "Thanks."

"Sure." I frowned. "But I can't guard the whole city."

"You said until this is over. What is going on? I'm not naïve in thinking the officials will work until everything is fixed, but I've never seen anything like this before. The police honestly don't care, and it's getting so bad I wonder if the fire department will even show up if something happens."

"I sure hope it doesn't come to that. Judging by the sirens whenever I step outside, they are busier than ever."

"Remember my friend, Deb?" She saw I was drawing a blank. "The paramedic?"

"Right. You worked on the same crew."

"Yeah. She said they're swamped with calls and it's getting worse."

"A lot of that going around." It was nice to be talking with her, but lately it just felt like creeping across a barely frozen pond.

She took my hands and I saw she was fighting back tears. "I'm sorry. I know what I said about your life hurt," she began.

"It's all right." Was it?

"But I wasn't lying. I still don't know if I'm ready."

"Okay."

"I don't know if it is, though. All this going on, and you've been so great, especially today. And as useless as the police and, hell, every official has been, your way of helping people seems less like a shortcut and more like common sense."

"I'm not saying I'm proud about everything we do. We're outlaws, when you get down to it. But I'm not going to say I'm ashamed either. We make tough choices and sometimes can't make a difference. But sometimes we do."

"I know. And I'm not sorry I've helped in the past. But it's just . . ."

"I understand. I think. I didn't pick this life. I kind of fell into it. You called it a shortcut? It felt like that for me until things went so sideways that the only way out was to get deeper into the life. Funny thing, along the way, I found out I was good at it. And scarier, I liked it. Not proud of that."

"Maybe it scares me too. For both of us." Sandy made sure we were alone and still lowered her voice. "We saved a hitman from bleeding to death. Some of my blood is in his veins. Does that mean some of his blood is on my hands?"

"No. Never. Cullen owns what he did, not you. You saved a dying man who collapsed on our doorstep," I said. "Did you ever feel guilty saving someone at a car crash?"

"Of course not."

"If a drunk driver was the survivor at a scene, you never considered withholding treatment, did you?"

"You know I didn't." She gave a little smile. "I see your point."

I kissed her. She kissed me back, and I almost forgot about Mr. Penney. When we pulled away from each other, I asked, "Can we pick this up later?"

"Sure. Come by my place."

"It's a date."

I went to the front where Mr. Penney was waiting. "Ready to go?"

It was an easy drive to get Penney back to his house. He didn't live far, but even during that short drive, his relief was palpable.

* * *

After I dropped Penney off, I doubled back to Old City, only this time I wasn't going to Sandy's rehab center. This time, I stopped off at the bike shop near the drugstore on Market Street where we'd been run over by the flash mob.

I pulled around the corner and took one of the owner's spots. Such access to parking around the city might have been the best perk of holding favors with many small businesses. I texted Mike the owner, who met me at the back door.

"S'up, Kyle?" Mike was a short guy in his early thirties. He had a bushy beard and wild hair that made his head look oversized on his slender body. His arms were interspersed with tattoos and road-rash scarring from his days as a bicycle messenger.

"Living the dream." I shrugged as we stepped inside. We were alone for the moment. He led me through the back area, where several bikes were in various stages of disassembly, and then out onto the front area, where he had a row of trail and race bikes and another wall with shelves and assorted bike accessories.

"Hang on. Lemme unlock the front again." Mike turned an old-style wood sign around to read that he was open and then turned the deadbolt. "Now. What can I do for you? Oh, and how's your girlfriend doing?"

The question hit me funny for an instant until I remembered he saw Sandy get flattened. "Yeah, she's good. Scary time, not going to lie."

"We're all feeling it." Mike gestured to the rows of bikes. "Worst fall month since I opened. It's like a January around here."

"Customers spooked?"

"Don't think it's my deodorant." His humor evaporated. "Is this why you're here?"

"I wanted to ask about a bike."

"Seriously?" I saw Mike glance at my stomach. "I mean, that's great. Biking is an excellent form of exercise, sir."

"There's still some muscle under here, you know," I said. I nodded at the front door. "You haven't been hit yet, isn't that right?"

"The mobs? Nah, those guys are more into running, judging by what I've seen."

"I notice you don't have bikes outside on display anymore."

"Imagine that. It's a bad look to have them chained up like Houdini."

"Makes sense." I walked over to the bikes and stopped by a heavy-looking rig with huge tires. "This looks like the monster truck version of a mountain bike."

"That's an e-bike. The Montara Crusher. Wanna try it? I bet you'd like it."

I took a look at the price tag. "Nine grand?"

Mike nodded. "Yeah. I was a purist for a while, but I got with the program and started stocking these. They're popular and, not going to lie, they help keep the lights on."

"So, someone checking one out from the street would know what they are seeing? If they're not a flabby neanderthal like me?"

"Yeah, if I was dumb enough to put my most expensive ride out there. They're also fast, damn near a getaway vehicle," Mike said. "Why are you looking at me like that?"

CHAPTER 14

Conshohocken, Pennsylvania, one hour later

I dodged some potholes on the road that snaked along the Schuylkill River just outside the city. I was on the way to what we called Steve's Skunkworks. After some lucrative operations, Steve teamed up with me to buy a run-down warehouse to give him enough space to embrace his inner mad scientist.

I hit a remote and watched the chain link fence roll open. The exterior of the main building looked as rough as when he first bought it. Rusting corrugated steel panels created a patchwork appearance, but a few visible cameras and fresh signs warned potential looters or squatters that the place was in operation and protected.

Anyone dumb enough to ignore the warnings would need to run an ever-shifting gauntlet of defenses I couldn't even keep up with. There might not have been bear traps or minefields—Steve was aware that those sorts of things were hard to explain to local law enforcement—but to say intruders would have a bad day would be a serious understatement.

Steve ran a repair shop for appliances and electronics, but that was just something to keep him busy during slow times. The place was mainly a cover for his real work.

I knew he was likely watching me from before I even opened the gate. The visible cameras were kept working because he couldn't stand anything not being operational, but they were more like window dressing. There were tiny cameras all over.

It wasn't that Steve was paranoid. Well, not very paranoid, anyway. The whole place was a proving ground for his gadgets. We got to practice our techniques on defeating his detection efforts, and we both improved as a result.

I texted *Knock, knock* just in case. I wasn't in the mood to get snatched up in a net or some other goofy booby trap.

My heart sank at the reply. *Not by the hair of our chinny, chin, chin.*

"Damnit! Come on, guys." Steve had converted part of the place to his living space, and VP spent a lot of her time there as well and had her own area for her computer gear. The message meant that I was about to be the guinea pig for some fun and games.

I got out of the truck and looked around, knowing they were watching and snickering. I stepped to the door, which opened by itself and left me hesitating in the doorway, feeling like an idiot. Rollie would love to be watching the screen with them. I could just hear him murmuring like a golf announcer that I was getting soft and sorely needed this practice.

Fine. I scooped up a stone about the size of a potato and jammed it in the open-door hinge so it couldn't close on me, then crouched and stepped inside.

As beat-up as the exterior was, the inside could pass as a reasonably presentable appliance showroom stocked with repaired washers and driers and other gear.

"Grab the teddy, and show you're ready," VP's voice came over a TV that flashed to life and I saw an image of a teddy bear on a pedestal in the middle of some open interior space.

Crap. I recognized Drone Alley, where VP practiced her indoor flying skills.

"Save me, Kyle! Save me!" VP cried out, in what was supposed to be a stuffed animal voice.

I strode past the repaired appliances and opened the door to the back. It wasn't locked, but I was careful when I touched the handle. I didn't think I'd get blown up or anything, but I was expecting something.

Nope, the door just opened. To the left, a wall ran down the length of the building where the rest of Steve's work went on. To my right, I saw the open floor that reminded me of a high school gymnasium. Right in the middle of the floor I saw the pedestal with the stupid teddy bear sitting like some sort of idol in an Indiana Jones flick.

Too easy, of course. Might as well get it over with. I stepped forward and the lights cut, plunging the room into darkness. I took out my regular phone to access the flashlight, but before I could turn it on, I saw a bunch of red lasers form a grid around the pedestal.

"Cute." When I turned my phone's flashlight on the light washed out the lasers, but I knew they were still there.

I took a couple steps forward and doused the light. The grid was the same. The squares were just large enough to allow me to step in the middle of each.

I took careful steps and tried to keep my balance. A few more and I'd have a chance to grab the damn bear.

I heard a soft buzz, like a huge hornet. Not good. Something smacked the back of my shoulder, and I jumped and pivoted, right though one of the beams on the floor. Then, I heard a loud beep, followed by what sounded like a swarm of bees.

The lights came on, and I saw I wasn't far wrong. I counted half a dozen tiny quadcopter drones hovering at face height and staring at me with their beady little camera eyes.

"Nice trick, guys. Game over?"

Apparently not. No response. Fine. I took two steps and plucked the teddy bear off the pedestal. I held out the bear toward the drones. The swarm drifted backward a foot and held its place.

"Catch." I tossed the bear at the middle of the swarm, but they parted like sardines dodging a shark and reformed as soon as the stuffed animal hit the floor.

"Now what?" I moved back toward the open door.

The swarm followed. I moved at them, and they gave way, always remaining just out of reach. "Suit yourself." I started back to the door.

Now, the swarm fanned out and encircled me. When I got closer to the door, the ones in my way didn't back off and instead began to flash and make an eerie chirping sound.

I felt a scratching sensation on my skin where I'd been tapped just before everything got especially weird. I reached back and felt something stuck to my jacket over my left shoulder blade.

I pulled it off and found I was holding what looked like a giant dragonfly with red and green LED eyes. It had wiry talons that it must have used to grip the fabric of my jacket.

I flung the thing away from me, and it skidded across the smooth floor.

In an instant, the swarm followed it and hovered above where it ended up, close to the pedestal.

I wasted no time going through the door into the office and slamming it behind me. I continued back outside through the front door, glad I'd made sure to jam it open.

Before my eyes could adjust to the sunlight, I heard another whirring sound. I spun around and saw another tiny drone right behind me. It held something right under its body, and before I could react, I realized it was a syringe. I tried to duck, but the next thing I knew it had squirted me in the face.

"*What?*" I wiped my face and looked at my hand.

Just water.

"Nicely played, Kyle." Steve stepped around the corner. He had a virtual-reality visor pushed up on his forehead and a drone controller in his hands.

"Are we done?"

"That was awesome. How did you figure out the targeting drone?"

"Are you kidding? Do you use fishhooks to make it stick?"

Steve nodded. "I wondered if it was too aggressive." He retrieved the drone that sprayed me.

I pointed to the drone. "And what was the point of that, other than to be a pain in the ass?"

"Call it a twofer. Good volunteers are hard to find. Check it out." Steve handed the drone to me.

I looked closer. I'd been right the first time. That was no squirt gun, it was a real syringe but without the needle. "Why?"

"We try to be non-lethal, right?"

"Yeah." We did try. Sometimes the other side played for keeps though, and we had to make hard choices.

"Well," Steve went on, "if necessary, we could load this with, say, ketamine, and have the target knocked out in a couple minutes."

Interesting. "Minutes, huh? So, not a gun-to-the-head hostage-type scenario, but a gentler way to disable someone." Rollie's experience as a sniper had saved me more than once when speed was crucial. Not my favorite memories, but I was glad to be alive. Still, an alternative that didn't leave anyone dead was worth exploring.

"It's still experimental," he said. "We're trying to figure out dosages, but I know you like having options."

VP stepped outside. "Dude, that was fun. How'd you like the swarm?"

"Scary. How did you keep them together like that?"

"They're programmed to keep space between each other, and I can lay in patterns or assignments for them to follow. The drone we stuck onto you gave them a focal point." VP smiled.

"I got that," I said. "What can they do?"

"Lots of stuff. We can put fixed points, and they can cruise around on guard. They can relay video and they can carry small items—nothing heavy, of course, but still useful."

I pointed to Steve's drone. "Hypodermics?"

She nodded. "They can be killer bees if you want. Um, I don't mean actual poison."

"But it could be."

"I'd never," she said.

"Others might." Fun was fun, but there was no sense losing sight of the fact that in the wrong hands, these things could be nasty.

"I know," she said. I could see the idea bothered her.

"We didn't invent drones," Steve said. "We're working on counter-measures, too, you know."

"What's a good measure without a balancing countermeasure?" I asked.

"Arms race, baby," Steve said. "And, since you mentioned non-lethal, I'm ready to show you the latest."

"Will it take long? I actually came out here for a reason, not just to be used for target practice."

"Sorry. We don't get a lot of company out here." He smiled. "What's up?"

"Any chance you could hide a tracker on that e-bike in my truck bed?"

Steve peeked at the shiny new bike I'd bought from Mike. I made sure to leave the sales tag on it. "Easy. Can I ask why? You know, so I can get the duration and range right."

J. GREGORY SMITH

I looked around out of habit. We were out of the way here. "All these flash mob rip-offs, we know they're organized. Maybe there's a way to find out where they're taking all this stuff."

"Love it," VP said. "But even if we found it, would the cops even bother to go out there?"

"I sure hope not," I said. I turned to Steve. "Okay, I've said my piece. You had another torture for me?"

"Follow me." Steve led me back into the open area and the back of the room.

I saw a heavy cart with a tarp over it and some stout power cords running to a fat outlet that reminded me of a heavy-duty dryer plug.

"Electrocution wasn't on my to-do list today." I was beginning to regret my use of the word "torture."

"Non-lethal. Remember?" Steve pointed to a spot near where the drones had chased me. "See the two lines of tape on the floor?"

I looked down. "Yeah." There was about twenty feet between them.

After fiddling around in the back of the machine, Steve pulled the tarp off. I heard a growing hum and got a very bad feeling. There was a device on top, mounted on a swivel. It resembled a block of concrete shaped like a stop sign. Steve climbed up and positioned himself behind the device. "Okay, when I say go, make like a rioter and try to reach the second line."

I really didn't like his use of the word "try." In fact, I'd lost all interest in this exercise, but I refused to look like a coward. "Can't wait."

"Bring it, Kyle."

I added yelling, maybe just to keep up my courage, and charged forward.

I couldn't hear anything over the racket I was making, but whatever Steve's machine was doing, it was quiet. But he sure triggered something. Just a couple feet into his makeshift "no-go" zone, it felt like I was running directly into the mouth of a blazing-hot invisible oven.

In an instant, it felt like the front of my body was on fire. I'd seen burn victims overseas and my reaction was instinctive: I raced to the side to get as far from the zone as fast as possible. My hands swatted at my chest to put out the flames, but the sensation of pain had vanished the moment I'd stepped away. No heat, no fire. I felt fine.

90

"You good?" Steve called over top of the device.

"I think so. What the hell was that?"

Steve switched everything off. "Zone is clear. System deactivated."

I reached my hand back into the area he'd taped off, ready to snatch it back. Nothing.

Steve climbed down. "That, my friend, is my home-brew version of what the military calls the Active Denial System, or ADS."

"Why don't they call it Pain in a Box? Now I know what it feels like to be microwave popcorn."

"Crazy, isn't it?" Steve smiled. "I had VP zap me with it."

"Whips and chains not getting it done anymore?" And boom, Steve flashed red. It was never not going to be fun to make him blush.

"But it isn't microwaves," he said, reclaiming control of the conversation. "Those could do real damage. This uses millimeter waves that stop right at the surface of the skin. They get a hell of a response from the nerves, wouldn't you agree?"

"I had to react," I admitted. "It was like dropping a hot potato. Not a voluntary choice: I had to get away."

Steve nodded. "Yup. Even knowing that it can't really hurt you doesn't help. Instant panic city."

I looked at the machine. "How'd you figure this out, and where did you get the gear to make it? Oh, and when am I going to lose you to a military contractor?"

"These things cost millions over ten years ago, but tech moves forward and all that. It still wasn't cheap. Plus, I cut some corners."

"This doesn't seem like the sort of thing that comes with directions. Or is even available, for that matter."

"I built most of it myself. And it depends on what you mean by 'comes with' instructions." He looked at the floor. "Maybe someone found the specs on a site that hadn't updated their cybersecurity."

I pointed at the transmitter or emitter or whatever it was called. "You didn't find *that* at a yard sale."

"Not exactly. Officially, it was an early prototype that got junked."

"Funny thing happened on the way to the scrapper?"

"Something like that. It wasn't functional, but some reverse engineering got it up to speed."

"Probably best I don't know more. But since I got hit with it, what did you mean by shortcuts?"

"It's a shadow of what the real military made, and whatever they have now has much tighter security. Not that I'd know or anything."

"Of course not."

"But, this one has much more limited range, and it can only be used in short bursts. It uses a ton of juice and gets overheated easily."

"So, you can't just leave it zapping a hallway or something to keep intruders out?"

"Not like an infrared detection or anything like that. After a full minute, maybe less, the main unit might catch fire itself."

"What if it only turned on when it detected something, you know, if it was paired with an infrared detector?" I was thinking out loud. I had no ability to make any of that happen.

Steve grinned. "I like how you think. But for this, even up and ready on standby takes a toll. Not like when it is firing, but a real power drain."

"So, it isn't portable." A shame.

Steve looked insulted. "I never said that. It's limited, but I'm working on a version that will fit in a van."

"Really?"

"Most of this box is a transformer, and the power comes from a wall."

"That's a lot of batteries. Wait a minute." I just realized something.

Steve grinned. "Now you know why I wanted that EV van."

"Those things are rolling battery packs, aren't they? Even so, that's enough?"

"It works, just not for long," Steve said. "And if you aren't careful, you'll wind up pushing the van home."

"Even so, I already know a little can go a long way."

"True." Steve put his hand on the side of the machine and decided it was cool enough. I helped him pull the tarp over it. "Let's get your bike set up."

CHAPTER 15

Old City, Philadelphia, the next day

I kissed Sandy goodbye. It was more than just a peck on the cheek, and last night was much better. Dinner together felt almost normal, and spending the night felt like it had narrowed that weird rift. "Will you need a ride home?"

"Nope," she said. "I'm covered. I'll let you know how the truckers work out." She hopped out of my truck.

I pulled around the corner to reach the back of Mike's Bikes. Before I texted him, I grabbed a burner phone and called VP.

"Yo."

"Bait's at the shop," I said. "I wanted to make sure the signal is working."

"Five-by-five. I have a clean record from when you left Steve's until you pulled in the lot." She paused. "Hey, did somebody get lucky last night?"

"Luck had nothing to do with it. I guess it works, huh?"

"Dude, we usually have to deal with limited power on the transmitters. With the e-bike battery, this thing is a flamethrower."

"Okay, how long do you need before we set the hook?"

"Well, you didn't say what we need to be ready for."

"I said be ready for anything."

"You know that's an invitation for Steve to pack the van with everything in the whole warehouse."

"All right. No need to bring a moving truck. If we get a bite quick— and these days, that's likely—we should be ready to follow and track the bike. Maybe stage at my place, since it's closer to Old City and you can still work if it takes longer than expected."

"We can do that. Will this be all recon, or do you think Rollie will join us?"

"He's working on a house in the neighborhood and left a bug-out bag at my place." Rollie's idea of being prepared involved less James Bond and more Rambo, but he had his own non-lethal kit.

"Right on. We'll be in place in less than an hour, and you can hit us up while we're on the move."

* * *

"You really think this can work?" Mike looked over the e-bike. "I hope you have insurance."

"In a manner of speaking." I told him about the tracker.

He checked over the bike. "I don't see anywhere where he put it. This is good work."

"I'll pass along the compliment."

"You sure we should trust it, though? I keep an aluminum softball bat under the counter."

"Or we could just call the police," I suggested.

"Fine. We'll do it your way. It just enrages me to sit here and watch these mutts steal everyone's life's work."

"You and me both. But we're trying to avoid just playing Whack-A-Mole."

"Even that would be an improvement, but I get what you're saying." Mike pulled out a framed whiteboard sign with a drawing of the bike with cartoonish speed lines and electric bolts trailing behind like it was in motion. A caption read: "New e-bikes in stock. Hurry because they go fast!"

"Nice. You would have made a good starving artist."

"I'm trying not to be a starving anything," Mike said.

We took the bike and sign outside and set them up right near the front door. Mike tied a rope around the frame and to a bike rack on the sidewalk. "Don't want to make it too easy."

I hadn't ridden the thing, just brought it to Steve and VP. "Does it need a key?"

"This one doesn't. There's a key to unlock and remove the battery, but it will run as is now."

"Let's go inside, and get a cup of coffee." Wasn't that what cops did on a stakeout?

* * *

Two hours later

We'd seen several people stop by to check out the bike. One came in and talked Mike's ear off about green this and that and how great e-bikes were. For a minute, I thought our decoy had netted him a nice sale. No such luck, the guy had been all talk.

Just when boredom had kicked into high gear and I was ready to pack it in for the day, we noticed a kid go by on a regular bike and take a picture of the bike on his phone. "Interesting."

"There's another one on a bike," Mike said. "I don't recognize them as customers."

I wasn't surprised as yet another bike passed by, and I noticed they all wore masks. "Stay cool. We aren't here for a fight."

"I am if they come in to clean me out," Mike said. He was a small guy but tough and fearless.

"I'll back you up in that case." I had a pistol on me, but the last thing I wanted was that kind of attention.

"It's starting to look like the start of one of the city social rides we organize."

He was right. No fewer than four bikes were riding back and forth.

I called VP to let her know to be ready. I pictured her and Steve hustling out of the house and getting into their van.

When I turned back, I saw Mike heading for the front door. "Mike, stay here," I hissed.

"They saw me in here looking. Won't look right if I don't." Mike opened the door. "Hey guys, looking for something I can help you with?"

Some of the "kids" were almost as big as me and most were larger than Mike. I felt my stomach drop and moved toward the door.

Two big guys rolled right up to Mike. "Nah, fam, we good."

As soon as the masked guy said the words, the dude next to him raised up a spray paint can and blasted Mike right in the face. He turned away with his eyes closed, and the red paint make it look like he'd been dipped in blood.

I ran toward the door and saw the flash of a knife blade cut through the rope. Another guy switched on the bike like he knew what he was doing and it accelerated down the sidewalk.

Mike swung elbows backward in a blind effort to keep attackers off him. One guy laughed and shoved him back through the door. I saw a couple more getting ready to charge into the store. I pulled Mike back inside, making sure he knew it was me, and stepped up to the entrance.

"You want some too?" the guy with the paint yelled and raised the can. I knocked it to the side and felt wet on my cheek but my vision remained clear. I pulled the revolver from my waistband and pistol-whipped the guy in the nose before aiming it at the rest of the group. Blood stained the guy's mask and the spray can fell to the sidewalk.

"Anyone else?"

I heard "Gat!" and the crew scattered. The guy I'd hit lost his taste for conversation and rode away on his bike a bit wobbly. I lowered the gun and retreated into the store, locking the door behind me.

"You okay, Mike?"

"Yeah. I kept most of it out of my eyes, but that shit stings."

"Flush it out quick. I have the front covered." I wiped the side of my face and used a mirror on one of the display bikes to check the damage. It looked like I'd gotten a severe sunburn on one side of my face.

"Did it work?" Mike yelled from the bathroom over the sound of running water.

I chanced a look out the front window. All clear. I stepped to the back of the store to see how Mike was doing. The white porcelain of the sink was a pale shade of pink. A pile of reddish paper towels filled the wastebasket.

"I think so. They're gone and so is the bike. Let me call my people. Is that any better?"

"Not as bad as real pepper spray, but it's a close second." He raised his head and squinted at himself in the mirror. "I'm not blind. I guess that's a win." He noticed my face. "They got you too?"

"Mostly a miss. My eyes are fine, and the guy that did it is enjoying a broken nose."

"Good. Glad you were here. I thought they were going to clean me out."

"Sorry, I didn't expect a feeding frenzy in response to our bait." It was scary how fast it escalated. I took out my phone.

VP picked right up. "Yo."

"Fish on the line?"

"You know it. We're close, do you want us to pick you up?"

I thought for second. "Why not? We're not trying to run the guy down. We want to see where he's going."

"Rollie?" I heard Steve say, presumably from the driver's seat of the van.

"Not yet," I said, "but give him a heads-up."

"You got it. See you in five." VP hung up.

"It's working?" Mike asked. "They know where this turd is going?"

"Yes, it is working, and as for the turd, that's what we hope to find out."

"You're chasing him now? I want to help."

I held up my hand. "You already did. They fell for it. And you got more than you bargained for in the process."

"They started it. I like to finish my fights." I could see the wild-eyed Mike from his daredevil bicycle messenger days.

"Not now. I'm not sure what our move from here will be, but I need leeway. We tend to color outside the lines, if you get me."

Mike gestured toward my waistband. "I didn't see anything." He held up a paint-smeared paper towel. "Perfect alibi. But if you need my help, I'm in, and you never know when temporary blindness might flare up."

I saw the van arrive. "Thanks, Mike. I may take you up on it. We need to stick together."

CHAPTER 16

Old City

I jumped into the van. VP sat at a custom-built workstation in the back where she had several laptops running. She turned toward me.

"Dude, what happened to you?"

I explained, "Keep an eye out for a guy with a bandaged schnozz."

VP pointed to one laptop that displayed a map of the area and a moving dot.

"That's the bike?"

"Yeah. Looks like he's doing about twenty miles an hour steady."

"Mike said they're pretty fast."

Steve spoke up. "I can do that on a regular bike, easy."

VP laughed. "For how long?"

"Until I puke," Steve said. "I assume you still want this guy to get where he's going? We could catch him."

The thieves were so organized, it made me think twice. Might get some good intel if we sweated him. "Nah, let's stick with the plan," I said. "He's a small fry."

"No problem on this end," VP said. "The signal is fire."

"As long as we don't lose him, this works for me," I said. "Where's he headed?"

"He went up Second Street for a while. Smart to go on the sidewalks against the grain on a one-way street," she said. "He's on Aramingo now. His speeds are up and down, bet he's getting more comfortable. Thinks he's slipped any pursuit."

"No reason not to think so. His buddies kept us busy. They would have cleaned Mike out too, but I changed their mind."

"Dude, be careful. One of these days, they'll just shoot back."

"You're right. It's getting out of control. But it was kind of spur-of-the-moment, and after smacking one of them, I needed to discourage the gang beatdown that was coming my way."

"Not judging," VP said. "Just glad you're okay."

"Me too. Steve, you don't have any paint thinner in here, do you?"

"Got enough to bathe in back at the shop, but that wasn't on my essentials list here."

VP handed me a bottle of hand sanitizer. "Try that."

I made sure to keep it out of my eyes. "Any better?"

"Yeah, now you just have a natural rosy glow from chafing your face."

"I'll live with it."

A few minutes later Steve pulled into an open space on Aramingo Avenue at VP's call. "Our guy is slowing down," she said. "Let me check the maps here. Steve, take the next left, Margaret Street."

"He's going up the street past these train tracks. Okay, now turning on Worth Street. Slow down. We don't want to catch up to him."

Steve put on the flashers, to the annoyance of a battered sedan behind us. I could see a railroad overpass ahead. He pulled over onto the sidewalk and ignored the angry gestures as the driver passed us.

VP studied the map. "He's a block down on Worth Street. Slowing again. He stopped. Should we move in?"

"Can we get closer without being spotted?"

"Who designed this city?" VP said. "Okay, Steve, down Worth for a block. Then, it's one-way in the opposite direction, and we have to turn down Orthodox."

Steve did it, and we could see the block where the bike had stopped. The next turn would put us around the corner and headed back toward the railroad overpass.

"The bike signal is still stopped. Looks like it might be moving inside a building now."

"What's down there?" I asked as Steve pulled off the road and partly up on a sidewalk. There were row houses on one side, and the wall of a building to our right.

"Looks like some old warehouses."

"That would make sense. A stash place for the bike?" I said. "Can we get a better look? Without being obvious?"

VP was already digging into an aluminum case. She took out a tiny quadcopter drone with a camera the size of a lipstick slung underneath. "Steve, mind doing the honors?"

Steve slid out from the driver's seat over to the passenger side and held out his hand with the palm up. "You have about six feet from the window to the wall. Go vertical right away, and you should be clear of wires."

"Cool." VP slipped a set of virtual reality goggles over her head. The copter buzzed to life and did a little up and down hop on her hand like a terrier ready to go to work. "Signal is clean. Here you go." She stretched her hand to Steve, who took the drone.

"Got it." He lowered the window and stretched his arm outside of the van. "Good to go."

"Drone away," VP said.

I sat back and watched them do their thing. VP had been a great drone pilot from the time I first met her, but she and Steve had gone next-level, that was for sure.

I watched the drone's progress on one of the open screens inside the van. First, all I saw was a blur of stone, then the brilliant sky as the tiny machine cleared the building we sat beside. It was disorienting for me when the drone spun around while VP got her bearings. I saw the expanse of railroad tracks and the rooftops of row houses. VP skimmed low over them and drifted over to get a peek at the street below.

"Okay, that's the one, the smaller warehouse that says 'Frankfort Storage'," VP said. She zipped the drone back over the house across the narrow one-lane street. The roof was flat, and VP landed and proceeded to sort of hop the drone forward until it reached the edge and the camera could observe. Just watching made me feel dizzy, but I guess VP had taken her virtual Dramamine.

"Think we'll be able to stay put for a little?" she asked.

I looked over at Steve and saw he'd donned a white plastic hard hat and was fishing through a stack of stickers he'd pulled from the passenger seat glovebox. He found a pair he liked and applied them to the sides.

"Amtrak?" I asked.

"Might buy a little time. Any nosey resident should believe that we're using drones to inspect the tracks." He pointed at the railroad bridge in front of us.

"How long can we watch with that drone?" I said.

"Now that it is parked, maybe an hour, just on camera," VP said. "I'll set it to auto return here in forty minutes just to be safe." She sat up straight. "Hey, we have a camera watching the front." The drone highlighted the security camera with a red box outline.

"Nice. Can you do a quick loop around the building so we can get a better idea of the exterior?"

"On it." VP launched the drone to fly a circuit around the warehouse.

I watched the screen. No red boxes on the roof, but one for a camera covering the back. "Is that a skylight I see?"

"Tasty." VP steered the drone back to its perch across the street.

"You're recording?"

"Of course. If anyone comes or goes, we'll get a shot of them. It's not high def but better than nothing."

The door to the warehouse opened, and a young guy stepped out. He turned back to the open door, and I got a glimpse of another person. This second figure leaned out for a moment and fist-bumped the young guy.

"Did you see that?" I asked.

"Yeah," VP said. "Is that the guy who took the bike?" We could see he was on his phone.

"Could be. They all wore masks, and I was more worried about Mr. Spray Paint at the time."

"What's our move?" Steve asked.

"Think fast," VP said. "Looks like our guy's ride is here." We saw a small sedan roll up, and the guy jumped right in.

"No back and forth," Steve said. "He must know him."

"Got in the front seat too. Doubt it is an Uber," I said.

"Window's closing," VP said. "If you want a license plate, I gotta fly and it'll be iffy."

"That's okay. He's not important. Right now, we need to see more of this warehouse. That's where the bait went."

"We need to see the inside," Steve said.

VP said, "You knock and when they answer the door, I'll buzz the drone inside. Think they'll notice?"

"I have something a bit more organized in mind."

CHAPTER 17

Fishtown, Kyle's place, midnight

We piled into the van with Steve driving, VP at what we called the mobile command center and Rollie and me in back.

"Kid, I hope I'm getting time-and-a-half for this," Rollie said. "You know we're up past my bedtime." He looked as strange as I felt, as we were both dressed in heavy firefighter gear.

If that wasn't enough, we were both wearing body armor under the thick waterproof coats. "Glad it's a short drive," I said. "I'll probably sweat out twenty pounds."

"At least you don't have to play mountain climber in this get-up," Rollie groused. All an act, he was as jazzed as any of us.

"You guys sure that's how you want to play it?" Steve said.

"Now he asks," Rollie said.

"We didn't get all dressed for nothing," I said, "and I had to call in a perfectly good favor to get this gear. They'll be pissed if we get bullet holes in them."

"Don't even joke," Steve said. He'd been hit once with a soft vest and knew how much it hurt.

"It's a good plan," VP said. "Considering we just threw it together."

"That's the spirit," I said.

* * *

Frankfort, near the Frankfort Storage warehouse

As we approached the front of the warehouse, we paused at the mouth of an alley a couple buildings before it. The first building presented us with a three-story brick face. Rollie followed my gaze.

"I told you, kid, the walls are lower next door, and it'll be easy to set the grapple," Rollie said.

"Remember the camera out back." I didn't know why I was getting a case of mother hen.

"I've done this before, and all the gear isn't too heavy. Give an old fart some credit."

"Just be careful." It sounded dumb to my ears.

"Where's the fun in that?" Rollie called VP. "Comms check?"

"Test, test, test," she said. Rollie and I nodded as her voice came back in through our earpieces.

"Check. Check," I said to nods all around, and Rollie's voice came in fine when it was his turn.

"We're burning dark, gentlemen," Steve called. "I figure after I drive past the front I better not again. Someone is on the other end of those cameras, and at this hour we'll draw attention."

"Yup, we'll circle around the block and grab a nice piece of sidewalk to wait."

"Time to go rescue a cat out of a tree." Rollie opened the door and stepped to the alleyway. He was unrecognizable with the red plastic fire helmet.

"Good luck," I said.

I returned to the van while Rollie moved down the alley.

"I hope these outfits are worth it," I said.

"I think the firefighter has a nice balance between official and non-threatening," VP said.

"I guess we'll find out," I said.

We cruised past the entrance, and I looked out the one-way window in the van's rear doors. All quiet, but we passed right through the camera's field of view.

Steve took us around the block.

"All quiet except a couple rats," I heard Rollie say in my earpiece. "Hooking up."

"I know I shouldn't worry," I said off-mic.

"Dude, he's old, but he's a stud," VP said. "I've seen him use the self-belay ropes at our place. I can't even do some of that stuff."

"And I can climb," Steve said, "but the combat part isn't my thing."

"And I'd probably just break the rope," I added. "I know."

Rollie cut in: "Climbing."

We sat in silence for next couple minutes. VP spread out the schematics for the building that she'd found online registered with the city. "The office space is toward the front, storage in back. The skylight should be over the open storage area."

"Top of the world, Ma." Rollie's signal that he was on the roof. Our plan had him move across two abandoned buildings and lower himself onto the target warehouse. This route ensured that he'd avoid the camera covering the rear of the warehouse.

"Quarterback, want a peek through the window?" Rollie was addressing VP. No names over the air.

"Why not?" She hit some switches, and a blank laptop screen came to life and showed first Rollie, who waved at the camera, then her drone's view as he turned it around to face the glass skylight.

VP pulled the drone controller rig over her head and donned the VR goggles. This drone was different from the tiny one she'd used earlier. While not big, the Sky-Champ was rugged and purpose-built to explore inside buildings and bounce off walls. It was a modified version of a police-grade unit.

"Can you see more than I can?" Rollie asked. The image on screen wasn't promising.

"Too dirty, Ninja," I said. "Good idea, anyway."

"Gimme a minute to get 'er open." Rollie placed the drone facing him on the flat roof. We got to watch him work a small prybar around the edges of the metal frame until he was able to lift the cover off. He set it down beside the opening.

"Ready, Quarterback? Like we discussed." From the camera, we could see Rollie attach a string on the drone.

"Good to go, Ninja," VP said.

We could see it was dark inside the large open space. Dim city light spilled into the room, but most of the windows were bricked up at ground level.

"I can't believe I didn't think of this," Steve said. It had been Rollie's idea to lower the drone into the room manually to avoid the buzzing sound of the rotors to alert anyone inside.

"All quiet so far." Rollie had reduced his voice to a whisper, but the comms picked him up fine. "I guess we'll find out if they have a motion detector."

We all held our breath as he lowered the drone. At about ten feet down, the camera couldn't see much.

"Switching to infrared," VP said. The room flared and appeared in stark black and white. "Spinning." She goosed the controls, and the drone whirled around, producing a dizzying view that she'd pause later for clarity. "Bring it up, Ninja."

"Secure," Rollie replied a moment later.

"Standby," VP said. "Okay, let's see what we have here." VP took the quick snapshot of the room and slowed the replay, so we could see more detail. The first thing I noticed, aside from shelves filled with objects, was that the room wasn't occupied.

"Hey, there's my bike." I knew I shouldn't interrupt, but I was surprised it was still in one piece.

"Jackpot," VP said. "Room looks stuffed with loot. Nobody in there."

"They're sure to be close by, but good to know," Rollie said. "Phase Two?"

VP and Steve looked to me. I glanced at the schematic. Given how much of the place the storage room occupied, the remaining office space couldn't be crammed with guards, could it? Two, three guys, tops?

"All quiet on the scanners?" I asked.

Steve nodded. He was monitoring the radio calls for police and fire. I put on my fire helmet. "Go to Phase Two."

* * *

After Rollie lowered the drone back into the room and down to the floor, he followed suit, rappelling through the skylight.

With him inside, we were committed. Fresh rivulets of sweat ran down my sides.

"Still quiet." Rollie's voice was a bare whisper. VP fiddled with some controls, and we could hear him better.

"Can you pan the drone?" VP said.

Rollie did. I knew he had a set of low-light goggles of his own, so we could all see the narrow hallway off the main storage room leading to the office area. It looked like the only interior door to access the room. We saw a closed loading bay door and a metal fire door leading to the back.

"Think that door is wired?" I asked. We'd all seen the alarm stickers out front, but given the apparent nature of their "business," it seemed unlikely they would want to draw the attention of the police to the place. On the other hand, it meant that as soon as we kicked the nest, they would respond with guns. No question.

Rollie went to check and left the drone facing the access hallway. "Dunno, but it's almost welded. They have locked chains all over it. They're lucky I'm not a real fire marshal."

"Guess I'm not getting in that way," I said.

"I see the power box. Gimme a minute, then I'll stir 'em up. Knock on the front on my signal."

We watched Rollie tie some cord to the wall down low and stretch it across the access hallway, so it was about a foot off the ground. After that, he moved across the room and opened the power box. VP had spun and landed the drone so it could shine an infrared light for Rollie.

"Okay ready," Rollie said. "Quarterback, get in position."

VP lifted off the drone, and it hovered ten feet in the air with a view of the doorway.

"Power out." Rollie ran back into view after he threw the main breaker for the whole building. With a little luck, this would kill their cameras. It didn't seem like a real high-tech operation, but we were ready either way.

Steve eased the van ahead. Now we were alongside the warehouse, and I noticed that the light in the window that I'd seen earlier was dark.

I could see Rollie take a spot using the wall for cover. Time stretched, and I began to wonder if the place was empty.

Nope.

"Someone's coming. I'll leave my comms open so you can hear." Rollie sounded cool as ever.

We all heard the metal door screech open. Weak flashlight beams stabbed through the dust in the air. I saw a pudgy hand paw at the light switch and flick it up and down like it would force the power back.

"It's off back here, too," the guy said to someone else.

The beam faded, and the guy swore and shook the flashlight, which coaxed back a feeble finger of light. "How old are these batteries?"

The man stepped into view, and he appeared to be a guy in his forties, bald and heavyset, and carrying a pistol in his non-flashlight hand.

"Target One is armed," VP said.

Rollie keyed his microphone in reply and left it on again.

"What's that sound?" The guy raised his pistol. "Len, get back here. Something's not right."

VP bobbed the drone up and down and the guy turned and waved the flashlight toward it. The second guy—named Len, apparently—came into view. He was younger and bigger. He also had a pistol along with his flashlight. "New target is also packing," VP said. "Showtime."

"There's a fucking drone in here," the first guy said.

As soon as he spoke, the drone erupted with a blast of laser light strobing into his eyes. He raised his hands to shield his face and moved forward into the open space. Or at least he tried, as he hadn't noticed Rollie's trip line across the way. He went down hard, and his flashlight went dark when it smacked the concrete floor.

"Oh shit," Len, the second guy, charged forward, but he paused to step over the trip wire. He raised the gun toward the drone as VP gave him a taste of laser.

At the same time, Rollie came out from hiding behind the wall. He stomped on the first guy's gun hand and kicked the pistol across the room.

Len caught the movement, though his vision had to be screwed up now. "Who's—"

He didn't get to finish the question because Rollie raised a taser pistol that fired with a pop and telltale electric crackle. Len's entire body seized, and he dropped both the flashlight and the gun, which Rollie sent skittering.

While still working the wire-connected taser with one hand, Rollie pulled out a hand-held stun gun that required direct contact and pressed it into Len's buddy. We could hear Rollie breathing hard over the screams of the two guards.

Rollie gave Len, who was still hooked to the taser, another jolt, and he spasmed on the ground. Rollie put the taser on the floor and pulled out some flexicuffs. He did the first guy's wrists amid howls of pain.

Len tried to pull out the barbs, and only got jabbed with the other stun gun for his trouble.

"Quarterback, can you check the front? Busy here."

"Yeah." VP sent the rugged drone over Rollie's head and bounced it down the hall. The last thing I saw of Rollie was him cuffing Len.

"I'm going." I pulled on an oxygen mask, which, in addition to the helmet, concealed my entire face in case that camera was still working.

I stepped out of the van, lumbered the few steps to the front door and pounded on the metal door. It was still dark in there and no sign of flashlights. I heard something hit the door from the other side and for an instant wondered if somebody had thrown a shot my way. Then, I heard a faint whirr from the drone's quadcopter rotors.

"Don't see anything up here," VP said. "There's an office door that is closed. Be careful."

I jogged back to the van and brought out a firefighting tool called a Halligan. It looked like a modified, extra-thick crowbar. With my outfit, I could skip subtle. I worked in the pry side, and as expected, the metal door was sturdy, but the Halligan was a leverage monster, purpose-built for rapid entry. The door squealed in protest but gave it up, and I was through.

I flicked on my own flashlight and remembered to hit a small infrared strobe that would tell Rollie it was me. I'd felt a taser before and didn't need a refresher.

Inside, the drone hovered like it knew me. The front room consisted of a simple counter and an open door leading into the building. I could see another closed door along the hallway. "Ninja, I'm in. You good?"

"Better than them. C'mon back."

"Clearing."

"Don't forget interrogation gear," Steve chimed in. It sounded more ominous than it was. We weren't planning on hurting these guys any more than we had, so we'd discussed ways to protect our identities. Steve's contribution was a portable voice-changer.

I climbed over the counter and almost fell in a heap on the other side. All the gear and body armor made me feel more like a hockey goalie than some half-assed action hero. I saw the office door VP had noted. The interior door was locked, but it was just wood. I probably could have shouldered it open on my own, but I'd taken a real shine to this Halligan bar. The door splintered open in seconds.

The office walls were stained yellow with cigarette smoke. I saw two chairs and a desk with a dark monitor for the cameras. No sign of anyone else here. I checked under the desk just to be sure nobody had decided to hide there.

No people, but a strange piece of plywood where the desk-sitter's feet would go. I dropped to my knees and pulled on the board. "Hello." It looked to be a floor safe.

"Bus driver," I called back to Steve in the van.

"Go ahead," he answered.

"Any chance you brought any skeleton keys with you?"

He perked right up. He took every locksmith class he could find. "Never leave home without it. Whatcha got?"

"Floor safe." I read off the make and model.

"Okay. I'll be there if you need me." Steve sounded excited. "I'll need a pinch hitter," meaning someone to stay behind the wheel.

"Quarterback, still quiet?" It was moot if they'd alerted the cops. I still doubted it.

"All quiet. No sign of cavalry either," VP said.

"Stand by." I moved back toward the door that led to the storeroom. I checked one more door that was half-open. I kicked the cheap hollow core wood door, and it slammed open. It was an empty one-toilet bathroom.

I got back to the storage area. Rollie had already taken down his trip wire. The two guards were trussed up and seated along the wall where Rollie had hidden. He'd put black cloth hoods over their heads. The two pistols were next to him, now unloaded, and he had the flashlights, their wallets and a couple pocket knives that told me he'd frisked them.

Rollie studied the driver's licenses he pulled.

He whispered into the mic in a voice so low I doubted the guys could hear him. "The big guy is Len. This one here is Paul. They can't see us."

I nodded and held up a finger. I wanted out of all this stifling gear, but Steve had set up his voice-changing "anonymizer" to be attached to the oxygen mask. I didn't want to break anything, so I just switched it on like he showed me.

I stepped to the guards. "Gentlemen, I'm sure you're wondering what all this . . . What the crap?" Every word I spoke sounded exactly like Donald Duck.

"Huh?" Paul said.

"Damn it," I said in a duck voice as I ripped all the gear off my head. "Can you hear me now, asshole?"

"Yeah," Paul said. "Is Mickey here too?"

Rollie shook his head at me. I shrugged and pointed at the stupid mask I'd shucked.

Rollie held up the stun gun and switched it on right next to Paul's head. It buzzed and crackled. Paul recoiled from the sound. "Got yer mouse right here," Rollie growled.

"All right, all right," Paul said. "What do you want? You're not bangers, already figured that out."

Len spoke up: "Do you have any idea who you're messing with? Who we work for?"

"You tell me, Len. Who runs this place?"

"You can find out. The hard way."

Rollie placed the now off stun gun against Len's neck. "Someone needs more shock treatment, I guess."

"Wait," Len said quickly. "We get paid to take stuff in and make sure it doesn't get swiped."

"Great job," I said. "Names, Len. We know where you live."

"The ones they gave us are fake, I'm sure," Paul said. "We do our thing, and we know they will take care of us."

Their comfort level pissed me off, but we weren't here to lean on them hard. Never been our style. "Len said you take in stuff. I see by the shelves that's true. Who brings it?"

"You seem like a bright guy, when you don't sound like a cartoon," Paul said. "Anyone who knows to come here knows they'll get covered . . ." He trailed off.

Finally, something useful. "Got it. So, you pay them for the swag. Where's it go from here?"

"How should I know? They pick it up, and more comes in, and that's the way it goes."

Paul wasn't there for his intimidating physique; he knew more, but we didn't have all night to sweat him. "What's in the safe?"

"What safe?" Len said.

"Under the desk. How about the combination?"

"We don't know that," Paul said. "We just work here."

Rollie looked to me, ready to zap the smug out of him, but I shook my head.

"Hold that thought for your bosses. I'm sure they will want to hear all about it." I whispered into the mic, "Bus Driver, Ninja will relieve. Your services are required."

Rollie understood and took another hood out and filled it with the guard's guns and other effects.

"Now what?" Paul asked.

"Now shut up." I had the stun gun, and while we didn't want to tear them up, I wouldn't hesitate to use it to keep them in line.

While I waited, I swept my flashlight around the shelves. They weren't all full, but some were crammed with designer bags, small electronics, and tons of sneakers. On other shelves, there were dozens of fragrance bottles, from fancy stores all the way to things grabbed from the local drugstore. Speaking of which, there were enough over-the-counter pills like painkillers and even baby formula to start a convenience store. Along another wall, I saw full golf bags and tennis gear.

"This place looks like an Amazon fulfillment center."

"Maybe it is, and you made a big mistake," Paul said.

Enough. I gave him a good zap on his inner leg, which kicked in time to his startled scream. I saw Steve race into the room and appreciated the backup. "I saw some batteries on one shelf. I can use this toy all night. Sound like fun?"

Steve took in the room and gave me a "You good?" look. I nodded and pointed to my wrist, then mimed turning a combination lock dial.

Steve shrugged and flashed his fingers to imply a half hour or more. I indicated to go ahead.

Soon I heard the whine of a high-speed drill. So did the guards. "That's a waste of time," Paul said. "Nothing in there."

I ignored him. I'd stepped away from them while keeping them in sight so I could speak to Rollie. I whispered an idea.

"You got it," Rollie said. "Quarterback will move HQ and post lookouts. Be right there."

I wasn't crazy about us getting so spread out, but I had a hunch it would be worth the risk. While Rollie brought some more gear and returned to help me, VP would move the van and deploy a few drones to perch on rooftops to monitor for any more bad guys arriving. Given the nature of the operation, we were less worried about real police showing up.

Rollie came back in with a bunch of lawn and leaf bags along with a whole box full of rolls of duct tape. "Who wants to play 'Silver Mummy'?"

I helped, and fifteen minutes later, the guards were wrapped chest to toe in duct tape.

"You know people are coming, don't you?"

"I hope so, for your sake," I said. "We're not staying to feed you.".

"I gotta use the bathroom," Paul said.

"It's right down the hall."

"Can you cut me loose?"

"Why? You said your buddies will be here any minute."

There was a short pause while the called-bluff sank in. "Fuck you."

I took out a rubber ball and stretched more tape. "If you can't say anything nice . . ."

I lifted just enough hood to access Paul's mouth, and soon I had him and then Len gagged.

"Don't go anywhere."

Rollie handed me a box of leaf bags. Soon, we were both scooping as much merch as possible into the bags and piling them by the back door. Rollie had also brought bolt cutters and with a few clips had the back door unlocked. I double-checked for alarm sensors and, satisfied, let VP know that she could pull around to the rear. Between changing drill bits, Steve had confirmed that the cameras were down for the count.

Rollie and I started with the most expensive items, especially the designer bags, which had to have come from a local place that specialized in exclusive luxury goods. The owner was on O'Brien's list and not part of a big chain.

I noticed the drilling had stopped, and then Steve appeared in the hallway gesturing for me to follow him back to the office.

"Jackpot, boss." He was sweating and aimed his flashlight down to the open safe.

I dropped to my knees and peered inside. Stacks of bundled cash sat under an open shoe box filled with watches, gold chains, rings, and bracelets.

"Can't leave that there with their safe in that condition. Something is liable to get stolen."

Steve grinned. "Agreed."

"We have enough bagged up by the back. Scoop all this up, and come on and help us. I'll let Quarterback know it's time."

Back in the storeroom, I saw we'd left quite a mess. I took the e-bike and rolled it by the door. I wondered if there'd be space in the van, but we could strap it to the roof, if necessary.

I leaned down to Paul. "Hey, you're right. There's nothing in that safe."

I couldn't make out his response behind the gag. Just as well.

Steve joined us with a pillowcase stuffed with the contents of the safe. He went outside to meet VP. That bag had top priority.

I flattened one of the cardboard boxes they had piled up for processing all the swag. I found a marker they used to label the boxes and wrote "No Honor Among Thieves."

"It looks like *this* place got hit with a flash mob. Tell your bosses this is only the beginning."

I picked up a large bottle of perfume from one of the drugstores, at least I assumed as I'd actually heard of it. When I saw we were about ready to leave, I dashed it to the concrete floor.

CHAPTER 18

Philadelphia, Frankfort

"Any signs of pursuit?" I said to VP who looked like a bag lady, surrounded by sacks. We were packed in tight with all the recovered loot. As I'd thought, we had to batten down the e-bike on the roof of the van.

"How should I know? My screen is covered in scarves." Some of the bags had ripped open.

"Do your best." I shoved some of the shifting cargo aside to get a peek out of the back window. "Looks okay from here."

"You in any shape for recovery?" Steve said to VP.

"Yeah, gimme a second. What the hell are we going to do with all this crap?" she groused.

"One thing at a time," I said. "Do you need help?"

"Yeah, hold some of these damn bags off me, so I don't crash the drones. Steve, you got room to catch 'em?"

"I'm pulling over right near the train trestle like last time, in case you can't see."

VP now had her virtual reality goggles on and was almost laying atop a pile of bags while she worked the drone controller. "Clean signal on the sentries," she said. "I'm spinning up the lead drone." She hit some switches, oblivious to the lumpy treasure pile she was perched on. "All three are in formation. I'm bringing them home."

While the rest of us were feeling the pressure to clear the scene, Rollie was curled up on top of some bags and looked like he was ready to fall asleep. "Lemme know if I need to shoot anyone."

"Will do." I knew he was only half joking.

"I see the drones," Steve said.

"Kyle, pass that silver case up to Steve," VP said. "Steve, I'm starting sequenced landings by your window."

I crawled to the front with the drone case, feeling like a little kid in one of those pits filled with plastic balls. "Here you go."

Steve dropped the window and leaned outside. "First incoming." He held out his hand, and the first tiny drone alighted on his outstretched palm. "One aboard." He set it in the foam nest in the case and repeated the process. The next drone landed, and soon each one waited its turn until he had the last one back in the van.

"I'm not sure if I'm more impressed or frightened," I said to VP.

"Why limit yourself?" she gave me a crooked smile. "Be both."

* * *

Conshocken, Steve's warehouse

With Rollie sacked out on a couch in Steve's office, the rest of us had decided to press on and get the bags of stolen goods offloaded.

"We can sort this out later," I said. "I want to see what we got from the safe." That was what I was most curious about, as we were going to keep the cash because it would hurt the right people. We knew the other stuff had been looted from local shops. It was just a matter of sorting it out and returning it.

"Let's spread it out on this table," Steve said.

VP sipped on an energy drink. I was sticking with adrenaline for the moment.

Steve dumped out the sack and among the loose jewelry and cash something jumped out at me. "Hey, I know this."

It was a gold cane top, snapped off with wood embedded where it used to be mounted. "That's Mr. Penney's. I'd recognize it anywhere."

"The old dude who got mugged?" VP asked.

"Yeah. God, I'd love to figure out who cashed that in," I said. "But no matter what, he's going to be thrilled."

"Yeah," Steve said, "well I wish it was going to be as easy to figure out where the rest of this stuff goes."

"We'll get there," I said. "The jewelers will know what's missing. I figure a solid description match ought to be good enough."

"Shh. Counting." VP had tucked into the stacks of cash. A few minutes later, she looked up from the pile. "Looks like just over forty-eight large. Not bad for a night's work."

"Best of all, we didn't touch off a firefight," I said. "On top of that, I don't have to pay for a bunch of bullet-riddled firehouse gear."

"We'll have holes in something if those guys ever figure out who we are," Steve said.

"Probably," I admitted. "We'll have to see to it they don't. This is bound to hurt them."

Steve yawned. "How long do I need to house the swag?"

"Not long. Let's all get some sleep, and then we can figure out from the tags they left on stuff where it came from. Maybe we can start with the priciest things first."

* * *

I drove Rollie home as the sun came up.

"That was good work tonight, kid. Mission accomplished, and everyone came home."

"Amen to that," I said. "Thanks to you. I hated leaving you alone for the entry."

"You did your thing. I did mine. Surprise was key. They won't make the same mistake again, if they're smart. I wouldn't."

He shook my hand and headed into his house.

I got to my place a couple minutes later and brought in the swag from the jewelry store. There had to be at least sixty grand in watches, and I don't know how much in gold and jewels. I figured whoever was behind the warehousing arm of the operation was paying cents on the dollar for these and the other goods in exchange for offering quick, easy money for the thieves and a one-stop shop to unload all the gear. Add to the fact that everyone associated with the scheme seemed to operate with total impunity, and it had to be a lucrative operation all around.

Until last night, anyway.

I tried to get some sleep, but despite feeling exhausted, my mind raced and wouldn't let go. I stared at the ceiling for a while and then gave up and got up to make some coffee. It felt a little strange not having Sandy there, but I'd mentioned I was going to work late last night and when she didn't ask me to elaborate, I figured she had a good idea I'd be up to something. Kind of obvious, as I no longer had anything to do with the port.

I itched to tell her that we'd recovered Mr. Penney's gold cane top, but that would either open too many doors that I didn't want to get into now or her forced indifference would mean our distance was only going to grow.

I finished my coffee and glanced at the clock. Time to get cleaned up and head down to Jeweler's Row.

* * *

Sanger's Jewelers

I stepped inside the store, and there was Derek Miller perched on his stool, in his police uniform.

"Hey, Derek. Don't you ever punch in with the city?"

"Funny," he said. "I'm on the three-to-eleven shift."

"Long day."

"Aren't they all?" He covered a yawn. "I can sleep when I'm dead, right?"

Saul must have seen me on camera. He popped out from the back.

"Morning, Kyle." He was all smiles, but I thought that was for public. I'd probably get an earful when we were in private.

He waved me back.

"All right. Now what? You want your cash back already?"

"No. But don't work that kid out there into the ground."

"Thanks for the tip." Sanger softened his expression. "He's good and works hard. I have another, but he only looks the part. What did you need?" He glanced at the hard case I was carrying, figuring it'd look more professional than a pillowcase.

"I found some things I need you to check for me." I opened the case. Watches rested on a bed of crate foam. Rolexes and Omegas. Then rings, bracelets, and gold chains. "See anything that looks familiar?"

"How . . ." Sanger took out his loupe and flipped the watches over one at a time. He shook his head and retreated to his desk, where he pulled out a sheet of paper. "Three of these are mine. Serial numbers match, not like I'm not gonna not know if I'm missing some Submariners."

"Good. What else?"

"These rings, I have the design specs, and I can tell you right now that these four"—Sanger slid the engagement rings to one side—"are Bernie Alman's work. I'd recognize the style anywhere. You know him?"

I said I did.

Sanger looked me in the eye. "What the hell is going on here? What do you mean, you 'found' them?"

"You know the old one about not looking a gift horse in the mouth? I told you the other day I wanted to help, and I'm trying. Between us"— I gestured in the direction of the front of the store—"let's just say that the rash of robberies are connected, and maybe they weren't too careful about their storage."

"We all figure they're connected, but the way they're going about it feels more like a feeding frenzy than an organized crime wave."

"You're right there."

Sanger looked back at the jewelry. "So, you're here to sell them back to me?"

"I'm here to *give* them back to you." I held up a finger. "But just what is yours. I have more stops to make, starting with Alman's, looks like."

"*Give?*" I knew it was part of his job to be cynical.

"It's your property, isn't it? I'm just glad it's out of the wrong hands."

Sanger took a deep breath. "You realize what this means?"

"That the assholes who paid the punks fencing this stuff have nothing to show for it?"

"So much the better." It was good to see him smile. "But it's more than that. I filed insurance claims on all this, but now I can take it back, which means I should be able to keep my policy after all." His voice went ragged. "I told you they were going to cancel me." He shook his head slowly. "After decades of business."

"Glad to help."

Sanger's expression made all the lack of sleep worth it.

CHAPTER 19

Kyle's place, two days later

Despite some busy days, I'd managed to catch up on my rest. I felt like my brain had returned from a sabbatical in the fog. VP and Steve were due to come over, and Sandy had just left. We'd had a nice evening, and she let me know how well the truckers were doing with helping her clients get safely to and from her office.

I heard a buzz on the security system and saw on one of the monitors that a van had pulled up to the house. I got up to let them in.

VP wore her usual hoodie, her standard uniform for being out in public. Steve had a long-sleeve T-shirt and he carried a pair of the trash bags with him. He looked like some kind of DoorDash garbage delivery service.

"Morning, guys," I said. "You didn't have to bring anything to eat."

"You can do whatever you like with it, but this is all that's left from 'Operation Restock'." Steve plopped the bags down.

VP pulled down her hood and cocked her head. "We good to talk?"

"Sandy's at work. And you can talk around her, you know that."

"Do I?" She didn't miss much.

"We're okay," I told her. "She just needs to catch her breath on the whole lifestyle thing."

"Didn't mean it so personal, dude. Just looking after the store, you know?"

I did and turned my attention to the bags. "That's everything? You guys did great."

"Steve did great. I insisted on staying incognito, so he did all the legwork."

"You helped with the triage. That was the hardest part." Steve pointed at me. "Plus, your name opened a lot of doors."

"It went down pretty easy," VP said. "Not too hard to figure out, when most of the stuff still had price tags." She shook her head in wonder. "Designer bags are insane."

"Irene at the Chic Shack said she owes you big-time," Steve said. "So does Irv at Peak Sneaks. He said some of the rare Jordans we returned represented a month's income."

"I'll never get it, but I understand they're worth a fortune," I said. "So, what's in these?" I pointed to the remaining bags.

"Drugstore stuff," he said. "I got nowhere with the manager. He acted like I was the one who stole them and the merch was poisoned or something."

"What?"

"I'm serious. He threatened to call the cops. Said the store had it covered, and the company didn't want any part of fighting customers."

"I didn't realize looters were considered customers," I said. "You didn't give him your real name, I hope."

Steve looked insulted. "Course not." He shrugged. "I guess insurance revenue is good enough for them."

"We found all the jewelry owners," I said, then explained their issue with insurance.

Steve nodded. "That came up more than once. The mom-and-pops were grateful."

"Good."

"Yeah, but what isn't good is that besides being grateful, they're still scared," Steve said. "And mad."

"I can't blame them. This could easily get out of hand. I wish we owned a store window glass shop."

Steve grinned. "Hell, I'd settle for the plywood concession."

"Well, if the drugstores don't want their stuff back, I guess we can give it to Franklin over at Strawberry Mansion. I'm sure some of the renters could use some discounted supplies. Maybe it'll help them pay on time." The places weren't five-star but a hell of lot better than the flat-out slums they'd been when I'd acquired them.

I glanced at VP, who'd dropped out of the conversation. She had one of her burner phones in her hand, and I watched her eyes pop wide. "Dude!"

"What?" Steve and I both said.

"The text number we got from that lead from the squatter place. You-know-who's rental?"

Cullen. I'd forgotten about the text code we'd cracked and figured it to be a dead end.

"Yeah, I remember," I said. "What have you got?"

"An address, and a time. Two-fifteen today."

Near as we could figure, this was a casting call for a flash mob at a store. My heart raced.

VP read off the address.

"You sure that's correct?" Steve said and VP nodded. "Shoot, I don't even need to look that up. That's the address for Peak Sneaks."

"Meaning they're just going to double down and hit it again?" I asked.

Steve nodded. "Those collectables are worth way more than their weight in gold. You think word's already out that they got restocked?"

"Are you supposed to reply to the text?" I asked VP.

"Doesn't look like it. Just an open invitation to a closed list."

Heat surged in my chest. I glanced at the clock. "We don't have a lot of time."

"What are you thinking?" VP asked.

"This time will be different."

* * *

Old City, Peak Sneaks

Irv Simms stood in the back doorway of his vintage sneaker shop while I tried to convince him. My team waited inside the van—Steve at the wheel with VP riding shotgun, and we'd brought Rollie along.

"You're sure about this?" Irv leaned against the doorframe, but I figured I must be making progress, as he kept looking over his shoulder toward the store showroom.

I nodded. "Sorry to say, it's pretty solid word, Irv. A source I trust says you're getting mobbed again this afternoon." I gestured to the van.

"I know it's a lot to take in, but if we're going to be able to help, we need your okay now. Unless you'd rather take your chances with the cops."

He made a face like I'd offered him a sip of rotten milk. "They don't care when it really happens. What are they going to say if I call in a hunch?"

I shrugged.

"Look, Kyle," he said, "I haven't forgotten everything you already did for me. Why put you and your people at risk? Maybe I should just close for the afternoon."

"Hear me out," I said, then I explained what we had in mind.

* * *

With less than an hour to go, I sat in the back of Irv's store with Rollie. VP had camera drones parked in the front and back to watch the street, and I fiddled with the earpiece awaiting reports.

I understood Irv's reluctance and had assured him we weren't going to turn his store into a battle zone. Our plan was simple: Gain whatever intel we could about how the mobs would form up, let them start their attack, and then, after they grabbed the bait—in this case, a ridiculously valuable pair of sneakers we'd just recovered—drive them off with a toy Steve had been dying to use. After that, we could follow the tracker back to their new storage facility, just like last time.

"Keep your ears handy, kid," Rollie said to me. "You ever have Steve try this on you?"

I nodded. "It's almost as bad as that damn pain-ray thing." Steve had rigged an acoustic device that sent deafening sound in a tight cone. In this case, he'd made it sound like a store alarm, but no security system was ever this loud. "I turned my bad ear to it and even that didn't help."

"Call me old school, but I prefer the classics." Rollie opened a canvas bag that concealed a pump shotgun.

"Don't let Irv see that. We'll lose his faith if we have to drag a body out of here."

"Relax, just beanbag rounds," he assured me. "The problems will limp their way out of the store. Anyway, it's just in case."

I pointed the butt of his .45 in a waistband holster. "And that?"

"Ain't gonna be my body that leaves the store."

Hard to argue with that.

* * *

Forty-five minutes later

Irv was sweating bullets. We'd seen customers come and go. He'd even made a nice sale, and I was glad the customer hadn't been interested in the tracker-planted bait shoes.

"Quarterback, how are we looking on the street?"

"Regular schmoes walking around. No suspicious gatherings." VP sounded bored. "I know I didn't read that text wrong."

"We all saw it," I answered. "It's not two o'clock yet. Maybe they're rallying somewhere else."

"Maybe." She didn't sound convinced.

The store sat empty. Irv wandered to the back of the shop. "How we doing?"

"Still quiet," I said. "You clear on what to do if it goes down?"

"Get behind the counter, stay low, and slip out the back." He rubbed his face. "I haven't wanted a cigarette this bad in fifteen years."

"You're doing fine." I waited for Irv to go back on the floor before I resumed pacing to stretch my legs. Rollie sat still and could have been meditating for all the stress he showed.

We all tensed when two o'clock hit.

"Quarterback, anything?"

"No," VP said. "Was this some sort of code for another time? Or another place, even?"

"Sounds complicated, given the bozos that make up the mobs, but who knows?" The same frustration I heard in VP's voice flowed through my body, along with something else that I couldn't quite put my finger on.

We waited fifteen minutes, then thirty. One young guy came into the store, and for a second, I thought Irv was going to vault the counter. I even glanced over to Rollie to make sure he wasn't reaching for anything, though I should have known better. I hoped he hadn't noticed me checking.

After the customer left with Irv promising to call him when some obscure pair of shoes came in, I officially began to feel foolish.

"Quarterback, no texts calling it off?"

"Yo, don't you think I would have mentioned it?" VP snapped. "Sorry, dude."

"Looks like we got stood up."

"Still got bupkis, front or back," she added.

I glanced at Rollie. "You're the vigil expert," I told him, knowing he'd camped out for days just to get a single sniper shot off during the Vietnam War.

"Don't mind waiting," he said, "but no point if it isn't going to pay off."

"Let's call it," I said. "Someone changed their mind, I guess. Let's pack it in, guys."

I explained to Irv, who wasn't exactly disappointed that a raging mob hadn't returned to ransack his store. "Just to be safe," he said, "I think I'll close early. I sent everyone else home anyway, and frankly, I could use a drink. Join me?"

"Can I get a rain check?" I asked. "Gotta get our gear stowed and figure out where we messed up."

We picked up all our stuff and slipped out the back while VP collected her drones. Just as I approached the van, the hair on the back of my neck stood up, and I spun around and scanned the parking lot. Just cars and Steve and Rollie loading the van. I glanced up and saw a window curtain slide back into place from a building overlooking the lot.

The urgent warning faded, but acid still roiled in my stomach.

"Yo, you ready?" VP called out, and Steve started the van.

I stared at the window another moment, but the curtains remained in place. I shook my head. It was a city. Lots of people and lots of windows.

"Well, that was a bust," VP said as I climbed in the van. "Sorry, peeps."

"Not your fault," I said.

"Longshots are called that for a reason," Rollie said. "They don't all pay off."

"But it was so specific," VP said.

Steve turned down a side street. I hadn't been paying attention. We'd just passed the gate to Chinatown. Two blocks later, by the convention center, he turned again onto Race Street and the wrong direction from where we were going.

Steve kept looking at the rearview mirror.

I glanced back and saw plenty of cars, no surprise this time of day. "What's up?"

"Not sure," he said. "See that silver Crown Vic?"

Rollie and I peered out the tinted back windows. "Cop car?" I asked, seeing the telltale spotlight mounted on the side.

"Once upon a time," Rollie said. "That's an auction car."

I looked again and sure enough, the paint on the hood was faded and peeling in spots. The car changed lanes and began to catch up to us. I noticed the police ramming grills still attached to the front. I turned to Steve, who was looking for holes in the traffic. "When did you notice them?"

"Back on Arch Street, but it wasn't until they followed us on a couple turns that I really began to wonder."

"At least we know they aren't actually cops."

"You sure that's a good thing, dude?" VP asked.

"Gives us more options," Rollie said as he reached into a storage area and started pulling out Kevlar vests. He tossed one up to VP, who fitted it around the back of Steve's seat, giving him protection from the rear, then put one on herself. I pulled mine on and watched out the window until Rollie was set.

"You sure we need these?" VP asked.

"No," Rollie said, "but this is the time to ask, not when it gets hot."

"Fair," VP conceded. We had a steel-reinforced "nest" for her to retreat to, so she could still watch a screen, if necessary, in relative safety. It helped that she was small, as it wasn't practical to turn the whole van into a tank.

"They're still back there," I said. We had two lanes in our direction, and our shadow was taking full advantage and gaining ground.

"Think they know we made them?" I asked.

"Hard to say," Steve said.

VP clambered out of her nest and crawled out with a phone camera. Rollie gave her a hard look. "I may need room to work, here." He was reloading the shotgun with buckshot shells. He saw my gaze. "Just in case. Jeez."

"I hear you," VP told him. "But if I can get their faces, it could be useful. Believe me, I'm gone if it starts to go south."

Rollie accepted that and gave VP space to perch by the back window. "All this tint," she complained, meaning for both our van and the car, which had plenty all over it. It made it difficult to get a good look at the people inside the car.

"Whoever they are, they're coming in for a closer look," Steve said. I noticed he'd scrunched down as much as he could with his lanky frame. "And there's a second car with them, I think."

"We're *sure* that's not police?" I asked.

"Uh, guys," VP spoke up. "Definitely not cops."

"Why's that?" I asked.

"They just pulled on ski masks," VP added as she slid past Rollie and me and slipped back into the nest, but not before she double-checked the vest on Steve's seat.

"Hold on." Steve hit the gas, but this thing was no Blue Bomber, where Rollie could outrun about anyone. But I knew we had some tricks up our sleeve.

The silver car was closing and traffic wasn't helping. We were in the heart of the city, which should have kept us safer, but all it meant at the moment was too many cars and bystanders.

"I'm running out of room here," Steve griped.

A glance at the road ahead showed a stale red light with lots of cars queued up.

"Silver wants to pull alongside us. Don't let 'em," I said. "I can see them reaching for stuff in there."

"Hell no," Steve cut the wheel and swerved halfway into the oncoming lane, then jammed the brakes.

"Shit!" I grabbed a safety bar in case the back door popped open. The car hit with a loud metallic crunch but the doors looked okay.

"Damn!" VP yelled.

Rollie had braced and held on with one hand and the shotgun in the other.

Steve hit the gas. The car fell back and then accelerated. The ramming grill took the hit and the silver car looked okay. Worse, I saw the white Crown Vic advancing fast.

"Can't turn yet. Too much traffic," Steve said.

The light turned, but the silver car closed and hit us hard. VP yelped again.

"Come on!" Steve yelled at traffic.

It felt like we were crawling forward. I watched for anyone running up the street. Nope, but pedestrians had heard the impact, and we had the attention of the whole block.

"Windows coming down, Kyle." Rollie watched out the back. "Get low, everyone! Steve, don't be too choosy about open space," he added.

Figures leaned out of the windows from the silver car's back seats and masked guys aimed pistols our way.

"Guns!" I called out and ducked down. Rollie racked a shell into the shotgun.

The back window exploded, and we heard a series of shots from the pistols. Slugs thunked through the back doors like tiny lights snapping on. We were close, not like they could miss the van.

Screams bounced off the close walls, and a quick glance said we didn't have much room to maneuver. Pedestrians scattered.

Steve hit the gas and just as fast hit the brakes. He screamed his frustration.

Rollie popped up, aimed the shotgun and dropped down without firing.

"Can't chance it, kid," he said to me. "Too many civvies." He began unloading the shotgun and putting the beanbag rounds back in. Less lethal didn't mean safe, but much more so, for bystanders.

I nodded.

The van lurched forward, and I felt us go up on the curb. We were on the sidewalk, and Steve honked the horn nonstop. More shots hit up higher and through the roof from inside. Pedestrians dove out of the way and scattered farther ahead, frightened by the sound of gunfire.

I thought Rollie clapped me on the back, then realized a round had hit me in the vest. It hurt like hell, but the Kevlar did its job.

"I see some daylight ahead," Steve said. "Hang on."

I peeked out the back window and saw the silver car following us on the sidewalk. One good thing was that all the bouncing on and off curbs had jostled the shooters back inside the car.

The van slammed into something with a wet thump, and I feared the worst.

"Just veggies," Steve called back, and I saw the stand outside a grocery store flash by. We were cutting through Chinatown.

"We're sitting ducks, kid. I don't have a choice." Rollie lifted the shotgun.

"Wait." I got an idea. "Dutch Boy," I said.

Rollie grinned. "Yeah." He put down the gun and rummaged through the storage locker.

I unlatched the back door but didn't open it. "Slow down for a second, Steve."

I loved that he didn't question, even in the face of fire.

"Here." Rollie handed me a glass jar.

I swung the door open just as the silver car followed us back onto the street. It was about ten feet back, and I whipped the jar right at the driver's side of the windshield. The glass shattered, and white paint splashed across the screen.

"Up!" Rollie yelled like a tank gunner ready to load another round, and I reached back for the next jar. Rollie slapped it into my hand, and then another as soon as I'd flung the last one. Thick blotches of paint covered the windshield.

The driver finished the job for me when he tried his wipers which spread the paint all over.

"Steve, go!" I closed the door and peered out the back. We jumped another curb, and the driver tried to follow, but saw the car ahead too late. He clipped a bumper then overcorrected into a storefront.

"Eat that!" Steve yelled. "Vine Street coming up."

"Don't celebrate yet," Rollie said. "Looks like his partner is still back there."

"Everyone okay? VP?" I took a deep breath. My shoulder and side were sore, but nothing like a cracked rib.

"I'm squished down here so tight you can just call me V."

Steve laughed, more out of relief. "Call out where the guy is. I'm gonna need to focus forward."

We took the turn for Vine Street just as the white Crown Vic power-slid into view just shy of Chinatown. So much for them stopping to check on their buddies.

"That car has some balls under the hood," Rollie said. He peeked into the container. "Sorry we don't have any more for a second coat."

I had another idea. I pulled out Steve's long-range Acoustic device. "VP, can you power this thing up?"

She popped her head up. "Bet. Gimme the cord." I tossed the plug. She had all sorts of power adapters near her computer and drone gear. She said something else, but I had my bad ear turned toward her and didn't catch it.

The white car was catching up fast. The driver had some skill, and I watched him weave around some cars, earning honks.

"Steve, keep him on our right side." I moved over to the slider door with the boxy device. "Rollie, get the latch."

Rollie crouched and watched for my signal. I waited until the car pulled next to us. Steve took a sharp turn left, and the tires howled in protest. The driver struggled to match the move, and a shadow told me we were passing under the expressway. I saw windows slide down on the white Crown Vic on both the driver and passenger sides.

"Now!" I yelled to Rollie and fumbled with the switches on the device. Rollie slid the side door open, and I raised the device and hit the switch.

Nothing.

"Hang on. Breaker popped," VP shouted.

The masked driver glanced at me, but it was the guy behind him that froze me. He raised a pistol, and time seemed to stop as I stared right at the muzzle.

The guy took aim, and I tried to lean back, away from the line of fire. It felt like my body wouldn't obey. Rollie moved like a cat and pivoted to the open door with the shotgun up and pointed at the car.

As I fell back, I saw the gunner's eyes go wide and he too recoiled away from a muzzle pointed at him. Rollie fired a blast, and I saw a flash of white when the beanbag round flew into the car.

"Got it. Go!" VP shouted.

I sat up and raised the device, now lit up, and hit the button. The driver had kept pace, but I heard the sound bounce off the car and side walls of the underpass. Even diluted, it was deafening.

The driver clapped his hand to his ear and veered hard away from the van, right into the overpass wall. My ears were still ringing from Steve's toy, so I was robbed of the pleasure of the racket it made.

I switched the acoustic device off and nodded to Rollie, who slid the door shut.

CHAPTER 20

Conshohocken, Pennsylvania, Steve's warehouse

After I'd confirmed that everyone was all right, while Steve wove through the streets as "fast casual" as a bullet-riddled van could move, we listened to the police and emergency scanners go crazy in the wake of our carnage.

When we got clear of the area and the locus of the search remained around Chinatown, we pulled into an alley for a quick stealth makeover that consisted of a couple magnetic signs for a lawn company and some New Jersey license plates. Rollie stuck some white putty into the most visible bullet holes. All in all, it wasn't great, but we managed to get to Steve's without getting pulled over.

Steve hit the remote to close the garage door after us. "Nothing to it."

Rollie checked our vests, which we'd stashed after getting clear, as they would've been hard to explain to a traffic cop. Something fell out of one, and he bent to the floor of the van and picked up a deformed pistol slug. Some fabric clung to the mushroomed chunk of lead.

"Who caught one?" He held the vest up and saw by the size it had been mine. "Kyle?"

"It's fine." Sounded better than to complain that my shoulder blade was throbbing.

"You got hit?" VP said. "Why didn't you say something?"

"Like what? 'Ow?'" I asked. "The door and the vest slowed it down—enough, anyway."

"Let's see." Rollie pointed to my shirt.

"All right." I raised the shirt. It hurt to move my shoulder, but nothing seemed broken.

131

"Yowch," was Steve's medical assessment.

"Looks like a paintball hit on steroids," Rollie weighed in. "You should have Sandy at least have a look, but my guess is you'll live."

"I'm not sure how she'll take the news that we've been in a gunfight."

"I wasn't wild about it, and I was there," VP said. "Glad it wasn't worse."

"Remember, they started it," Rollie said. "I'd say they got the worst of it. But yeah, we got lucky."

"We walked right into their trap," I said. "VP, can we look at the footage from the front and back cameras?"

She nodded, glad, I think, to have something concrete to do. Getting shot at is an awful helpless feeling. "Yeah, they had to be watching us. Maybe we'll see them."

The adrenaline began to wear off. "Rollie, thanks for saving me back there when that guy drew down on me. I thought sure I was going to catch one in the head."

Rollie waved it off. "So did that masked marvel. He's lucky he jumped back when he did."

"But I thought you had one of those beanbag thingies," VP said.

Rollie scowled. "Yeah, but they're not filled with beans. That's the number nine lead shot, and they pack a punch, especially at close range."

"Did you hit him?" I asked.

"Right in the ribs," Rollie said.

"That must have hurt," Steve said. "Crashing couldn't have been pleasant either."

"He shouldn't have pointed a gun at my friend," Rollie said. "It would've been buckshot and a trip to the morgue if there weren't bystanders around."

* * *

One hour later

"Yo, I think I got something." VP stepped into the garage area, where Steve, Rollie and I were stripping down the van. After such a public spectacle, we all agreed the thing was radioactive, so after we finished pulling all our useful gear out, the van could make one last, disguised trip to a friend's scrapyard.

We all followed VP back to her office space, where she had split-screens of the video feed from the sneaker shop.

"Check it, I saw this dude out front when we first set up, but he went by like the rest of traffic." VP pointed out a lone figure on a scooter moving past. He looked over at the shop but otherwise didn't seem to slow or stop at all.

I wasn't getting it. "I don't see what—"

"Hang on." VP reversed the footage and froze the video when the guy looked at the shop. She zoomed in on the still, and when the image had sharpened, she pointed again. "Look at his helmet."

We all leaned forward. Rollie pulled out a set of readers. "I'll be damned," he said.

"A GoPro," Steve said.

"Yup." VP smiled. "We were busy, so I didn't notice this until just now." She pulled up another video clip, this one showing the view from the back of the store. We could see our van and the small parking lot. I watched as I got out of the van along with Rollie and met Irv at the back door of the sneaker shop.

"You gotta get my good side." I wasn't sure what she was seeing here.

"Maybe *she* did." VP fiddled with the controls and focused the screen several stories up to show the building that overlooked the parking lot. The back of my neck tingled. She froze the shot and zoomed in. "See anyone you know?"

It wasn't just a person in the window. It was a woman aiming a camera down at us and speaking into a phone. "Shit. That's Rose Thorn, isn't it?"

"Unique looks have a downside," VP said. "I cross-checked the tat on her right arm. It's her."

"Last, but not least." VP pulled another clip that showed the front of the store and the street. "This is almost out of frame, but we got lucky." The uppermost edge of the frame showed the distinctive front half of a silver Crown Victoria up the block but in sight of where we pulled out from the parking lot.

"Well, we don't have to wonder if it was some sort of coincidence," Steve said. "She's into a hell of a lot more than just giving bad advice to squatters."

Rollie's expression hardened. "I won't underestimate her again. Either that scrap of paper was bait she left at the house all along, or she set this up to figure out who the stranger was texting her."

"Either way, she made us for sure," Steve said, "and wasted no time putting a target on our backs."

"She comes off as pretty radical, but this is all on another level," VP said.

"Huh?" I said.

"Her public persona is all fight the power, anti-police brutality, hero of the little guy." The words were flip, the delivery, not so much. VP sounded sympathetic.

"And you buy that crap?" Rollie said.

VP bristled. "Not all of us worship at the feet of authority. I'm not a boomer, in case you forgot."

"Nobody's perfect," Rollie shot back. "You slipped my question."

VP took a breath, thought for a second. "If you meant do I buy Rose's persona? After she just tried to kill us all, that's a no." She looked down. "Thought you were ripping on what I believe."

Rollie's tone softened. "Your beliefs are your business. And it's freedom I worship at the feet of, if we're keeping score."

The two of them locked eyes, nodded. I was glad they'd wound it down on their own, without me having to remind them we were on the same team.

"We just survived a brazen attempt to kill us," I said. "Right on the street." I still was having trouble believing they'd launched their attack in the middle of the city. Not a care in the world about the chance the cops would pitch themselves into the fray.

Steve stepped to another set of computer screens. "The radio calls went nuts for a while, but now they've settled down, and I see nothing but standard-issue reports of suspected gang activity and hit-and-runs, no serious injuries reported." Steve looked over at us. "And no arrests."

Rollie shook his head. "Of course not. And no reported injuries means just that: none were *reported*. I tagged that guy hard. He'll be out of the fight for a while."

"So, does this mean Thorn is in charge of all this?" Steve asked. "She's organized the flash mobs?"

"Maybe. Or she's just the highest-placed player we've run into so far," I said. "The Irish pulled me in to all of this because they're having problems with the new DA."

Steve nodded. "He's doing a great job keeping crime down. Nothing is reported or prosecuted, voila, low crime rate."

Rollie pointed at Rose on the screen. "She feels safe in the city. If it was just her, the Irish would have solved the problem a while ago."

Fury built in my chest. "Maybe she doesn't have to worry about getting prosecuted, but after today, that's the least of her problems."

Rollie frowned. "Think it's time for a face-to-face?"

He was serious and it forced me to slow down. "I guess it depends on what we mean. Remember, she's an attorney, and if she has some sort of protection from city prosecutors, that means she can bring heat on us from the authorities."

"And if I meant something a little more persuasive? I'd consider it self-defense," Rollie said.

"Guys, we'd need to find her first," VP pointed out. "She's from out of town, and right now I can't come up with a location."

"Rose Thorn can't be her birth name," Steve said.

"It's not, but she legally changed it years ago. She's got a bright trail all over Washington and Oregon. Arrested at protests, but nothing ever stuck and her law license is in good standing."

"But still hard to find?" I said.

"I don't exactly have a list of hotels and their guests. I could try some hacks on credit card databases, but that would take time. I have to be careful."

I didn't know all her tricks, but whenever VP spoke like that, I knew it was a big ask. "We don't even know if she's paying with her own card. It could be her organization's. For that matter, we're only guessing about hotels."

"True," Steve said. "But if she's running these goons, she probably has a place to stay."

"We'll find her," Rollie said. "The question stands, what then?"

I took a few deep breaths to let my anger and adrenaline subside. "Shooting back is one thing, but going on a proper hunt after the fact is another."

"Sometimes," Rollie said. "And other times it boils down to timing and semantics. Think she'll quit after today?"

"If she's even part of what's running the shitshow going on in the city right now, then her escalation tells me we must have struck a nerve when we hit that warehouse."

"So, that's a no?" Rollie asked.

"Correct." I thought about this location and home. "What do you think she might try next? Our homes?"

VP spoke next: "There's good news, at least I think."

"Yeah?" I said.

"Well, you two never said your real names around the dirtbags at Cullen's place or around her, right?"

"True," Rollie said. "Though to be fair, I think she figured out we weren't really Mutt and Jeff."

"So, for now at least, she knows you by face, but not by name," VP said.

"As far as I know," I said. "We should be careful."

"Hard to guess what she might pull to draw us out again," Rollie said.

"Or maybe she's counting on us thinking just that, and we'll have to lay low," Steve said.

I raised my palms. "We can 'what if' ourselves to death. Let's get some rest and regroup tomorrow. If we can find her first, we have a chance to catch her off guard."

Steve nodded. "You got it." He pointed to the van. "Right after I get this thing to the knacker."

"Yeah. Good idea," I said.

We didn't just fly off into motion, though. All of us just sat there, still computing.

It was me who broke the silence, thinking aloud: "If she can get the cops on her side, that could be a real problem. No matter how well she's connected, though, I doubt she can move all that fast. We gave them a bloody nose today and left them with a hell of a mess to clean up."

CHAPTER 21

Kyle's place, the next evening

"What happened?" Sandy had just hugged me in the wrong spot and hit the bruise on my back shoulder blade, and I winced hard.

I caught the lie before it reached my lips, but she caught me doing it. "If you want to hear, I'll tell you," I said. She had her out.

After a short pause that felt endless, she said she did.

"Shot."

"What? How?" She started to lift my shirt to see.

"Vest stopped it. Just hurts. I was lucky."

"You call that luck?"

"Actually yes, all things considered."

"What does that mean?" Her chin quivered.

"Last chance," I said. "You wanted some distance." I didn't mean for it to sound like I was throwing her words back in her face, but pain made me cranky.

"Tell me. And don't you need a doctor?"

"It didn't fracture. No need to bother Doc Crock." She'd dealt with the Irish Mob's favorite disgraced sawbones before. What he lacked in actual licensing and permission to practice medicine, he more than made up for in discretion.

I filled her in on the last couple days. "So," I said in closing, "if the random violence wasn't enough, now we have to worry about the targeted kind."

Her jaw set. "I won't run away. If my clients have the guts to get here, we'll be there for them."

"Good. As far as I know, you have nothing specific to fear. This Thorn woman sicced her dogs on us, but she still isn't sure who she's up against. If that changes, I'll tell you right away." It was only fair. "The truckers are still doing all right, though?"

She touched my arm. "Yes! They are heroes. You should hear Mr. Penney go on about them."

I smiled. "Nice to get one right now and then."

She hugged me, making sure to be gentle on my back. "Is that okay?"

"More than okay," I assured her. "I think you fixed it."

* * *

Kyle's place, the next morning

Sandy left early, and it was amazing how seeing her had melted the stress away.

That lasted as long as my first cup of coffee.

VP called, and I grabbed the phone. "Hey."

"Dude, put on the news."

"What channel?" I was still waking up.

"Doesn't matter. Call me back in a few." She hung up.

I flipped it on and saw the "Breaking News" banner.

Officer Shot

I knew the reporter doing the live feed, but that wasn't the only thing I recognized. The coffee turned to acid in my stomach.

"This is Jill Williams reporting. Here's what we know so far. This morning, just after Sanger's Jewelers opened, a so-called flash mob rushed into the store with the intent to rob it. Unfortunately, they were surprised by an off-duty but uniformed police officer."

Oh, no.

"The officer confronted the robbers, and that was when one of them pointed his gun and the two exchanged shots. Both the officer and the alleged perpetrator were struck."

Alleged, my ass.

"First year officer Derek Miller was rushed to the Temple Hospital Trauma Center and is said to be in critical condition."

The station flashed to what looked like Derek's Police Academy graduation photo.

"And the shooter? Sorry, alleged shooter?" the anchor asked Jill.

"He was arrested when he sought treatment for a gunshot wound to the shoulder."

No picture, I noticed.

"Any information on his identity?"

Jill shook her head. "Police aren't releasing anything just yet, and the security around the suspect is said to be tight."

She went on to cite increasingly alarming crime stats and skyrocketing incidence numbers and other such information I knew all too well. I called VP back.

"I'm sorry," VP said. "I know he's a friend."

"If you need me, I'm on my way to the hospital," I said.

"Anything I can do?"

I was about to say no, but had an idea. "Yeah," I said. "They're not IDing the shooter. Think you might be able to find anything out?"

"I could try. How hard do you want me to push into the police computers?"

"Maybe another angle: If I can get a copy of the security camera footage, do you think you could work with that?"

"Yeah." She paused. "Dude, that's going to be rough to see. Want me to clean it up before you look?"

Cold anger filled my body. "No."

* * *

Temple Hospital Trauma Center

That disinfectant smell. From the Sand Box medical tents to Doc Crock's converted dining room operating room to this world-class Level One trauma center, that odor conjured more memories than I cared to remember. This time my body was fine, but when I got inside, I could see I shared a helpless feeling with an ever-thickening crowd of police officers.

I looked for someone I knew as I made my way to the ER waiting room. I knew better than to try get any closer, but the last I heard, Derek was still up in an operating room.

I never knew his parents, but I saw a cluster of civilians over in one corner of the room and by the number of police and officials around them it was clear they were family. Jeez, his dad looked just like him.

Their faces were blanched the color of the polished floor.

I wasn't about to go near them, but I did move closer to a knot of young officers. "Any news?"

They all pivoted toward me and gave me hard stares. "Who are you?" said meatiest, most red-faced of them. I knew he couldn't have been any older than Derek, but he already had that hard-bitten, perpetually angry look cop-work brings out in some men.

"I'm a friend," I said. "Well, he used to work for me before he went to the Academy."

"Yeah? And?"

I could see I was at risk of serving as a lightning rod for their stress, and this guy in particular would be all too happy to light me up.

"I'm not a reporter, if that's what you're thinking." I pointed at the knot of press who were kept at bay across the room.

"You're not family either," another said.

I was ready to back way off and rethink why I was there in the first place. I couldn't help Derek right now, and he was in the right hands. Still, I felt like I had to do something, and my instincts said to come here. Now I felt more useless than ever.

"Lighten up, guys. He's okay." Sergeant Barry Daniels, an older cop I knew, had come over. He nodded to the officers, who moved away from me.

I'd seen Daniels at a distance, but not all of the ones I knew wanted to be seen with me. Just part of the business I was in, I tried not to take it personally.

"Thanks," I told him. "Horrible morning, not their fault."

We stepped out of earshot of everyone.

"He's a good kid," Daniels said. "You know him or something?"

I explained about his work at the port. "Did the docs say anything?"

He shrugged. "Nothing good. The ones who know are still in the operating room."

"I saw on TV you got the guy."

"It wasn't in my district. They say he's going to be okay. He's getting moved to the medical wing of the detention center." Daniels dropped his voice so low I almost missed it: "For now."

It was the *way* he said. He looked defeated.

I knew I shouldn't press but couldn't help myself. "What do you mean?"

"The guy's an adult, but with this DA, that may not matter. I don't even know why we bother making arrests anymore."

"I've been hearing that around, but not for something like this."

He just stared at me. His eyes looked dead. "I guess we'll see, won't we?" He walked back across the room.

I spotted a lone familiar figure slumped in a chair at the far corner of the waiting room. Saul Sanger. He looked tiny in the chair, like he was just melting away.

I went over to him. "Saul."

He looked up like he'd been drugged. "Kyle?"

"I just heard. I came down to . . ." I started.

"To what?" Saul spoke in a soft voice. "What can anyone do?"

"I wish there was something."

"I wish none of this happened. If I hadn't hired him, he wouldn't be here."

"Maybe not, but you and your other people might have been here instead. He was doing his job."

"None of them can do their job. At least he tried." He shook his head and stared at the floor. I wish that punk had been the one shot in the head."

"Maybe with this guy off the streets the attacks will slow down." I didn't even believe myself.

"Plenty more where he came from. Besides, you really think he will be locked up for long?" Saul said.

"They have a sure case. It was on your security camera, wasn't it?"

"That was the first thing they took, right after they carted that poor boy off," Saul said. "Want to bet me it will get lost long before the trial?" He gave a smile that didn't really resemble a smile.

That gave me an idea. "You keep copies, don't you?"

"They'll probably seize those as soon as they think of it."

I stepped closer. "Do you have someone watching the store right now?"

"Of course. There are cops there—crime scene and all—but I don't trust them."

"Be right back." I went over to the reception desk and borrowed a pen. I scribbled an email address on a scrap of paper. It was one of VP's throwaways.

Saul watched me return, and I noticed he had more life in his gaze. Good. "Listen, can you call your guy at the store and send a copy of the footage to this address? It's safe and will be a dead end even if they look."

"What do you want with it?"

"Insurance? Hard to sweep things under the rug if they wind up on the news." I didn't add that I wanted to know who the prisoner was.

Saul nodded. "Yeah. I mean, don't get me wrong, these guys here are as mad as anyone, but I just think the city won't have the stomach for a big trial."

"I hope we're not that far gone, but . . ."

"Got a phone I can borrow?"

As a matter of fact, I did.

* * *

Temple Hospital Trauma Center, an hour later

Dozens of cops came and went to show support. Saul sat with a cup of coffee in a hand that still shook.

VP called back.

"What's up?" I asked her.

"How is he?"

"Still in surgery. I'm not sure if that's good or bad." Didn't feel great, that was for sure."

"He's still fighting," VP pointed out.

"So, it went through?"

She paused. "Yeah. I thought it'd be rough." Her voice hitched. "I wasn't even close. But you know about that part."

"I guess I do," I said.

"You also know the shooter," she added.

"What?"

"You'll see it yourself, but it's your flash mob buddy Andre 'The Giant' Rogers."

"You're sure?"

"Even if he hadn't lost his mask after he got shot, you'd know it was him. Got a solid face still and it leaves no doubt."

"They haven't shot anyone up to now." Then, I remembered our little adventure in Chinatown. "Except for us." I shuddered, thinking a few inches higher and I might have been right here on a table. Or a slab.

VP blew her nose like she'd been fighting tears. "They didn't have to here. You can see Derek draw his gun and confront the lead guy. They didn't expect it, you could tell, but just as he moved to deal with that guy, in comes Andre behind him, and he was just going to execute him from the back."

"It's okay, I can see it later," I said.

"No, this is too messed up. Last second, Derek must have sensed the guy behind him, and he moved fast. He whipped around and aimed just as Andre fired. It might have messed up the big guy's shot, but"—she paused—"you can see it go through the skull. It's awful. But Derek fired at the same time, and it hit Andre's shoulder."

"Okay. Can you have a copy ready to go to the press? I'm hearing a fear that this might get downplayed."

"How is that even possible?"

"They pegged our rolling battle through the streets as just a gang dispute, remember?"

"Shit. Yeah, you got it," she said. "Just say the word."

"Not yet. I'll keep you posted."

* * *

Temple Hospital Trauma Center

It was past lunchtime, but I couldn't eat. I'd seen people hurt, killed right in front of me, even, but something about this forced me to stay at the emergency room. I knew it couldn't help Derek, but I still couldn't make myself leave.

A sudden commotion from the press told me that something was up. I stood and saw a throng of reporters surge forward. Just as fast, a blue wall of police met them. The police formed an impromptu wall, and all I could see behind them was a gurney getting pushed across the hallway in the distance.

The reporter complained, but the police never let the cameras get close. They gave up when it was clear that Derek had been moved to the ICU.

The line of police parted, and some captain or another emerged in his pressed uniform and identified himself. I stepped closer so I could hear.

"Again, Officer Miller is out of surgery and is in the Intensive Care Unit. The doctors say he is still critical, and we'd ask for your patience and understanding in this difficult time."

Still alive. I exhaled; didn't even realize I'd been holding my breath.

Reporters bombarded the captain with questions, and he deflected them like he'd spent time as a public information officer. I stuck around long enough to hear if he'd say anything about Andre, but not a word. So far, the reporters didn't seem to know the guy's identity, but I doubted it would stay that way. In fact, if the police brass played too many games with withholding Andre's name, I'd make sure of it got out. But not yet.

When the questions and answers began to sound so repetitive they could have been on a recorded loop, I slipped away. Sergeant Daniels broke from the group and followed me until we were by the vending machines.

"I hope they'll post guards at the door," I said.

"Better believe it." Daniels studied the drink choices like I wasn't there. "That family has enough to deal with without worrying about seeing Derek all over the front page, like he is *now*," Daniels shuddered.

Just the way he said that curdled my stomach. "Hear anything more than the sanitized version on Derek's condition?"

Daniels's head dipped. "It's bad. They did as much as they could, but Jesus." He took a deep breath. "They say the next few hours will be key."

"Just keep that prick locked up, huh?"

He looked at me, his eyes blazed with anger but also with grief. "If it were up to most of us, we'd draw straws for a firing squad." He looked around like he was worried a reporter might have overheard him. "Not really, but God, you know what I mean."

"I get it." I was glad he wasn't the one answering questions.

"It'll be up to good old 'Catch and Release' Castle. It's the DA's world. We just work in it." Daniels left without buying anything and returned to his fellow officers.

After the flurry of activity, the throng of reporters settled down into what could only be described as a death vigil. They didn't dare leave in case the news broke that Derek passed away. I hoped he'd make them wait sixty years. I pictured Derek on life support that long and reconsidered.

At any rate, I decided not to bother Jill Williams, who'd helped me break a story or two over the years. I wasn't ready to tease any info on Andre, and I still thought that would take care of itself.

Other serious cases came through the doors, and the doctors dealt with accidents and unrelated violence. The police presence remained heavy, but they did a good job keeping out of the staff's way.

I decided to take a walk outside and stretch my legs. That was when I noticed a large figure across the street. He leaned against a road sign and puffed on a cigarette. He wore a dark straw hat that shaded his features, but I'd know that hulking shape anywhere.

Cullen.

I crossed the street trying not to look like I was heading right for him, which I was. Spit dried up from my mouth like I'd pulled a drain plug, but I couldn't stop my feet. It wasn't right. If this poor kid pulled through, I couldn't just stand by and let him get snuffed out like this.

But the bigger burning question than what did I think I could do to stop him escaped my lips as he watched me approach.

"Why?"

Cullen continued to stare toward the emergency room entrance, but his head tilted like a quizzical dog's.

I repeated my question.

Now he looked at me. I felt a chill and blurted out, "The place is full of cops. They won't let anyone get close."

"I hope not." Cullen ground out his cigarette and faced me.

"You still haven't told me why."

"First off, just because I know you, doesn't mean I owe you shit." His face relaxed. "Second, I have no idea what you are talking about."

Now it was my turn for head tilts. I lowered my voice. "Why would you want to visit Derek? You can't have anything to do with those thugs."

Fury clouded Cullen's features before he regained control. "I'm nothing like that trash, even if you and the rest of the world brand me some sort of monster."

I didn't nickname the guy "Killer," and it fit.

"And for your information, you have it all wrong. For someone with the rep for knowing everything in and out of Fishtown, sometimes you're a real dumbass."

"Huh?"

"Derek is my cousin."

"Your . . ."

He shook his head at me. "The whole family isn't mobbed up. He knows about me, but I always kept my distance."

"Must be awkward at holiday time."

"Don't be a prick," Cullen said. "Being the black sheep made it easy to stay away from them. But that didn't mean, he didn't hear the same rumors as anyone."

Aside from his reputation, I knew Cullen had been investigated and questioned over the years, but nothing had ever stuck. "But if you weren't close. How come you're here now?"

"He's still family. I've watched him over the years. He was one of the good ones. He didn't deserve this."

"He might pull through," I said the words and didn't believe a single one. Cullen cut his gaze at me. No sale.

"Not if he's lucky," Cullen whispered. "I saw they have the mutt that did this."

Now his gaze would have pinned me to the sidewalk if it were possible.

"I heard the same." My pulse rate had picked up.

"Yeah? What else have you heard?" He stared hard at me, and it occurred that this would be a bad time to try to lie to him.

"He's locked up at the detention center hospital."

"No shit. I know Derek winged him. Don't waste my time, Kyle."

Fine. Not like it'd stay secret, and I had no reason to cover for the bastard. I gave Cullen the name. "I've run into him before. Literally," I explained. "They're organized. We hit one of their warehouses full of swag. They tried to hit back." I shared our recent Chinatown adventures after the trap.

"You been busy." As close as Cullen came to being impressed. "I thought that was just gangs."

"Don't believe everything you read in the papers."

"Pretty bold right in the open, in the middle of the day."

"We thought so too. Part of the reason we may have let our guard down. They don't seem worried about the authorities."

Cullen indicated the hospital. "Maybe that'll change."

I took a deep breath. "Not all my contacts on the force are convinced."

"That punk better hope he stays right where he is."

"You going in to see Derek?"

"Funny guy. This is close enough. My other cousins have enough on their plates." Cullen shoved his hands in his pockets.

"I understand," I said. "And I'm sorry."

"Thanks. For everything." Cullen resumed his vigil.

CHAPTER 22

Fishtown, Kyle's Place, two days later

"Is it on yet?" I'd just returned to the house after taking Sandy in to work. That she hadn't given me a hard time about being overprotective said everything about how completely insane things had gotten in town.

"Not yet," VP said. She sat next to Steve in the living room where we had a big screen TV tuned to the local news.

"How was the trip?" Rollie had wanted to ride in with us. Another sign of the deteriorating conditions.

"Not bad," I said. "I think every troublemaker is down at the courthouse."

Onscreen we could see my reporter friend stand at a distance while the camera panned the streets. A huge crowd swelled the sidewalks, and it looked like a matter of time before the flimsy sawhorses and low metal barricades would burst like a dam and the mob would take over the street.

"This is Jill Williams. I'm here at the courthouse standing in the shadow of City Hall. This simple arraignment has more of a feel that the entire city is on trial as we wait to learn the status of accused police officer shooter, Andre 'The Giant' Rogers."

In the background, we could see mobs of scruffy-looking young people screaming and waving signs. The camera zoomed in on one placard that read "Justice for Andre." Another, "End Police Brutality" and "Giant Mistake."

Steve shook his head. "Nothing says spontaneous demonstration like professionally printed signs."

I thought the same thing. "Are we any closer to figuring out exactly who, or even why, something like this is being funded?"

Rollie nodded. "VP, you're recording all this, right? We might find some people we recognize."

"Yeah," she said. "Anything good, I can run through the facial recognition. Lot of masks, though. I'd love to have our own drones, but with this circus, forget it."

"At least I didn't need to worry about spilling his identity to Cullen," I said. "I didn't think it would take long."

"You saw these clowns at the detention center?" Rollie said. "Someone spread the word about him."

As if on cue, the news report showed footage from the day before when the protesters had tried to swarm the entrance of the hospital wing of the detention center. Crowds of men and women dressed in black from head to toe led by some guy with a bullhorn raced across a road and blocked traffic. A scrum of officers with long clubs marched to meet the ragtag group and it looked like a football squad versus the Frisbee team.

They looked to be at an impasse until some of the guys in the back lobbed fireworks and started to throw water bottles.

"Cute trick. Notice those water bottles are frozen?" Rollie pointed out.

The prison guards sure did, and the next clip showed them charge as a line and push the crowd back. One masked guy cut loose with a big can of bear spray, and a couple of the guards on the edge broke ranks and chased the guy down and bashed him with their clubs.

Jill Williams cut in. "We've been told by the Philadelphia Office of Public Affairs that the two officers apparently involved in the incident at the detention center have been suspended without pay." She glanced over her shoulder when a siren whooped as a police car drove past. "The Fraternal Order of Police has said they will be filing an appeal."

The news anchor asked about Derek.

Jill nodded. "We spoke to the Temple Trauma Center, and Officer Miller remains in critical condition in a coma. The team refused to speculate beyond that at this time."

"You'll know soon, you damn ghouls," Rollie said. "Shit, guess I'm one, too, aren't I?"

"We all want to know," I said.

The camera returned to the live shot of downtown. The crowd grew. Police lined the entrance to the court and the garage entrance for vehicles. "They're not getting too close to the protesters, are they?" I noticed.

"Can you blame them?" Rollie said. "I wouldn't stick out my neck, or my pension, for these goobers."

Now a couple individuals moved behind the press section and began waving signs and screaming over the reporters. "Let him go!"

The mob knew Andre had been moved to the courthouse after receiving treatment for his much less serious wound to the shoulder.

"They expect them to just release the guy? He shot a cop!" Rollie shot a hot glance at VP.

"Dude, don't look at me. Yeah, I'm no police groupie, but this is a crazy I can't begin to translate."

"And no idea who might be behind it all?" I asked. "They may not all be professional protesters, but this is not spontaneous."

Jill moved a few feet closer to the building. She didn't try to chastise the protester. Smart. However, no cops rushed out to keep them away. The protesters noticed, and about a dozen more came forward with the intent to take over the broadcast.

Jill fell into motion. "We're going to move inside, where we expect the arraignment and bond hearing to begin soon."

"Stay safe, Jill." The anchor put on her best concerned face.

Only when the news crews got close to the courthouse entrance did the police step forward to ensure their access. The protestors backed off, but for a second, it looked all hell was going to break loose.

* * *

I muted the TV while the talking heads rehashed what was known about the case at the time. We weren't too interested in all the finer points of the legal wrangling anyway. But I did want to get a look at Andre when he came into court. The charges all were serious enough to keep him locked up until trial.

Eventually the TV stations all tapped into the single video feed permitted by the judge, a cadaverous-looking fellow with skin that looked thin as parchment.

We saw the deputies bring in Andre, who was wearing a sling for his shoulder so oversized it looked like Derek had tried for an amputation with a chainsaw rather than winging him with a single bullet.

"Couldn't find the big bandage, I guess," Steve said.

Andre's attorney stood next to him and set out paperwork. The feed was off to the side and not very good. The camera on the judge must have had better lighting.

"Is that . . ." VP began.

"I don't recall the pantsuit," I said, "but yeah, she looks familiar."

The judge reviewed the charges and addressed Andre and his attorney.

"Ms. Thorn, I have entered your client's not guilty plea. Do you have anything to say before I rule on the bond?"

"Yes, Your Honor." Rose faced the judge.

"I almost didn't recognize the voice, since she wasn't screaming," I said, "but that's her, all right."

"Shh," VP said.

"Your Honor, my client acknowledges his role in the recent incident," Rose began.

Incident?

"However, we would urge the court to consider that he is an established member of the community with years since his last arrest." Rose smiled at the judge. "Moreover, with the event in question, he maintains that he reacted in self-defense when Mr. Miller aimed a gun at him and his response was simply instinct where he felt he was given no choice."

"What?" VP muttered. "That's bullshit."

"A lying lawyer," Rollie said. "What *are* things coming to?"

Rose went on to paint a fantasy of Andre as being in the wrong place at the wrong time. I knew this was only a hearing and not where the case would be tried, but I kept expecting the prosecution to jump in that they had hard evidence to the contrary.

"What about the security tape?" I said.

"Who has time for that?" Steve's voice dripped sarcasm.

VP wheeled on me, her face flushed red. "Dude, you *can't* make me sit on this." She meant our copy of the video of the "incident." I'd watched it, and it had been every bit as difficult to stomach as she'd said it was. It also negated the fairytale Rose had spun.

"I hear you. Let's see what happens first."

We sat through the tedious legal procedure. I did note that Rose was able to come across as competent and professional. Another reminder that we shouldn't underestimate her.

VP was as angry as I'd ever seen her. We all were, and I was having trouble thinking of a good reason not to send the video to the press.

"Hang on guys," I said. "I think the judge is winding down." I turned up the volume.

Judge Cadaver scribbled on a paper. "And so, the defendant will be released on a bond of ten thousand dollars."

"Ten *thousand*?" I think everyone else in the room said.

The crowd in the courtroom went into full agitated hubbub-mode, and he glared at them until they piped down. "Further, Mr. Rogers will wear a GPS tether as a condition of his release."

"*What?*" we all said in unison again.

I just looked at VP and nodded. "I'll let Jill Williams know it's on the way as soon as she goes off the air."

* * *

The news hit the crowd outside the courthouse soon after, and the cheers and celebrations were grotesque. More fireworks and chanting made the jubilation appear to only fuel the aggression.

And the crowd had grown. Whatever the agitating pros were doing to stir things up was working. The protest was shifting into a volatile and dangerous mob.

The line of police looked every bit thin and blue, and the officers were not in proper crowd-control gear. The few who did wear helmets belonged to the motorcycle patrol.

"Look at them," Rollie said. "You can't appease a mob. They just smell weakness."

"If *we* know that, why didn't they figure it out?" VP pointed out.

"Great question. Whoever gave the orders put those men in danger."

He was right. The crowd edged forward. With each passing minute, they grew bolder.

The motorcycles tried to line up in the street to keep the crowd on the opposite sidewalk, but there weren't enough of them, and individuals slipped in between and around them.

One officer rushed forward from the line by the courthouse and tried to grab a guy. The protester was skinny but stronger than he looked. He pulled out of his shirt, leaving the cop with a handful of grimy fabric.

One of the motorcycle cops gripped the guy by the arm from behind, but the protestor snatched his arm away—it was obviously slick. He had to have oiled up his body on purpose.

At the same time, another guy ran up and kicked the cop's bike hard enough to topple it over from its kickstand perch.

The motorcycle cop right next to the falling bike revved his engine and dashed forward to avoid a domino-like chain reaction. Just then, two masked guys rushed up to the bike and grabbed the handlebars. One switched off the ignition, and the other shoved the officer, who managed to keep himself and the bike upright.

Then, a third protester reached for the cop's sidearm. Bold little turd.

"Oh no," Rollie said.

The cop clapped his hand down over the holster but in the effort to retain the weapon lost his balance and went over with his bike.

We could hear his cry of pain over the noise of the crowd and no wonder. The full weight of a Harley on one leg must have been excruciating.

The scream was like blood in the water to sharks. More protesters ran forward, and then the line of police behind the motorcycles charged as one. They all pulled out nightsticks, and when they reached the guys kicking the fallen officer, they began to club people off him.

"About time they gave out some wood shampoos," Rollie said.

With the scrum around the trapped officer broken up, several cops lifted the bike up and they were able to get the man out from under it. He looked to be okay but wasn't going to run anywhere for a while. A couple of cops helped him back toward the courthouse.

The officers in the street formed a line, and those with pepper spray began to hose down the leading elements of the mob.

"Why didn't they arrest those guys?" VP asked.

"They need every person out there and then some," Rollie said. "It takes one or two to bust them and take them away, and it might get worse."

"They weren't ready for this at all," I said.

When the spray cans were empty, the cops pulled tasers and stood shoulder-to-shoulder while backing up in a controlled retreat. Water bottles flew in from the back, and the mob cursed at the police. The remaining motorcycles formed an echelon and used the diagonal line to push the lead elements of the crowd back. One guy was dumb enough to try to grab a bike, but without space between the bikes, he only got himself knocked over at low speed. He scrambled to his feet and ran back to the safety of the group.

I was glad the camera feed from Jill's crew was behind the action. Just as the crowd seemed spurred to greater fury, cop reinforcements erupted from the courthouse. It was probably only about twenty guys, but they looked like they could have played for the Eagles. These guys were football player big and wearing full riot gear.

"Courthouse jail guards?" I asked.

More sirens in the distance told me the cavalry was on the way.

Now the riot squad began lobbing a mix of tear gas grenades and flash-bangs. The crowd wasn't expecting it. They fell back wailing about medics and police brutality, and only one guy tried to kick a tear gas cannister back and went down when we heard the boom of a shotgun.

He fell from the impact but staggered to his feet and ran away.

"Beanbag round?" Steve asked Rollie.

"Yup," Rollie said. "Told you they hurt."

Our front seat to the action soon retreated to the courthouse, and Jill's report was cut short by a coughing fit when she got a whiff of the tear gas.

I looked at VP. "We might want to give her a minute before we drop our own bombshell on her."

"Yeah. That was insane."

"Crowds can turn into a living thing," Rollie said. "Crazy, mean and dangerous as hell. Remember what you saw here, gang. We do not want to get caught in one of these."

"Sold," VP said.

Rollie wasn't done. "This isn't going away. You all need to understand how fast the game can change, and we need to do whatever is necessary, and yes, I mean live ammo. Second place can mean dead."

"Okay." I knew Rollie didn't make idle threats. "But do we know exactly what that mess down there is about?"

Rollie pointed at the wide shot coming in from a helicopter feed. I noticed it was a hell of a zoom as the responding police choppers hovered in the sky over City Hall. The press helicopter had to be half a mile away. "Lots of brotherly love down there." He looked at me. "But this was organized. Those agitators had training. They looked like drugged-out kids, but there were professionals in there. They knew just what buttons to push, when to lie, when to fan the flames."

The fireworks, the frozen water bottles. "Yeah."

"You mean Slippery Sam wasn't on his way to come in last in a body building contest when he found the protest?" Steve said.

"Somebody wants all this, for whatever reason," Rollie said. "The sooner we find the head, or heads, of the snake and . . ." He shrugged. "Well, the sooner we get our city back."

CHAPTER 23

Kyle's place, later that morning

After it looked like the protests had dispersed, I checked in with Sandy. She wasn't right next to City Hall, but not far away either.

"Yeah, I saw it," she said. "We've already had some cancellations, and one therapist doesn't want to come in."

"But you guys are okay?" I hated the helpless feeling when things spiraled out of control.

"We're fine. How could they let that guy out? You don't believe that lawyer, do you?"

"Keep an eye on Channel Twenty-Seven." I explained about the tape.

"Oh my God," she said, and she didn't even know how bad it was.

"Yeah, the lawyer is trouble," I said. "She's the same person who sent the goons after us after the sneaker shop."

"What? Can't you have her arrested?"

"I can't prove it. I still don't think she knows exactly who I am, so you should be okay. But if you see her anywhere near you or the store, get away and tell me."

"Okay." I heard enough fear in her voice to know she took that seriously.

* * *

I dialed a private number for Jill Williams. I got her voicemail, as expected. Not only was she going to be super busy, I was on a burner.

"It's me. Call me back." She knew my voice. Even though I didn't leave any clue what I wanted, she knew that I didn't ring her up to waste her time.

Ten minutes later, she returned my call. "What's up?" I appreciated that she didn't say my name over the line. Some days I felt paranoid, others not enough.

"Are you having any luck seeing the security tape of the shooting?"

"How did you know we've been trying to get that?"

"Because you're a good reporter," I said. "Let me guess, they're stonewalling you?"

"My source said it's coming straight from the prosecutor's office." Her frustration, and maybe remnant tear gas, made her voice raspy.

"I saw you out on the street. Are you okay?"

"Fine. Comes with the territory. So, what did you need? Kinda busy."

"I can't help with that, but what would you say to a copy of that security footage?"

There was a pause.

"You're serious?" she rasped. "How?"

"Sources and methods. But it is legit." I lowered my voice. "And raw. No way you can air it uncut."

"Don't worry. If it's real, we'll take care of that."

"She's lying," I said, meaning Rose. "This was damn near an assassination. And they know it," I said. "Nothing about any of this shit feels spontaneous."

"I agree. You know I'll do what I can. When can you get it to me?"

"Give me a secure email, and you'll have it in five minutes."

I scribbled the address and handed it to VP, who had been pacing in front of me the entire call.

* * *

After we sent the tape I didn't hear back from Jill, not that I expected to. I figured she'd see it soon, and then she'd get to battle with her bosses at the station on how best to get the footage on the air. It occurred to me that the station might choose to bury it, but we'd all agreed (Jill included) that if that happened, we'd make sure all her competition had copies, and it'd become a race to the airwaves. As it was, Jill and I had a good working relationship, and this would mean she owed me a favor.

It was only a couple hours later that the breaking news banners had us scrambling to unmute the TV. It wasn't on camera. I wondered if she was working on what we'd sent.

"This is Stacy Bett. We're just getting word that Andre Rogers is about to be released." The reporter stood outside the courthouse.

"No way, dude. This is such bullshit," VP said.

"That punk has powerful friends. Wish we knew why," Rollie said.

"Stacy, what are the crowds like?" the Ken-doll anchor asked from the studio.

"Almost nonexistent. After this morning, we now see a strong police presence." The camera panned to show a couple lines of officers in full riot gear. They could have been lining up for a parade, there were so few protestors. It looked more like office workers on their lunch break.

"Weird," Steve said. "I'm no expert, but it seems a lot easier to whip up a crowd than to hit some magic off-switch."

"Here he comes," Stacy said.

Rose came out with Andre on her arm. Now in addition to the oversized sling and bandage, Andre wore an enormous bulletproof vest over his torso.

Rose paused by a cluster of microphones. "We will be making a more comprehensive statement later, but as you can see, our primary concern right now is my client's safety. We appreciate the wisdom of the court to grant him the chance to clear his name without fear of reprisals while in custody of the very system that has it out for him."

"I'm not sure if she's more irritating as a radical or a lawyer," Rollie said.

"She kills it in either role," I said. VP shot me a smile.

The police allowed a van to pull up, and Rose joined Andre inside and they drove off.

"I'd love to tag that van with a drone to see where they go," VP said.

"Not exactly a low-key environment," I said. "Think it'd be worth chasing them with traffic cams?"

VP considered it. "Nah. We know his address, but they'll move him away from there, I bet. Unless you were thinking of trying something." This was usually when she'd try to be the voice of reason if I seemed to be overreacting.

"Not that he wouldn't deserve it, but that's not our call and he's a little high-profile, don't you think?" I said.

VP nodded. "You know I didn't mean it"—she paused—"much. But I'd frame a picture if they crashed and burned."

"I'd probably ask you for a copy," I said. "Also kidding. Sort of."

"Nice trick, her throwing shade on the cops like he was some sort of victim," Steve said. "You know, we could set up on his house. I'm sure we could get in and out without attracting attention."

I shook my head. "He's too hot right now. He's caught, more or less, but at least we know he's tethered." I looked over at VP. "Hey, any chance you can hack in to his ankle-signal?"

Steve and VP shared a look. Steve spoke first. "That's some pretty spicy tech. I think it's possible, but it might be more trouble than it is worth."

"Why?"

VP stepped in. "If we're talking going in cold, the first thing we'd need to do is get a sniff of the signal and then break it down so we could isolate for sure what was the monitor versus some other phone or system that uses GPS."

"I see." I didn't, of course, but I was raised to be polite.

Steve nodded. "Yeah, so we'd have to get in close, and even then, we'd have some homework. But as you said, it's risky to move in close while he's so famous."

"By then, it'd be simpler to tag his car or even him with our own stuff," VP said.

"If we find him, why do we need to track him anyway?" Rollie asked.

I held my hands up in surrender. "It just feels like this is the first step in this guy getting away with it."

"Come on, have a little faith in the system," Rollie deadpanned. It wasn't that funny, but it got a round of weary laughter. It had been a tough couple of days.

* * *

Kyle's place, that evening

I spent the better part of the day watching news stories related to the Andre Rogers case.

It was a relief when Sandy decided to come over after work. I knew she didn't like me trying to protect her all the time, but with days like today, I think even she saw where I was coming from.

She sat with me with a beer in hand and the early broadcast recapped the craziness of the day.

"We now have an update on the unrest of this morning, and our own Jill Williams was on hand to witness the events. Jill?" The anchor tossed to her.

"Thanks, Al. We'll have an exclusive report in just a moment, but before we do, we have just learned that even as Andre Rogers was being released, the police department announced the immediate suspension of two of the officers involved in the violence on the streets. These fresh suspensions are in addition to the officers who were involved in the prison hospital disturbance."

"Which officers?" the anchor asked.

"The police union has not released the names, but I am told they were part of the actions to assist the fallen motorcycle officer, who I personally observed had been and was continuing to be assaulted."

"Was it a question of excessive force?"

"The police spokesman said they are reviewing the incident and have placed the officers on unpaid leave. The union has promised to file another grievance in the morning."

A "Breaking News" banner splashed across the screen. "In light of those developments and the claims of self-defense by accused shooter Andre Rogers, we stay with Jill Williams for this News Twenty-Seven exclusive."

"News Twenty-Seven has obtained shocking footage of the actual shooting of Officer Derek Miller. We must warn viewers with young children to turn the channel." She paused, as though letting that all sink in.

"Now everyone's bound to stay tuned," I said.

"We have verified the authenticity and edited the following to adhere to broadcast standards, but again, it is still quite graphic."

Sandy gripped my hand while we watched. I'd seen it already, and they didn't change much. They blurred the exit wound from poor Derek's skull, but it was plain to see that it was a miracle that the man was still even breathing at this point. Also clear was who shot who first, putting the lie to Rose Thorn's ridiculous yarn about self-defense.

"We are told that the city prosecutor's office has a copy, and that they refused to provide News Twenty-Seven with access to the footage. In fact, we never even heard back from the office until they threatened this reporter with arrest. I want to thank the station and our own legal team for the courage to stand by me and promise that we will protect our sources."

"Good to know," I said.

"Are you going to get in trouble over this?" Sandy asked.

"Me? Not a crime to hear a rumor. Whoever sent the file certainly wouldn't have used anything linked to me."

She nodded. She understood the game, even if it wasn't her favorite these days. "Seems like they are going after all the wrong people," she said.

"It gets harder to tell who the good guys are all the time," I said.

One of my burners rang. VP.

"Did we mess up?" she asked when I picked up.

"We'll be fine. It's the damn city that messed up. Did you see the earlier report? They leaned harder on their own people than on this clown."

"Maybe the vid will help," she said.

"It might. I hope so. I don't know if that judge will change his mind."

CHAPTER 24

Kyle's place, the next day

The last couple of days of breaking news felt like moisture feeding gathering storm clouds. Staying glued to the news seemed like the best way to gauge the danger.

Today's serving came from the dueling press conferences in reaction to the release of the security tape. First up was Rose Thorn, any pretense of her keeping a low profile was gone.

Rollie perched on the edge of the couch beside me like he was about to spring out of his seat. "This ought to be good. You have any luck on where she is staying?"

"Not yet. She's awfully exposed these days."

"Yeah, right. But I really want a chance to thank her for sending those amateurs after us."

"You and me both. She's raised her game now, sending an army of them after the whole city."

"Yeah," Rollie agreed. "But why?"

I could only shrug. "At least we're getting a handle on some of the important players. I can see how feeling invincible to the cops or prosecutors makes crime sprees easier, but targeting cops? Makes no sense."

Rose stepped up to the podium. Other than her trademark now-toned-down magenta hair, and glasses, she looked like a different person. Her anarchy tattoo was well-covered by long sleeves.

After a brief introductory speech, she got to the point. "And now, we are seeing our worst fears unfold in real time. My client is being tried in the media with every inflammatory report that poisons the jury pool against him."

Someone asked the obvious question about the security tape.

"That's just the thing, isn't it?" Rose pounced. "You people can edit and cherry-pick leaked recordings from who knows where, and those become the narrative before the process has even begun. Not the way it is supposed to work in this country."

"Cute," I said.

"You gonna believe me, or your own lying eyes?" Rollie mocked.

Rose batted down a couple more similar questions before leaving the podium in an indignant huff. The media didn't have much time to chew on this before the announcement from District Attorney Castle.

"Convenient timing, wouldn't you say?" I asked. "What is she, the warm-up band?"

"I don't believe in coincidences," Rollie agreed. "Is the DA sympathetic to her points, or is it more than that?"

The news feed changed to the DA Castle's office. He was a short, thin, bald guy in his late fifties with wire-rimmed glasses.

"He looks like the world's most arrogant accountant," I said.

"Head chef for cooking the books," Rollie said.

Castle sat behind his desk and read a statement. It droned on about the principles that provided the foundation of his office and the integrity of the solemn oath he'd taken and crap like that. I was glad Rollie's reaction was similar to mine, or else I might have begun to worry that I was becoming jaded.

"He ever going to say anything?" Rollie groused.

Finally, he did.

"Despite enormous pressure to rush to justice, this office will uphold the rights of everyone, including the accused. We have a process in place, and we will follow it according to the law, *not* the rule of the mob."

"How fair of him," Rollie said.

"And we will also not tolerate any abuses of those rights by those in the city entrusted with the powers of enforcement. I am announcing an investigation into the conduct of several officers who are alleged to have overstepped their bounds during crowd control while citizens were exercising their right to protest."

"So," I said, "he's saying they won't revoke Andre's bond despite it being obvious what he did?"

"Yeah," Rollie said. "Andre is a trustworthy cop-shooter. That's what I heard." He rubbed his closed eyes, hard, with his blunt fingertips. "We are now officially living in Bizarro World."

I turned off the TV. "I can't take any more of this crap. I'm going to go down to the hospital and check on Derek. Do you want to come?"

Rollie shook his head. "I don't know him. I'd feel like some kind of rubbernecker. Will they let you in to see him?"

"I don't think so. That's not important, and God knows his family has enough to deal with. But I just feel like I should do something," I said. "There will be cops around, and maybe I can pick up some info if I see any I know."

* * *

I think Rollie understood my desire to go down to the hospital. Hell, I knew there wasn't anything I could do for Derek, and it's not like he was alone there, whether he knew it or not.

Also, I figured I'd run into Barry Daniels, the sergeant I'd talked with earlier at the hospital. We'd traded favors in the past, and he was dialed in to what was going on with the rank-and-file cops.

When I arrived at the trauma center, the first thing I noticed was a handful of cops at the front entrance. They glared at a cluster of punks across the street who marched while holding signs, preprinted signs, with the usual *End police brutality* and the like, but one in particular made my blood boil and explained the expressions on the officers.

Miller Shot First

The thought crossed my mind to call Rollie in to join me in for a paintball editing session on those signs, but while fun, it wouldn't have helped anything. That said, I doubted the cops I saw would have interfered. They looked to be of the mind that it was about time to *start* some police brutality.

* * *

The cops at the door gave me some hard looks, but it was clear I wasn't part of the hostile crew across the street, so they let me pass.

Inside the waiting area, there were more police, and I knew Derek's room would be guarded. I looked around and didn't see Daniels, nor did I see Saul Sanger. I knew he was worried, but he still had to run his store. It was ironic that only now did Sanger get the police protection he'd needed during the buildup to all this mess.

I took a seat, again wondering what I hoped to accomplish. I decided to give it an hour and if I didn't see anyone I knew, I'd head out.

I noticed a couple of stringers over by the vending machine and decided it wasn't worth talking to a freelance reporter for crumbs of information. I was selective about getting myself on any reporter's radar, but they were a necessary evil sometimes. Jill Williams was a rare exception, but it had taken time to build that trust. She and the other main TV reporters were off covering other stories as the days dragged on. Cold, but that was the business, I supposed.

About fifteen minutes into my vigil, I heard a commotion at the door. The stringers popped up and moved closer. At first, I thought maybe the protesters from across the street had decided to push their luck.

Then, I recognized Derek's father and brother coming inside the hospital. I was surprised that they weren't already inside. They must have taken shifts. Then, I saw who was with them and my heart sank.

A priest.

A pair of officers escorted the trio, and one of them headed off the stringers, calling for privacy. The reporters moved away, less out of respect than a rush to spread this latest development.

I suppressed an urge to call someone, but who? Rollie? Sandy? VP? I wasn't sure, but I guessed I wanted some sort of connection in the moment. I also knew it would look ghoulish, so I just sat and stared at the entrance doors to the ICU.

The Miller family members and the priest hurried through the doors, and then, like an alarm had been pulled, police erupted out into the hall. I spotted Barry Daniels among the officers.

I caught his eye and cocked my head. His gaze flattened a little, but then he glanced toward the vending machine area where we could speak away from the others. He met me there.

"Was that what I think it was?" I asked him.

"It wasn't for confession." Daniels ran his fingers through his short gray hair. "I don't know what else we expected. The kid fought hard—his body did, anyway—but I think he was gone when they rolled him in."

"Damn. I wish there was something more we could do."

"Out of our hands now." Daniels face turned hard as ice. "Now we get to grab up that mutt who never should have been released. Not much, but it's all we can do right now."

"At least he should be easy to find." I thought about his ankle monitor.

It was a throwaway comment, but it seemed to galvanize Daniels.

"I'd love to chat more, but I'm going with the team to pick him up. He'll hear the news and might decide to take off, monitor or no. Wish me luck that he tries to resist." Daniels turned away.

I thought about going after him when he spun on his heel and came back.

"Don't get the wrong idea," he began.

"You were clear enough."

"I'm pissed."

"We all are," I allowed.

"Yeah, well, despite it all, we are professionals, so know this and don't get it twisted: If we catch the suspect and he surrenders, we'll take him in."

"Yeah?"

"Yeah, smart guy. But if he pulls a gun, we won't wait for him to drill another officer first." He stepped close enough that I could count the whiskers on his cheek. "Tell me you wouldn't do the same if it was you."

* * *

I left before the word got out to the rest of the world. I hoped they had a plan to get the family out of the hospital before the media frenzy returned. Derek wasn't in pain anymore—if he'd felt anything to begin with—and I hoped that knowledge would bring some comfort to them, but I knew all too well that it took time. If ever.

I took the long way back to my truck, so I wouldn't have to go anywhere near the small knot of protesters who hadn't gotten the news yet that Derek was gone. This wasn't the time to go looking for a fight. Seeing them celebrate might be more than I could take. Once in my truck, I called Rollie.

He listened in silence as I filled him in.

"I'm sorry," he said.

"Me too. Wish I owned some favors that could make a difference here." I was just babbling.

"Sure," he said, letting me vent. "What now? This won't exactly calm things down. The mob will feel empowered with what they see is a win and will flip out when Andre gets taken in. Or taken out."

That landed and cleared my head. "You said a mouthful there." I told him what Daniels said about the cops going on the hunt for Andre. "He promised to keep it fair."

"I hope so, for their sake, but I hope the guy reaches for a piece when they catch up to him. But his lawyer will probably just make arrangements to have a limo drop him off."

I hadn't thought of that. "Might be the safest play, but I think I'd be breaking out a hacksaw if I were him."

"You and me both," Rollie said. "You coming back to your place? I can't picture too many outcomes that will deescalate the situation. Things might get weird."

"Probably an understatement. I'll give Sandy a heads up and see if she won't close up early."

"Be safe." Rollie hung up.

I called Sandy and brought her up to speed. "His poor family. This is awful. He never had a chance, sounds like."

"I guess not. He fought hard, anyway." I asked if she wanted me to come by.

"You go ahead. We have some more clients to finish up. *Them* I can help. We'll keep an eye on the news here. And I'll see you later."

Bunkering up might not have been the best idea to suggest. She was right. Though I expected Rollie was also correct and things were going to get "weird," as he put it, it made sense to see how this played out.

I decided to get back to my place as quick as I could to see how this would get covered by the media.

CHAPTER 25

Kyle's place

"How do they manage to cover anything with so many damn commercials?" Rollie sipped his coffee. Even though it was only the afternoon, I thought he'd accept a beer. That he hadn't told me he was opting to stay in ready-mode. I was too, I suppose, by feeling dread at the unfolding coverage.

"Gotta keep the lights on," I said. We were tuned to News 27. I didn't much trust the news but figured Jill Williams would be on, since she was the lead reporter on this story, and she was as fair as they came.

We'd seen the breaking news banners about Derek's death. That had hit the air before I got home.

I did see that the protesters were no longing preening for the cameras across the street from the hospital. I'd wondered if it was out of decency before realizing it most likely meant that they were going to be redeployed by whoever was moving them around the chessboard. Maybe back to the courthouse, which was where Jill had been sent.

One of the breaking news banners had been that the court had convened an emergency bond hearing and that Andre was required to attend. That was a couple hours ago, which struck me as moving at lightning speed for the court system. Of course, the fact that Derek had died meant that murder of a police officer was now on the table.

"I'm not going to lie," Rollie said. "I didn't think this candy-ass judge had it in him."

From the TV view, we saw a car pull up and Rose Thorn get out. Alone.

She was instantly bombarded with questions from the throng of reporters, but she skipped her usual camera-hog routine and headed right inside.

Not long after, the coverage flipped to the camera feed inside the courtroom.

After the preliminaries, the judge got to the point and asked Rose where her client was.

Rose stared at the floor until the judge repeated himself in a much sharper tone.

"Your Honor, I'm afraid I don't know. I have left messages on his phone and at his residence. I must say that this has been very short notice. If you could issue a continuance until next week, we will be sure to appear."

The judge wasn't having it and issued a bench warrant on the spot ordering Andre to appear.

"With respect, Your Honor, are you sure that is safe, given the inflammatory circumstances surrounding the case?"

The judge sat up ramrod straight at that. "What do you mean, Ms. Thorn?"

"She means she's worried the cops might be pissed off at the guy who just killed one of their own," Rollie yelled at the screen.

He was right and Rose said as much to the judge.

"They are expected to behave in a professional, ethical, legal manner, as are you. Your client is not here. Bond is revoked, and this warrant is effective immediately. Court is adjourned until such time as your client can be brought in." The judge signed the paperwork. "And, Ms. Thorn, if you are so concerned about the police, I suggest you find a way to reach Mr. Rogers and persuade him to come in on his own. Given he is on a tether, I don't think you have much time."

"A little late," I said, "but nice to see him rip her a new one, I guess."

I called VP knowing that she and Steve would have been watching. "Now I wish we were able to see the monitor in real time," I said.

"I think I can do the next best thing," VP said.

"Yeah?"

"Can you guys go down to the bunker? I can patch through the police monitor chatter. Should be active, if they're as gung-ho as I think."

"Great idea." I pointed to the basement stairs, and Rollie got the picture.

The bunker was an overengineered collaboration between VP and Rollie. It was a reinforced concrete safe room complete with armor plating and a working escape tunnel that led to the shed in my backyard. We called that the subway. It was also a high-tech nerve center where VP could work her magic when she wasn't home and I could monitor the similarly overbuilt security system.

Most of the time my low profile was enough protection, but once in a while some crooks took things to the next level. Rollie hadn't let me rest until I let him indulge in what he called "home improvement."

Down in the bunker, we sat in comfortable office chairs, and I opened the connections to VP's place.

"Okay, I got it," VP said. She was on one speakerphone, and the sound system would play the police scanner feed. "You can put the speakers on."

It sounded like it was coming straight from a police radio—which, knowing her, it probably was. "You were right," she said. "They have a special unit calling the shots."

"I do what I can," I said. I didn't have the tech knowledge she had in her pinkie and tended to hit my thumb as often as the nail when trying to build things, but I could leverage connections like nobody else.

VP sent over a screenshot with a cheat sheet of police codes.

"Nice." Rollie peered over my shoulder. "Print me one of those, Kyle."

The printer woke up and spat out a sheet before I could even nod my head.

"Thanks, Quarterback." Rollie waved to the security camera in the bunker that VP was surely seeing.

"De nada," VP said over the speaker.

I heard an officer, presumably from the special unit, addressing the officers in the chase cars: "Subject on the move again, now heading northwest on Germantown Avenue."

"Copy. All units stay close." The other cars checked in. It sounded like at least three other cars, at least by the chatter.

"He's still heading up Germantown Avenue. I think we have visual on the car. Watch for a blue Accord. Wait for my order. We want to be sure."

Be sure? "What does that mean?"

VP answered: "We've played with similar gear. It's pretty accurate, but there's a thing called 'Urban Canyon Effect' that can distort the signal. Lots of cars around, so they want to be certain they have the right one."

"Makes sense," I said.

The radio cut in: "Target stopped. Okay, confirmed: it's the blue Accord. All units, we'll take him at the next intersection." The officer called out the intersection and some police codes that Rollie got to work on.

"Oh, snap!" VP called out.

"What?" Usually, it was something good.

"Dude, I know where that is, and they have a traffic camera."

"Can you—" I didn't get a chance to finish the question when one of the screens in front of me flipped on and showed a momentarily peaceful scene of cars and pedestrians. The lunchtime crowds looked unaware of what was unfolding.

Rollie whistled. "They just called in SWAT and a police chopper. They are not playing."

Fine by me. But as much as I wanted to see Andre get his, the bystanders all around didn't deserve to get caught in a crossfire.

The chatter grew thick, and I lost track of all the codes and commands rattling by. I had to assume the cops knew what was what. VP found a couple camera angles that she had zeroed in on the intersection, and I realized one was a security camera for a store and another had to be a Ring-style doorbell camera.

"Now you're just showing off," I said.

"I do what I can."

Show-off or not, she'd served up a perfect view.

We could see a blue sedan approaching in the distance, but from here it was still small and could have been any blue car. VP offered up other angles, and then we could see black and white vans converging. The first one to arrive pulled over. No flashing lights, I noticed. Soon others moved into position, and then cars began to pull over, and when nobody emerged and smoke curled out of the tail pipes, I figured they were also Philly PD unmarked units.

We lacked sound, so it was playing out like an action film from the silent movie era. The police radio provided the narration.

The blue car approached with no indication that Andre suspected the trap closing in on him. Since there was no sound, I couldn't tell how close the helicopter was until I saw some pedestrians look up. One guy put down his hoagie to point toward the sky.

As the car neared the intersection, I became frustrated by the tinted windows. No way to see inside. "Can you zoom in?"

VP laughed. "I'm just borrowing these cameras, dude. You want a close-up, I'd have to get a drone on scene."

I laughed too at the imagined reaction of all that police attention interrupted by the arrival of a strange remote-operated kibitzer.

The radio chatter erupted, and the adrenaline behind the speakers was evident with all the yelling and distortion.

A moment later, every vehicle we could see that had crept up erupted with blue and red flashing lights and I assume screeching tires and blaring sirens. People on the sidewalks jumped and scattered. They might have had no idea what was happening, but they all seemed to agree they wanted no part of it.

The blue car had just entered the intersection, and police cars swarmed in. Dust erupted from the middle of the street and napkins flew off tables. A loose baseball cap bounced down the sidewalk as the diners raced away from the intersection. I realized that had to be the helicopter, dropped about as low as the pilot dared. That area had plenty of suspended wires overhead, so a pilot would have had to be crazy to try to land there.

The pilot didn't try to land, but he might have been crazy after all. I saw several objects bounce on the road next to the now-stopped car. "Are those—" Before I could finish, I saw the telltale flashes and was glad the sound was off, and *really* happy we weren't there in person.

"Yup," Rollie said. "Not close enough to break the window, looks like."

Cops in body armor and helmets burst out of one of the cars that skidded to a halt behind the Accord. One cop held a long triangular stick that he tossed right behind the back wheels. One of the SWAT vans went nose-to-nose with the car and another cop advanced behind a ballistic shield until he was close enough to throw a stick by the front tires.

"Stop sticks, very good," Rollie said. "If he runs, it won't be for long."

"I don't think it'll be an issue," I said. More police had erupted from the vans and formed a semicircle around the car, rifles and shotguns pointed at the vehicle, which had not moved.

The officers paused, and I noted that all the bystanders had cleared the streets.

One cop held up a megaphone. We couldn't hear it, of course, but I was familiar with the process. They were giving instruction to the driver. Even desperate and afraid, or crazy or stupid or all of the above, Andre had to realize that he wasn't leaving. The only real questions were, would he decide to suicide by cop and go out in a blaze of glory? Or, would Daniels be good to his word and accept a peaceful surrender? Surely, he knew the cameras were all around?

The tinted driver's-side window lowered, and a pair of hands emerged.

"What the hell?" I said. Those were not Andre's hands.

"Did you notice a passenger?" Rollie asked.

The driver tossed the keys to the car out the window and then kept his hands in view. With slow, deliberate movements, he eased open the driver's door and stepped out of the car.

Not Andre. Not even half the size of Andre. The guy placed his hands on top of his head and sank to his knees. I think that was on command, but given the saucer eyes even the traffic camera picked up, it might have been from pure terror.

"Who the hell is this guy?" Rollie said.

Cops rushed forward and cuffed him. Others swarmed the car, snatching the other three doors open and pointing rifles. Last and apparently least, they opened the trunk and found nothing more than some dirty laundry and some bottled water.

Rollie face-palmed. "What a cock-up."

The radio chatter mirrored our confusion in more code-speak, but it was the same idea.

They confirmed a strong signal from the ankle tether.

They began a more thorough search of the car. By now, the cops on scene shifted their task to securing the perimeter and traffic control. The news media had gotten wind of events and vans had begun to accumulate on the side streets.

While the search continued, we got word over the radio that the guy they arrested was claiming to be an Uber driver. As soon as VP heard the name called out, she went to work.

"What," I said to nobody in particular, "Andre called for a ride and just slid out of his monitor?"

"No way, Kyle," Steve piped up. "We have a couple of those for, um, research. They aren't indestructible, but as soon as they are cut off or damaged for removal, they signal tampering. A person would need to cut off their ankle to slip it off intact."

"I don't think Andre is that hard-core," I said.

VP came back on the line. "Confirmed the driver is an Uber driver, been one for over four years and has no arrest records, not even a traffic ticket."

A moment later, we heard the police dispatcher come back with a similar report.

"You're faster than the pros," I said.

"I don't get paid by the hour," she said.

A number of officers had gathered at the trunk on the car. One leaned in and then wriggled out and held up what looked like an intact ankle tether.

"I didn't hear any reports about blood all over the back of the car, did you?" I asked.

"No," VP said. "Really weird. So how did it get there?"

"Good question," I said. "Even better question, where the hell is Andre?"

Chapter 26

Philadelphia, Jeweler's Row, one day later

Rollie and I pulled into the back way behind Sanger's. The old street was barely as wide as an alley. I noticed the cameras just as we'd both commented on how almost every store was boarded up like they expected some sort of hurricane to sweep up Sansome Street. When we parked Rollie's Blue Bomber, I called the store before we got out of the car. The guy who answered peppered me with questions and wouldn't put Saul on until he knew our names and I'd described the car.

Saul finally picked up the line. "Okay, Kyle. Come on through the back door." He sounded ten years older.

We got out, and Rollie and I both carried pistols hidden in our waistbands. When Rollie had insisted on riding shotgun through town, he meant it literally.

As we approached the back door, I saw another camera above the frame, and I looked at it and waved. A sign that matched the one on the front read "By Appointment Only" and "Armed Security on Duty."

After a brief pause, the lock buzzed and we were able to open the door. We were greeted by a spotlight that blinded us, so we could not see down the hall.

"Wait for Mr. Sanger, please." The voice's tone made it clear it was not a request.

A minute later, I heard another door open and the first voice spoke again. "Do you want them searched, sir?"

"No, and I'm just Saul. You don't have to suck up to me. You already have the job."

I wanted to be on the safe side. This guard sounded tense.

"Hey, Saul," I said as Rollie and I held out our empty hands, like we'd agreed to earlier. "Just so you know, we brought our own protection. I hope that won't be a problem. It's a little nuts out there."

"Put that down," Saul said to the guard, and Rollie and I froze.

"Yes, sir."

"How do you turn this damn thing off?" Saul asked.

"Let me, sir." The spotlight died and when my vision cleared, I could see a fit guy in a security uniform with a sidearm holstered and a pump shotgun at his side. He looked just like the guys I was used to seeing over in the Sand Box.

Rollie bit back a laugh and when Saul stepped closer, I could see why. Saul, all five feet of him, wore his own holster with what looked like a cowboy revolver with a barrel so long it threatened to scrape the floor.

"Make your jokes," Saul said. "I can see it on your faces. But you said it yourself. It's nuts out there."

"The gun store didn't have one with a longer barrel?" I asked.

Saul smiled and shrugged. The guard didn't do smiles, it appeared.

"Murray's Pawn," Saul said, "and this was one of the last pieces he had in the place. He said he's never seen such a run on weapons."

"Can you use that?" Rollie said.

"Who knows? It isn't loaded, but you can't miss it, can you?" Saul gestured to the guard. "That's why he's here."

"What's your name, son?" Rollie asked. "You look like you served."

"Army MP, sir. Separated from service last year." He stuck out his hand. "Name's Grimes."

"Can't all be jarheads like me, but it looks like you know your stuff. Try to keep the boss from blowing his foot off, huh?"

"Standing orders, sir," Grimes said.

Rollie grinned.

"Saul, we came by to make sure you were okay and to say, you know . . ." I trailed off to avoid saying the obvious, that the last guard was killed on duty.

Saul nodded. "Thanks." He led us back to his office. "Grimes is costing me a fortune," he said after he closed the door, "but I almost wish that monster would try to come back here. He won't surprise anyone this time."

"I think he already has. We can't figure out how he slipped the tether without it being detected."

"If he's smart, he's headed to Mexico. I wasn't kidding about what Murray at the pawn shop said. It's the same all over. People have had it, and if the cops can't fix things, the whole city is going to be an armed camp."

"It already looks like a war zone up and down the street," I said.

"Can you blame them?" Saul said. "It's reached the point where an unbroken window is an open invitation to become the next target."

"I wish I had an easy answer," I said. "I know the cops are combing the city for Andre." I hated this helpless feeling.

"I'll bet they are. If they catch him, maybe they'll put a tether on both ankles before they let him out again."

"I'm glad to see you have some help. Anything we can do for you?"

"Pray?" Saul said.

I didn't have those kinds of connections, but then again, it couldn't hurt.

Just then my VP burner began to ring. "Excuse me." I stepped into the hall.

"What's up?"

"Where are you?"

"I'm at Sanger's. Why?"

"Got your regular smartphone on you?" VP sounded out of breath.

"Yeah, why?"

"It's on the news right now."

"C'mon. What?"

"They found Andre," she said.

"He's caught? Where?"

"No. He's in pieces." She let that sink in.

"A shootout?"

"No. Some guy found a leg in a dumpster and called it in. The police found the rest of him all chopped up. Looks like we know how whoever it was got the tether off."

"Holy . . . Do they have any idea who did it?" I could hear shouting in the background. "Wait, where are you?"

"You won't like it, but we had to take a chance. Your favorite girl is about to hold a presser. This could be our best shot to track her."

"You're down at the courthouse? In the crowd?"

"I knew you wouldn't like it. Got a hidden camera in my hoodie and a tracker with her name on it. I'm gonna put it on her car before she leaves."

"We never talked about this." I knew I sounded like a concerned parent, and I guess that's how I felt. Rollie looked at me from across the room.

"Dude, there wasn't time. We heard the chatter on the police scanner and cooked it up last minute."

"Why not have Steve . . ." This was all too fast.

"Seriously? Who else of us can blend in here?"

"Fine, but this is too dangerous."

"I'll be careful. People are showing up in droves. Want the feed or not? I gotta move closer, and I'll have to watch what I say."

Would she bail now if I insisted? And what if it worked? "Put the feed onto my smartphone." I ran back to Saul's office, where Rollie looked like he'd already said his goodbyes. "Do you have a TV?"

"Of course." Saul pointed to a set of monitors showing camera feeds. "These get cable."

I told him about the news and the condition of the body. I would have thought he'd react more positively.

Saul fiddled with a remote until it showed regular television, and he set it a network breaking news report. "Bad business."

I motioned for Rollie to follow me outside the office and whispered to him what was happening. My smartphone buzzed, and I accepted the video call. I could see Steve was on it as well, muted.

"That girl is nuts." Rollie frowned in concern, but I heard admiration as well.

"Not much we can do for her from here," I said.

* * *

The feed started with VP working her way in from the edge of the crowd. The camera appeared to be well-hidden. I could see just the barest outline of VP's trademark hoodie as she slipped around people, looking side to side. She was right: many of them looked like people she might've hung out with—bare-faced, with assorted piercings and bright-colored hair and tats.

As she got closer to the heart of the scrum, I could hear some of the people next to her murmuring. Words like "fascists" and "lynch mob" and "racist pigs" and such kept popping up. VP would nod and mutter agreeable sounds.

"Civilians are getting riled up," Rollie said.

One guy with a purple mohawk looked right at VP. "I heard they butchered him like an animal."

"So did I," VP said. "Had to get down here."

The guy fist-bumped her and moved on.

"Yo, there's the car," VP whispered to us. She moved closer to the street, and she was able to get about thirty feet from the sedan when she stopped. "Check it. Pros."

We could see a group of black-clad guys in masks, some with signs, others with backpacks. They were watching the crowd, and we could see some of the bystanders run up to them to talk in their ear before melting back into the crowd.

"There goes my boy," VP said, and sure enough the guy with the purple mohawk checked in with one of the Black Bloc-looking guys.

"They're covering that car tight," Rollie observed.

VP heard him. "I see 'em. It's not over yet. I only need a second."

My stomach went into knots.

* * *

VP took up a vantage point that showed the courthouse and the stand of microphones massed in front of a podium. Moments after exiting the car, Ms. Thorn, all geared up in her "Respectable Rose" outfit, stepped up to the microphones.

Wasting no time and ignoring all shouted questions, launched into her spiel: "Ladies and gentlemen, our worst fears have been confirmed. On behalf of my late client and his family, we condemn the frontier justice inflicted upon Mr. Rogers at the hands of the police."

The group forming across the street gasped at the amplified accusation. Reporters tried to cut in, yelling questions about evidence.

Rose held up her hands for silence. "I'm sorry to be so blunt, but Mr. Rogers was last seen alive in fear for his life after the news of the untimely passing of Officer Miller, which I might add, while tragic, we would have proven was the direct result of his own actions."

The crowd was getting spun up and began to yell in response. "Yeah!"

"Now, barely a day later, a young man will never get his day in court as he was murdered in cold blood, chopped into pieces and thrown away like garbage." Rose was working the crowd, and herself, into a proper frenzy.

"Who else but by the police, who even now look ready to celebrate?" She pointed to the row of officers who had come out to shield Rose and the courthouse from the ever-growing crowd.

"Booooo!" the crowd shouted.

"Is that 'to protect?'"

"Noooo!"

"Is that 'to serve?'"

"Nooo!"

"She went from press conference to rally in a heartbeat," Rollie said.

So much for Respectable Rose.

"They're eating this up," VP said.

VP glanced between Rose and the crowd, which was turning into a mob. We could see she was raising her fist along with all the others and could hear her shouting along. At least nobody was taking any notice of her.

The blue line of officers in between the two sides was looking thin, indeed.

Rose began shouting and raising her arms over her head. Her sleeves pulled down, and I could see a tattoo of a clenched fist on her inner forearm.

VP turned around, and we could see that more people had arrived and what had been dozens of scraggly-looking protesters had swelled into hundreds. A couple cops started to attempt traffic control to keep cars off the street in front of the courthouse altogether.

"Justice!" Rose screamed.

The crowd echoed her.

"For Andre!"

They roared the name back.

"No justice!" she prompted.

"No peace!" came the response.

More people filled the sidewalks and spilled into the street. The police went shoulder to shoulder, but this reduced their footprint and the protesters surrounded them. They moved closer to the reporters and cameramen. One cop jogged up to the press area, and we could see him speak to Jill Williams. She looked like she wanted to argue, then the first water bottle came in from the edge of the crowd. It burst open with a splash. At least it wasn't frozen.

"Oh shit," VP said.

"Can you get out of there?" I said over the phone.

"Kinda stuck right now." VP didn't sound so cocky.

Jill faced the camera and fought for composure. The cop returned to the line, and I admired his courage because his eyes betrayed fear.

We watched as the reporters shuffled to the courthouse doors. In the background, Rose continued to whip up the crowd.

A group of police in riot gear lined up and rushed out the door. The police may have been outnumbered, but they weren't outgunned. The cops had riot shields and heavy batons. They formed a semicircle with Rose at the center, where she continued to egg on the audience.

The original line of police fell back to form a second line of defense.

We saw some more police emerge, including an older cop in a dress uniform.

"That's Commissioner Rains," Rollie said.

Rains gestured to Rose to step down, and she began to scream even louder.

Rains spoke to a civilian, and a moment later all the podium microphones went dead. Rose didn't miss a beat. She kept up the chanting and enough people in the audience could hear her to get the echoes going.

Rains pointed at Rose and motioned for her to come down. He reminded me of a father scolding a defiant daughter.

Rose flipped him off.

"I think Counselor Thorn has left the building," I said. She was Rosie the Rebel now.

"More like about to go to the pokey," Rollie said as Rains had had enough and ordered his men to get her down.

"Sorry, guys, I don't think Rose is leaving by car anymore," VP said. She looked to be sardined inside the growing mob.

Rose didn't put up much of a fight, but we could hear her screams.

The police cuffed her and led her into the building.

And the mob went berserk.

CHAPTER 27

Philly courthouse

Despite all the jostling, VP had a clear view of Rose being carried into the building after going limp like a little kid who didn't want to get picked up. The last thing we heard was her bellowing at the top of her lungs that she couldn't breathe.

As dumb as that sounded, it worked like a charm on the frenzied mob. They began screaming obscenities at the police, and more water bottles rained down on the officers like a plastic cloudburst. One bounced off Commissioner Rains's head and knocked off his hat. The crowd whooped in delight and fury.

"I'm out," VP whispered and began to wriggle through the thickening mass of people. I felt my heart go into my throat when she hit a human wall and got pushed back toward the line of police.

"Yo, medic coming through!" VP glanced at her arm to show us she had put on a makeshift protester version of a Red Cross armband.

It seemed to work, as the people nearest to her gave way just enough for her to slip by.

"Clever," Rollie said.

Just then, someone bumped VP and the camera went out.

"Hey, you guys need to see this," Saul called to us from his office.

"I'll be right there." I motioned for Rollie to go ahead.

A couple tense moments later, my burner rang. I picked up and heard shots and mayhem all around. "I'm okay," VP said, "but gotta get clear. Talk later." The call cut out.

I arrived at Saul's office to see the fireworks going off at the courthouse on the TV he and Rollie were watching. I remembered the backpack on the Black-Bloc guys. Popcorn crackles and loud booms thundered through the doorway, and the police advanced to drive the protesters back.

The TV view appeared to be from the inside of the courthouse through a ground-level window.

The problem was that the crowd had grown to the point that there wasn't much room for the people in front to back up if they wanted. Elements in the rear pressed the others forward and soon there was nowhere to go but into the wall of police. VP had escaped just in time.

A minute later, I received a text from her saying: "Clear, RTB" meaning returning to base. I showed Rollie, who looked as relieved as I felt.

The cops pushed back anyway, and more objects showered onto the lines of police. Water bottles gave way to glass bottles and small stones. While the rocks bounced off the shields and helmets, some landed on the less prepared officers of the second line. Their cries of pain spurred the front line of cops to surge forward in a push that looked like a human version of a bulldozer blade.

Some of the protesters at the head of the crowd grabbed the shields and wrestle with the police. One-on-one they were far out-muscled by the burly cops, but they had the numbers. One cop trying to regain his shield had his helmet yanked off and was smashed in the face with it. The sight of blood gushing from the man's nose triggered a frenzy. The mob clawed at the police who began to use the heavy clubs with abandon.

As soon as one rioter—and a riot is what it had become—fell, two more took his place. I saw a large paving stone arc over the lines, and it dropped onto Commissioner Rains, striking him on the shoulder and driving him to his knees. The crowd surged ahead, and the lead officer of the riot squad ordered the men to fall back and regroup. They did, though many left their shields behind.

The second line divided into two groups, one to aid the front line and the other to escort the commissioner back to the courthouse. He was able to walk but cradled his left arm with his right. I suspected he might have a broken collarbone.

Rains refused to retreat and turned back to the crowd. He yelled some orders to the riot officer who shouted into his radio. The cops from the second line joined their brothers into one line, and anyone who got close was pepper-sprayed or clubbed. Nobody bothered to try to make an arrest.

Finally, Rains allowed the officers to lead him back to the courthouse. Some cops cleared the way, but I was still able to see the camera shot through a window to the street. Rains came in the door looking pale and grimacing in pain. Someone brought a wheelchair from the courthouse.

Rains waved it off but accepted a regular seat. Another uniformed officer ran up to him and whispered into his ear. Rains's face contorted in pain, but he nodded, and the news crews' microphones picked him up saying, "Do it."

Soon, some staffers with a rolling cart piled with gas masks rushed the door. Right behind them, a few officers with several grenade launchers slung over each shoulder ran out like dystopian golf caddies.

The police outside had managed a shaky perimeter, but the crowd seemed to be catching its breath. It hadn't thinned much, and, in an even more ominous sign, I realized that most of them had put on masks. Just cloth, but it was clear they didn't want to be recorded doing whatever they were planning.

At a shouted command, the riot-geared cops donned masks they carried, and the other cops fell back to mask up from the cart. The launcher caddies ran forward and handed out the launchers and bandoliers of ammunition.

The crowd taunted the cops, and now that they were out of water bottles began throwing anything they could get their hands on. From my vantage point, it looked surreal, like a movie or play. Right until several well-tossed stones shattered the window in front of the news camera. Thick chunks of glass fell out of the frame.

Someone pointed to that hole in the window and spoke to Commissioner Rains and the officer. "Clear 'em out, then," I heard, and with that, the cops on the street shouldered the launchers, and the launchers erupted with a chorus of thumps, and smoke streamed from cannisters as they arced into the crowd.

Some in the building must have gotten a whiff through the broken windows, and they began to cough. Court staffers led people away. The press was allowed to remain, it appeared.

Even from this distance, I could see the tear gas take immediate effect. The crowd scattered from the smoke, and I heard the rotor of a helicopter overhead. The police reformed ranks and pressed ahead, now fully across the street.

At first, I could hear that the chopper was broadcasting a message, but it was too hard to make out. Then, Jill and the cameraman stepped out the door, and an officer handed them a pair of gas masks from the cart. After some audible coughing from the cameraman, both of them donned the masks.

"I wonder if she will get one with a station logo on it if this keeps up," Rollie joked.

"She should get a helmet too if she's going out there," I said.

"She should get back inside, is what she should do." Saul made the most sense.

Still, with her and the cameraman back on the street, we had a front row seat to the action. In this case, I was relieved to see that the crowd was breaking up and the cops were advancing at more of an organized jog. They clobbered anyone who tried to rush them, and those attempts quickly petered out, then stopped altogether. I could make out that the helicopter was repeatedly ordering the area cleared.

Somehow Jill managed to work her microphone under the mask without allowing enough gas in to choke on. "As you can see, the protesters are moving off and"—she paused to cough—"and scattering. The police are ordering everyone within earshot to remain indoors until the gas clears." She coughed again. "That's good advice."

Jill and the cameraman returned to the courthouse where the police were rotating back inside. They maintained a presence.

A makeshift trough had been set up for officers to flush their eyes. Not all got their masks on in time, it appeared.

"Just before we came back to the courthouse, we could hear numerous car alarms and breaking glass." Jill looked like she could use some treatment herself, with her raspy voice and red eyes. "One of the officers told me that some of the crowd decided to cause as much damage as possible on the way out."

"Thanks, Jill," the station anchor said in his best concerned-for-his-colleague voice. "Come back safe."

"I guess the show's over," Rollie said.

"Sorry, my friend," Saul said. "I'm afraid it is just getting started."

CHAPTER 28

Cullen's rental, two days later

It felt strange to be back at Cullen's rental house, but a deal was a deal. We needed to finish up fixing the place after running off those twerps. After meeting Rose here, it felt like returning to the scene of the crime. I wish we'd known what a psycho we were dealing with. Not that we'd have been able to do much about it.

Speaking of psychos, Cullen was due to meet us here to go over the work. He'd told me to be here alone, but after all Rollie had done, before and after, I let him know that we were a team and also, he was the one to fix anything he didn't like. I was a little surprised when Cullen agreed.

"A little more to the left," Rollie was saying. He had a new entertainment center set up to go with the new TV after the idiots trashed the old one. I'd gotten a great deal. Cost a favor but worth it.

We both heard the key hit the lock before either of us had any idea someone was on the porch. We were pretty much armed all the time these days but had agreed that we would not do anything to make Cullen react to by mistake.

The door opened partway, but I didn't see anyone.

"Hello?" I called out. "We're in here." I wanted to be ready to take cover but fought it.

Cullen's huge body filled the doorway. How could such a big dude move like a cat? I noted one hand was on the door and the other in his pocket. Rollie and I kept our hands in sight.

"I saw your truck outside." He entered the foyer and took his hand out of his pocket before he closed the door.

He glanced around at the fresh paint and the furniture in the family room. "This is better than new. I thought I said not to break the bank."

"No broken bank." I handed him a list of everything, complete with a very favorable price list. "See? Under budget."

Cullen frowned at the figures. "I'm not a charity."

Rollie stepped forward. "We had to be kind of active, driving those idiots away. That meant some of the damage was us. I don't cheap out when I fix something I broke."

"Well, you do good work," Cullen said. He turned to me. "I want to talk to you."

"My cue to leave?" Rollie looked at me as if to say he'd watch my back if I asked.

Cullen looked at Rollie and shrugged. "Doesn't matter. I know you have more talents than carpentry. You'd probably hear about it anyway."

I didn't bother trying to deny it.

Rollie stayed put. "I mind my own business. And, just so you know, not 'cause I'm scared."

For some reason, that seemed to amuse Cullen.

"So, what's up," I asked, "besides the city blowing apart at the seams?"

"You want to ask me something," he said, "and I need to get it out of the way first."

"Me? No."

"Stop. You don't think the cops did that piece of garbage who killed Derek, do you?"

"No," I allowed. "They probably wanted to, but they weren't the only ones."

"I won't miss him," Rollie said.

Cullen did that non-smile smile thing with his lips again where they pressed together and pulled back for an instant. "Was that a pun, Marine? I know it wasn't you. You're known for confirmed kills."

"Not all of them," Rollie whispered. Then louder. "And not this one." We knew too much about each other, but it just came with the circles we travelled in. Like it or not.

"Well, it wasn't me either," Cullen said. "I wish it had been." He shifted on his feet. "Don't either of you find it hinky, the way he was found?"

I did but wanted to see where he was going. "Cut-up bodies aren't unheard of, correct?"

Cullen didn't flinch. "True enough," he said, "but isn't the point usually to get rid of, you know, evidence?"

Weird hearing the same line of thinking coming from both him and Saul. "Yeah. Maybe it was someone who was new at this."

"*Really?*" Cullen wasn't having it. "Someone pops their cherry and goes straight to the butcher shop?"

"Maybe not. But that leaves someone who wanted the body found."

"You're not always a dope." Cullen reached into his jacket, and I felt a zing of adrenaline. Rollie locked onto him but held still.

Cullen pulled out a folded piece of paper. "Read."

I let Rollie look over my shoulder. It was a police report about the discovery of Andre's dismembered corpse.

"Skip the foreplay," Cullen said. "See the name at the bottom?"

I skimmed the text to where the witness was named. "Lin Campbell?" I glanced up and gestured to the house. "Our Lin? The renter who kicked all this off?"

Cullen gave a slow nod. "The same."

"Jaysus." Rollie blew out a breath.

"Do you believe in coincidences?" Cullen didn't bother to wait for an answer. "Which brings me to the next one. Our girl, Rose."

"Yeah, you're right." I thought for a moment. "How did *you* know she visited your house?"

"I gave you a job, but didn't you know I'd be keeping an eye on things?"

Fair enough. "So, Lin just happens to find Andre's dismembered body, reports it, and right away his attorney is all set to light the city on fire."

"Almost like they'd been planning to use Andre right to the end," Rollie said.

"Almost," Cullen said.

"Lin didn't seem like the killing type," Rollie said. "An asshole, to be sure, but like you said, that's a big step and what happened to the body after is some next-level heinousness."

"You get used to it," Cullen said under his breath. "But I agree. I don't think it matters whether he did it himself, or Rose, or one of her people. Whatever group she is leading—"

"Or taking orders from," I put in.

Cullen shrugged. "There's always another boss. My point is that this is all part of a bigger thing."

Rollie nodded. "I'm no stranger to paranoia, so you've got me sold me there. But what the hell's the purpose of just creating havoc all over the city?"

Now Cullen smiled. I thought his lips might split. "Hell if I know. But I can think of someone who might. I'd love a chance to put the question to her."

"Current events say she's being held for inciting a riot, or whatever they call it," I said. "If you can get in and out of the jail after a nice chat, you are better than I realized."

"I wasn't planning on signing the visitor log, but now that you mention it, any chance you could get me a list of who *does* visit?"

Even if I could, did I want to put them on Cullen's radar? Taking the fifth wouldn't cut it when he wanted information. "I'm not sure."

"I'm surprised she hasn't been released already with this prosecutor," Rollie said.

Cullen nodded. "So am I. Another reason I'm here," he said.

"Well, it is your house," I said. No smile there. "But what did you mean?"

"We all know that unless there's some reason to hold her, the clowns in charge will let her out. Don't you think it's strange the riots haven't spun up to free their revolutionary leader?"

"Calm before the storm?"

"No doubt about that," Cullen said, "but even so, why not right now?"

"I don't know what they are waiting for, unless it's to stock up on bricks and fireworks," I said. Then, I got an idea: "No promises, but what if we could tail her after she leaves?"

"I assume you don't mean we follow her out the door?" Cullen said.

"Actually, that's exactly what I mean. But—and it's a big 'if'—if we can catch up to her and uh, insist on a conversation, could you promise not to go too hard? It's not really our style."

"Your 'style'?" Cullen said. "My old stock-in-trade usually didn't feature much in the way of conversation. My bosses had other people for that sort of thing."

"Yeah, well," I said, "we all have lines we don't want to cross. So if we're able to deliver her, will you promise?"

"Promise what? You're a little open-ended, there."

He had me. "All right. We're talking about you kidnapping her and forcing her to give information. Can you promise not to hurt her too much, if hurting her some is what it takes?"

"Tell you what. I won't hurt her at all. You get me her location, and I'll bring her in to you."

"And?"

"And nothing. Then, you ask her your questions and use all the harsh language or waterboarding or whatever doesn't offend your little style. I'll stay out of it."

"I didn't mean—" I started.

"Yeah, we did," Rollie cut in. "You got a deal. We find her and we all go get her and we can get answers." He glared at me. "She got us shot at. Kyle took one in the vest. That's on her, and so's a hell of a lot of other shit, near as I can tell. My city is on fire, and you're damn right we're going to get some answers."

Cullen pointed at Rollie and said to me, "You should listen to him more. If you keep trying to straddle the fence, you're just going to end up falling on the pickets, balls first."

CHAPTER 29

Fishtown, Power Cemetery, near Kyle's place, one day later

Despite the cloudless sky, the air felt pregnant with ozone. One of my sources on the city police called me on a burner, and before I knew it, Barry Daniels was on the line and wanted to arrange a meeting.

Normally, I'd ream the contact out for breaking protocol, but they were called burners for a reason, and moreover if Daniels had gone to such lengths for a discreet conversation, it had to be important.

Daniels knew where I lived but couldn't afford to be seen near me, even though he hadn't worried about it much back at the hospital. Another clue this was no social call. I agreed to meet him at a small historic cemetery just around the corner from my house.

I wore a light windbreaker and a hat and glasses to try to blend in. I was carrying a pistol but not because I didn't trust Daniels. It was the whole damn city these days.

I saw a lone figure over by a headstone. He carried flowers and was dressed in civilian garb, an Eagles hoodie and mirrored aviator sunglasses.

I strolled up to him. "This is different. I assume it isn't to let me know about Derek's wake."

"Would you believe that asshole Kennett told—not asked—the Miller family to 'wait on the funeral until things cool down'? That's an exact quote."

"Since when does the mayor get to dictate to families how they bury their kids?"

"Since never, but he knows it will be with full police honors, and he's afraid that there will be some sort of counter-protest, especially after the piece of crap who shot him was killed."

"Does Kennett think one of you guys was involved?"

"Who knows what he really thinks?" Daniels growled. "What matters is that he's all about kissing the asses of that mob."

"It does seem that way," I said. "Any luck on figuring out who did kill Andre?" Worth a shot.

"The crime scene got trashed, and we had two officers injured trying to secure it." Daniels took off his sunglasses and cleaned them on the sweatshirt. "Those anarchist-looking pricks called it a shrine and filled it with junk and touched everything. A dumpster. Can you believe it?"

I could. "As if someone or some group didn't want the case solved?"

He met my gaze. "More than a few of us think so. I can tell you this, despite the guy getting what he deserved, his murder couldn't be worse for the force."

"Why?"

Daniels looked around to confirm we had the little cemetery to ourselves. "That's why I wanted to meet."

I waited.

"You didn't get any of this from me."

"I hear that a lot," I said. More like all the time.

"You saw all the crap that went down when Rose went out of her way to make Andre, and I guess herself, into a martyr?"

"Sure. I hope Jill Williams wins an award."

"The mob is screaming police brutality and DA Castle is right there with them."

"You saw what I saw. This looked staged or at least instigated by professional agitators. Castle can't be that dense."

"He's going to bring charges on every officer who went out there."

"But Commissioner Rains was out there," I said. "I saw him get clobbered."

"Broke his collarbone. Tough old dude."

"What does *he* say?"

"Kennett told him to suspend those officers, but what he really meant was fire them. 'A fair trial followed by a first-class hanging,' and all that," Daniels said.

"I didn't count them," I said, "but that's a lot of people."

"Most of our best crowd control. I'm sure Kennett thinks we can get the meter maids suited up in riot gear and not miss a beat."

"Wow. But why are you—I mean, why am I learning this from the graveyard spirits?"

Daniels let out a long exhale. "I know you aren't with the Irish, not exactly, but you play a role in this part of town with keeping things working."

"Sometimes I know people who know people who can be helpful and so on. C'mon, Daniels. What do you want?"

"This hasn't leaked yet, but it is about to come out. Commissioner Rains is refusing to even suspend the officers. He said we can't spare them with all the crap going on."

"Brave, I guess. But what am I supposed to do about it?"

"Buckle up."

* * *

Kyle's place

Rollie sat with me to watch the press conference. I shouldn't have been surprised, but I felt a knot of anxiety build in my stomach while we looked over the cast of characters around the podium. Commissioner Rains stood at the microphone. He wore a dress uniform despite his left arm being immobilized with a sling. Behind him were Mayor Kennett and DA Castle.

"It has been my great honor to serve alongside some of the bravest men and women this fine city could produce," Rains read from a prepared statement.

"He's really going to do it," Rollie said.

"It looks like it," I said. I didn't know Rains personally, but for a guy in a position that required politics, he didn't seem too bad. The cops I knew respected him.

We listened as Rains thanked and praised his colleagues. When he got around to Mayor Kennett, I saw the man's jaw muscles bunch like his body didn't want to release the words.

"I know the force will be in good hands as Mayor Kennett continues to implement his vision to transform our city into a model for the future," Rains finished up.

"Guy looks like he wants to puke," Rollie said.

"Can't blame him."

Mayor Kennett approached the podium and the two shook hands. Kennett wore a Cheshire Cat grin the whole time. Rains stepped back and took a seat while Kennett lauded him with insincere praise.

"Can't just let the guy go. They have to kick him in the ass on the way out," Rollie said.

"The mayor is marking his territory," I said.

"And as we turn the page," Kennett bloviated on, "I am pleased to announce the appointment of interim police commissioner, R. J. Simms."

"Who?" Rollie said.

I had a laptop handy and searched the name while a slender man with wire-rimmed glasses and a shaved head joined Kennett at the podium.

I found the guy's profile right away. "Oh shit."

"More good news?" Rollie quipped.

"This clown works in DA Castle's office."

"That's cozy. He doesn't look like a cop, that's for sure."

Simms babbled about the great opportunity and the importance of reconnecting with the community, all while Rains had to sit there and listen to his tenure get trashed by implication.

Simms leaned into the podium with a super-serious expression. "But we face challenges right out of the gate. We must secure the trust of the people despite a fresh spate of abuses."

"Might as well turn around and point at Rains," Rollie said.

"I will work closely with DA Castle's office. For too long the prosecutors and the police have worked in opposition. That ends today."

"Smug bastard, isn't he?" Rollie said what I was thinking.

"So, as my first act as commissioner, I am announcing the suspension of each and every officer involved in the egregious display of excessive force we all saw the other day." Then, Simms did look back at Rains. "With the exception of Mr. Rains, who is no longer on the force."

Rains stared straight ahead and refused to acknowledge the remark.

"Moreover, as DA Castle often says, justice must be tempered with mercy. As such, we will be requesting that his office drop all charges against Ms. Thorn for her role in exercising her right to free speech."

Castle's smirk and nod told me all I needed to know about how long Rose was going to remain in custody.

On cue, my VP burner rang.

"You seeing this shit?"

"I am. Is what we talked about possible?"

We didn't discuss operations over the phone, so I understood her pause. "Already on it, and we will see you in an hour." She hung up.

I thought she'd forgotten something when I heard the phone ring again. No. Another phone. It was the burner for my contact in the police.

"Yes?" I wasn't sure who was on the line.

"Do whatever you need to do." I recognized the voice as Daniels's. "And . . . I'm sorry."

"What do you mean?" I asked, but the line had gone dead. I looked at Rollie as I snapped the burner in half. I had an acid bucket in the basement for destruction later.

"Short and sweet?"

"Short. Sounded like Daniels. A really dejected Daniels."

"What does he expect from us? We don't owe him anything, do we?"

"No, we just swap info sometimes, and otherwise we just kind of kept the lines of communication open."

"So he just tried to give us some kind of heads up? A specific or two would be nice."

"Maybe he meant about Rose," I said, "but he has no control over that."

"No. But we might," Rollie said.

* * *

One hour later

"Dude, I wish we had more time." VP and Steve had arrived right on time, and Steve helped her carry in several aluminum suitcases.

"More time than rushing into an angry mob? Even so, we might have even less than you think," I said. "They already announced that Rose will be back in court today. We assume so the prosecutor can ask the judge to release her, as there are no longer charges."

"News radio said that people are already starting to gather around the courthouse," Steve said. "Funny—and I mean weird—no mention of a line of cops keeping the streets clear or anything."

"Let's assume it'll get dicey the closer we get," I said. I looked at VP. "What do we need from your end?"

"Closer the better but, you know, not too close. Been there and done that." She glanced to Rollie and opened the cases, where I saw a total of four drones nestled in foam. "Rollie, the basic plan is that each one will carry a magnetic tracker. When we get a chance, we will fly it over the car and plant it on the vehicle roof."

"Won't everyone see it?" Rollie asked. "The drone, I mean."

"That's the hard part," Steve said. "We have to give the car a chance to get clear of the mob but not the chance to outrun our coverage."

"How fast can these things go?" Rollie looked skeptical.

"Faster than you think," VP said, "but we brought the small ones, so they aren't obvious. A big, long-range one would be as subtle as a flying pizza box."

Steve pulled out a map of the area near City Hall and spread it out on my dining room table. "That's the tradeoff. These guys don't have much battery life, but they're small and fast."

"Too bad Kyle cheaped-out on the satellite, huh?" Rollie pointed to the map. "So, what are you thinking?"

Steve leaned over the map. "Here's the courthouse door. She will probably come out here. We will have a drone parked on the edge of the parking lot building across the street. We can also keep one by the back, in case they try to sneak her out."

"Will we be able to see that far?" I asked.

"We should," VP said. "Also, we can use the coverage by our friends in the media."

"Good point," I said. "Then what?"

"If she gets her ride from the regular entrance, it's one-way streets." Steve traced his finger along the lines leading from the courthouse. "They'll have to turn left here, then we'll have one block before they could go in any direction."

"Sounds like that's the place," Rollie said.

"Hey, it isn't perfect," Steve admitted, "but the crowds may be thinned out by then."

"After that?" I said.

Steve spoke. "You and Rollie will be in the chase car a ways off and we will direct you in. Then, you know what to do better than us."

"I'm sure we'll think of something," Rollie said. "Let's get moving, check comms on the way. Use cells as a backup only, and keep it vague."

"Yo, take your laptop," VP told him. "I can share the feed."

"Will do."

We headed for my truck. I decided to throw a fake contractor placard on the side along with bogus license plates. It wasn't the best cover, it but beat having nothing.

CHAPTER 30

Philadelphia, Center City

I knew we'd rushed just about everything on this op, but it still felt like it had taken forever to get everything into place.

I was driving, and Rollie was riding shotgun, in every sense of the word. We were circling near City Hall and the courthouse in a slow, traffic-choked orbit around the Philadelphia Convention Center.

"Dropped again, dammit," Rollie groused at the feed from the drones perched on nearby buildings like high-tech gargoyles. "Every time we go through these overpasses."

"Can't help it. It's like going through a tunnel." I put my shades back on when we got to the other side.

"Yo, you there?" VP said.

"Yeah, same deal. Maybe we should just pull over if we see a spot," I said. "Not like I see any traffic cops around."

"Dude, the crowd is getting thicker. You seeing it?"

"I am," Rollie said. "What I don't see is any crowd control, do you?"

"No," VP said, "and the news stream is saying they are being told to stay inside the courthouse. They're running their cameras from in there. Why would—" She cut herself off. "Wait, something is happening,"

"Screw it. I'm pulling over to hold the signal." I wedged my truck in by a fire hydrant and put on my hazards.

We could see people pouring into the narrow streets. VP added some of the TV coverage, and even with a glitchy feed, I could see the sidewalks filling with people. "God, this is well orchestrated," I said.

"How do you mean?" VP said.

"They're all wearing masks."

* * *

"Here she comes," VP said. The news feed showed Rose emerging from the courthouse. Poor image quality or not, her smirk came through. We had the car radio on. The reports confirmed all charges had been dropped, and she was to be released.

"I don't see a podium," I said. "A small favor."

"I'm not surprised after the last time," Rollie said. "Look at all these masked-up pukes."

There were uniformed police inside the courthouse but still none outside.

"So far the natives aren't restless," I said.

"Course not, Rollie said. "They're getting what they want, aren't they?"

"Hey, I see a car coming," VP said. She must have repositioned the drone, as the picture jumped around then settled down.

"Ah, crap," Rollie said.

The car was an SUV. With flashing lights. It crawled through the crowd with the siren yelping in short bursts.

"Why would the cops want to give her a ride?" I asked.

"Under new management?" Rollie said.

"Dude, this changes things," VP said over my earpiece.

I had to think fast. We'd been expecting a private car to whisk her away. They really wanted to make sure she got away from the courthouse. "All right, team. Keep phase one. Tag the car if you can."

"You're not thinking about—" Steve began.

"Phase two is modified. We can still follow and observe." I didn't want to get too specific over the air, even with our scrambled circuits, but I wanted to make sure they didn't think Rollie and I were crazy enough to take down the police vehicle just to get to Rose.

Right in front of the courthouse, the news showed Rose and her lawyer step outside. The SUV pulled as close as possible. I saw a split-second shot of the officer driving.

He looked terrified.

The crowd whooped and roared when Rose emerged. Another cop popped out of the courthouse to open the SUV's rear door, and the attorney got inside.

Rose stepped on the running board, but instead of getting in, she boosted herself up and climbed onto the roof of the police vehicle.

"This chick is crazier than me," VP said.

Rose straddled the flashing light-bar, creating a weird effect on her legs like she was at a club or something. While she danced, the crowd went nuts. They surrounded the vehicle, and a bunch stood in front of the SUV, grabbed the ramming grate and gyrated like the siren was a techno beat.

The mob began to rock the truck, and Rose surfed the rolling motion.

"What phase is this?" VP said.

"Snafu phase," Rollie said.

With the crowd thick around the SUV and no sign of the cavalry, Rose turned toward the courthouse and gave it the double bird. Then, she stood up tall, spread her arms and, holding herself ramrod straight, tipped back into the waiting mob.

"Aw, hell no," I said.

Rose crowd-surfed away from the SUV and then vanished into the mass of humanity.

"Anyone see which way she's going?" I said.

Suddenly, blankets draped over a half dozen people and each figure went in a different direction.

"Shit, dude," VP said. "I got nothing. Could be any one of them or none of them."

I kept the explosion of profanity to myself and took a deep breath. The crowd held the SUV in place and then, one by one, the shrouded figures disappeared into the city.

"She'll pop up again," I said at last. "Let's cut our losses and take it back to base."

* * *

Kyle's place

"That went well, don't you think?" VP let her snark beat her inside the house.

Rollie and I made it to the house before them, as we didn't need to take time to recover the drones. The crowd had receded and melted into the city along with, it seemed, Rose Thorn.

"We didn't have much time to plan," Rollie said.

"Yeah," I said, "well I'm not sure any of us would have come up with a David Copperfield crowd-surfing illusion as one of the contingencies."

"Sometimes longshots don't pay off," Steve said. "The good news is that, as paranoid as Rose seems to be, we didn't tip our hand that we are looking for her."

"I guess that is something," I conceded. "Like I said, she'll have to turn up."

"She will," Rollie said. "You saw the way that mob moved. She's driving some sort of agenda, and they are her army."

"So, we'll see her leading the charge at, what?" I asked.

"Not sure. But I doubt we'll have to wait long. Rabid mobs don't just hang out on retainer."

As usual, he was right.

CHAPTER 31

Kyle's place, two days later

Sandy and I sat on the couch after dinner, and we watched the news, or the "Disaster De Jour," as she called it.

They were running a report filed by Jill Williams on Channel 27. We saw a clip of her from earlier in the day. Jill stood near a parking lot, and in the distance, we could see a police cruiser parked and a pair of cops just sitting.

"Officers I spoke to call this 'patrolling in place' and all over the city, frightened citizens are seeing similar passivity from the police." Jill cut to some man-on-the-street interviews.

One guy who simply called himself Joe said, "It's bad. Ever since that new guy came in and had his own people arrested, it's like the rest of them are just phoning it in."

Jill continued her narration. "Newly appointed Commissioner Simms made good on his pledge to suspend and arrest the officers most actively involved in crowd suppression at the courthouse."

I wondered if Jill would get into how she'd seen it all with her own eyes, but she stayed above the fray.

"Commissioner Simms declined to be interviewed, but his office did release a statement that read as follows: 'Officers are expected to report for duty and carry out their assignments.'"

"Wow, bold stuff." I sipped on a beer.

"Where does it end?" Sandy said.

I hugged her tight. "It'll probably get worse." I thought about our new routine. She didn't want to go to her place lately, which was nice for me. But the fact that she didn't get mad or try to talk me out driving her into work was a first.

"I'm scared, and so is the whole staff. Some are taking vacation, but I know it is just staying away. The only way we can keep up is that clients are starting to no-show."

"Even with the transport?"

Sandy nodded. "I didn't want to complain."

"What? Don't tell me any of the drivers are bailing on you?" I thought I knew those guys.

"No. Not them. Mr. Penney said the muggings around his building have gotten so bad that a lot of the older folks barely go out anymore."

"I didn't know." I felt like a jerk being so out of touch. "How are they living like that?"

Sandy smiled. "Your guys didn't tell you?"

"I guess not." I didn't like being the one in the dark.

"All three of those guys are heroes. When they aren't getting clients to the center for therapy, they're running groceries to the building. Mr. Penney said the lobby looks like a warehouse."

"Damn. Was that their idea?"

"Collaborative effort," Sandy said. "Actually, it started when Mr. Penney mentioned that some of them were worried about getting their meds from the pharmacy at the grocery store. After that it was kind of a 'While you're there, can you . . .' kind of deal."

"Incredible. Guess I owe them all a raise."

She smiled. "They didn't bat an eye." Her expression darkened. "I'm still worried about the residents. It's like they're being held hostage."

Hon, if this keeps up, we all will be, I thought. "Any chance we can get you and your team over to the building to do some house calls?"

"We can't move the equipment. I guess in a pinch we could do basic exercises and stretching. Better than nothing. But ideally, we need to bring them in."

"Hard to do that if they refuse."

"They're scared, and who can blame them?"

"Nobody, but it sounds like we need more than just drivers now. More like an armed escort."

Sandy looked like she wanted to disagree but couldn't. "Maybe."

"We're stretched thin," I said. "But let me see what we can do."

* * *

The next day

"Nice to meet you, Rollie." Diesel Dan picked us up at my place in a van. They shook hands. I saw Rollie's gaze cut over to the shaved patch of hair from when he'd gotten beaten up when his rig was hijacked. Dan also noticed.

"Nope, not a lobotomy," Dan said. "Just a fashionable reminder that the bad guys don't play."

"Roger that," Rollie said. "We don't either."

Dan raised his shirt to reveal a revolver. "The first one was free, but the next one will cost 'em."

"If we move fast, we should be okay," I said, hoping that was true. I'd already brought Sandy and Bitsy to their office. As much of a pain as Bitsy could be, I had to give her credit. She was going to show up for as long as clients needed her help.

The back of the van was piled with full grocery bags, and it smelled like Dan had looted a farmer's market. Apples, bananas, and fresh berries perfumed the interior.

The ride to the Sugar Mill apartment building wasn't a long one. It was still in the Old City neighborhood, but given the age of these clients and the fact that they needed physical therapy, even under good conditions, they required some sort of transportation.

And these were far from good conditions.

"I guess traffic lights are suggestions now," Rollie said.

"Worse today than just a few days ago," Dan said. "Word spreads fast." He leaned on his horn, and the driver flipped him off before scooting across the intersection. "Makin' friends," he muttered to himself.

"How many we got today?" Rollie asked.

"Just four, so as soon as we get the grocery bags in, we'll get the folks loaded up. I can manage pretty well if you guys have my back."

* * *

The minute we began unloading the van, I could tell that the residents hadn't been overreacting. Rollie hung back by the van, and Dan

204

and I hauled the bags. Each bag had a different name scribbled on it. It must have been a nightmare trying to fill each order like this.

A cluster of older folks including Mr. Penney watched and peered out of the doors like refugees.

Several shifty types appeared in the alleyway and watched our every move.

"You seeing that?" I asked Rollie.

"Of course."

"They don't look like Rose's crew." I hoisted a single bag this time to keep one hand free.

We were armed but had other treats if the natives weren't looking for anything life or death.

"Agreed," Rollie said. "More addict than anarchist but desperate enough."

Dan came out and saw us watching the alley. "Yeah, that's a favorite hangout. Watch out for ones not too far gone. Some of them are fast."

"Let's get the rest of these, then we can escort these nice folks to their appointments." I took a second bag knowing Rollie had us covered.

"Bless you boys," said a woman I recognized, named Jenkins. It appeared she was helping Mr. Penney distribute the groceries from the lobby.

I looked over at Mr. Penney. "That's the last of the food. We're ready for the passengers, I think."

Not so fast. Three guys had wandered over to Rollie. They looked like they wanted to surround him, but he kept his back to the van so he was able to face them.

"Just a minute," I said to Penney. I caught Dan's eye, and we disengaged from getting handshakes and hugs from the grateful residents.

Dan and I had just started to pick which one to take when the guy talking to Rollie made his move. The twentyish in ratty clothes said something about "sharing grocery money" then lunged in and tried to grab Rollie by the front of his shirt.

Rollie had been waiting and shifted his body to the side and gripped the guy's wrist with his left while he lashed out with a sharp blow to the guy's elbow. The attacker howled and staggered back. Rollie had a short dark object in his hand that explained the guy's reaction and told me what to expect next.

Rollie moved again to try to keep the injured guy between him and the other two. They tried to get around their partner but were so focused on rushing Rollie that they didn't realize Dan and I were coming in hot behind them.

I already knew that Rollie hadn't seen a gun or a knife. If he had, the three men would likely all be dead by now. This made things simpler and far less traumatic for the besieged seniors.

I reached into my pocket and slipped my fingers into a solid brass "paperweight" that bore an uncanny resemblance to old-fashioned knuckle-dusters.

Rollie moved left and right, and neither of the other two wanted to take him on alone. The guy in the middle cradled his arm squealing about it being broken. Probably so.

Dan and I both got close, and that was when I saw a small box cutter in the guy on my side's hand.

Oh no you don't.

I pulled my hand out of my pocket and shifted the grip on the knuckles to absorb the shock without hurting my own fingers. The tricky part with those things was to remember less is more—and more is way too much, unless I wanted to kill the guy, which I didn't.

I threw a quick jab to the back of his head. It felt like a practice punch, but it made solid contact. The guy's arms fell to his sides and the razor hit the sidewalk. His legs buckled like a string-cut puppet.

Dan reached his man an instant later and boxed his ears from behind with open palms. The guy spun around and covered his ears, and Rollie took advantage of the opening and cracked the guy in the ribs with his blackjack. Ouch.

The guy with the broken elbow decided he could take his suffering somewhere else and shambled back toward the alley. He was followed by the one now nursing damaged ribs and a balance problem. They weren't fast, but looked motivated and not in the least concerned about abandoning their fallen comrade.

I heard cheers from the lobby, and the four seniors going to physical therapy moved almost as fast as the two departing would-be muggers.

A guy I knew named Henry called out, "How 'bout *them* apples?"

"All aboard," Dan called out and helped the folks onto the van.

I checked on my guy, making sure the dude was still breathing, and very relieved to catch a strong pulse. I showed Rollie, and he verified what I'd felt. "He should make it. Take an arm." Neither of us was a doctor, but we'd seen plenty of casualties.

Besides, they'd started it.

He didn't weigh much, and we let his heels drag on the sidewalk as we moved him closer to the alley.

"Eyes peeled," Rollie advised.

All I saw was the last of the two we'd fought, and they saw us and must have figured we were chasing them. The one with balance trouble stumbled into a trash can and yelped in pain.

My guy groaned and stirred a little—a good sign. We left him just inside the mouth of the alley.

"We better not see you here again," I told him, though I don't know why I wasted my breath. He wouldn't remember it. But on the plus side, he wouldn't remember me either.

When we got back to the van, Dan had loaded our passengers. I'd been worried they would be terrified to go through with the trip.

"What are you waiting for? Let's roll," Henry said.

Rollie smiled. "Not a thing." Dan hit the gas as soon as we were aboard.

"Thank you, boys." A nice lady with a bad hip named Myra patted Rollie on the shoulder.

Another man named Bill looked positively jazzed. "That was *great*. Twenty years ago, I'd have joined you three. A nice ax handle across the shins would fix their wagon."

Henry watched as Dan steered around some double-parkers. "You can just run that light. I always knew it would come to this. I thought I'd be gone before it all kicked off."

"We're not beat just yet," I said.

Henry turned around in his seat to look at me. I heard his spine crackle with the effort. "Beat? Who said anything about beat?"

"What did you mean?" I wasn't sure where he was going with this.

"Civilization is bowing out, for now, anyway. This is the time for the good people to stand up for ourselves without the damn government getting in the way."

"Sounds like anarchy," Rollie said.

Henry glanced at Rollie. They'd met a few times before. He gave him a respectful nod. "For some, but for us decent folks it is a chance to fix it."

Rollie thought about it and gave me a look like he was stumped.

"I'm more interested in surviving," I said.

"Yet here you are," Henry said, "when you could be holed up in your homes, turning them into forts."

"Yer right," Rollie said. "I was never a 'wait for the alligator to eat me last' kind of guy."

"Exactly!" Bill said. "Sorry we're too broken down to help much."

"We appreciate all you are going through for us," Myra said. "We can still be your eyes and ears for our part of town. The roof of the building has a great view of Old City."

I thought about some of the flashpoints in the city and how the crowds had gathered and shot to critical mass to start trouble. Any advance notice could help. "That means a lot, thank you. I'll talk to Mr. Penney about working on a sort of rooftop watch system. I wouldn't ask you to go out alone on the streets."

"Father time may be turning our bones into glass," Henry said, "but we just make up for it with experience and treachery. Any way we can help, you let us know."

Our fourth passenger, Niles, had been quiet for the whole ride. "Maybe it's time for the Pinkertons," he said now, looking sad and resigned.

* * *

Old City, Sandy's physical therapy center

When we got to Sandy's, we pulled right up and even onto the sidewalk to minimize the walk. Dan helped everyone off the van, and Rollie and I watched the streets. Down here, it felt more like a bank holiday, with some businesses closed and others open, but with some sort of sign indicating customers should knock first. Sirens wailed in the background, and I took an odd comfort that despite an emergency, it meant that someone was still responding.

"You'll be back when we're done?" Myra asked.

"Of course," I said. I looked at Sandy.

"We'll be all done in a few hours," she said. "That okay?"

Dan nodded. "We have another quick job and should be back in plenty of time."

CHAPTER 32

Blue Bell PA, outside of Philadelphia

"Right on time." Cab Calloway leaned his slender frame out of the tractor trailer. He really did look like the jazz legend.

The back doors were wide open, and I could see we were in for some heavy lifting. The truck was filled with an eclectic mix of food and supplies to keep some of the struggling independent businesses in Fishtown going.

"This is basic stuff," I said. "You're sure these guys will pay our rate?" I jokingly called it our "smugglers' surcharge". Not much of a joke, as it was about accurate.

"Sand Box service. Sand Box prices." Calloway pressed a thick envelope into my hand. "Prepaid and everything."

"Maybe we *are* Fishtown's answer to the Pinkertons," Rollie said. "Armed escorts don't come cheap."

I waved the envelope. "This is a lot for these guys. They must be desperate."

Calloway nodded. "None of their trucks want to come into Philly right now. Three rigs from big-box and chain stores have been hit already and the smaller truckers don't dare."

Dan closed up the back doors and secured them with a padlock thick as a baby's wrist. "Maybe it is a lot of money to them, but I value my skin and this is fast turning into a Wild West situation."

We were joined by Shred Davis, the last of the drivers I knew from overseas who'd been helping Sandy out. As beefy as Calloway was lean, Davis had thick, strong arms and the neck of a football player.

"I got the list," he said. "You guys know the drill?"

"Dan will follow with us in the van. We'll keep your backside covered," I said. "Let's gear up, we don't have a lot of time."

"Feels like the good old days." Davis pulled on his body armor, and we followed suit.

We all drank some water, and I knew we'd need plenty more. These outfits weren't designed for comfort unless you took a round, and then they beat simple Kevlar, as my bruised back could attest.

"Let's saddle up." I'd given Davis a radio, so he could stay in touch. "Don't be shy if something looks hinky."

Davis grinned. "You ever known me to be shy?"

* * *

The short ride to the city limits was smooth enough, but when we crossed inside Philadelphia proper it was like passing through an undeclared border.

Rollie pointed out pairs of people standing at corners. At first, I thought it might be dealers staking out a new territory, but the figures were closer to middle-aged.

"Neighborhood watches?" Rollie said.

"Maybe," I said. "Think the cops will come outside the city proper?"

"I don't see why not. I can understand the locals being worried about things spreading."

I saw some smoke hanging above parts of the city. At least not in the direction of Fishtown where we were headed. We turned down Broad Street.

Davis came in over the radio. "We're getting a lot of kids with cell phones pointed at us."

I saw what he meant. "I see them. Good Samaritans like before?"

Davis laughed over the air. "More like lookouts. Feels like when we left the Green Zone."

"Roger that. Stay frosty." I'd slipped into the lingo like we were back in Iraq. More developed—not as hot, but the air tasted like danger. Hard to explain it, but worse to ignore it.

"Cab says he's not going to stop for reds if the traffic allows it," Davis said. "He said ten out for our first delivery."

The thought of large numbers of bandits getting texts about a juicy truck made my scalp tingle.

"I see a cop," Davis said. "First one in a while. Just sitting at that gas station."

When the truck passed the station, we saw it too. It was a marked Philly police SUV with two officers inside and the engine running.

"What is he doing?" Rollie called out, and I realized Cab was sailing through the intersection just after the light had turned, right in front of the cops. Worse, cars had just begun to enter the intersection, as they now had the light.

"Not leaving my wingman," Dan shouted and punched the gas. Car horns blared and brakes squealed as we blasted by them at near paint-swapping distances.

I grabbed the radio. "Are you nuts?" I glared at Dan. "You too. We're going to get popped before we make one delivery." There was enough gear in Rollie's footlocker in back to get us thrown *under* the jail.

"Kyle, look behind you." Cab had the mic and sounded ice cool.

I did. The cops hadn't budged. We'd almost caused a chain reaction crash right in front of them, and I'd seen officers inside that car.

"Gentlemen, we are on our own," Cab radioed.

* * *

Fishtown

"First stop coming up," Davis said. "I called ahead and they are expecting us. They'll help with the load, so it shouldn't take long."

"I hope not." Rollie scanned his side of the van and behind us. I knew he wasn't worried about the police. Like the rest of us, we were worried about *no* police.

I stretched and pulled on an oversized windbreaker. It made a warm outfit even worse, but at least it wouldn't look like the Marines had landed—though counting Rollie, they had.

The first several stops were tense but uneventful, with the exception that a kid on a bicycle passed close enough to get yelled at by Rollie when he began videoing as he rode past.

* * *

Chief's Taproom, a nice local place owned by a retired fireman, was our last stop. The brakes on the truck hissed, and Rollie and I jumped out of the van. Davis climbed down and went to the back to remove the giant lock and open the doors.

The front door to the place had been barricaded, and there was a sign with a cell number to text for entry. It seemed they were only catering to regulars for right now.

The doors opened, and a red-faced, heavyset guy strode out, followed by some younger men and women I recognized as staffers.

"Hey, Chief. You touching freight now?" I noticed he wore a pistol on his hip, and he scanned the street in all directions before I got a quick handshake.

"Whatever it takes." He pointed at my getup. "You weren't kidding about riding heavy."

I nodded to his pistol. "You too. Bet that does wonders for customer manners."

"They're not the problem, like you don't already know."

Davis and the workers swarmed the back of the truck, and I admired the way the guys had loaded the trailer in order of stops for maximum efficiency. They worked so fast that I would only get in the way. Calloway remained in the driver's seat with the engine running, same as Dan.

I pointed to the nearest smoke plume. "How are your brothers doing?" Meaning his old firefighter colleagues.

"You're seeing it. Those pricks attacked one engine yesterday, and I heard the guys spent as much time keeping the mutts away with the hose as they did on the fire itself."

"Even *they* can't get police protection?"

"Less every day. This 'Blue Flu' is becoming an epidemic. There's nobody to call. Nine-one-one is a joke right now. Same thing with ambulances."

"Seriously?"

"Look at you. Loaded for bear just to drop off some beer and hot dog rolls for Christ's sake," Chief said. "First responders want to make it home alive like the rest of us."

"Heads up," Rollie said. He had the back doors to the van open and the footlocker unlocked but was looking off down the street.

Chief and I turned, and we saw half a dozen young men on motor scooters round the corner and buzz toward us. Not good.

Then, a van followed them, nice and slow.

Worse.

"Get your people inside." Rollie spoke over his shoulder and lifted a shotgun he'd retrieved from the footlocker. I drew my Beretta and held it at my side.

"Need my help?" Chief asked after waving his folks back to the bar.

"Nah, tend your flock," Rollie said, never taking his eyes off the group. "We got this."

The scooter group saw Rollie and fanned out and maintained a distance. They blocked traffic, and I saw the masked goons carried pistols of their own.

The cars behind them noticed and began to bail down side streets and reversing into each other in a crunch of metal. A couple of the thugs turned and played anarchist traffic cop, waving the cars away and probably making sure they weren't about to get run over.

All the body armor felt about right.

"Pleasure doing business, Kyle," Chief called out.

"Always." I saw the last of the staff had made it indoors. "Tell everyone to stay low for a bit. These guys might get froggy." So far, they were being cautious. So far.

"Would you believe we have sand bags behind the bar? Now get out of here, will ya'?" Chief ducked inside and slammed the door.

The goons just circled their scooters at what they thought was out of range. Rollie's shotgun was set up for short distances, but it could reach that far, though it would also hit lots of other things. They hadn't fired, so neither would we. By now, Davis was back at the truck, but he had a huge revolver in his hand. I gave him a hand signal to stay put. Dan was still in the van, and he leaned out the window. "Guys?"

"I know," I said. "Radio Cab it's time to get out of Dodge, and it might get bumpy."

Dan nodded. "I think he guessed the last part."

I circled my hand to let Davis know we were rolling, and he climbed back into the big rig.

"Get in, Kyle," Rollie said. "I'm gonna ride in the back." He backed toward the open doors.

The scooter boys began to hoot at us, but they weren't aiming their pistols just yet. I still couldn't believe this was going down in broad daylight in my town. Maybe they were deciding a softer target might be better.

I got into the front seat. "Don't spill Rollie out," I said as Cab moved the truck out. There was almost no traffic ahead of up, and it looked like a big mess behind the line of scooters. Of course, no sign of the police. The thin blue line had gone from dotted to nonexistent.

Rollie backed into the van and clambered aboard. He slammed first one then the second door. "Hit it."

Dan punched the gas to catch up to Cab. The radio crackled, and we heard Davis: "Thought for a minute you weren't coming."

"No soldier left behind," I said.

"Ah, damn," Rollie said. "Heads up, kid."

I looked back. The scooters were following us. These weren't super-fast, but in a clogged urban setting, they could beat traffic and they could keep up with a tractor trailer around town.

"We need some highway." I took out a phone and called VP.

She picked right up. "Yo."

I gave her a very short version of our situation. "We were going to get out of town on North Broad. Any chance we can switch to I-95?"

"Hang on. Going map mode. Real-time loading."

I glanced back, and the scooters were stalking like a pack of wild dogs on the hunt.

"Crap," VP said. "Looks like a big jam-up at all the entrances."

"No coincidences," Rollie said.

"We'll go out the way we came in, then," I said. "Thanks, and if you see anything we need to know, don't be shy."

"Bet. Be safe, you guys." VP hung up.

I got on the radio and updated Cab and Davis. "Let's skip the manners. Any way you can get outside the city, and don't take no for an answer."

"They're still back there," Rollie said. "We can't outrun them at this speed." He looked back at me. "Might have to get messy."

"If they can't take a hint . . ." I let the rest hang in the air.

The scooters shadowed us as we barreled forward along West Girard Avenue toward North Broad Street. The only good thing was that the traffic was light. Folks too scared to go out.

"We got more scooters ahead," Davis called over.

"Pack hunting," Rollie said.

Davis came back on. "Whoa, they're jacking a car. Some lady just got pulled out at gunpoint. They're using her car to block the intersection."

"Anyone else in the car? Can you see? Any car seats?"

They got my point. "Negative. It was just the driver. Scooters on the sides, waiting for us. Driver getting dragged away by her hair."

"Ram through it," I said.

Just as Cab began to speed up, we could see what they were talking about. I spotted the lady, and the scooters behind were closing in as well. The ones waiting for Cab looked ready to snatch him out when he slowed.

"Dan, stop. That lady," I began.

"I know, but that's what they want." Dan was already on the brakes. Masked scooter riders closed in.

"No, it isn't." Rollie handed me the shotgun. He pulled out another gun. This one was a suppressed Ruger .22 with a long magazine. "I'll get her. Keep 'em off me." He gestured to the footlocker.

The van stopped in the middle of the street. The scooters sped toward us as Rollie jumped out the back and moved toward the corner where the lady struggled with the goon.

I raced around to the back, and the group of scooters slowed. That was my chance. I snatched up a couple cylinders, pulled the pins and lobbed them at the bunched group, who tried to turn and flee while they bounced down the street toward them. The two flash-bangs went off, one close enough that the driver overreacted and fell off his scooter. Two others collided and tipped over in a tangled heap. The rest were in full retreat, at least for now.

I heard the crash and saw Cab had smashed through the makeshift barricade. The lined scooters up there cleared off just in time. Then, I looked over to Rollie and the owner of the totaled car.

The lady was fighting the guy for all she was worth, but he was stronger. He slapped her hard across the face and pushed her to the ground. As soon as there was some daylight between them, Rollie stopped and raised the little carbine. With the suppressor, it made almost no noise, but it sounded like he'd unleashed a swarm of bees.

And they stung.

The attacker lost interest in his victim as he clutched his wounded legs then fell to the ground. Rollie walked forward. The guy reached for his waistband. Mistake.

Rollie paused and took aim. More bees and at this range, even I wouldn't miss. Three or four rounds into the guy's elbow ended whatever he had in mind. He rolled over in pain, and Rollie sprayed his other arm and resumed his approach.

By now, the forward scooter guys had split up. Half went after Cab and Davis. The other had noticed Rollie and pulled into the road to go after him. Rollie got closer, and the lady had regained her feet. I saw a nearby store had opened their door. So did Rollie, and he pointed and yelled at her to get inside. He didn't need to tell her twice. For the first time, I noticed all the faces in windows staring out in fear.

While Rollie was distracted, one scooter guy had seen enough and raised his pistol and fired a couple shots. Rollie dropped, and for an instant, I thought he'd been hit.

I raised the shotgun and fired a blast. I hated to do it in the middle of the city, but the lead was already flying. I knew I'd caught the guy's scooter, as I saw the front headlight explode. But it turned out I'd peppered more than just the guy's wheels. He dropped the pistol and clutched his leg before he fell to the ground.

A loud crack screamed by my head. One of the remaining forward scooter guys had an angle on me. I dove closer to the van to use it for cover. I spared a glance at the guys behind me. They were still disoriented, but one had decided he wanted in on the fight and had his pistol out but seemed undecided what to do with it.

I reached back into the open rear door of the van, grabbed another flash-bang and chucked it. This one rolled right into the clump of men and scooters. The three of them collapsed like I'd thrown a real frag at them. They'd live but might be deaf.

I heard a closer pistol shot and realized it was Dan firing out of his window. Return fire smacked into our vehicle, and a side window shattered. I peeked around the van and saw my attacker had almost reached me. I picked up the shotgun but not in time. Dan had hit the guy in his left arm but must have only been a graze. No more shots, so he may have emptied that little revolver. The guy was close.

"What's up now, bitch?" he said to me with a grin.

Instead of shooting me, though, the guy's gun fell from his fingers, and he face-planted in the middle of the street. I'd lunged forward and shoved his pistol out of reach before I saw the two tiny neat holes in his temple.

"Dan, you with me?" I yelled from the back.

"I'm good," he answered. "He missed, barely, but we need to go *now*."

I had my shotgun and made sure to rack a shell in it.

"The others bugged out," Dan said.

I climbed in. "Where's Rollie?"

"He's coming. Close the door. I can't even see the truck anymore."

Rollie reached the van and Dan screeched the tires as soon as he was aboard.

"You okay, kid?" I saw Rollie take in the shattered window next to Dan. "How about you, son?"

Dan nodded.

"Yeah, thanks to you," I said.

Rollie shook his head. "Had to do that. Thought I was going to be too late." He raised a hand and stuck his finger into a bullet groove in the driver's seat headrest. "I see you brought your lucky rabbit's foot."

"I felt that one go by," Dan said. His hair waved in the wind created by the open window.

Rollie glanced back. "Crazy shit. I hope those assholes have fun trying to get an ambulance."

"Anarchy has a downside," Dan said. "Who knew?"

I loved these drivers. Cool under fire, just like always.

I reached for the radio.

Nothing. I tried again. "Cargo One, do you read?"

"Hang on." Dan slewed the van hard left, and the tires shrieked through an intersection while we turned onto North Broad. Not that it seemed to matter much, but the traffic lights here were all just blinking. Most of the vehicles we saw looked like frightened civilians trying to escape.

"Is that them?" Rollie pointed to a truck about half a mile up the road. It appeared to be jinking around stopped vehicles. They weren't exactly built to slalom, but if anyone could, it was Cab.

Finally, the radio crackled to life. Davis sounded out of breath. "Little busy here, Wingman. On North Broad, if you're not doing anything . . . look out!"

"We see you," I said. "One minute out." I let him go.

"Look!" Dan said. We passed a scooter wrecked on the road. The engine was smoking, and the driver was stretched out nearby. The guy's mask had fallen off, and blood was coming out of his mouth.

"He alive?" Dan asked.

"Maybe," I said. "Who told these fools we were a soft target?"

A quarter mile farther on, we began to do a similar slalom around abandoned cars. One was on fire, and I saw packs of young people who looked much less organized. "I think these are free agents."

"Nature abhors a vacuum," Rollie said. "The cats are away, and the mice see an opportunity."

I thought about how large parts of LA were in chaos for days during the Rodney King riots with residents on their own.

"There's another," Dan called out.

On our left, we could see a flattened scooter along with an equally flattened rider. "Wrong tool to run a truck off the road," I said.

We could see the truck ahead of us. One scooter was trying to keep up, but we all saw bigger problems. A pair of fast Japanese bikes whipped back and forth behind the rig.

"He's shooting at the tires," Rollie said and swapped mags on the .22. "Can you catch them?"

Every time bikes tried to come up on the right side of the truck, we saw Davis stretch his arm out with his big magnum. The bikes would hit the brakes and pull back in behind the rig.

"I could if the last scooter would quit getting in the way," Dan said. "What do you say?"

I didn't get a chance to answer because the scooter guy began to weave and shoot at us. The rider was firing blind, but we were still hard to miss. This van wasn't built for this.

"Screw that." Davis didn't need to wait for me. He mashed the accelerator and bumped the scooter, hard. The rider went one way and the scooter the other. Now, it was just us and the two fast bikes. These guys wore helmets, so I couldn't see their faces. It was clear they were pro riders.

Chunks and strips of rubber flew up with each destroyed tire. The riders dodged the debris with ease.

"Into popping tires, are they?" Rollie said. "Get as close as you can," he said to Dan.

"Can't ram 'em, they're too quick." Dan floored it and swung left. Cab saw us as we went into the other lanes and nodded like it was a pleasant Sunday drive. A couple saucer-eyed drivers in the oncoming lane headed right at us but swerved at the last second. Other than that, it looked like citizens were staying off the streets.

Dan pulled back onto our side of the road, and the two bikes shied away. One rider took a moment to draw and aim a pistol.

Rollie didn't hesitate. He leaned against the open passenger seat window frame and unleashed a string of shots.

The rider flinched at the sight of the little rifle pointed at him, and then his bike wobbled, then lay down as the rear tire burst. The rider had just enough time to get his leg clear and skitter off the bike. I saw he wore a vest with a skid plate, and he looked like a flipped turtle sliding down the road on his back.

The second biker saw what happened and decided to call it a day. He flipped us off and raced away like we were standing still.

That was everyone as far as I could see. "Everyone good?"

Rollie and Dan said they were. I jumped on the radio. "Cargo One?"

"Yo, thanks for the assist. City line is coming up."

"And Cab?"

Cab took the microphone. "Riding rough, as you can see." The truck was listing left like a ship taking on some water. "Nothing I can't handle. Feels like the Sand Box."

"Too much so. Good job. Let's get clear, and we'll rally. Beers are on me later."

We crossed the city limits, and the citizen watch group—or whatever it was called—had grown, and they weren't trying to hide the rifles and shotguns slung over their shoulders. Police from the local towns parked in a row and left the citizens alone. Except for no barricades, it looked just like a checkpoint.

As we passed in our bullet-pocked rig with its shattered windows, the watch group stood and cheered. One guy did the fist-pump trucker salute, and Cab obliged with a long horn blast.

"Did the sign back there say Twilight Zone?" Rollie asked.

CHAPTER 33

Conshohocken

We led the truck to VP and Steve's warehouse. After introductions, they set off to work on getting spare tires put on the truck, not to mention patching holes in the body.

"Dude, you sure about going right back into town?" VP said after hearing about the rest of our adventure.

"We're late as it is," I said. "Can you guys at least tape over the bullet holes? Hate to scare our customers."

"On it," Steve said.

I called Sandy to let her know we'd be running a little late, but in case she hadn't noticed, the conditions were deteriorating and no matter what, that the clients must wait for us.

"That's fine, but . . ." Sandy said.

"What?"

"Please hurry. It was a long session, and a couple of them are overdue for their meds."

"Shit. Hadn't thought about that. Is it urgent?"

"As long as you are coming now, it should be okay. They left them at their place, but I confirmed that at least they have them when they get back to them."

"Thank goodness. Bad time to do a pharmacy drive-through in town."

"I hear you," Sandy said. "I checked with Mr. Penney, and he will have everything waiting, so we can make sure everyone gets what they need. Sometimes Niles forgets."

"You're the best. See you soon."

"Should we go in with you?" VP asked when I returned to the group.

"We're getting low on vehicles, aren't we?"

Steve came back with a empty roll of first aid tape that sort of matched the color of the van. "Good as new. Are we running escort?" he said to VP.

"He doesn't want to scare the old people," she told him.

Steve laughed. "No offense, Kyle, but you look like the Michelin man goes to war. If that didn't scare them . . ." He trailed off.

"I'm sure we'll be fine . . ."

"But?"

"While we run these guys home, maybe you can take some more toys to my place. I used up some flash-bangs, and Rollie's stash skews to the lethal. Do you have anything running? Preferably one that doesn't attract looters."

"I have something out back that should be good. Get out of here, but stay in contact. Half the cameras are down in the city, and some of the reports we're hearing are crazy."

"I still can't believe how fast this is unravelling," I said. "Rollie, are you up for another ride?"

"Try to stop me." He came over to the van.

"Mind if I drive?"

He shook his head.

"I do," Dan said. "I'm not leaving you guys to have all the fun."

"You did your bit. You saw how it can get out there."

"Yeah, and I want to make sure these folks get home. Or are we taking them out of the city altogether?"

I was relieved he wanted in, but it had to be his choice. "Good question," I said.

"You think you'd get those folks to budge even if you asked?" Rollie said.

"Probably not," I said. "Fair enough, we'll skip kidnapping and get them, Sandy, and her people out."

* * *

Philadelphia

Rollie stared out the window. "It's happening faster than I expected."

Whatever we saw on the way out of town in terms of locals banding together was not a one-off.

"Real easy, Dan," I said. "The last thing we need is to scare anyone."

"I heard that," Dan said.

As we rolled back into town, each of the neighborhoods we passed had established its own checkpoint. The main roads, which were so quiet it was eerie, were open, but every neighborhood had blocked its side streets and set up a single point of entry guarded by locals carrying weapons in the open.

I tried to reach some of my own neighbors, and my frustration mounted as I couldn't get through. Calls either dropped or just rang through to voicemails. There was a haze in the sky punctuated with dark smudges of thicker smoke in the distance.

I tried to call Sandy and didn't get further than her picking up before the call cut off. "Dammit." I tried texting instead. At least if there was a brief connection, it should go through.

That worked. I let her know we were on the way. She replied to hurry, as some of the folks were feeling the lack of their meds. She confirmed the landlines were out.

I tried to call VP with the same results. It must have been the cell towers in town. I went to texting, and she wrote back right away.

I warned about the checkpoints and told her to use my name if it would help. Some places it would, others would say, "Kyle who?"

When I relayed that the older folks were needing their meds, she had a great idea.

"Guys, VP said they are going to meet us at the Sugar Mill apartment building."

"Why?" Dan asked.

"Well, if we have trouble, they can get the meds to the people. Hard to do from my place. Second, if we're in a jam, they will be a lot closer to help out. If all goes well"—I paused, as "well" was a relative term—"then we have some safety in numbers to get back to my place."

* * *

We rolled down Market Street. Earlier we'd passed a firehouse which had makeshift barricades in front of the doors for the engines. A plywood sign read: "Out of Service. Do not approach. Intruders will be shot."

"Hope nobody's cat gets stuck in a tree," Rollie said.

When we drove by the federal courthouse, it looked ready for a siege. Cops on the roof and bags and barriers. But they showed no interest in anything outside the property line of the courthouse.

In just a few hours, the place had turned in a movie set for a disaster flick. On a normal day, the side streets were a confusing mess of narrow, one-way streets. Now many were blocked by cars, some deliberate, others due to wrecks.

"Bandits left," Rollie called out. We saw a group of about twenty masked guys. A couple were smashing into parked cars and grabbing whatever they could. Others were more discerning and picked out local shops.

"Hey, I see some over at Mike's Bikes," I said. Mike had replaced his windows with plywood, and bike racks were piled by the entrance. I could see some writing painted on the wood but couldn't make out what it said.

"We need to focus on the mission," Rollie said.

"He could be in there." I knew Rollie was right, but still.

"Maybe, but we know for sure where there are people who need us."

"Get down!" Dan yelled, and I heard several muffled reports as we got near the storefront. Dan hit the brakes, and I saw chunks of wood burst outward. One guy with a crowbar about to work on prying off the piece changed his mind. He dropped the bar and dove to the sidewalk. The rest of his group of five scattered.

I could make out the writing on the board: "You Loot. We Shoot."

"I guess he's in there," Rollie said.

"Yeah, okay. Hey, we're attracting attention." I noticed the car-smashing group was fanning out toward our vehicle. The lead guy pulled a pistol from his waistband and bellowed, "Out of the car!"

Rollie got out and levelled the shotgun at the guy's face before he could figure out where to point his gun. I got out and had my own pistol sweeping the group. If I saw a gun pointing at us, I was going to open fire.

"Drop it or die," Rollie said, and I knew the guy was about to get a twelve-gauge ticket to hell.

Rollie could be convincing, and the guy let go of the gun like it was hot. "Chill, old man. You got it." He yelled over his shoulder. "Ay! They strapped. Let's bounce."

They backed off and worked themselves around a corner. Again, I saw faces in upstairs windows. Anyone on the streets was probably up to no good.

A voice from above shouted down. "That you, Kyle?"

I looked up and saw that Mike had raced up to the roof, and he was holding a rifle. "You okay?"

"Yeah. You?"

I gave him a thumbs up. "Need a lift?"

He shook his head. "No chance. Got my life's savings tied up here. Not giving it away."

"Be careful." Whatever that meant right now.

"Kyle." Dan was back in the van. Rollie was ready to get in while covering me. Several people peeked around the corner at us.

"I'm coming," I said.

We reached Sandy's physical therapy center a couple minutes later. They were waiting for us, and she had mop handles and bicycle chains to reenforce the front doors.

"Rollie, you and Dan stay here. I'll get the patients and move them over. Sandy and Bitsy can help get them in." I grabbed a walkie talkie, as I wasn't sure about the phones.

At the door, Sandy put on a brave face for the older folks and to her credit, so did Bitsy. I'd been expecting her to be as much trouble as the actual patients, but she was a pro. Scared like the rest of us, but a pro.

"Someone call for an Uber?" I called out, shooting for breezy reassurance.

Sandy took a look at the scrapes and dents on the van. Most of the bullet holes were covered. "What happened? Are you all okay?"

We were interrupted by a burst of gunfire in the distance. I pointed in that direction and at the hazy sky. "Yeah, but it's a beautiful day in the neighborhood." I glanced at the folks in the lobby. "Good thing it's a short ride. Everyone ready?"

Bitsy gave Niles some water. I didn't like his ashen color. Of the four older people, he looked to be in the worst shape.

"Hey, folks," I said, "sorry for the delay. It's been a crazy day."

Henry stepped up to me. "We're not all senile. The whole city has turned to shit. You got a gun I can borrow? Mine's at home."

"I want an ax handle," said Bill, the other feisty senior.

I smiled. "I think we have it covered, but I'll keep it in mind. Thanks."

Bitsy pep-talked the clients toward the door. Myra seemed hesitant. "What on earth happened to the van?" Her eyes were wide as saucers.

"Lost a window on the way," I said. "It'll be a bit breezy, but it won't take long."

I looked over to Sandy and spoke in a low voice. "Anything else you need that we can grab now? Going to be hard to lock the place up tight."

"I have what I need." I saw she clutched some pepper spray. She had a handbag and a satchel with a stack of paperwork. "Hard drive is copied in here." She patted the bag.

"VP would be proud of you." I smiled and got a peck on the cheek.

My walkie talkie cracked to life. "Yeah?"

"Uh, Kyle," Dan said, "I think we've got a little problem."

"Be right out." I ran to the front of the center.

Dan was wrong.

We had a big one.

CHAPTER 34

Old City, Sandy's center

There was a small park across the street and next to that an old church with a historic graveyard. I recognized some of the guys we'd just run off. Worse, I saw a guy on a motorcycle with a rider on back wearing a shirt with the back scraped off.

"Those are the same guys who attacked the big rig." I turned to Dan. "See the one on the bike with the wrecked shirt?"

"He's got a wrecked bike to match."

"I don't think he's up for exchanging insurance info."

"Considering a bunch of his buddies got racked up or crushed while trying to get us, I'd say that's about right."

They were directing people to take up positions around the old stones and setting up using a brick wall as cover. I stepped outside with a hand on my pistol.

Rollie had his shotgun out. His head was on a swivel as he assessed our situation.

"Whatever they are saying about us, it must be bad," I said.

"The biker twins have been on their phones," Rollie said.

"Hope they had as much luck as I did with my phone."

"Don't bet on it." Rollie pointed, and we watched more and more people arrive. It looked like a mix of people, but the bikers seemed to speak mostly to the antifa-looking types. Plenty of others showed up on scooters and bicycles. I looked up the street and saw another cluster of people pointing in our direction.

"That looks like an AK," Rollie said.

"Thinks we can bug out before we're cut off?" My whole scalp was tingling with the danger closing in.

Rollie looked left and right. A few guys appeared at the path back to Market Street.

"Guys?" Dan pointed the other direction, and we saw some people pushing a car across the narrow street. We might have been able to ram our way through, but the van wasn't a tank and our passengers were in their seventies and eighties.

Rollie shook his head. "Nope. Time for a tactical retreat. Get the footlocker inside. I think we're gonna need it."

"Dan," I said. "Nothing sudden—don't let them think we're panicking—but would you mind giving me a hand?"

Dan never took his eyes off the mob—that was what it had become—at the edge of the park. "You got it."

We didn't have far to go, but the footlocker weighed a ton. That was comforting but still heavy.

"Slow and steady wins the race," I said. With my back to the crowd, my skull buzzed.

"Double-time, gentlemen." Rollie slung the shotgun over his shoulder and held the .22. "I'm going to take out the AK in a minute. Might piss 'em off. Get ready," he said.

I saw Sandy was ready to hold the door. Thank God, they hadn't tried to rush all the old folks to the van. They could see the same thing we did. I glanced over my shoulder. Rollie used the open van door to brace the rifle. Even though it was a small round, in the right hands I'd already seen what a .22 could do and Rollie was an expert. An AK round would go through most of my armor except for the strike plates, and I didn't have so much as a baseball cap on my head.

"Ready?" Dan asked.

I nodded, and we shuffled as fast as possible toward the door. I heard a roar from the crowd like we'd triggered an attack reflex. I guess we had.

"Here they come." Rollie sounded calm. "Hurry up. I'll be right behind you."

We focused on moving to the door. Sandy held it open, and we put the footlocker down and slid it into the foyer. "Get everyone way inside, and stay low."

I glanced back and saw at least twenty guys sprinting across the open park. I spotted the guy with the rifle, and he was running along the cobblestone and firing from the hip. Loud booms accompanied the muzzle flashes, and I was back in the Sand Box for a second. One round hit the pane glass front of Sandy's center and screams filled the room. Another hit well wide of Rollie and into the van's side.

Rollie didn't even flinch, and I saw the little bolt cycle with his steady rapid fire. The AK guy dropped the rifle, and his hands flew to his face. It had to be a reflex, as I think he was gone before he hit the ground.

Another goon swerved to pick up the rifle and took a couple hits in the neck. He flopped to the ground and blood seeped through his fingers.

Others took note and avoided the AK sitting in the grass. I drew and fired my pistol. I was no marksman, but they were too close for comfort and running across an open space. One guy went down and clutched his leg. The rest hit the ground and realized how exposed they were.

We'd stopped the charge, and Rollie waved for me to get back inside. He switched to the shotgun and let loose with a couple blasts. The sound of the shotgun did the trick and the attackers fell back. Rollie let them go and used the opportunity to make it to the door.

"Eat it!" Henry had crept back to watch and was hollering after the fleeing attackers.

"Get out of here," I yelled.

"Stay out of the way." Rollie's glare did the trick and Henry retreated. "Anyone hit?"

"I don't think so." Rollie and I dragged the footlocker farther inside.

He stared out the window. "Gave them plenty to think about, but they aren't leaving," he said.

"Guess we aren't going anywhere for a while."

More people were arriving, but they kept their distance. Funny what a couple bodies could do for morale.

Sandy came from in back.

"Hon, it isn't safe up here." I saw her expression. "What? Someone hit?"

She shook her head. "It's Niles. He needs his insulin. He's getting shaky. Much longer and he could go into shock."

I stared out the window, and the glass above me shattered. Sandy screamed, and I dropped down. Now more shots rang out, and the van shuddered and leaned. Rollie peeked out. "Tires. Someone is thinking." He raised his .45 and fired a couple of shots.

"Did you get them?"

"Not trying," he said. "Just giving them some more to think about."

"The van option is looking rough," I said.

"It's going to be dark in a while. They might wait to make a move."

"Why are they so interested in us? What are they going to loot in here anyway, exercise equipment?"

"My guess is that when we tangled with those biker leaders, they took it personally," Rollie said. "Who knows what they told this mob? Whatever it was, has them all fired up."

"Doesn't matter right now. We have to do something. I don't think Niles has much time."

"But the wrong thing could get us *all* killed." Rollie tapped the footlocker. "We can do some damage, but we can't take them all out, even if we wanted."

Definitely not.

I tried 911 just to see what would happen. I got a recording asking me to hold on due to a high call volume. I looked over to Rollie. He was reloading .22 mags and stuffing shells into the shotgun.

"Any luck?" he asked me.

"My call is important to them." I hung up and tried VP.

Her voice popped on, sounding like she was underwater: "Yo, you guys okay? Listen—"

The call cut out before I could answer.

"Damn." I tapped out a text asking where she was and telling her that the med situation was serious.

She wrote back, *Almost there. We were stopped at a checkpoint. Used your name, but it was scary for a minute.*

I texted, *Under siege here, blocking the roads, maybe a hundred or more.*

She responded, *At building lobby. Mr. Penney is here and remembers me. He has the meds.*

Don't come. Too many bad guys here. Frustration surged in my chest.

There was a pause. Then my phone rang. "Did it work?" she said.

"I hear you," I said.

"Rerouted the tower it uses. This other one works for now. Dig it, Penney wants to gather a posse from the local militia. They have a lot of guns and a lot of, um, *experience*, if you catch my drift." I gathered Penney or others could hear her.

"Experience like Rollie or just geezers with guns?"

"The second," she said. More interference and I thought I'd lost her. "Dude?"

"Still here. Signal is weak."

"Never mind," she said. "Got an idea. Can you get to the roof?" The call dropped.

I texted her back that we could, and she replied with a thumbs up.

Dan and Rollie were moving equipment by the windows. No more shots for now. I could see steam coming out of the front of the van.

I relayed what VP had said.

"Can Sandy go?" Rollie asked. "We can meet her up there when we get down here a little more secure." He dug through the footlocker. "Wish I had my rifle." I knew he meant his tricked-out sniper piece.

"You're doing okay without it," Dan said. "Kyle, little help?"

Dan and I rolled and pushed a couple weight machines and then some treadmills.

Before long, we had at least a minimal barrier to slow down an attack. These weren't mindless zombies (I hoped) so if we had to drop a couple more trying to get in, maybe the rest would take the hint.

Dan took the shotgun and hid behind cover. "The back way is blockaded. You guys go up to the roof, I got this for now."

Rollie and I went up the stairs and then climbed up the ladder to the roof. On the way there, I could hear Bitsy talking to calm the clients. Henry was less agitated, and Niles hadn't said a thing for a while. Myra kept asking why the police wouldn't answer.

Up on the roof, Sandy paced. She peeked over the edge, and I was glad to see she kept her head low. "Anything new?"

She jumped, and I felt bad for startling her. "Sorry." I let her know what we'd done to secure the front.

"What are we waiting for, exactly?"

I shrugged. "I don't know. I trust VP said it for a reason."

"I should get back to the people, see if there's anything I can do for Niles. Call me back here if you need me."

231

I kissed her and watched her descend the ladder.

Rollie was peering over the ledge. Every few seconds, he dipped down and changed positions. The sun began to sink in the sky. I tried not to let my spirits follow it. Rollie took out a small mirror on a telescoping mount that reminded me of a selfie-stick. He tilted it back and forth.

"How we looking?"

"Let's just say I won't have to be worried about missing targets. Too damn many right now. How many nines do you have?"

"Three full mags plus the rest of the spare box in the footlocker," I said.

"So, about seventy-five. Okay. We have a couple dozen shells for the shotgun and maybe a hundred rounds for the .22. and about forty .45, plus maybe twenty for Dan's .38."

"Not too bad," I said.

"We'll see." Rollie didn't look happy. "Goes quick when it hits the fan. Did you bring any flash-bangs?"

I pulled out a half-dozen that I'd stuffed into my pockets. "I left a few downstairs for Dan."

"I've ID'd some of the leaders. Haven't spotted them all. Maybe I could pick some off, but .22 at close range is one thing. Farther out, might be tough."

Before I could answer him, my phone chimed with a text from VP: *Heads up.*

I heard a loud buzzing, and we both looked up to see six drones in formation directly overhead. They flew to the center of the roof and descended. In their little carrying claws, four of them each held a small paper bag. The drones landed and released their payloads. Two of them held small, mountable cameras.

I looked inside the bags, and my heart raced when I saw prescription bottles and a little medical kit. One look at a pill bottle and I saw the name "Myra."

Rollie smiled. "I'll be damned."

I ran to the opening and bellowed for Sandy to come right away.

* * *

"He's doing better," Sandy called up the hatch to the roof.

Relief surged through my body. Niles had been going downhill fast, and the insulin kit had arrived just in time. We now had enough for more than a day, and as long as the power held out, Sandy had a small fridge to store it. If we were still stuck here for more than a day, I didn't think insulin would be our biggest problem.

"And the others?" I asked.

"They're okay. We had some snacks in the breakroom, so now they're just a little scared and mad."

I thought about Henry asking for a weapon. If it got much worse, I'd have to consider it. Davis and I had seen combat but only as civilian contractors. Rollie was the only real former soldier among us.

* * *

Rollie had been monitoring the situation from the roof. We'd mounted the cameras front and back, and VP had patched us in to the feed. We had a safe way to look out without worrying that someone might take a shot at us. Rollie had also bashed some loopholes through the edge of the roof that would enable him to shoot without exposing his head.

I texted VP the latest report. *You guys are lifesavers.*

You're not saved yet, she replied. *Almost dark. Make sure Rollie knows how to toggle the infrared display."*

I called that out to him and he gave a thumbs up. "Looks like a damn rock concert down there, and we're the main act."

VP reacted. *He's right.*

How did you—

She typed faster than me and answered my question before I could finish it. *Forgot to mention, cameras have a mic, so I'll hear what you have to say. No speaker, so I can't answer until we get into radio range.*

I stepped to the front camera. "Don't be stupid. You see the crowds. You guys will get trapped. Better we fight our way out back and slip away where we have a shot at pickup."

You got zombies in the alley too, she wrote. *Besides, drones are low on juice. They won't make it all the way back here for fresh batteries. Carrying cargo wears them out fast.*

"We'll keep them safe here."

Hold the fort. I have an idea.

CHAPTER 35

Old City

Now that it was fully dark, what was a concert without fireworks? The mob alternated between chanting and firing commercial-grade fireworks at the building. Sandy, Dan, and I took turns on guard duty and fire control. We still had water and a few fire extinguishers, but with every broken window we risked having a rocket land inside and set something ablaze. At least the stupid fireworks weren't accurate.

Smoke filled the air with a gunpowder stench. Under cover of loud reports and darkness, the goons tried to advance to the front of the building. Rollie watched from the roof and unless the goons were equipped with night vision, he had an advantage. Added to his edge, the suppressed .22 might not have packed a wallop, but it was so quiet they didn't even know he was shooting at them until one of them got hit. He was careful to conserve ammo, but it would take a few hits, especially in the noncritical areas he was targeting, to discourage a single person. They'd fall from a knee or leg hit, but Rollie usually had to send a few messages before the attacker realized that several of them were on the ground in pain.

Rollie radioed down to me. "The drones just took off and flew away."

"Somewhere there's a joke about drones leaving a sinking ship." Or maybe there wasn't. The day weighed hard, and I was getting punchy. "Looks quiet from here." Parts of the city seemed to be blacked out, and orange firelight flickered in pockets. So far, we still had power.

"Been a few minutes since I had to discourage some scouts," Rollie said. "We're due for something. Hang on." A second later, I heard a series of loud crashes and frightened screams toward the back of the building. I pulled my Beretta and ran back there. Bitsy was with the seniors, who looked terrified and tired and not improved from the stress, but worlds better than before the meds had arrived.

"You there, kid?" Rollie sounded out of breath.

"They're coming for the back door." I ran down the hall that led to it.

"Stand down," Rollie said. "That was me."

"*What* was you?"

"I was worried about a blind spot back there from the camera. I checked, and a couple of the little shits had crept over to it and were working on picking the lock."

"What was the racket?"

"I brought up some of the dumbbells from the exercise room. They dropped in a nice straight line."

"Did it work? Did it scare them away?" I still thought we might have a chance to fight our way out from the back as it was so narrow.

"You studied physics, son. It worked, but they sure aren't scared. I hope the second string will think twice when they see what is left of their friends."

"Damn." It just leaked out of me.

"They weren't coming to ask for spare change."

That hit with a cold dose of reality. "You're right. I guess I wasn't going to mess around if they got in."

"Better not be any guessing about it. I don't plan on any of us burning to death today."

I checked the door and saw it was still locked, as well as barricaded.

Dan cut in on the radio as the fireworks started back up: "Guys, eyes front. This is new."

I pictured Rollie's dash across the roof. He'd been covering all sides of the building for at least an hour, and he must be exhausted.

I raced to the front. Sandy had joined Bitsy, and she just looked at me. I squeezed her hand as I went by.

Like something out of a bad war movie, we saw a line of firework shooters through the gaps in our makeshift barricade. Black-clad masked goons came out of the darkness and stood shoulder-to-shoulder with thick cardboard launcher tubes like anarchist soldiers preparing for old-style musket volleys. Another line flashed laser pointers at the doors and windows. The beams stabbed through the lingering smoke like a stage show. For an instant, I thought they were laser sights, but then realized they were like one of VP's drones, trying to dazzle us. It looked stupid and annoying, but if one of those pricks knew where we were and hit us with one, it could wreck our sight picture and even damage our eyes.

Some of the firework launchers concentrated on the rooftop. What typically burst high in the sky now just arced across the park and scattered colorful burning fragments over the rooftop. I heard a loud report.

"Rollie, are you okay?" I forgot all radio protocol.

"I'm pissed off now. They've been trying for that hit all night. Nothing to ignite up here except me."

"Can you do anything about those lasers? Hard to draw a bead."

"Yeah—ah, shit. Bigger problems. Stand by."

Before I could wonder what he was talking about, we saw it. Several of the firework guys had made it close to the entrance. Between the barrage and the damn light show, we'd missed them sneaking up. Now they held bottles with rags and were lighting them. Lasers danced all over the front windows.

"Molotovs!"

I squinted and fired blind out one of the shattered windows, not really caring if I hit someone else standing out there. We hadn't seen a friendly in a while.

Dan did the same, but really all we were doing was adding to the noise with our eyes all but closed.

Above us, Rollie took advantage of the distraction. As the first guy reared his arm back to throw his cocktail, his bottle burst into a spectacular bloom of fire. I saw his body outlined for an instant before he was engulfed in flames and raced away, then threw himself to the ground and commenced rolling madly back and forth.

This gave the others pause, and the lasers stopped. One more would-be Molotov-chucker lit and threw his, and Dan, now able to see, fired with the shotgun. He missed the bottle, but hit the guy and spoiled his throw so it fell short but landed right on the van. Smoke and gasoline fumes wafted into the room.

A third hadn't lit his yet when Rollie hit the bottle and then the guy's knee. He tossed away his lighter and crawled away from ignition sources.

I aimed low and took a guy in the shin, and he crumbled. Dan fired another blast and hit two laser guys standing next to each other who were about to start up again. They went down and stayed down.

"They're backing off," Rollie said.

"About time," I said. "Freaks. They have to be on something to not get scared off."

"Doesn't matter right now," Rollie said. "Watch that van. Nothing to stop it from going up."

The heat from the fully burning van came through the broken windowpanes.

"Kyle," Dan said, "we might want to take a step or two back."

"Yeah." I imagined what would happen if the van's gas tank blew. The car next to it was smoldering, and its windows shattered from the heat.

Sandy came forward. "Oh no." One of the front windows collapsed from the heat, and it was like a furnace blasted us as smoke roiled across the ceiling.

"We're going to have to try to get out the back," I said. "If the van blows, the place will go up." I radioed Rollie: "Rollie, better get down here. We're going to catch fire soon. Gotta try to get out, even if we have to crawl over a pile of bodies."

"Roger, I can feel it up here. At least they won't come in through the front door."

We were talking on the radio which meant that VP could hear everything we said on hers.

"Dude," she said, "drones are back with fresh batteries. Let me scout the alley for you."

"Can you send one or two up here?" Rollie said. "I can hook up a couple flash-bangs if you can drop them."

"Bet, should have thought of that," VP said. "Fire is looking bad."

More smoke was getting in but not too much in back. It stunk of burned rubber. I hoped Sandy and Bitsy were getting the seniors ready. Henry and Bill walked okay, but we might have to carry Niles if we had to run.

I looked at Dan. "How many more shells?"

"I just topped off, so seven in the gun and six more in my pocket."

"Yo, can you make it to Front Street?" VP said about the road that faced I-95 that was on the block behind Sandy's office. We could follow the alley to the bottom which ended on Front Street.

"I think so," I answered. "Gonna be a long block."

"Yeah," she said. "The crowd is spreading out but definitely not giving up."

Sandy came into the room. "We're ready, if you are."

"Good. Once we're in the alley, take everyone to the right and lead them to Front Street. VP and Steve are coming." I gave Sandy's hand a quick squeeze.

Just then we heard and felt an explosive roar from the front. We would have been cut to shreds from all the flying glass if we had still been up there. Then barbecued. Smoke billowed into the room.

"Rollie! Bugging out!" I pointed for Sandy and Dan to get down and to go now.

"Go, kid, I'm right behind you. Get 'em out."

The back door was also near where the fire stairs let out. I saw Dan had un-barricaded the door and was waiting to burst out.

I looked at Sandy and Bitsy. "You guys are doing great. As soon as we clear the doorway move everyone to the right toward Front Street, okay?"

Both nodded.

"Quarterback, how is the alley?"

"Hang on." She was flying multiple drones and talking on the radio. I'd have lost my mind. "Okay, got some fire blocking the front. Shit."

"What?"

"Hurry. One jumped through, and they are putting it out with blankets, lots of them waiting around the corner. Go on my signal," she said.

I was about to ask what the signal was when we heard first one then another flash-bang.

"Dan, go," I barked. "Take the left side. I'll take the right." We were crouched down as the smoke filled the room. I prayed the fire stairs kept it out, or Rollie would be in trouble.

Dan had a crazed look in his eyes I remembered from the Sand Box. Again, we were drivers, not warriors, but the line could get blurred. Like now. He shouldered open the door and leapt out. He fell down, and I heard a pistol shot ring out.

Dan raised up on one knee and fired two quick blasts. I heard screams and stepped out. I almost tripped over the same body Dan just had. The guy had been brained when Rollie had dropped the dumbbell. To the right, it was clear. To the left, the close quarters allowed Dan's shotgun to wreak havoc on the bunch of attackers. One of the lead victims still clutched a pistol. Others just had whatever they could get their hands on.

More swarmed at the mouth of the alley, and I got a crazed vision of some sick duck-shooting carnival game with the targets darting across, waiting to get hit. After the first wave got caught by Dan, they seemed to bunch up on either side.

"C'mon." I beckoned Sandy and Bitsy. "Stay by the wall, and keep low, everyone."

I positioned myself next to Dan and made sure if any rounds came this way, I had a chance to catch them, preferably in the body armor. My heart pounded in my chest, and I must have sweated off ten pounds.

Henry grabbed my arm. "I want to help!"

"Get your friends down this alley, and you will save lives," I said to him, and I saw it sink in.

A shot whined off the bricks above us. That shot some pep into Henry's step and sent him hustling down with the rest. Bitsy looked terrified but moved like a pro. Sandy, bringing up the rear, was as tough as they came.

Dan fired several blasts and then swore. "Reloading. I put down some suppressing fire with my pistol. It was hard not to fire too fast, but I knew I had to conserve. The rounds at least raised convincing sparks when they hit the pavement."

Thicker smoke was pouring out the back door. Where the hell was Rollie?

"Loaded," Dan said. "Not much ammo left."

I heard coughing from inside, then a crash and two pistol reports. "Gotta check," I said to Dan over my shoulder. "Bail if you need to."

"Hurry." Dan fired a blast.

I crawled inside and saw Rollie on his knees struggling with a young goon. Another body lay on the floor along with Rollie's .45. Both were coughing, but it appeared the younger lungs were winning.

"Where that crate of jewelry, old man?" the guy screamed. "Tell, and I'll let you go."

Those bikers must have told these idiots we were Old City's answer to Fort Knox.

I held my breath and plunged in. I didn't dare shoot for fear of hitting Rollie. I reached the pair and pistol-whipped the attacker. My lungs began to burn.

The guy let go, and Rollie collapsed. I hit the guy once more and shoved him away. He looked stunned but stayed low enough to be under the smoke.

I let out my breath and took in way too much smoke. I was wracked with coughing spasms but ducked down for some better air. Spots danced in front of my eyes.

I fought them off and grabbed Rollie by his vest and dragged him to the door. I pushed him out, and he tumbled into the alley. The hair on my neck danced, and I rolled over and sat up with my pistol in a two-handed grip. The wiry punk had recovered enough to crawl after us, and he'd found Rollie's gun.

I fired three times, and he twitched and died just as something in front of the building let go, sending smoke and hot embers into the room.

I pulled myself out into the alley. The air tasted impossibly sweet and cleared my head in a flash. Rollie was still coughing, but he was on his knees and seemed to be recovering.

I looked at him, didn't need to ask.

"I'll make it," he assured me. "Bastard surprised me when I came out of the stairs. Got one of them, but I guess he brought a friend." He slapped at his waistband. "Dammit. My piece!"

"Forget it. I'm not gonna get you out twice."

"Come on!" Dan yelled and fired another blast ahead of us. I heard a scream. He glanced over his shoulder and saw Rollie and nodded to him.

We scrambled into the alley and could see that the group had made it near to the other end. "We need to move," I said to both.

Dan held up three fingers, and I realized that what he was down to for shotgun shells.

"Save 'em," Rollie said. "Still got your .38?"

"Yeah. Want it?" Dan said.

Rollie shook his head. "Cover our ass. I'll be all right." He was breathing heavily. "Getting old."

"Maybe quit smoking burning buildings," I said.

He nodded as if storing away this advice. "What's the plan?" he asked.

I pointed. "Make it to Front Street. VP knows that's where we're headed. We have to get clear of this crowd."

Rollie picked up his microphone and pressed the button a couple times. "My radio is shot."

I tried to raise VP on mine. No luck.

"Okay," I said, "if we're alone out there, I say we try to make it just past Front and onto I-95." The main highway was right next to this section of Old City.

"Maybe," Rollie said. "Either the traffic will shield us or the riot will cause wrecks, and we can grab a vehicle."

Dan started working his way down the alley toward our people.

"Uh oh," Rollie said.

I'd gone back to covering the alley mouth. When I looked back, I saw Sandy and the group coming back toward us.

CHAPTER 36

Old City

"What are they doing?" I waved to get Sandy and Bitsy's attention.

No luck. They were busy herding the seniors back up the alley and glancing over their shoulders toward Front Street. I kept looking to the other end we were defending. I saw a little movement, but they were being cautious.

"Kyle," Rollie said in a low voice.

"What?" I followed Rollie's gaze, and I knew why the group was returning. A huge crowd stepped into sight behind them, filling Front Street. They blocked the whole street, let alone the alleyway exit. I saw baseball bats and the glint of blades along with skateboards gripped as clubs.

I checked Dan behind us. He still faced the top of the alley, which was next to the front of Sandy's building. I got on the radio. "Uh, Quarterback, if you can hear me, Front Street is a trap. Stay away, but if you see another way out, we need one. We are stuck."

"Hang on," was all VP said, and then I heard the whirr of a couple drones over our heads. I'd just lifted my eyes when the drones opened up with laser dazzlers aimed at the top of the alley by Sandy's building. Those guys would get a taste of their own medicine, and anyone peering around the corner would get blinded, so we could act first. Maybe we could break out by the front of Sandy's if enough of the goons had circled around to the other side of the alley to cut us off. But we couldn't move fast.

"That's great, but I say again, large crowd on Front Street. They will be ready for you," I said.

"I don't think so," VP answered.

* * *

Dan, Rollie, and I met Sandy and Bitsy and their crowd in the middle of the alley. Sandy's place was engulfed in fire, and flames and smoke poured out of the back door. I imagined Rollie's pistol would cook off.

"I think we're gonna need more Pinkertons," Niles said.

"Yeah," I said. "We're going to give them all we've got. Stay low, everyone."

Now a bunch streamed into the alley from Front Street. They had the numbers, but I still couldn't believe the lack of fear. Had to be on something. I raised my pistol and squeezed off a couple rounds aimed high.

The mob paused and some of them tried to flatten themselves against the wall. I fired again and some began to back off.

"Stop wasting ammo," Rollie said. "Either drop a couple or hold fire. If they charge, we'll need every round."

'Watch out!" Dan called out. From the top of the alley, they were getting smarter. They began to toss Molotovs blind around the corner. At this point, it didn't matter if they were lit or not, with so much fire to work with. The no-look throws didn't go very far, but they did push us back closer to Front Street. On the plus side, it also made a decent barrier to block that side from both directions.

Someone grabbed my hand, and I spun around. It was Myra. She had a soot smudge across one cheek. Tears shone in the firelight. "It's okay. You did your best."

"Not yet, but thanks." I took the lead, facing the approaching mob from Front Street, as I had the most armor. "Try to stay behind me, everyone."

I checked my ammo and found I was down to five rounds in my pistol and one spare mag.

"Rollie," I called, "I got about twenty left." Even if I could shoot better than him—and I couldn't—we'd be overrun if the mob just charged.

For now, our last bit of shooting scared off the goons, and the bottom of the alley looked clear. But they hadn't gone far.

We could hear the mob doing rhyming chants and revving itself up, and then some of the craziest would dash in and out of the bottom of the alley. I fired at them, but the skinny ones were hard to hit. A couple shots and they'd back off, but not for long.

"Down to one shell and five in my snubbie," Dan called out. "Can't find my speed loader."

"Kyle, let's have it." Rollie held out his hand. I gave him the gun and spare magazine. He ejected the one in the weapon and replaced it with the full mag. He tucked the partial mag in his pocket. He handed me the blackjack. It was a leather-wrapped pound of hurt. "Don't screw around. Make it count."

A breeze shifted and pushed the smoke back toward the top of the alley. The wind carried a weird chemical odor from Front Street. It smelled like nail-polish remover and vinegar.

Sandy turned to me. "Know what that is."

She'd seen it all, working in an ambulance. And smelled it too. I knew it as well.

"Meth," she said. "A bunch of them must be doing it all at once."

Rollie gestured with his pistol and spoke to Dan. "Forget scaring them now. Every shot is for keeps." He pointed to the shotgun. "When you run that dry, use it as a club."

Dan didn't look like he needed convincing.

Rollie and Dan took the lead. I was just behind. "Use me for cover if they start shooting," I was serious. At least the blaze behind us protected our backs, for now anyway.

The crowd began screeching. "Here they come." Rollie dropped to a knee. I turned to make sure Sandy and the rest were on the ground. We couldn't run even if we'd been able, so this was the best we could manage.

Adrenaline coursed through my veins, and I gripped the blackjack. I was the last line of defense.

They came in twos and threes. Most had bats or other clubs. I saw a knife or two. No guns, but this wave was so crazy, firearms might not have done them any good.

Their eyes bulged with fury as they sprinted up the alley. Rollie fired with a cold precision and dropped one at a time. Dan held fire, ready to blast anyone who got through.

One by one, the crazed cannon fodder went from shirtless maniacs to switched-off corpses. Rollie hadn't been kidding about making every shot count. Some of the attackers hurdled their fallen comrades without any pause. Rollie dropped the empty mag and put the final partial magazine in. "Almost hand-to-hand," he said, like he was calling out bingo numbers.

Dan stepped up and let his last shotgun blast fly. Some pellets hit a guy running and others sparked off the brick wall. I glanced behind us, but that fire showed no sign of letting up. I noticed the drones had stopped dazzling and were just hovering. Auto-pilot?

Dan unloaded his revolver at the next wave. He wasn't Rollie but did okay.

Fear gave way to anger inside me. Why the hell did they want us so bad? I felt an irrational urge to beat the answer out of one of them. Maybe more than one.

After a brief pause where the wounded crawled away, sobered by the pain maybe, we heard a growing chorus of "They're out! They're out!"

Rollie tossed my empty pistol aside and drew a Ka-Bar knife. "Sell my soul for a couple of frags," he muttered. I knew he didn't mean flash-bangs either.

Following Rollie's instructions, Dan gripped his unloaded shotgun by the barrel. The plastic stock wasn't as good as solid walnut, but we were making do with what we had. I put my hand through the leather loop on the blackjack handle. Now I didn't have to worry about dropping it.

I checked behind. Nowhere to go, it still looked like the gates to hell at our back. Henry had found an old broomstick, and it had a sharp end where it had snapped. Good for him. Sandy had her pepper spray, and I saw Bitsy clutched her car keys in her fist like tiny claws. Bill was scrambling around, apparently collecting chunks of concrete big enough to throw. Niles had found a loaded trash can and had it on its side, ready to roll it toward the attackers.

Last was Myra, who had found a stick too thin to be used as a club, but she had wrapped it in some rags and moved up the alley where the fires raged long enough to return with a serviceable torch.

"Come on, then!" Rollie shouted, taking a knife-fighter crouch. Several shirtless guys charged forward, and I saw a whole bunch right behind them. The second row wore masks, and one raised a pistol.

I ran straight at the shooter making myself as "big" as possible with my arms out like I was trying to scare a bear or something.

The lead guy of the Meth Brigade tried to swing his skateboard, but it did nothing to my body armor. As roasting hot as it was inside it, I was very glad for it right now.

"Come on, bitch," Skater Boy taunted, but I snatched him up in a bear hug and carried him toward the shooter. No fear in him, but no meat on his bones either. This guy was a hundred fifteen pounds, at the most.

I closed the distance to the shooter, who looked surprised. Not as hopped-up as the kid in my arms, I guessed.

He recovered his wits and aimed the pistol.

When I raised Skater Boy so I could get my head behind him, he cried out, "Lemme go!"

Then, the shooter opened fire, right through his own guy. And when I say "through," I mean it: I felt both rounds come through and strike my armor. I had strong plates up front, so it wasn't a problem. Couldn't say the same for Skater Boy, who spasmed and shook. Cannon fodder to the last. I launched him at the shooter, and he got tangled up enough to spoil his next shot and give me space to swing the blackjack hard at his head. I was off balance, so it was a glancing blow, but the guy was still out before he hit the alley.

I fell down just as another shot rang out nearby. Another guy in a mask had gone for a head shot and would have got me if I hadn't dropped. I struggled to get to my feet, but the armor slowed me down. Not good.

But then I heard a buzz, and the second gunman was clawing at his face as a drone blasted lasers into his eyes. He mastered himself enough to try to aim at me, but I found a chance to swing into his knee. He buckled and dropped the gun, which bounced out of sight.

Back on my feet, I caught the guy in the jaw, and he was done. Two or three guys tackled me then, and what I think was a pool cue dealt me a glancing blow to the head. I wrestled them but they were heavier than Skater Boy.

Nearby, I heard a voice say, "Stab him!" and someone did, but the vest saved me.

"Cut his throat!" I heard—and then the weight came off me.

Dan had raced forward to clobber the guy about to end me, and the other one turned at the last second to take on Rollie in a knife fight. Rollie sidestepped the thrust and buried his Ka-Bar in the guy's sternum.

I regained my feet and was confronted with a massive crowd at the bottom of the alley. A hundred? More. Then, I heard a whistle like a referee might use and a loud, clear command, "Everyone, get them!"

Time felt like it slowed down. The crowd charged forward somehow both all at once and in slo-mo, like it was the start of some kind of big-screen apocalyptic footrace. The only thing that helped was that they couldn't all squeeze into the alley at the same time. Wouldn't matter, it was all a numbers game now.

Rollie and Dan stood shoulder-to-shoulder with me. Rollie made a guttural sound I'd never heard before as he gripped his bloody knife. Dan swore nonstop under his breath.

My head whirled.

Then, we all heard screaming, but it was no battle cry. It was agony. The bulk of the crowd, which was still in the street, sprinted out of sight to our right. About ten of them made it into the alley, and those who did, stopped screaming as soon as they were clear of the street.

Where had I seen this? It was hard to think.

A moment later, I saw what looked just like a TV news van pull across the mouth of the alley. Screams continued in the distance.

I saw a familiar octagonal shape of a transmitter mounted on a swivel atop the van and, better, an even more familiar person behind it on the roof of the vehicle.

Starvin' Steve.

No time to celebrate: We weren't alone. The ten inside the alley with us were fine, and I remembered how fast Steve's Active Denial System went from unbearable pain to nothing. At this instant, the guys were confused as hell and looking back to the van.

The three of us sprinted toward them. I didn't see any guns, and rage filled my chest.

Rollie moved like a man twenty years younger. He grabbed one guy from behind, who'd still been checking himself to see if he was on fire. I remembered the feeling. Rollie learned much more than sniping in the Marines, and the guy was done in a second.

Dan wrestled with a guy holding a bat. He ended up knocking him out with a headbutt.

Rollie got hit in the shoulder with a skateboard and dropped his knife. He grabbed the guy by the throat and kneed him in the groin.

I had two guys come at me, one with a knife and the other with a bicycle chain with a lock on the end. All I could think was to protect my head.

I ducked a vicious swing at my skull and saw the knife guy come for my legs. I stepped away, but the guy was quick. Not quick enough, turned out, as I heard a smack and saw one of VP's drones shatter against the knifer's face. He dropped his blade to care about his new broken nose.

I closed on the chain man, and he hit me, but I got in too close for him to get a good wind-up. I came under his chin with the blackjack, and he lost some teeth along with his consciousness.

A swing to the knife guy's jaw put him to sleep.

That left the three of us facing down five more, but their attitude told me they weren't jacked on meth. I saw the shine of fear.

And then, we all heard AR rifle shots, and Cab Calloway stood silhouetted at the mouth of the alley.

"Git!" He ran at our remaining five, and Steve stayed on the transmitter. I assumed VP was inside, but in all the fighting, my earpiece was gone and the radio was busted. Still, the remaining attackers now had a guy with an AR to deal with as well as Steve, Dan, Rollie, and me.

They panicked.

The guys ran away from us, but that meant straight at Sandy, Bitsy, and the seniors. Our people pressed against one side, and Sandy and Bitsy tried to shield them. Henry and Bill weren't having that, and Myra held out her torch to fend off anyone getting too close. Niles held back behind his trash can.

We gave chase, but I was already exhausted and never fast on a good day. Rollie could cover ground but, tough as he was, he was still north of seventy. Dan had the physique of a truck driver, so he was no speedster. Still, the attackers saw us coming, and they only sped up, especially knowing. Cab was behind us, carrying enough firepower to drop them all.

The guys ran straight for the top of the alley and the inferno raging there. The wall of flame looked smaller, but it was still plenty hot. They paid no attention to the six people along the wall.

But the folks along the wall sure noticed them and came at them in waves as they raced past: Sandy emptied her pepper spray can at their faces. Myra poked her torch at them, and one tripped up on the stick. Niles rolled his trash can in front of another, and the half-blinded guy took a header to the rough concrete. Henry stepped up to the tripped man and jabbed him with the broken broom handle.

The cries of pain spurred the last of the guys to run harder up the alley, and they didn't hesitate to run through the flaming wall. The ones who didn't do so well with the senior gauntlet regained their feet and limped after their comrades. They sped up when they reached the fire—the power of adrenaline—but it looked like they had to drop and roll on the other side to put out their clothes.

The seniors cheered like it was an Eagles game.

Cab caught up to us. "C'mon," he said. "It'll be tight, but we can all fit in that van. But we gotta go now. That was a big crowd."

Rollie clapped Cab on the shoulder. "Outstanding cavalry work, son." I don't think he realized how scary he looked or that he'd just put a bloody handprint on Cab's shoulder. Rollie's knife hand was covered in gore up to the elbow.

We helped the seniors who were less mobile. I picked Myra up in a fireman's carry and double-timed it toward the van. Sandy and Bitsy made sure Niles was doing okay and able to move.

As we got closer to the waiting van, I saw Steve leaning away from the Active Denial System antennae and saw the reason. Heat shimmers came off the unit, and I remembered what he'd said about how much power it drew and how hot it would become.

I'd have been concerned, but he had a crazed smile on his face. Davis came out of the driver's side and waved us on. A single drone passed us overhead and hovered by a side door to the van which opened, and VP landed it on her own arm like some sort of high-tech falconer. She flashed her trademark lopsided grin.

"Thought we were done for real this time," I said.

"Me too," Rollie said.

"Later," VP said. "We still need to get out of here."

We loaded everyone, and Cab was right. It was a very tight squeeze, but nobody was complaining. Sandy squeezed my hand on the way inside, and I gave her a hug and then one for Bitsy, a first. "You guys were amazing."

"Do you guys think my car will be okay?" Bitsy's laugh had a hysterical tinge, but she reeled it in. I'd never underestimate her again.

"All aboard," I called to the front.

Davis turned the all-electric van around. "Tell Steve to go easy on the ADS. We are way low on juice."

I relayed the message. Steve gave a thumbs up. "Surprised it didn't catch fire already."

The streets were mostly empty, and it wasn't far to Sugar Mill Apartments. Civilians were in hiding and small packs of looters flitted about, but we could hear occasional single shots ring out, none at us. The large mob had scattered, and we left it behind. Random small fires acted as unintended streetlights where power was out.

When we got close to the apartment building, we saw the street barricade. Davis slowed, stopped, and got out of the van with his hands raised. I could see rifles pointed at him, and others pointed at us.

Henry peered through the windshield. "Toll roads now? We're late for dinner."

The vehicles blocking the road moved aside at a command from whoever was in charge. Davis moved back to the van, and Steve waved. The guards peeked inside.

"Welcome home, you guys and gals," one of them said.

CHAPTER 37

Sugar Mill Apartments

We'd made it to the building, and the area around the apartments was quiet. The local militias, if that was the right term, appeared to have proven effective in walling off the chaos. Once the defenders had demonstrated their resolve, the roving mobs would go after easier pickings.

We'd received a hero's welcome at the building, and it seemed half the residents wanted to feed us all at once. More than food, I'd wanted nothing more than a hot shower and a change of clothes. The building generator was running, and I got both.

Now wearing a T-shirt and baggy sweatpants, I saw Rollie and the rest of us dressed the same way.

"I see you got the new uniform," Rollie said with a smile. Despite the unusual garb, Rollie looked like himself again. I'd barely recognized him when he'd let his killer side loose in the alley.

"So where do we stand?" I asked.

Steve came over. "They are letting us hook the e-van up to a charger. It's only a trickle, but by tomorrow, we should have enough power to get back to your place as long as we don't try to ADS our way out of here."

"That thing was amazing," I said. "Last I heard, you hadn't made it portable."

Steve gave me a sheepish grin. "Worked well, didn't it? Plenty of bugs to work out, but you should have seen that crowd scatter. They ran a whole block."

"I saw enough. You know half of them were pumped on meth?"

"Yeah? Didn't help them a bit, I'm sure. That pain can't be ignored."

"I'm just glad it worked."

VP came by and fist-bumped me. "That was intense. You sure you guys are okay?"

"Thanks to you guys. Steve said we can go back to my place in the morning—at least, if we can get through no-man's-land."

"I've been monitoring the news," she said, "and the outside stations show that it's bad but not nearly how bad."

"What do you mean?"

"They're describing it as widespread looting and some gang-to-gang fighting, but then, when they mention that parts of the city are calmer, they barely mention neighborhood watch groups keeping an eye on things." VP air-quoted the last part.

"That's what they're calling gun battles and arson, eh?"

VP shrugged. "All the news that's fit to sweep under the rug, I guess."

"But why?"

"We're getting a weak signal, that's for sure." She cocked her head. "You do have contacts in the media, don't you?"

Indeed. I took out a phone and decided the one bar would have to do and called Jill Williams of Channel 27. "Their building is right in Old City. I'll be surprised if they didn't hear our rumble live."

I left a voicemail in my usual minimal style: "Call me back."

Rollie plopped down next to me on a couch in the lobby. "Good to feel human again. Can't wait to get home. I heard we have a good group looking out for the block."

"Yeah," I said. "Our adventure notwithstanding, it sounds like the hard targets are getting a pass. Soft targets, not so much." Smoke lingered in the air.

"That's never going to be me." He showed me a pistol. "Steve said they picked up a few guns from the battlefield." I wanted to smile at the term, but that's what it was, wasn't it?

"I saw your .45 get caught up in the fire at Sandy's," I said. "What happened to the .22?"

"I shot it dry on the roof and didn't want it to slow me down trying to get out of there." He took a deep breath. "You know, I've been in more than my share of firefights. Not all of them with you either." He smiled. "But I've never seen such a fearless—no, wrong word—*reckless* bunch of fighters in my life."

"Some was the drugs."

"Yeah, I've run into that, and you save time not bothering to try to reason with it. But this was more. We sure pissed off their leaders when we took out some of the scooter guys after Chief's Taproom." He meant the biker guys who we ran off and had seemed to be directing the attack.

"I'd say. They must have told people to be on the lookout for a shot-up van."

"More than just that," Rollie said. "Did you hear that guy I was fighting with in the burning building?"

"Something about gold and jewels?"

"Yeah. The place coming down around our ears, and he's on some bogus treasure hunt."

"Clever to tell the crowd that, I guess, considering so many of these goons flocked to town to loot the place," I said. "Now that you mention it, what do you think went through their minds when they saw Dan and me haul that heavy crate into Sandy's building?"

Rollie nodded. "Not weapons."

"Well, you said yourself how dangerous a mob can be."

"I'm old, but I don't think I'm the one who came up with that one."

"Think we'll have to fight our way back to the house?"

"I hope not," Rollie said. "I need a beer and a nap."

My phone rang. It was Jill, returning my call. "Hey," she said. "Where are you?"

"Close to you," I said, "but we probably should skip a meeting in public."

"I doubt we could pull it off, anyway," she said. "We're relocated outside the city. I hear the station got ransacked." She sounded close to tears.

"What about your security?"

"Oh, they're right here," she said. "Management thought it would look bad if we fought back. But they did try to call the police. Can you believe it?"

"So, what do you hear from where you are?"

"Media is frozen out. The mayor's office is secure, and they're telling us it will be under control soon. Their line is that some frustrated people are lashing out due to systematic oppression or something, but that it will blow over and the city will reunite stronger than ever."

I remembered I was talking to a journalist. "Off the record, okay? I'm only 'sources'?"

"Of course. What's happening inside?"

"We were targeted by the mob that started it all, but this has gotten bigger than that, hasn't it?"

"I know that much," Jill said. "Gangs are taking full advantage, and news of the police stand-down is everywhere. People are pouring in and fighting with local crooks and then the civilian defenders in the neighborhoods."

"Don't I know it. I nearly got burned, shot, stabbed, you name it. And hell, I see from the news coverage that you know firsthand how many other first responders are out of the picture, given the paltry response to your station's own arson attack. It's true that nobody got hurt from that?"

"Amazingly, yes. You can see fires all over the city, and the smoke looks like one of those wildfires from Canada."

"I've seen it," I agreed. "Right now, the only thing keeping the crooks in check is their own fear of getting shot. Otherwise, it's anything goes. Someone brought in a train car full of meth, it seems like, and they could be at this for days. Where the hell is the National Guard?"

Jill let out a long, frustrated sigh. "Again, the mayor's office is downplaying things like crazy. What I hear is that they refuse to ask the governor to authorize the deployment."

"Can't the governor send them in anyway? He outranks a city mayor."

"He can, but usually they only will if asked. Bad optics to run roughshod over the largest voting bloc in the state."

I heaved a sigh. "We're so screwed."

"Yeah. But to be fair—and don't tell anyone I said this—but I think that the governor isn't getting the whole picture."

"You want a snapshot of the whole picture?"

"What do you mean?"

"There's an alley full of bodies right off Front Street. A bunch more in Wilson Park off Market. Send those pictures to the governor."

"How do you know that?" It sounded like that just slipped out.

"Bye, Jill. And be careful."

* * *

We all slept, despite the strange circumstances. Mr. Penney found Sandy and me our own room. We all had more to process than we could get our heads around, but exhaustion won the day.

In the morning, I found Steve, VP, and Rollie already awake. Mr. Penney and some of the residents brought us food and coffee.

Steve came to me. "We have almost half a charge. More than enough to get to your place."

I looked over at Bitsy, who had been very quiet. "Hey, are you doing okay?"

She looked up and gave me a weak smile. "I'm alive. So, better than expected."

"So are all the folks you helped. You should be proud." I didn't want to say she looked older. More mature was the better term—and stronger—but I couldn't come up with a way to say anything else that wouldn't probably land with a thud, so I put a sock in it.

She ended up responding as if I'd found a way to communicate it, anyway. "Didn't know I could do that," he said. "It just happened, and I reacted."

"You were amazing. I didn't know you had it in you." Crap. The sock popped out. She took it in stride, though.

"Me either," she said, and if it's all the same, this once was more than enough."

"I hear you. Looks like we can get out of here. If I can swing it, want to go home? You live outside the city, right?"

She nodded and her eyes grew shiny. "I'd love that."

Steve wasn't sure that the e-van had the range for that just yet, but Rollie had overheard us. "Get to our place," he told me, "and I can get her out of town in the Bomber."

We packed up and said goodbye to the Sugar Mill residents. We also talked to the guys guarding the neighborhood. I was impressed with their logistics and rotation. They were ready to dig in. Only the fatigue around their eyes told another story.

There was a lot of that going around.

CHAPTER 38

Fishtown

I barely recognized Girard Avenue. Rows of cars blocked the entire street, and men and women sat behind a line of sandbags. A large, hand-painted sign read: "STOP! Residents Only" and "Final Warning."

A couple bodies outside the perimeter bore mute but powerful testimony.

I saw some smoke, but whatever had been burning was extinguished. I even saw a firetruck willing to help within a protected border.

The short ride over here had been a patchwork of fortified neighborhoods and a horror show of business areas. Cab rode atop the van next to Steve, holding his rifle in plain sight. The raging mobs were nowhere to be seen. A few rough-looking stragglers left us alone. They looked as wary as us. Out here, there were many teams and no rules.

When we approached the checkpoint near my place, I said "Let me do this one" and stepped out with my hands in clear sight. "Yo, resident here. Can we come in?"

There was a tense pause before one of the figures popped up. "Kyle?"

I recognized Dave, the owner of a bar just down the street. "Yeah. Busy night," I said. "I'd love to put my head down without an extra hole in it, you know?"

Dave turned to the other guards. "Stand down. You see him, don't you?"

I recognized most of them, and they all looked like they hadn't slept in a week. Bet I didn't look so great myself.

He greeted me with a handshake and a hug. "I was worried about you. We have the area bottled up pretty good. Went by your place a bunch of times."

"Unavoidably delayed. You hear much about the rest of town?"

"Nothing good," he said. "How long can this last?"

"Heard talk about the National Guard. And delays. Can't go on forever. What do you all need? No promises, but it's yours if I have it."

He scribbled a list for me, and I told him I'd see what I could do.

When we got to my place, I looked over the exterior doors first. Nothing wrong that I could see. The security system, which had backups, had read all clear, but in this unhinged time, I didn't want to take any chances. At least the power was still on.

Rollie and I went through the place. Once cleared, we waved everyone else inside.

Steve hooked his van up to a charging cable. Sandy and Bitsy went to the living room and flipped on the news. VP wanted to get down to the Batcave to monitor events, but that was more than we wanted to share with outsiders to our inner circle, so she grabbed an energy drink and watched the news in the living room.

"Doesn't look so bad, according to them," Sandy said. "If I didn't live here, I might think it was just a wild weekend."

"When clubbing turns into *Night of the Living Dead*," VP said.

"It all still feels like a bad dream," Bitsy said.

* * *

Rollie, Davis, and Cab were going to walk the few blocks with Bitsy to Rollie's house. There, after they cleared the house, they would take the Blue Bomber to get her home.

I gave Rollie the list Dave had passed to me. "If you can find any of this on the outside, the guys at the checkpoints could use it."

"You know I love a good secondary objective," he said.

Bitsy gave me a quick hug. "I'll let Sandy know when I get there safe."

"They going to be all right?" Steve asked me. "I can have the van ready if they need backup."

"They should be. Fishtown seems contained, and they have a checkpoint to get onto I-95."

Dan had taken a spare bedroom to crash for a bit, and Sandy asked for some space to try to process all that had happened. VP went to the basement to monitor as much as she could. I sat down in the living room and ignored the television. I closed my eyes for just a second.

* * *

One of my phones jarred me awake. Story of my life. My back ached from falling asleep in the chair. I must have been out cold as I tried to answer two other phones before I found the one ringing. "Yeah?"

"Tell these clowns playing soldier to let me in," said a low, gravelly voice that made my blood freeze. "We need to talk."

Cullen. He was on a new phone, no caller ID.

"Who's on the checkpoint?"

"How would I know? They said to get you on the line so you could vouch for me." Cullen sounded impatient, which was to say, normal.

I talked to the guard and said Cullen was okay, which was better than telling the people tasked with guarding the neighborhood that they should just go ahead and let in a guy headed to the hitman hall of fame.

When the phone went back to Cullen, he said, "I'm coming up to your place. Just you. No, wait. Just you and the sniper."

I knew better than to ask why. He wasn't one to waste words.

* * *

"Sure, send everybody over. They can have a party," Rollie said when I let him know why I had to clear out the house. He lowered his voice. "I'll be right there as soon as they're tucked away here."

Sandy held me. She knew Cullen. "Are you sure I can't stay?"

"I'll have Rollie with me. And how bad could it be if he was nice enough to call first?" She just looked at me. I kissed her. "I'm sure it'll be safer if he doesn't know you heard whatever's on his mind."

I was glad she understood.

CHAPTER 39

Kyle's place

Cullen must've waited until he saw everyone leave and Rollie showed up. He was at the door just minutes later. It appeared he'd brought a friend. In a big-assed sack.

I opened the door fast and hoped no neighbors were watching. "You giving out samples now?"

Cullen took the giant duffel off his shoulder and lowered the body to the floor at Rollie's feet. "Are we alone?"

I pointed at the bag. "Yes, lucky for you. What are you thinking? And who was that?"

I was sorry I asked when he squatted down and unbuckled the top of the bag to reveal Rose Thorn. "Not was. Is."

She was unconscious but still breathing. "Holy shit. How'd you find her?"

Cullen pulled her gently free of the duffel. Rose was dressed in simple shorts and a T-shirt. It didn't look like the kind of clothes I would have guessed she'd even own. "I watched her pull that disappearing act at the courthouse," he said.

"Right, we all did. Pretty slick."

Cullen looked annoyed. "Bet you tried to follow her."

"You know we did and how it turned out," I said.

"I could see she had it all planned out, so I didn't bother with her."

"So what did you do?" Rollie asked. He kept glancing down at Rose, but she was out cold.

"I followed the cop car that was supposed to take her away."

"Why?" I asked. "She wasn't in it."

"Just when I thought you were wising up." Cullen shook his head. "Her lawyer was still in it."

Oh.

"I tailed them for a while, and eventually they dropped him off. He didn't know she was going to pull that stunt."

"How can you be so sure?"

That got me another look of disgust.

Oh again. Maybe Cullen was right.

"So, you managed some alone time with the attorney," Rollie said. "I'm guessing you found a way around attorney-client privilege."

"He went to some so-called safe house guarded by a few of those street punks."

I had no time to worry about what happened to them. And what was done, was done.

"He was talkative once we reached an understanding," Cullen said. "I learned a lot about what is happening and, best of all, how to find this one." He nudged Rose with his toe. She stirred but remained out.

"Where is he? In the trunk?"

He looked at me with dead eyes. "This is *my* show, not twenty questions."

"What's next then?" Rollie sounded impatient too.

"Let's get her somewhere safe. Got a basement?"

I had to think fast. We had a nerve center down there that doubled as a safe room, but I didn't want Cullen to know about it. Even more, I didn't want Rose and her flying monkeys to know anything about my home.

I caught Rollie's eye. "Yeah. One basement is just like another. Rollie, can you go first and make sure she won't see anything to ID the place?" He nodded, and I saw he understood. The Batcave had a secret door that looked like a plain wall when closed.

Cullen hoisted Rose over one shoulder like she weighed nothing. So much trouble in such a small package.

Rollie had made the basement look like an ordinary basement and added a chair along with some lengths of rope. Ever the Boy Scout.

"Cozy," Cullen said as I eased Rose into the chair. Her hands and legs were already bound. I was surprised she hadn't been gagged, but he must have been more worried she'd suffocate.

"Now what?" Rollie said.

Cullen took out a leather pouch and unzipped it. Inside I saw syringes. Made sense.

He swabbed her arm and injected it, then stood behind her. Soon her breathing sped up, and she smacked her lips. Finally, her eyes fluttered open. She squinted at me, trying to focus. Then, she turned to Rollie, and confusion swam in her expression.

"Wha? How?"

Recognition came as she seemed able to focus both her eyes and mind. "You! How?"

Cullen stepped into view, and him she recognized in an instant. Her scream told me her memories of him were most unpleasant.

"You remember what we talked about?"

The terror in her eyes told me she remembered that and much more. Gone was the fierce anarchist fighting the power. She looked like she'd aged twenty years.

"Answer," he said, just the slightest edge to his tone, and she recoiled like she'd been slapped.

"Yes, I remember."

"Good. Tell them what you told me."

That she began to speak without hesitation made me shudder to think what Cullen must have done to break her. Then, I thought of all the bodies from the recent violence. All the senseless deaths.

"We caused all of this," she said in a robotic tone. "The city was ours, and we needed the chaos to bring about meaningful change."

"We?" Rollie asked.

"All our followers fight for justice to remake society to serve the—"

"No slogans," Cullen cut in. "Plain English."

"Sorry." I didn't know she knew that word. "We are funded by the World Citizen Project. There are many shell organizations, but that's at the top. They are shielded. They funded the district attorney, the mayor, and one of us is police commissioner."

Rollie and I needed a few seconds to wrap our tenderized brains around this neat little summary. Holy crap.

"If you won everything," I said at last, "why is the city burning to the ground? Why destroy your prize?"

Her expression clouded. "That which is destroyed can be rebuilt." She glanced at Cullen in fear. Drifting toward more slogans, I guessed. "But we lost control of our animal."

"Animal?"

"The people. We have many followers, but not everyone out there is with us. And it is getting worse."

"I thought you had the police," I said.

"That's the problem. We thought the police would follow orders. Isn't that how they are trained? We didn't count on them striking."

"Wait, back up," I said. "You had the DA and the mayor bought and paid for, but to get the new police commissioner you needed riots and that all started after Officer Miller was killed and then Andre. How'd you plan that?"

Did I see a trace of proud smile?

"We didn't," she said. "We adapted to the situation."

"Andre was yours, right?"

"Yes, a local, but he was with us."

Anger swelled in me but I held it in check. "And you ordered Miller killed? Why him?"

"No. Our army is organic. They were allowed to operate with latitude, and an army is an animal that needs to eat. Also, after our distribution center was robbed, we were all under pressure to recover our losses. In this case, Andre went too far with the security guard."

"But you went all in to protect him afterward?" Rollie said.

She nodded numbly. "Until we didn't. His mistake was an opportunity, so we used that. After Miller's death, he became too great a liability. He didn't know everything, but he knew too much. He got scared."

"So, you just threw him under the bus?" I asked.

"Andre was sacrificed," she said in a bland voice "We made the best use of him, given the situation. We needed to put the blame back on the police and destroy the sympathy from Miller's death."

Cullen tensed at that, and I wondered if she knew they were cousins. It didn't matter now.

"How are you supposed to get things back under control?" Rollie asked.

"I can't do anything. I'm here now." Her voice had that same detached, drugged quality.

"And if you weren't? If we changed that?"

Cullen's expression told me this was a false hope.

"I don't know," she said. "Gangs are doing whatever they want. Our people aren't safe either."

"What a shame," Rollie said.

"If you have lost control, then why doesn't the mayor reach out to the governor for the National Guard?" I asked. "That's what's got to happen. Not even the police, if they came back, can get a handle on this right now."

"He's lost right now. He has no guidance. Like they say, failure is an orphan. The WCP is washing their hands of it. The mayor and DA don't even know that yet."

"They both got a lot to learn." Cullen's voice dripped with menace. "I'd especially like to teach the mayor."

"Mayor Kennett is afraid," Rose drifted on. "The mobs around City Hall aren't our people anymore. They're from all over. He's operating out of a secret office location several blocks away. We have people providing security."

Cullen looked at us. "All the security details he had from the Philly PD got the same Blue Flu. He thinks those mutts will keep him safe."

"Where is he?" I asked.

Cullen shut Rose down with a glare. "*I* know," he said to me. "And now you know why I'm here and you got the real story."

"You need our help," I said.

"Three of us should be enough." Cullen put his hand on Rose's shoulder. "Well, four. It's the only way."

"If nothing happens, the Guard will have to get called in anyway."

Cullen shook his head. "The politicians are cowards. They will delay, and the city will keep burning for days, maybe weeks."

Rollie met my gaze. "He's right. We can make a difference."

I couldn't get the image of all those bodies in the alley out of my mind. That and Sandy's center, which had to be a smoldering pile of rubble by now.

"I'm in," I said.

Cullen turned to Rose. "You did okay. Just a little more and you can earn your Philadelphia freedom. *If* you behave."

"But they'll kill me," Rose said, shedding her sleep-walking tone all at once.

"We'll protect you," Cullen said. "But if you try to backstab us, I'll do your friends, and then make the last couple of days with you feel like pattycake."

He looked at Rollie and me, daring us to say something.

Rose nodded and shook like a leaf.

* * *

Cullen asked Rollie to take Rose to his car. Once she was out of earshot, Cullen stood close to me and said in a low voice, "When we reach the mayor, this is the play. Listen carefully . . ."

It was Cullen's show. If we pulled it off, it'd be a good one.

CHAPTER 40

Philadelphia, Rittenhouse Square

If the neighborhoods around town had become fortified islands, the more commercial districts were more of a no-man's land. Of course, there were buildings with residents trapped in them, and office buildings either abandoned, barricaded, or burned. Hand-painted signs abounded warning of lethal consequences, and, for the most part, the warnings were being taken seriously.

I was sure it was an unintended consequence, but the divisions between the various bands of criminals also led to no single group taking full control.

The upshot, while still chaotic, made it possible to move through the city.

I drove Cullen's car with Rose sitting next to me and Cullen right behind her. Her right arm was cuffed to the door handle.

Rollie hadn't come from his place emptyhanded. He sat across from Cullen in the back with a suppressed Ruger .22 in his lap.

"I thought you left that on the roof at Sandy's," I said to him in the rearview.

Rollie looked disappointed in me. "Two is one, and one is none." He also displayed another .45 in a holster.

Cullen seemed to approve. "Kind of like shark's teeth."

"Here." Rollie handed me a Beretta. "Was saving it for your birthday, but you need it now."

I took the gun. I also had my brass knuckles. We didn't ask Cullen for an inventory of what he had on him.

* * *

"That's the building," Rose said.

"The Arts Council?" I was leery of a trap.

"Inside, there's a tunnel that goes under the street and comes out to a dentist office. The mayor has space there that he uses for secret meetings or hookups or whatever he wants."

"If you're lying," Cullen growled.

"I only went there once because he really didn't want to be seen with me," Rose said.

One way or another, we were about to find out. "All right, guns down. Here's the first checkpoint." The guys were not kids but dressed at the height of anarchist chic. Lots of all-black hoodies and masks. Some red armbands with clenched-fist insignias and stripes that must have represented some sort of rank. One started moving toward us. They must have been used to some level of visitors because they weren't freaked out by a carload of people.

"I count four," Rollie whispered from the back. "One shotgun, two with holstered pistols and . . . is that a cavalry saber?"

"Must be the leader," Cullen said. "Know him?" he whispered to Rose. "Do not lie."

She nodded and put on a fake smile. "His name is Carlos."

The guy approached the car with caution. The shotgun man watched, but the weapon still rested on his shoulder. He relaxed when he saw Rose.

"Hey, where have you been? You okay?"

Cullen, low from the back, said, "Get it right."

"I am now," she said.

My stomach tensed.

"These guys saved me, and they drove me here," she said. "I need to see him."

"What happened?"

"Bunch of randos grabbed me, but these guys saw it happen and drove them off. Could have gone bad."

"Thanks for that," Carlos said to me, but he eyeballed me more than I liked. "Do I know you?"

I didn't know him but began to wonder if Rose had gotten hold of our pictures somehow and told her goons to be on the lookout. "Nope. Must just have one of those faces."

"Yeah. Well, you guys can hang out here. Rose, if you're good, you can go through. I'll let them know you're coming."

"Sure, no problem." I smiled. "I should stay with the car anyway."

"Problem," Cullen whispered after Carlos stepped away. "They can't call ahead. Mayor will bail."

I got out of the car with Rollie. This got all of their attention. The guy about to run the message inside stopped, and his hand dropped to the butt of his pistol.

"Easy," I said. "We have some supplies and were going to ask for a hand."

"It's heavy," Rose chipped in. "Won't take a second."

"What is it?" Carlos said.

"See for yourself," I said. "You guys can have some, of course." I popped the trunk and pointed as I slipped my fingers into my brass knuckles. Carlos moved around to the back, and when the trunk blocked the other's view of him, I made my move.

"I don't see any—"

I caught him flush on the jaw. It made an awful crunch, and he folded like a lawn chair. Rollie snatched up the Ruger and went right for the guy with the shotgun, who had moved forward. The barrel had just come off his shoulder when Rollie put three quick shots into his face while the other two were still off guard. I drew my pistol and got the drop on one. He saw and took his hand off the butt of his pistol. The other guy watched me and drew his but dropped it when Rollie shattered his elbow with a well-placed round.

"Don't shoot," my guy said and raised his hands.

Rollie ran up to the wounded one and put his lights out with his blackjack. I made my guy turn around, and Rollie disarmed him and knocked him cold. We dragged all of them including Carlos along the far side of the Cullen's sedan and stretched them out at their post.

The rest of the street was quiet. Team Anarchist seemed to have the area somewhat pacified.

Cullen came out of the car with Rose, who was now in tears. "Losing her poker face," he said over his shoulder.

"Not much more," I said to Rose. "Lead the way."

Rollie was next to me. We stepped inside the Arts Council building entrance and found one guy there, peering out the window.

"Rose? What happened to the guards?" He reached for a phone.

"This." Rollie smashed the phone with the blackjack and followed up with a blow to the side of his head, depositing the dude to the concrete floor. I was beginning to see why so many places outlawed blackjacks.

The three of us pulled ski masks over our faces. We were done being subtle, and I didn't need to be the star of a video for a raid on the mayor. Maybe, as his secret lair, he avoided recording here, but best to be safe.

"Which way?" Cullen asked Rose.

"Down here," she whispered.

We took a staircase, and then she pointed out a spot on a wall that pushed in to reveal a lit passage. I didn't see cameras, but that didn't mean anything. No stopping now in any case. We jogged ahead.

We saw a door ahead. It had a peephole.

"Front and center." Cullen pushed Rose to the door. He tried the handle, which of course was locked, then knocked and crouched down.

I saw the peephole darken, and then the door opened a crack. "Thorn? Where have—"

Cullen brushed Rose aside and drove his full weight against the door. The metal door slammed into what looked like a frail aide barely out of college and sent him flying out of sight. Rollie and I had guns up, and I dragged Rose with us. Cullen sounded like an enraged bear. By the time we made it through the door, I saw two more bureaucrat-looking guys sprawled on the floor.

The place looked like a conference room and had a couple more doors on one side. At the head of the table, I saw a familiar face sitting in a thick leather swivel chair with his mouth agape. Mayor Kennett.

"Wha, wha, what do you want?" he stammered out, his pol's gift of gab deserting him.

I nodded to Rose while I guided her to a seat. "We know everything. It's time to do the right thing."

"What's that?"

Cullen snatched him up out his seat. "End this shit. Call in the Guard."

"Sure, whatever you say."

We all took turns looking at each other. Then, Cullen yanked the mayor to his feet, spun him around, and shucked his suit jacket off him.

"Now . . . now what—" Hizzoner sputtered, then fell into gaping silence as Cullen ripped one shirt sleeve off him from the shoulder seam and deposited him back in his chair. "Now listen, I don't know what you—"

"Zip it," Cullen took out his hypodermic kit. He swabbed the mayor's pudgy white arm and snarled at Kennett when he tried to pull his arm away. "Sit still."

Cullen filled a syringe and injected the man.

"What was that?" Kennett asked then began to hyperventilate and sweat through his shirt.

"Let's call it an insurance policy," I said.

"I don't understand. Who are you people?"

"Concerned citizens." I glanced at Rollie, and he guided Rose out of the room. He'd make sure the coast was clear when we left and then make sure Rose wouldn't hear what we had to say next.

Once they'd left the room, I found a bottle of water and gave it to the mayor. "Who we are isn't important. What we want is."

"I'll call in the Guard, okay?" He was running a little hot and ragged. I was thinking we might need to make him breathe into a paper bag. "Please, what did you do to me?"

"If you play ball, then we did nothing," I said.

"I said I'd do it. What more do you need?" He sounded hysterical.

"Focus." I put two fingertips to my mask's eyeholes to give him a target. "Listen carefully. We gave you a designer formula made by the people we work for to prevent backsliding once we leave the scene."

"You poisoned me?" His head lolled in the seat.

Cullen grabbed the water bottle from him and poured the rest of it over the mayor's head. "Snap out of it."

Kennett sputtered and stared at us.

"I don't get all the science behind it," I said, "but this stuff is harmless for about three days. After that, it breaks down in the body into a potent neurotoxin. It won't hurt, at least that's what they say." I'm not proud that I enjoyed his reaction.

"Why?"

"Hush. Here's the good news: There's an antidote. It's very specific. Don't try your own doctors. They will probably trigger the breakdown early, and you'll be dead in minutes."

Cullen leaned into him. "We are going to give you several specific demands. If you back out of any one of them, you'll never hear from us again, and you are a dead man."

"And what happens when I do what you ask?"

"You will be given a location where you will find a vial of the antidote. Inject it, and the poison will become inert and you can live the rest of your days in retirement."

We gave him maybe three seconds to process this, but that was it. We were on borrowed time and had to get out of there as soon as possible.

"Retirement?"

Cullen had heard enough. "Listen up. One, you get on the horn and tell the governor you need the Guard, like yesterday. Do that first."

"Yes, all right."

I spoke up. "Two, you fire that clown Simms and rehire Rains. Then, pray you get a police force back for him to command."

"What if he won't take the job?"

"You make the offer," Cullen said. "We will know if you don't."

"All right." His shirt stuck to his skin, more sweat than water. I hoped we weren't going to give him a heart attack.

"Last," I said. "As soon as these actions are in place, you resign. Don't waste time either. You are on the clock."

"But it will take time to get things under control. A few days isn't enough."

"It's all you have," Cullen informed him. "You think our people want you sticking around after you fucked it up in the first place?"

I leaned in. "Just get the ball rolling, and then step aside. Or else."

We'd made our point.

* * *

Rollie looked like he was ready to climb the walls by the time we got back outside. He kept a grip on Rose's shoulder, and his other hand held the small, suppressed .22 carbine. He could one-hand the thing almost as well as a pistol. The pack of us left the Arts Council building and moved to the car. I was a little surprised nobody had messed with it, but we'd parked snugged up to the checkpoint, and it appeared they had this area under control.

The ones we knocked out were still out, and the shotgunner Rollie had shot was down forever. We'd all made it into the car when Rose whipped around in her seat to speak to Cullen. "Wait," she said. "You didn't finish off the rest of those guys."

Cullen looked puzzled in the rearview mirror. "Why would we? They're not a threat, and we are leaving."

"But they saw me," Rose said.

"So?" Cullen said.

"They saw me!" Rose yelled at Cullen.

"Oh. Well, that's too damn bad for you. But it should be even more reason for you get out of town and never come back." Cullen caught my eye in the mirror, almost to say "See? Told you I'd spare her."

"Can I go now?"

"After these two get home," Cullen said.

"That reminds me." Rollie pulled off his ski mask. "No offense." He tugged it over Rose's head, backward so it covered her eyes. "Look down toward your lap please," he added.

I switched the driver's seat with Cullen when we got to my place. The last we heard was Cullen warning her that if she gave him trouble, he'd hog tie her and toss her in the trunk.

CHAPTER 41

Kyle's place, two days later

The first thing I noticed was the helicopters that dropped pallets of supplies to the neighborhoods and were broadcasting warnings all over the city, especially to the no-man's-land business areas.

Next came news that the National Guard had formed a perimeter around the whole city and, with their own checkpoints, had stemmed the flow of crooks coming in from other states to take advantage of the chaos.

The news covered the announcements and the guardsmen—who were soldiers, not cops—rounded up anyone they caught after the curfew and put them in temporary tent cities. Soon after that, we got word that Commissioner Rains had been rehired on the condition that charges would be dropped on the cops who had been fired.

Last night, my friend on the force, Daniels, let me know that his brothers in blue were itching to get back to work, "Now that we can do our jobs."

On this morning, Rollie came over for coffee. "The smoke smell is much better, don't you think?"

"Definitely. The armed escorts for the fire trucks are making all the difference."

Rollie lowered his voice. "Anything left of Sandy's center?"

I shook my head. "The entire building collapsed. Filled that alley with debris."

"Funeral pyre," Rollie said, shaking his head.

Then one of my phones went off. The third burner I tried came up a winner: it was Jill Williams. Their news operation was still sharing space with a sister station outside the city. "Guess who is about to hold a press conference?"

I had a good idea.

* * *

Kyle's place

Cullen leaned out of his car window. "Take a ride?"

"Don't mind if I do." I climbed in.

The streets were much safer these days, but I still open-carried a gun, and I wasn't alone.

"Now that Kennett has resigned," Cullen said, "I imagine he's interested in hearing from us."

"Time sure flies, doesn't it? I prepared this, but would you like to do the honors?" I handed him a manilla envelope with a glass vial inside. There was also a photo of Kennett's house with the following written on the back.

Citizen Kennett,

Now that you have kept your promises (a first!) please find in the vial the same harmless saline solution that you received two days ago. No antidote required.

May you live a long life in the private sector. As you can see, we know how to reach you if we ever need anything else.

Sincerely,

Your long-suffering constituents

"We might give him that heart attack yet." Cullen smiled and took the envelope.

"And there was something else," I said.

"Go ahead." I could see he knew what was coming.

"I heard they found Rose's body. Near the courthouse."

"I heard the same thing." Cullen waited for an accusation. "You think it was me?"

I weighed my answer. "No. But I doubt you care what I think."

"I'm not sorry she's gone, but curious why you don't blame me."

"They say she had a sign around her neck that said 'Rat,'" I said. "Didn't seem like your style."

Cullen nodded. "Visited many rats in my career. Didn't take time to label them."

"So, I guess her friends caught up to her before she could leave town."

"Looks like," Cullen said and lifted the envelope I'd handed him by one corner. "Hey, it's been fun, but I better drop you off and get this to the ex-mayor."

CHAPTER 42

Old City, one week later

Sandy and I walked down the street hand-in-hand, interrupted every so often by business owners who came out to shake my hand or let me how their repairs were going. It all reminded me of the urban version of an old growth forest recovering from a terrible fire.

There still wasn't much traffic, but the new mayor had already spoken about lifting the curfew soon. National Guard trucks rolled through the city, but now it was more of a symbolic show of force.

"I guess it sounds strange to be so happy to see the police around," I said.

"Not at all. We got a good look at the alternative, didn't we?"

"Too good. I just got used to working around them, is all."

"It won't be long until everyone will be complaining about the traffic and crowds," Sandy said.

Her hand was still in mine, but I swear I could feel it slipping away. We finally stopped in front of the mound of rubble that had been her rehab center.

The elephant in the room—or on the street, as it were.

"You said you were still thinking," I said. "I'll say it again: I can find you another perfect location. Some great spaces have opened up." I was trying to keep it light, but the words pulled all the air from my chest.

Sandy turned and hugged me tight. When she let go and stepped back, her eyes shone with tears. "Starting over is hard enough."

"And I want to make it easier." The thread of hope was so thin it could be cut.

"But not here. It's not you. You know it's not. It's . . . the whole thing." It sounded like her words were costing her as well.

"But you help so many, right here. You wouldn't have to be part of any of the other . . ." I shrugged. "We'll try to do our best, in our own ways."

She kissed me. "You're a good man, and I know you really do make a difference, no matter the cost. But I can help others somewhere else. A simpler life."

"So, I'm too complicated?" I forced a smile.

"This town is too complicated. And it's as much a part of you as your arms and legs. When I said you could come with me to Lancaster, I might as well have suggested relocating to the moon."

"Maybe not the moon." But she had me there. "You can see the work we do matters."

"And that's why you can't leave it. I'm not sorry for helping. And that's part of it. The clowns in charge may be down for the moment, but it won't be long before a fresh crop replaces them, and it'll be the same story again."

"Not for a while, I hope. VP found funding connections from the top city officials and the World Citizen Project. You saw that DA Castle is stepping down?"

"Yes, and I noticed he had a beauty of a shiner. Just a coincidence?" Sandy asked.

"Maybe not," I said. "Wasn't me."

"Were you surprised to see it?"

"No." No point trying to fool her. I didn't add that the guy was lucky to be alive. Cullen had been cleaning house since the last time I saw him. Between the return of the police and some leaders who weren't in their pocket, the anarchists had gotten the message and decamped for another city to plunder.

"A win for the good guys, or the regular guys or whatever, but it can't last," she said. She shook her head. "It never does."

"Can I visit?" I asked her.

"Of course." We let the illusion linger in the air. "I wasn't built to do this for life," she said then paused. "But I think you are."

I wanted to disagree, but I couldn't and knew the reason why. This proud, broken city needed me and my people coloring outside the lines. Way outside, if needed.

The End

ACKNOWLEDGMENTS

As always, I have to thank my wife (and first reader) for her constant support. She has a sharp eye for detail and for the flow of the story. She keeps the characters (and me!) on their toes.

I also want to thank the terrific group of editors starting with David Downing of Maxwellian Editorial Services and the proofreading and excellent cover design from Ebook Launch.

NOTE FROM THE AUTHOR

Thanks so much for reading. If you enjoyed this book, I would greatly appreciate a review on Amazon or Goodreads. These can go a long way to help reach new readers.

You can find out more about new books at my Amazon page below or searching for "Author J. Gregory Smith"
https://www.amazon.com/stores/J.-Gregory-Smith/author/B002VW9IIU?ref=ap_rdr&store_ref=ap_rdr&isDramInt egrated=true&shoppingPortalEnabled=true